Suzannah Dunn

is the author of six other books of fiction: *Darker Days Than Usual*, *Blood Sugar*, *Past Caring*, *Quite Contrary*, *Tenterhooks* and *Commencing our Descent*. She lives in Brighton.

From the reviews:

'In each of her previous novels, Suzannah Dunn has filled me with admiration... She writes with extraordinary depth of understanding. *Venus Flaring* is a wonderful affirmation of her talent and originality. She has created two characters so real you feel you come to know them better than your own friends... Their story is by turns funny, moving and, at times, harrowing in its intensity.'

MARTYN BEDFORD, author of *Acts of Revision*

'*Venus Flaring* treats familiar themes to a witty and original overhaul. Dunn marries plot and themes, to create a haunting, melancholy tone perfectly suited to the sense of loss which afflicts even minor characters.'   *TLS*

'Veronica and Ornella... grow up and apart, but Veronica has a great desire for reconciliation. "Losing a friend is worse than losing a lover," she reflects, "because everyone expects to lose lovers... But why should a friend stop being a friend?" Dunn describes the relationship with acuity, wit and wisdom.'
Daily Telegraph

'After reading *Venus Flaring* no other book will strike quite so close to your soul... Dunn time after time stuns the reader. This is a vital, refreshing, terrifyingly brilliant novel that demands to be read.'   *Finetime*

further reviews overleaf

'That stark feeling of betrayal is at its most potent when it has bitten away at a lifelong and seemingly solid friendship. In this cruel gem of a book, Suzannah Dunn writes with economy and flair. If a pacey intelligent read is what you're after, dip in and let her prose penetrate your nightmares.'   *The List*

'Real changeling stuff here... Powerfully written, there are enough twists and developments to keep the reader constantly alert.'   *Dorset Evening Echo*

'Edged with insights and observations that glitter darkly... The novel's last fifty pages are unbearable to break and have to be read at one sitting.'   *Impact*

By the same author

venus flaring

suzannahdunn

Flamingo
An Imprint of HarperCollins*Publishers*

Flamingo
An Imprint of HarperCollins*Publishers*
77–85 Fulham Palace Road,
Hammersmith, London W6 8JB

Flamingo is a registered trade mark of
HarperCollins Publishers Limited

www.fireandwater.com

This edition published by Flamingo 2000
9 8 7 6 5 4 3 2 1

First published in Great Britain by
Flamingo 1996

First paperback edition published by
Flamingo 1997

Photograph of Suzannah Dunn by © Claire McNamee

ISBN 0 00 649792 6

Set in Linotype Sabon by
Rowland Phototypesetting Ltd,
Bury St Edmunds, Suffolk

Printed and bound in Great Britain by
Clays Ltd, St Ives plc

For Charlotte

THE SUN IS fierce, low in the sky over the water. My face smoulders. Today is the last day of October but this drooping sun is burning me in a way that the even shine from a high summer sun would never do. Across the path from me, two elderly women slow down and turn, a muted kerfuffle of their walking sticks in the mud. They turn to look over the lake, swinging shadows from their heels. I smile to recall from my childhood that the sign of a ghost was a lack of shadow: these elderly women, then, are alive and kicking. I am sitting on this bench for a few moments while my daughter is with her father. By the lake, he is showing her something, but I cannot see what he has in his hands. Cupped, his hands are very long and luminous like those of saints and mournful men in medieval illuminations. But he is laughing, explaining something to her: he has squatted beside her and their heads are lowered together over his hands. Their heads are different colours, he is dark but she is blonde. But not as blonde as I was, when I was three. And not many years, now, until she is not as blonde as she would like to be and she starts to mess with dye. Not many years until she stops listening to her father and this park becomes one of the very last places where she will want to spend an afternoon.

A few moments ago, I watched someone else's daughter:

she came along the path behind a woman who, I presumed, was her mother, who was brisk and competent in drip-dry slacks and sturdy walking boots, the crook of her arm looped with a windcheater, her hands full of foil-wrapped sandwiches. But the girl – how old was she? she could even have been my age – was all wrong: her walk was difficult for her, drastic; her hair was short, shapeless, flat on her head; her mouth was wide open and her teeth decayed. Her eyes were lit but unfocused. The woman strode ahead of her to one of the unoccupied benches, shouting cheerfully, 'Over here, out of the sun,' enthusing, 'Let's have this lovely bench over here, away from the sun.' The girl barked with excitement. The bench was shaded from the dizzying sun, but was also the very furthest away from the path, from other people. For a moment, I thought of what I would like for my own daughter; I indulged in the luxury of thinking about the many possibilities for her future. My parents had been very keen on education as the key to success, to a profession, to the chance to earn a good living: first generation upwardly-mobile, they did not quite achieve this for themselves but were hopeful for me and my sister, paid much more than lip service to the notion. A discredited notion. I was lucky, I do what I want to do, and I have money. But what I want for my daughter is happiness. I want her to be happy-go-lucky. My wish is for her to be liked. Not loved, not *only* loved – this is not my wish because someone *will* love her, there will be *someone*, and I will love her, her father will love her – but *liked*.

My daughter and I have fed the ducks, we threw bits of bread and the ducks flew to us, their splash-landings like hands skimmed over and into water, the sound of fun. Now, out on the lake, in silhouette, they look like miniature Nessies. As they cross the pooled sunlight, they tow trains of glare. Away from the sun, the ripples are much less spectacular, mere goose-pimples or grazes on the surface of the water. An occasional flare signals a diving duck. And then I can see the underwater duck in my mind's eye, pushing through the darkness with its sleek head. The duck pops back onto the surface surprisingly far away. I am bewitched by the gilded ripples on the sludge-coloured water; their crests are diamond, hard and brilliant, and yet I know that they do not exist, that they are blinding tricks of the light.

The light, away from the lake, in the shadows of the trees, is old, smoky with the dust of dead leaves, dense columns of yellow air between the thinning branches. As we walked through these ghosts of the summer on our way to the lake, there were occasional thuds – falling conkers – which made us jumpy. And our jumpiness made us giggly. This autumn air is both sharp and musty, like an apple. Today I feel an odd mix of melancholy and exhilaration. This is the high summer of my life: tomorrow, I will be thirty-three.

A few days ago, I began to think about my best friend again, about my loss of my best friend. This time, I wondered how I had *found* her, how we had become friends. Which was difficult for me: she simply *was*, she had simply been *there*, a fact of my life for nearly twenty

3

years. I knew her from school: she had been in my year, but not in my form. I knew *of* her for years before I knew her; I knew her name, everyone knew her name: *Ornella Marini.* She was half Italian. She had a brother, Guido, in the year above us. My memories were clear, vivid, but initially they came slowly, one by one; taking time before they joined to become the story of how I lost her.

GAMES: HOCKEY, AND I am in position as a back. My favourite position. Which is not saying much. Today, there is no sky, only cold cloud. Recent rain wheezes in the soil between the studs of my boots. *Why* the school campaign for an All Weather Playing Pitch? Why would anyone *want* to play in All Weathers? Why would anyone want to play in *any* weather? I tend to avoid the sporty girls, except for Debra Taylor, the sprinter who spends every lunchtime sitting with the rest of us behind the cricket pavilion listening to the Head Groundsman's radio and sharing his cigarettes; and Cathy Sykes, a highjumper with four earrings in one ear and a boyfriend in the Sixth Form.

Today, numbers are low. My friends Abi and Dominique are off with flu. And Bev is spending Games in the library because her kneecap slips. So Miss Stringer has sent Alison Beardsley into goal, which promises no fun. Behind me, she is slamming her hockey stick

4

impatiently into the mud. And Ornella Marini has been sent to be the only other back. If I remember correctly, she is a member of the cross-country running team. I have seen her running, or finishing running, rolling up to the changing room: the soft arms of her tracksuit folded around her waist, and a sweatband frowning beneath the damp dark ribbons of her hair. But now she is wearing a PE skirt, because Miss Stringer insists that we wear skirts for hockey. Miss Stringer probably likes to see our bruises. Ornella stamps the chill from her body, and I see that her tough little legs have a metallic sheen. The sleeves of her sweatshirt are pulled down, held down, over her hands.

I watch a honeyed shine slipping up and down the length of her hair. She is turning one way and then the other. More often the other. Turning her back to the game. Perhaps she is so sporty that she can sense the approach of the ball. But now the ball comes closer. Sure enough, Ornella turns. But she spins the stick, tucks the crook into her armpit, and lifts to take aim. The aim is Miss Stringer. A low puff blows from Ornella's pout; simultaneously, the hockey stick jerks, very authentically. Steadily, she repeats the action, twice.

'Ornella,' I try carefully, 'Stringer will see.' As I finish, I can see that Miss Stringer *has* seen: she is peering across the field towards us, realising that she has been shot. I can see that she is bemused.

Ornella turns to me with an identical expression. 'So?'

I glance nervously back to Miss Stringer, and am relieved to find that she has decided to disbelieve her own eyes. In the lull in gunfire, she has returned her attention to the ball.

Ornella turns the stick into a Fred Astaire cane and begins to prance. She squelches the mud rhythmically with her studs. I notice that my own stick is twitching in time. Breathlessly she calls to me, 'How can we make sure that Gamesy is given the sack?'

I presume *Gamesy* refers to Miss Stringer. I glance into the herd to find her. As if grounds for her dismissal will become obvious to me. Which, of course, they do not: she is bouncing impeccably around the principal players, gently encouraging them and now very fairly mediating a dispute. Ornella leans heavily onto her stick, glowers at me, forcing me to answer.

I muse, 'I don't know. I think she'd have to beat you up, or something.' I add, 'Very badly.'

She snaps upright, chucks the stick high into the air, then catches it. 'I could say that she has been interfering with me in the showers,' she says.

For a moment I do not know what this means. I see *showers*, the school version, the long line of thick plastic curtains; I hear the thud of them in the air when they are drawn. And then I realize. But, watching me, Ornella's face splits into a laugh. I breathe with relief. I do not know what I would have said if she had been telling the truth. Gratefully, I inform her, 'Rumour has it that she was interfering with Rickman on the skiing trip whenever his wife was stuck on a black run.'

'Really?' she thirsts, gleaming. 'Really, honestly?'

I shrug, disowning the rumour. 'So someone told me.'

She watches me closely, for fractionally too long, before casually flipping her eyebrows. 'Well,' she says, conclusively. Or inconclusively. Then, much more definitely, 'He's yummy, isn't he: Twinkle Rickman.'

Is he? He is a man, probably thirty, perhaps even older. And he teaches Science. How can he possibly be 'yummy'?

She notices my reticence, and clasps the hockey stick to her sweatshirt, throws back her head, murmurs, 'Those eyes!'

I object, 'Ornella, whenever I see those eyes they are twinkling over a dissected frog.'

She concedes, barely, with a shrug, and begins to pace. 'So,' she calls out in her wake, 'we have something on Stringy.'

I idle the tip of my stick in the mud. 'You mean Rickman? No. Not enough.' And I have been meaning to ask, 'Anyway, why do you want Stringer to be sacked?'

She whirls around, incredulous. 'You *like* standing here?'

'Well, no. Of course not.' I take a few steps towards her, to reason, 'But getting rid of Stringer won't solve the problem. She'll be replaced.' And anyway, is it fair to blame Stringer? Surely she is only doing her job.

Ornella minces towards me through a particularly bad patch of mud to stress, 'We are standing here because of String-baby. Which is as much as I need to know.'

Momentarily savouring the smell of mud-drenched grass, I watch Miss Stringer. All our female Games staff are short. Does their shortness cause them to become

Games teachers? And if so, is this due to genes, or to feelings of inferiority?

Ornella says, 'Strings-Attached is the type of woman your mother warned you about.'

My mother has never warned me about any type of woman.

Ornella continues, happily, 'The woman is a monster.'

'She doesn't look particularly like a monster.'

'And you'd know one if you saw one?' Ornella's hockey stick has been dropped to the ground whilst she stretches, cupping her hands for the length of hair at the back of her neck. The hair sprouts in the rising hands, then falls free. 'Don't waste your time defending her, she wouldn't do the same for you.' Then she groans, 'My God,' and yawns, hugs herself, 'the bus stop.'

I try to track the line of thought to the bus stop. Which bus stop?

'I mean,' she whines, 'we have to stand here in the freezing cold for a couple of hours, then go for a luke-warm shower in a freezing cold changing room with no hairdryer, then rush outside again to wait for a few more hours in this sub-Siberian wind at our poxy bus stop.'

Oh, *that* bus stop: I agree, 'They should build us a shelter or something.' My words sound strange because the cold air is solidifying inside my nose.

'They should try building us a *bus*, first,' she wails in outrage and disgust.

'A centrally-heated shelter.' The cold has soaked beneath my skin.

'With armchairs,' she insists.

'Centrally-heated armchairs.'

She laughs listlessly. 'Oh, well, yes. Goes without saying.'

'And hot chocolate.'

Arms folded, Ornella is rocking toe to heel on top of the abandoned sinking stick.

'Served by a butler.'

'Oh, yes.' Her voice is shivering but her eyes are dreamy. 'A butler with a silver tray.'

'Food,' I say definitely. But it is also a question, an invitation: *what shall we have?*

'Toast,' she answers.

Of course. 'But I want my own toaster.' This is important: 'I want to make my own toast. *Very* underdone. Very *porous*.'

We both know that we are talking butter. Her brown eyes slip towards me, and she nods solemnly. 'Personal toasters,' she agrees.

'Television,' this is something else that I want.

'Personal televisions,' she continues in the same tone.

'No, no –' we have to be realistic '– we could have one huge screen.' Which is a much better idea. 'Like a cinema. We could have films.'

She groans. 'Personal cinemas, please. I don't want to sit through the boys' Bond films.' Beneath her absently rocking boots, the thin dry stick is worked into the mud. Archaeology in reverse.

'What about baths?' I continue, 'Deep hot baths, and towels, lots of them, soft and warm?'

9

Her eyes are huge in the huddle of her body. 'I was assuming that we'd have baths,' she says. 'And all the rest. A sauna.'

I wonder whether Ornella has ever had a sauna. But surely Swedes, not Italians, have saunas. Because Italians have sun.

'We have a problem,' I confide.

'We do?' She smiles to herself.

'When the bus finally arrives,' I explain, 'we will have the unspeakable horror of leaving our shelter . . .'

'A special, heated walkway,' she says, quickly.

'Conveyor belt,' I correct. 'But then we still have the horror of the bus itself.'

'You're right. What's the point of all this if the bus comes along with no free seats? And then takes half an hour to cross town?' She turns from me and gazes into the dripping distance, towards the main road. 'I want to be home *now*,' she says desperately.

I tell her, 'We don't need a bus, we need Concorde.'

In the unfocused foreground, a figure halts, hands on hips. 'Ornella Marini!' It, she, Miss Stringer, shouts crossly in our direction, 'Where's your stick?'

Ornella steps off the stick, bends to pull it from the mud, muttering to me, 'I know where I'd like it to be.' Straightening, she shouts amicably in reply: 'I dropped it.'

Miss Stringer reproaches us, 'Girls! Put some effort into this game!'

Ornella mutters, 'Quite right,' positions the stick, and bends deeply at the knees. She is poised impeccably for a shot. A parody of a shot. The game is miles away. She shouts gamely to me, 'Come on, Veronica! Let's see some effort!'

'Ornella . . .' I glance fearfully, but Miss Stringer has returned with overwhelming excitement to the game. Am I afraid for myself, or for Ornella? Now that we are *Girls*, together. Probably for myself, because I have already had a warning this week, for taking a detour into the Duplicating Room with Dominique to sniff the purple inky chemicals.

Ornella drops the pose and tips her nose into the air. 'I don't care.'

Obviously not.

She jolts me by bowing again, this time with speed and a brief cry, 'Jesus!' For a fraction of a moment I wonder if I am watching a prayer, an Italian, Catholic, ritual. But now, even more frightening, I realize that it was a cry of pain. She is doubled up. Is this another act, like the assassination of Miss Stringer, and the dance display? I approach, warily. 'Ornella?' As if I am calling into a black hole.

She twists to look up at me, and commands breathlessly, utterly convincingly, 'Get Stringer.'

Panic washes the walls of my stomach. I turn, vaguely, but see that Miss Stringer has already been alerted. She is jogging towards us, a rapid but even pace. In the background, the field bobbles with the watchful faces of a large number of girls, a distant crop of daisies. I step back from Ornella, clear the way. 'She just . . .'

Miss Stringer places a hand on the green dome of

Ornella's back, and leans rather too heavily. 'Ornella?' The tone is harsh, but possibly because the name comes on one of her surprisingly blunt and foggy breaths.

A small, pained voice sounds inside the dome. 'I'm sorry.'

Miss Stringer avoids my eyes, bends lower. 'Ornella?' she brays. 'What's the matter?'

The small faceless voice wavers, 'I've been feeling rotten all afternoon . . .'

Miss Stringer looks up into my face.

I do not know what to do, so I nod in confirmation.

She returns with renewed vigour to Ornella. 'What is it, love?' she bellows. 'Is it a pain?'

Slowly, Ornella unfolds. Her head turns towards Miss Stringer. 'I know what it is,' she says calmly, even serenely.

Miss Stringer says, 'Oh, your monthly,' then glances feebly to the hedgerow horizons in search of help or inspiration; glances forlornly over her shoulder towards her assistant, Miss Farthing, who is leading the netball game in the distance. Miss Farthing remains oblivious. Her teams swell behind the tall wire fence, their arms raised as if they are on a demo.

Miss Stringer looks sharply at me and demands, 'Can you manage to take her to Sister?'

Somewhere inside, I shiver with pleasure: *I am going indoors.* This time, I nod vigorously. Miss Stringer dips again and starts explaining into Ornella's ear – 'I can't leave the others, Ornella, so . . .'

And I savour my last look around the field. The stationary players appear shocked by the swift settling of the cold air on their skin. They wander, dazed, in small circles.

Ornella is rising, retaining the deep bend in her body. And Miss Stringer is stepping back. I hurry forward to drape my arms over Ornella's low shoulders, to guide her from the pitch. Held together, we slow each other down. My head is very close to Ornella's, but I hear nothing from her. Below us I hear the stumblings of two pairs of mud-slippery boots. The cricket pavilion looms over us, our first sighting of dry land. Suddenly there is the creak of our boots on concrete.

And Ornella springs from my clasp. 'Yippee!' she sings ahead of me, turning to face me, trotting backwards.

However much I expected this, it is still a shock. Piqued, I can think of nothing to say but, 'You can only do this a certain number of times.' Nine lives.

'No,' she says mildly, unruffled, after a moment of consideration, 'From now on, I can do it *monthly*.'

True. Good idea. Can I? No, because now, after this, Miss Stringer will be suspicious. Ornella has used one of my lives.

She laughs, 'Race you to the bus stop.'

'You have to go to Sister,' I call to her.

She stops.

'I have to *take you* to Sister. Remember?'

She turns, dismayed, drained; her face, a swirl of cream. She insists slowly, 'But there's nothing wrong with me.'

'I *know that*. But Stringer will go to Sister to check. It's her job to check.'

To my surprise, Ornella agrees immediately, with a big loose shrug of her long green sleeves. 'Okay. To Sister.'

'But there's nothing wrong with you,' I protest. 'And she'll give you aspirin. And you can't take drugs for no reason.'

She complains, 'For God's sake, Veronica.'

And I follow her in the direction of Sick Bay, because, after all, I am taking her.

Ahead of me, she barges through the swing doors into the main Hall. The Hall is a short cut to almost everywhere in the main building. On the door there is a notice, *The Hall Is Not A Right Of Way For Pupils*. As I catch the swinging door, I hear from the stage, 'There are many different ways to sit on a chair.' Must be Drama. Mr Partridge is standing on the stage amid chairs and Fifth Form pupils, frowning furiously at us. Ornella shouts breathlessly in explanation: 'Sister.' Which is equivalent to flashing a blue light. Mr Partridge lowers his eyes respectfully. I cringe and curse Ornella under my breath as I hurry along in my PE skirt under the Fifth Form gazes.

As we approach Sister's door, Ornella drops behind me. The door is ajar, but I stand to attention and knock. Instantly Sister is in the wide open doorway. Her face ripens into a smile, and she says a long swoopy, 'Hellooo.' She is my friend Bev's mum. She is very pretty, for a mum. At school she wears her hair in a bun, a shiny conker. Her eyelashes are so long and tough around the dark seeds of her eyes that I wonder if they are false. I have never seen her without a frosting of lipstick on her lips. At school her legs are always bare beneath her white housecoat, because Sick Bay is so hot, but they are not like our teachers' legs, they are not uncooked sausages, nor fake tan, but lemony. I am ushering Ornella in front of me. Sister is soothing, 'So what have we here, the walking wounded?' and, 'Come in, come in.'

She indicates that the drooping Ornella should sit on the couch. I stay by the door, pressing myself back onto the radiator. The couch almost fills Sick Bay, with Sister's small desk and the two-tier trolley, silver kidney bowls on the top, holding tweezers and scissors, and on the bottom a kettle, cups and saucers, and a biscuit tin. The small white medication cupboard is on the wall. The couch is prepared with a pillow, dazzling and undented like a huge tablet, and loose soft blankets, crochet, more suited to a cot. Sister kneels so that she can look up into Ornella's face. 'Now then,' she breathes.

Ornella blurts tearfully, 'It's nothing, it's my period. I felt awful, and Miss Stringer sent me.'

Only the tips of her toes touch the floor.

Gently, Sister asks, 'Do you have cramps?'

'No. Not really. Not now.' Ornella's chin crushes into her neck, and she mumbles, 'It was just . . . all that standing around . . .'

Sister hums agreement. 'Would aspirin help?'

Ornella peeps at her, and wrinkles her nose. 'I hate the taste,' she confides.

Sister rises, with a wobble and a grunt of exertion. 'Okay,' she pronounces, 'no aspirin, but you'd better rest here for a while.' She checks with me: 'Veronica, do you want to go back out there?'

And *I* wrinkle *my* nose. 'Not really.' Not at all.

She sparkles before lowering her eyes down to her watch. 'I've decided that it's too late to send you back:' the official version. Dropping her arm to her side, she ventures, 'Anyone fancy a cup of tea?'

We both murmur appreciatively.

'I was just about to have one,' she tells us, 'when you arrived.' She indicates that I should sit alongside Ornella on the couch, and then, flicking the switch on the kettle, she exclaims, 'Have I had a day!'

We are silently respectful.

Clattering cups, she asks thoughtfully, 'Shall I phone your mother, Ornella? To fetch you.'

Watching me, Ornella replies, 'No, thanks. I'm feeling much better. My brother Guido can see me home.'

'Ah, yes, Guido,' sings Sister, pouring milk. She replaces the milk bottle gently on the steel surface of the trolley. 'Tell you what: if you two can manage to wait until I've finished, then I can run you home.' She flicks a glance at Ornella. 'Whereabouts do you live, Ornella? Down by . . . ?'

'Yes, the park.' Ornella's face is fresh with hope.

No doubt mine is the same.

Sister shifts her smile from Ornella to me, and back again: 'Well?'

'Oh, yes, thanks,' we babble.

'Biscuits?' She wrenches the lid from the tin.

'Oh, yes, thanks.'

Showing me the sandy interior of the tin, she asks, 'How's your sister?'

She will have known from Bev that my sister, Juliet, who is six, has had chicken pox. 'Oh, fine, thanks.'

'Back at school?'

I have to reply through a mouthful of biscuit: 'Mmmm.'

'Good, good . . .' Sister turns away to organize some tea bags, and sighs heavily as she drops them into the little silvery pot. 'What a day!' Waiting for the kettle to boil, she turns to us and complains, 'Do you think that it should be my job to do the registers? To collect them every day, to go through them all and count the absentees? To chase up the notes from yesterday's absentees?'

Obviously she does not think so. Her eyes are spiked with indignation. Gravely, I frown my sympathy.

'What am I, a glorified secretary?' She tilts the kettle; the boiling water gobbles inside the squat steel pot. 'If I had wanted to be a secretary, I wouldn't have applied for the job of Sister, would I?' She lowers the kettle and turns her attention to the pot. The lid yaps. She turns to us, swinging more words past us: 'They'll milk you for all you're worth, here.'

I nod, knowingly. Ornella's toes begin to brush the tiles, rhythmically. Sister produces a hot water bottle from nowhere, and fills its lifeless form with the remaining water from the kettle. Her firm fastening of the plug produces a kaleidoscope of muscles in her arm. 'For your tummy,' she says to Ornella.

Prompted, reaching cautiously for the bottle, Ornella gazes into Sister's face. When the bottle is transferred into her hands, she retreats, lowers the flame of her eyes, turns them briefly to me. She holds the bottle reverently in her lap.

Sister sighs, much more softly this time, and pushes the skin around her eyes and temples with her smart enamelled fingertips. 'And it's not as if I don't have enough to do.' After a moment she says, 'I had The Eternal Triangle in here today.'

Katy Murphy, Thomasina Gardener, and Neil Kean: everyone in the whole school knows that Neil Kean has left Katy Murphy, after two or more years, for her best friend, Thomasina Gardener. Neil Kean is Head Boy, Thomasina Gardener is Head Girl, and Katy Murphy is Head of Sixth Form. All three of them look very miserable. Sound very miserable, too: often when we walk past Sick Bay we hear one or both girls crying to Sister.

I have inside information, of course, from Bev. She lets me know whenever they have been to see her mum in Sick Bay, she lets me know what was said: Neil loves both of them, he does not know what to do; Thomasina did not mean to hurt her best friend, it just happened, and surely it would have been worse to deny it; Katy's whole belief in human nature has been destroyed, and, yes, they do both say that nothing was going on beforehand, but why should she believe them?

Sister solemnly hands us our cups of tea and confides, 'It's exhausting. Mind you, if it's exhausting for me, then imagine how much worse it is for them.'

I murmur my thanks for the tea.

Ornella follows, then chirps, 'What's going on now, then? Is he back with Katy?'

Sister reels back with a thin high laugh. 'I can't gossip,' she protests jollily. 'I'd lose my job.' She raises her cup in front of her face, lowers her eyes, sips. Then she says, 'No, he's not.'

Her phone rings. She stretches across and hauls the receiver to her ear. 'Sister here.' She fastens her gaze onto ours and hitches her eyebrows: firm pencil lines, normal distribution curves. She tells the receiver, 'Okay, I'll come over.' Released, lowering it onto its olive green base, she sings a sigh and peers critically at her wristwatch. 'I'm afraid you'll have to excuse me for a while,' she tells us. 'You'll be alright in here?'

An enthusiastic murmur of affirmation.

She swipes the tin of biscuits from the trolley and slaps it onto the couch between us. 'And there's more tea in the pot.' She smiles in the doorway, and then she is gone, having closed the door behind her.

Ornella and I turn to each other, look properly at each other for the first time, eyes very wide.

'*Well...*' breathes Ornella. She wriggles backwards on the couch, lifting her feet, arranging herself cross-legged beneath one of the cotton wool blankets.

I bite into another biscuit, chocolate chip.

THE BELL RANG several minutes ago. There is nothing tinkly about our school bell. It sounds like a burglar alarm, or even several burglar alarms. We are sitting in the sun on the porch of the cricket pavilion, watching everyone returning from the field. Suddenly someone slips from the crowds onto the porch: Ornella Marini. I have hardly seen her since our afternoon in Sick Bay, several weeks ago. She saunters in front of us, peers through the smoke, announces, 'You need to smoke banana skins.'

Cathy Sykes queries, 'Banana skins?'

'Instead of cigarettes.' Suddenly, she is sitting above us all on the back of our bench, her shoes next to me on the seat. 'For hallucinations,' she says.

Cathy protests, 'Who wants hallucinations?'

Abi laughs, 'Which end do you light?'

Ornella says doubtfully, '*Dried* banana skins.'

Bev chips in, 'I had hallucinations when I had pneumonia. The floor was falling away.'

'Pneumonia?' Cathy is sceptical.

But I know that Bev is an expert on illnesses, having

had them all, courtesy of her mum, who is Sister.

Dominique says, 'Sounds more like dizziness, to me.'

'No,' Bev thinks hard, frowns hard. 'Because I could see armadillos below the floorboards.'

'You knew that they were armadillos?' I am fascinated. 'I'm not sure that I'd know an armadillo if I saw one.'

She thinks – frowns – harder. 'Somehow, you just know.'

Ornella says, 'I think you scrape the inside layer from the banana skin and smoke it.'

Abi laughs, 'Do bananas have filters?'

Ornella complains, '*Filters*! What's wrong with raw smoke?'

Cathy asks her, 'Who is your brother going out with, at the moment?'

She shifts above me on the bench. 'Diane Blake, presumably. Unfortunately.'

The porch echoes agreement with this sentiment.

Ornella continues more happily, 'Is Mrs Hallett pregnant? She *looked* pregnant, this morning.'

Mrs Hallett, like all other young married women teachers, is always the subject of this particular rumour. I shake my head. 'I reckon you've been misled by her smock.'

Ornella stretches her legs beside me, catches the edge of the seat between the heels and soles of her shoes.

'And,' I continue, 'she rows so badly with her husband . . .'

'How do you know?' The shoes click back into place on the seat, and she leans so far forward that her hair brushes mine, her brown on my murky blonde like branches on water.

'If they lived in your street,' I explain, 'you'd know.' For no reason, I add, 'He's a teacher, too, somewhere. RE.'

'RC?' asks Ornella, surprised.

'RE.' What is RC?

Bev rises, rickety. 'We're late.'

Cathy leads the way, strides across the porch. Dominique picks up the cold dead nub of our cigarette, mottled filter-brown, and buries this evidence in a crumpled tissue which she slips down into the front pocket of her bag.

'I'm *sure* that Mrs Hallett isn't pregnant,' I tell Ornella, 'I have a gut feeling.'

'Talking of gut feelings,' she says to me as we follow the others, 'I'm starving. Guard the gate for me while I run to the shop.'

We are not allowed to leave the grounds during school hours. There is one door in a wall which is hidden from view, but for which only the groundsmen have a key. Without a key, the door will open from the inside but not from the street. Without a key or an accomplice, it is the point of no return. Why me?

'Oh, go on,' she pleads. 'I'm starving, I'm fainting.' Then, more reasonably, 'What do *you* want from the shop?'

'Nothing. I'm on a diet.'

'You're a *gazelle*.'

'*Because* I'm on a diet.'

'What do you want?'

'Rolos, please.' I reach for my purse.

She stills my hand with her own. 'Later,' she says, turning away, somehow turning me with her.

We kick through the dandelions on our swift and secretive way to the wall. Reaching the door, reaching for the latch, Ornella promises, 'Two minutes, max.' Her eyes, in mine, are two teaspoons of dark honey. '*Don't leave me*, okay?'

It is too late to argue. 'Okay.' I glance around the empty courtyard, and the door closes. I lean back onto the warm brick wall. When I hear the footsteps, I realize that my eyes have closed. They are not Ornella's footsteps. They are on my side of the wall, across the courtyard, and they are slow, aimless. I open my eyes. The walker is invisible, behind a bush. I manage to stop breathing but I am helpless to quieten my heart. And now Mr Law steps from behind the bush, sucking hard on a cigarette. When he sees me, his eyes flare. 'Veronica.' He holds the cigarette away from himself for a moment, down, before it drops from his fingers to the ground. He walks over it towards me. 'What are you doing here?'

'Looking for an earring,' I say quickly, kicking the dusty paving stones, 'I've lost an earring.'

Coming closer, he groans a laugh. 'And what were you doing around here, in the first place, to lose your earring? If not cavorting with one of our groundsmen?'

And you should know about cavorting. There is a rumour that, years ago, he had sex with a Sixth Former, and that she did not quite consent.

I see his shoes stop in front of mine, and he lifts my hair away from my face. 'To lose *two* seems rather careless, wouldn't you say?' he laughs smokily, looking at my naked earlobes.

I flinch from the smoke on his breath. 'I only ever wear one. Like a boy.'

And I dare to glance up, to check the success of my ridiculous lie.

A mistake. His face flattens slowly into a smile. 'But you're not a boy,' he breathes, appreciatively.

Behind me, the door rattles with several knocks. Mr Law cringes, and hurries to open it. Ornella comes through, amazed, looking from him to me. Mr Law's hard breathing split into an unconvincing cackle. 'Aha! And Veronica was just telling me how she was searching for a lost earring,' he hisses, scathingly.

Ornella looks wistfully at me. 'Well, yes,' she sighs. 'But it's not over there, I'm afraid.' She smiles humourlessly at Mr Law. 'We thought that someone might have picked it up and chucked it over the wall,' she explains, world-wearily. 'Because they do, the boys, you know. No respect for us.' Suddenly she squats. 'Oh, look, down here!'

We all look. I follow her finger, bend with her, scan the gravelly stone surface. She is running her hand through the dirt. 'Found it!' Triumphantly, she passes an earring to me.

Pushing it into the vacant hole in one of my earlobes, I manage, 'That's *fabulous*, Ornella.'

An enormous smile bursts onto her small face.

Left out, Mr Law hoots, 'Yes, well. Perhaps we can go back into school now.' He ushers us away from the wall, but is soon leading the way across the field, striding faster and further away, turning occasionally, grudgingly, to check that we are following. When he is far enough away, I unhook Ornella's earring from my ear and hand it back to her. 'How did you do that?' I ask, in awe.

She slides two packets of sweets from her skirt pockets. 'Very *quickly*,' she laughs.

ORNELLA HAD SAID, 'Come to the fair.'

But I told her, 'I hate fairs.'

We were in the Cookery Room, which stank of steak and kidney pie. She was flicking her hands over her forearms, brushing off the flour, showering me with it. Luckily our Cookery teacher, Mrs Stuffy, requires us to wear the aprons which, earlier in the year, she had required us to make in Needlework, when she was our Needlework teacher. Here's-one-that-I-finished-earlier. Or not, in my case, because my apron lacks a hem. We have to do Crafts as well as our O level courses. At some point during each Cookery lesson Mrs Stuffy tells me, *Veronica, we need to sort out a hem for you, so come back and see me at the end of the day*. Which I do not do, because I do not care. And she forgets. Until next time.

Ornella said to me, '*Please* come to the fair.'

And Mrs Stuffy's voice slapped across the room from her desk, 'We'll make "pinwheels" now with the leftover pastry, your children will love them.'

We locked gazes of disbelief and amusement; and Ornella whispered the shared thought: 'We don't *have* any children.'

Overhearing, Mrs Stuffy bellowed, 'But you WILL have children, Ornella Marini.'

Which sounded so much like an order that we laughed.

'And it's NOT funny. Get ON with rolling your pastry, you two. No more chit-chat.'

Turning her back on Mrs Stuffy, idling a rolling pin beneath her fingertips, Ornella implored me, '*Please* come.' Her knees twitched with passion beneath her neat hem.

'But I *hate* fairs.'

She grinned, to lighten the tone. 'But you don't hate *me*, and I'm asking you.' Another grin, but weaker: 'You *don't* hate me, do you?'

'No . . .'

'Well, then.'

Mrs Stuffy began to sound the usual warning of the hem: 'And Veronica . . .'

I raised a hand to stop her. 'End of the day,' I confirmed cheerfully.

She was dubious: 'Can we remember, this time?'

Was this a genuine *We*, or the nursey version?

I returned to Ornella, to hiss happily, 'See? I can't come to the fair because I have to stay behind to stitch this hem.'

'*Evening*,' she stressed. 'We're going in the evening.' Turning vigorously to the clots of leftover pastry, she murmured, 'Eight o'clock, my house.'

And, so, somehow, I am here. She opens the door to me, smiles a greeting and peeks behind me, scans the empty road. 'Did your Dad bring you?'

'My Dad is in Saudi,' I say. 'As usual.'

'Oh.' She closes the door behind me, slowly, puzzled.

'Working,' I explain. Or fail to explain. Wiping my shoes on the mat, I protest, 'And, anyway, what about my mum?'

She frowns, the creases silting with make-up. I have never seen Ornella in make-up. I can see from the careful but heavy application that this is a new experience for her.

'Couldn't my mum have brought me?'

Ornella shrugs, unconcerned. 'Did she?'

'No,' I admit. 'She can't drive.'

Ornella flickers with irritation, strides past me along the hallway, flings open a door. I have never seen her out of school uniform. The jeans and jumper make the make-up even more strange. She announces through the doorway, 'Veronica,' followed by, 'Trustworthy enough for you?' Which tells me that there has been some trouble.

I balk.

A voice is coming from beyond the doorway; a man's voice, very foreign, but slow, sleepy: '*Not* with your face like that. Please remove it.'

Ornella lunges, grabs me, hauls me into the doorway in view of a man in an armchair. 'Paps,' she announces, to me.

'Hello . . .' Obviously I cannot say *Paps*. I do not want to say *Mr Marini*, in case *Mister* is wrong: I do not know the Italian for Mister.

He smiles, and purrs, 'Aaaah, Verrrronica, yes?'

Yes what? I smile nervously, eager to agree to anything and everything. Because I am terrified that he will say more and I will be unable to hear through his accent, or even that he will speak to me in Italian. I am dizzied by his foreignness. His dressing gown is rusty tartan, and his sleek slippers have the unnerving pinky-brown shine of hide. The centres of his watchful eyes are so dark that they seem to be something other than the stones which are stuck in the eyes of other people. The grey in his hair is pale blue. Ornella yells, 'Mum?'

In the dim distance, on the dark side of the lamp, a door opens. A woman walks towards us, her legs swinging straight from small hips, her knees peeping from the hem of her skirt. The lining of the skirt whistles around her legs. She is dressed up, but not for a fun-fair. But surely not for staying home, not even this home. My mum never bothers with shoes in our house, especially not shoes like this: long slim heels and toes.

'Veronica,' announces Ornella again, now noticeably bored.

I smile.

In return, she smiles down on me, and says, 'Hello, dear.' But she seems not to see me. Is this because, to her, I could be anyone? Or should she be wearing glasses?

Her hair, in a loose low bun, makes me think of silk. Spun silk. The colour of raw silk.

Ornella shouts, 'Okay, we're off,' and yanks me back through the doorway. She whispers fiercely into my ear, 'Wait a moment.' The stairs boom beneath her feet. Alone in the hallway, my nervousness increases. So I decide to follow. I climb slowly, unsurely, heavily, sending warning creaks ahead of me. Turning from the top stair onto the landing I see Ornella in her parents' bedroom. I know that it is their bedroom because the bed is big and there is no mess, there is nothing but bedroom furniture. She is slotted onto a stool in front of the dressing table. She glances expressionlessly at me, and reaches across the shiny surface into a dark box. In her rising fingertips is a huge pearl, which she presses to her earlobe. She repeats the action, more speedily, with the other one of the pair.

'Ornella!' These pearls, for a trip to the fair?

She turns instantly, frowning, pressing silence all over us. Her face is illuminated by the two pearls. She slips from the dressing table, walks soundlessly towards me into the glowing hallway and passes me onto the stairs, perfume buzzing.

She hurries down the staircase by swinging on the banisters, lowering herself over several stairs each time and then landing with both feet: swing-thump, swing-thump. She calls back to me, 'Did you stay behind?'

'Where?'

She has reached the foot of the stairs, so she turns, in front of the small hallway window, to look up at me. The pearls are the colour of the evening sky. 'Stuffy,' she says. 'Cookery. Needlework.'

'Oh. No.' Now I wince at the realization, 'Oh *no*,' but rapidly console myself: 'Why should I care? What's the point of a hem?'

Her eyes twinkle, despite their dusty lids. 'If you don't know by now,' she says into my ear when I reach her, 'then I'm not sure that I can tell you.' And now, much louder, to the hallway, she exclaims, 'Here they are!'

I turn unsteadily in the humid cloud of her perfume.

'Guido,' her voice rings, 'and Jean-Marie.'

Her brother is filling the hallway, scratching his hanging head. Behind him is another boy whom I recognize as a member of the French Exchange Group which has been roaming our school for the past few days and causing trouble in the Tuck Shop queue.

'Jean-Marie is staying . . .'

'Yes.' I have detected something in the way that she says his name. (But did she really say *Marie?*)

'And they're going to the fair tonight.' Her tone is tinkly with surprise, and her smile ripples the make-up around her eyes.

What a coincidence.

Guido opens the front door. My lungs deepen, trawling the evening air for its smokey smell of freedom, but without success. Suddenly I do not feel free. Ornella screams back into the empty hallway: 'Okay, we're off.'

Her mum's voice warbles from somewhere, 'Don't talk to anybody.'

On the doorstep, closing the door, Ornella leans into me to confide in a thrilled whisper, 'But, Veronique, I *must* practise my *French*.'

As we walk down the path, I can hear Ornella's dad singing: a repetition of two words, names. 'Ee-stan-bull, Con-stan-tee-no-pel.' Istanbul, Constantinople? Are they in Italy? Passing through the front gate, Guido turns and spits, 'Don't follow us.' And the French boy, behind him, copies his expression of loathing.

Ornella's red smile glistens in reply. 'Guido, dear, there is one way, and one way only, to the fair.'

The echo is lower: 'Just don't follow us.'

Ornella slows our pace, dawdles. When the two boys are further ahead of us, she demands excitedly, 'Isn't Jean-Marie *gorgeous*?'

Unfortunately, the answer is no. Which is harsh. So I say nothing.

'He's so *sexy*,' she enthuses.

Sexy belongs to the sixties, and *Hair*.

'I can't stay away from him; I want to . . .' she flounders flamboyantly, surrendering to helplessness with a huge shrug, '. . . breathe the same air.'

I resist the obvious retort about garlic. To be fair, I did not detect garlic. Garlic is not the problem. His trousers are too short. I watch him scuffling alongside Guido. His T-shirt is orange. He has nothing even faintly resembling a haircut. Although I cannot see from here, I recall his upper lip, the damp stain of a virgin moustache.

I manage a careful, polite, interested, 'And his name is Jean-*Marie*?'

She replies mildly, happily, 'Oh, Catholics *do* that.'

'Do what?'

'Call their boys Mary.'

I look sideways to discover if she is joking. But she is gazing insensibly ahead.

'Mary,' I repeat sceptically.

She glances reluctantly at me. 'Yes.' And switches back to Guido and Jean-Marie. 'My mother's brother's middle name was Mary,' she muses.

I do not believe this, but I try, 'Was he picked on? At school?'

With a switch of the pearl button, her face turns to me. 'It was a Catholic school,' she says flatly. 'So they were all called Mary.' She loosens with a shrug. 'Well, lots of them.'

I venture, 'Are you a Catholic?'

She says a word which I fail to catch.

So I gloss over this, move on to, 'And your parents?'

The same word. This time, I catch it, realize that it is *lapsed*. And she is asking me: 'You?'

'I'm not anything.'

She dismisses this, murmuring, 'You have to be something. You're born into something, even if you spend the whole of your life ignoring it.'

'Well, I wasn't.'

'Well, lucky old you,' she says, suddenly scathing, bored, utterly unconvinced.

Now, after a long moment of silence, she asks cheerfully, 'Are you an Arab, then?'

'*What*?'

She turns on me, affronted. 'Your dad,' she urges. 'Saudi.'

'*Working . . .*' I manage.

'Well, Arabs *do work* in Saudi, don't they?'

I laugh. 'Ornella, my Dad was born and bred in Stevenage. He's a plumber, and for some reason they want British plumbers in Saudi.'

After a brief pause, she asks, 'They have water in Saudi, then?'

'I suppose so.'

'I thought it was desert.'

We ponder this, until I cannot resist challenging her, 'Do I *look* like an Arab?' I do not look like an Arab because I am blonde, and I have never seen a blonde Arab.

We cross the road behind the boys, and when we reach the other side, she asks me, 'Do I look Italian, half-Italian?'

'Yes.' But why? Brown eyes, brown hair? No. If I did not know about Ornella's Italian blood, then I would not know. I open my mouth to retract, to explain, but her gaze has leaked back into the distance and she is sighing, 'I'm not *foreign*, though, am I; not *really* foreign, like him.'

In one sense, no; but in another sense, to me, yes, very. Wonderfully foreign, I realise with surprise.

The boys have stopped, are waiting for us, with frowns

of impatience. I realize that I have been hearing, although not listening to, the drone of the fairground for some time. Now I listen to the disco beat – two discos, two rhythms from different parts of the fair, one following the other, forming a heartbeat, ba-boom ba-boom – and the careening of the ghost train. The fairground is behind a thick wall of silvery caravans. Ornella quickens her pace, our pace, and Guido shouts angrily from a gap in the caravans, 'See you here at nine. *Here*, okay? *Don't* try to walk home on your own in the dark.'

'Guido,' she pants, the pearls wobbling on her earlobes, 'It's dark *now*. Nearly.' Panic has drained all expression from her face. But her panic has nothing to do with nightfall. It has to do with losing Jean-Marie.

Which Guido knows, because he sighs viciously and enjoys shouting, 'Just don't leave the fairground and you'll be fine.'

'Guido!' She rushes to bob breathless in front of him and Jean-Marie, pointing into the fairground. 'Come on that big thing with me.'

She is pointing to a machine which resembles a Big Wheel. But it is not the kindly Big Wheel of my childhood trips to the fun-fair. This wheel carries small wire cages. Although I cannot see, I presume that there are people locked inside these cages. The machine spins, the cages spin. The people spin. Their stomachs, too, presumably. And brains. And eyes, even, in their sockets.

Guido says, 'Go with *her*,' meaning me.

'Oh no,' I say immediately. 'No. No.'

I turn to Ornella. 'You promised me that if I came, I wouldn't have to go on anything.'

'I did,' Ornella says excitedly to Guido. 'I *did*.'

'*Well*,' mimics Guido, breathless. 'That's *your* problem, *isn't* it.'

I check on Jean-Marie. His face retains the frown which he flexed at us from the garden gate. He understands nothing except that Ornella is trouble.

Guido says smugly to Ornella, 'Have a nice time with your friend.'

Ornella is furious with him. So she protests, 'She has a name!'

Guido is turning away, granting me my wish, to *Leave-me-out-of-this*. But Jean-Marie is fractionally too late in copying him. Ornella snares him in her wide eyes. She gestures towards me and cheerfully pronounces, 'Veronique.' A belated introduction. He frowns at me through the original frown, and nods in greeting. Which is ridiculous. But I have to smile in return.

Ornella says, 'Candyfloss.' Hurrying after the boys, she shrieks, 'Le candyfloss! Des candyfloss! Guido!'

Guido halts, stiff with fury. Jean-Marie idles, confused. Now, inside the wall of caravans, I find that the fairground is very crowded. The crowd is made of groups of people, large groups, complete sets of people from grandparents to babies. I have never seen so many children in the open air so late in the evening. Where has everyone come from? This is a small town but I do not know these faces. Groups wash around Guido and Jean-Marie, between them.

Ornella is shouting over the throbbing motors, 'Jean-Marie can't come to the fair and not have candyfloss.'

Unease flickers in Jean-Marie's frown because he has recognized the sound of his name.

Loudly, Guido sighs, 'Christ, Ornella.'

And the machines: who makes these machines? Spinning, speeding, rising and falling machines; huge, with rows of seats, with safety bars. And everywhere knobbly with fairy lights which run staccato sequences of murky red and green flashes. Are there factories where these machines are made? Or do fairground people build them?

Ornella is asking me, 'Candyfloss?'

'Oh *no*.' I wrinkle my nose, which unfortunately heightens my sense of the nearby hot dogs.

'Guido?'

'I *said no*.'

Which, in fact, is untrue; he has not said no. Not to candyfloss.

'Jean-Marie,' she says, decisively, and marches alone into the crowd.

Guido glances warily at me. We do not move. I swivel and watch a man reaching into one of the tiny stalls with a long thin cane, reaching past the proprietor and hooking one of the cheerful bathtub ducks from the slowly rotating centre. He pores over his catch, joined now by a woman: together they flip the duck, fix on the inky black number on the bottom. No luck: they reel away, faces slack, leaving the duck in the hands of the stallholder. All around him hang the prizes, goldfish, each one set into a small shiny lump of water. As the couple stomp away, these silvery bells wobble soundlessly in the breeze.

Ornella reappears beneath a pink cloud. I doubt that candyfloss would feature in Mrs Stuffy's list of Important Dietary Components. But, then, for Ornella, this is probably a point in its favour.

Passing me, she challenges, 'What does Stuffy know about life?' She has read my mind again. And me, hers, too, I suppose.

'Ornella,' I laugh after her, 'if the way to a man's heart is through his stomach, then you're making a big mistake.'

She flounces towards Jean-Marie. Guido hurries to shout to her, 'We're off. Stay with your friend and meet us *where* I said, *when* I said.'

She purrs, 'Yes, big brother. But first . . .' And she stops in front of Jean-Marie. 'Candyfloss,' she says to him, instructs him, very slowly, carefully, gently.

Flummoxed, he watches her lips to follow the word. 'Candyfloss,' he echoes, unsurely.

Her lips soften slowly into a big smile. Then she hands him the brittle cloud, murmuring, 'Mmm,' probably to confirm that it is edible. Or supposedly edible.

Guido sneers, 'Not having some yourself, Ornella?'

She tips an amused glance in Guido's direction and follows the candyfloss with her lips, sucks a mouthful of pink crystals.

Jean-Marie smiles, perhaps due to the wispy stickiness on Ornella's chin, and says, 'Thank you.'

Ornella shrugs jauntily, and asks all of us, 'Who's for a wheel-on-the-wild-side, then?'

She knows that I will never agree to a ride. And I suspect that she knows something about Guido, too. Because his expression is suddenly even more sour.

'Jean-Marie?' she asks sweetly. And she points through his confusion to the wheel.

He grins stickily and shrugs the candyfloss.

Ornella soothes, 'She'll hold it for you.' She is looking at me: '*Veronique*,' she pronounces thoroughly.

His eyes shift from Ornella to the wheel and back to Ornella again. Suddenly he thrusts the candyfloss towards me. 'Veronique,' he says, nearly as perfectly as Ornella's version.

Ornella spins towards me, crowing an untranslatable, 'Attaboy!'

Reluctantly, I take the candyfloss. At least it will not melt. As Ornella bounces past me I halt her with my free hand. 'Do you really want to go on that thing?' I am genuinely curious.

She laughs. 'At least I'll be in safe hands.'

Well, *hands*, anyway.

Jean-Marie follows her, his shoes crunching flat the dried tracks of vehicles. I watch them approaching the base of the wheel, the tiny gaudy ticket office.

'You afraid of heights, then?' Guido asks me.

I turn to him. 'No, not heights.' But something tells me that this was the wrong answer. The levelling of his mouth, perhaps, or the thickening of his eyelids. He *wants* me to be afraid of heights. *He* is afraid of heights.

I try hurriedly, but truthfully, 'Not heights, but the spinning.' I try harder: 'The speed.'

He sneers, 'Speed.'

Stepping towards me, he confides, 'Ornella's a bitch.' It
was said matter-of-factly, and perhaps even admiringly.
'She goes for the jugular,' he explains mildly. 'She knows
your weaknesses and she goes for them.'

I do not know how to respond, so I stare at him. Then
I manage, 'She wasn't interested in *us*; she wanted *him*.'
I nod towards them, stepping into their wire cage.

A sigh torches Guido's lungs. 'And, God, yes, *why*?
He's such a wanker.'

'Is he?' I meant, Do *you* think so, too?

Guido stretches his eyes wide open, and they bulge
hard and shiny. 'Well, what do *you* think?'

Well, yes, but, 'Why didn't you want Ornella to come
with you? She could help you with him.'

'Help to keep him here for hours, you mean.'

I turn to the wheel to search for Ornella and Jean-
Marie, but they have been spun invisible. There is solely
the wheel, trailing its frill of fairylights in costume-
jewellery colours.

Guido accuses, 'Anyway, why did you come along if
you knew?'

Knew what? 'About Jean-Marie?' Amused, I admit, 'I
didn't know.'

'Oh, well, there you are, then,' he mutters. 'Jugular.'

Which particular jugular? Good faith, perhaps? Trust?

Or is it Ornella who trusts? Lately I have been less and
less able to refuse her.

We turn to wait for the wheel to slow, to stop. Eventually, through the crowd, I see pairs of people disembarking from the wire boxes, hauled and steadied by a man in oily jeans. These people have been shrunk by the spin. The man seems unsurprised, decants them very definitely onto the wooden platform where they puff up in the fresh air. My eyes dodge the crowds to find Ornella. I have not seen her being pulled from the wheel by the man. But suddenly she is hobbling towards me, with Jean-Marie. Clamped onto Jean-Marie's arm. Smiles have been spun across their faces.

'Are you alright?' I ask, 'Are you alright?'

She passes me, they pass me, hurrying ahead together with the determined, rough steps of the three-legged racer. I follow, with the candyfloss, with Guido, realizing that this is going to be a long evening.

I PEER THROUGH the rusty leaves of the rose-bushes onto the front lawn. Ornella is sitting on the grass, draining a bottle of wine. At last, I have found her. Stepping away from the thudding house, I warn her, 'If you knock-it-back like that, it'll knock-back-up.'

She swivels giddily, delighted, and proclaims, 'Veronique! Niquie!'

'*Nella*,' I reply, flatly. 'I'm *serious*.'

'Well,' she confides as I kneel down beside her, 'don't be. This is a *party*.'

Correction: '*This* is a front lawn. And *these* . . .' I point to the surrounding houses, one-by-one, '. . . are neighbours. Why don't you come back inside?'

Someone clatters onto the doorstep. 'Veronica? Vonny?' Cathy Sykes' voice.

I stand up.

Cathy calls, 'I *thought* I saw you coming out here; what are you doing?'

I shrug, which is easier than saying that I have followed Ornella and that I have no idea what *she* is doing.

'Anyway,' rushes Cathy, who is obviously not interested in the answer, 'do you have any nail polish?'

I peer into the darkness. 'Haven't you already painted your nails?'

A handful of pearly nails flickers in the porch. 'It's not for my nails,' she explains, admiring them. 'It's for my stocking.' She thrusts one leg through the doorway, switches the skirt on her thigh and pin-points the silvery scratch of a ladder.

Below me, unseen, Ornella murmurs, 'This one will run and run.'

Cathy straightens, totters on the doorstep, calls into the darkness. 'Who's that?'

'Only Ornella. And, no, I haven't. Got any nail polish. Sorry.'

'It's my mum's stocking, actually.' Cathy has shrunk, worried. 'I suppose you don't have any nail polish, do you, Ornella?'

41

Ornella says, 'The smell makes me puke.'

'Well,' she says coldly, 'thank God we're not all so sensitive.'

I suggest, 'Surely Spencer's mum has some nail polish.' I scan the façade of the house, looking for a small high window of crinkly glass trailing a sparse sleek vine of pipes: bathroom, bathroom cabinet, and Spencer's mum's make-up collection. But I see no bathroom window here, on the front of the house. The downstairs window is wobbling with the silhouettes of drunken dancers, like a giant lava lamp.

'Spencer's mum is vegetarian, or something,' Cathy replies wearily.

'So? I didn't say that she *eats* the nail polish.'

'It's something to do with animal testing. No make-up.' And suddenly she is gone.

Below me, Ornella says, 'They paint the rabbit's claws and see how long until the polish chips off.'

'Not funny.' I have a rabbit, called Felix.

'I'm sorry. And apologies to Felix.'

Forgiving, I kneel again. 'Nella, what are you doing out here?'

Despite the darkness I can see that she is suddenly alert, 'Do you have any food?' she asks me, almost conspiratorially.

'Do I *look* like I have any food? What are you doing out here?'

She disappears, drops backwards into the darkness to lie on her back on the grass. 'Escaping Philip Marshall,' she says up to me, 'And dreaming of Hugh Gleeson.'

I am sick of hearing about Hugh Gleeson from her. He is in the Upper Sixth, we are in the Fifth Form: two years' difference, so she has no chance. I tell her, 'When I walked past Spencer's dad's study half an hour ago, you seemed to be enjoying yourself very thoroughly with Philip Marshall in the swivel chair.'

Her voice trickles warm from the dusk-damp grass: 'It was nice while it lasted.'

I protest, 'You've had your eye on Philip Marshall for quite a while.' Swiftly I preempt, 'Well, half an eye.'

'A fraction of an eye,' she says pleasantly, dreamily. 'And I can no longer be unfaithful to Hughie-baby.'

I start, '*Ornella* . . .' A gentle warning, a soft fog-horn in the dew-stewing darkness. But how do I continue, what do I say? How do I tell her to give up on her dream?

She concedes, 'Unfaithful to the *fantasy* of him, I mean.' But the tone was happy. Because she is drunk.

I drift my fingers slowly through the rooted spiders of grass. 'Fantasy will get you nowhere.'

'Ah,' she sighs, 'but it's fun.'

I shrug: *If you say so.*

I listen to the desperate whine which is jangling the speakers, *Having, The time of, Your life, Oo-oo-oo-oo, See that girl.* I tell her, 'I think I'll go in for a dance.' To blow-dry my dewy bones.

She says, 'He looks like a rodent, don't you think?'

'Who?'

'Phili-pipi Marshall.'

'*Rodent?*' I laugh. 'Why not just say rat?'

'Because the connotations are all wrong,' she replies.

Her eyes follow me as I stand, they slot backwards in their sockets, focus upwards. 'He doesn't look like a *rat*. Not *that* sort of rat. I mean, he's *not* a *rat*. But he *looks* like a *rodent*.'

I have had enough of her drunken musings. I take a step back.

'Do you know about out-of-body experiences?' she asks me calmly. Her eyes have not yet let me go. 'Where you watch yourself from the corner of the ceiling?'

'Yes,' I reply, wearily.

She sits up in one stiff movement, one Frankenstein sit-up. 'Do you?' she yelps excitedly.

'*No*, not *personally*,' I correct irritably.

'Oh.' She does not move. 'Well,' she resumes eventually, 'When I was swivelling with Philip, I tried hard for an out-of-body experience. But he . . .' she shrugs, '. . . was pulling me back, I suppose.'

'Well, yes,' I confirm, briefly having been a witness. She says no more.

'So you went for an out-of-house experience, instead?' I sense her smile. 'And it's working,' she says.

'Poor Phillip.' I am distracted by the shadow-puppets on the newly drawn curtains.

'*You* have him, then,' drifts the small voice.

Trying to identify the distorted figures on the curtains, I narrow my eyes. When I was small I had an annual in which there was a page of secret writing, the letters so long and thin that I had to narrow my eyes and tilt the book to be able to read them. 'You know very well that Adam Rawlings is the love of my life.' I sigh: 'Or not.'

'*Why* not?' This comes soft and low: Ornella is switching to listening mode.

I turn my attention from the leaping shadows, lower myself for a moment to squat beside her. 'I think that he's after Gilly Lawson.'

'Gilly Lawson!'

'Shhh!' *And do the listening.*

But, 'Nooo,' the burning denial hisses in my face. 'Why would he fancy Gilly Lawson? Why would *anyone* fancy Gilly Lawson?'

I smile to myself, momentarily refreshed: yet another person who thinks that Gilly Lawson is unfanciable. But Ornella simply fails to understand. Often I feel that I have to translate our world for her, to tell her what is going on in front of her eyes. And now I have to inform her, 'I'm afraid that all the boys are after Gilly Lawson.'

'Why?' she blasts. 'Why would anyone fancy her? She's so *stupid*.'

Which seems harsh. I flinch, and counter, 'It's not what she *is*, Nella, it's what she *does*.'

For a moment, there is nothing from Ornella. But now, '*Does* she?'

'Does she what?'

'Do it.'

I realize that *Dancing Queen* is repeating. For the second time. Who is in charge of the music, in there? 'No, not *it* it.'

'*What*, then?'

I did not expect to be questioned for specific details; I am surprised to find that I do not know what words to use. Not for Ornella. There are the words that I use with my friends, but Ornella is somehow different.

'*Tell* me,' she urges.

Suddenly she relaxes, to tease me: 'You don't *know*.'

'I *do* know.'

'So, tell me:' sweetness and light, suddenly, from my shadowy interrogator.

'Use your imagination.'

She leans back onto her hands, half-way between sitting and lying. 'Dangerous,' she says cheerfully.

'What is?'

'You telling me to use my imagination.'

'Why?'

'Because you don't know how bad my imagination is,' this comes in the same cheerful, sensible tone, 'And I might come up with something far worse than a blow job.' She starts to muse, 'An inaccurate term, because you don't *blow* . . .'

'Yes, thank you, Ornella.'

She turns to me. 'Why don't you try to beat Silly Gilly at her own game? Can't you grit your teeth, or something?' She stops herself with a snorted laugh. 'Oops, no, not a tactic designed to win you many hearts.'

Suddenly *Dancing Queen* grinds to a spectacular halt, the needle ripped noisily from the groove. After a moment of stunning silence, the replacement is *The Wombles' Song*. 'My *God*!' I shriek at no one in particular, 'Who brought *this*?'

'A mole?' And she enquires, conversationally, 'Who's your favourite Womble?'

46

Emphatically, I tell her, 'I don't have a favourite Womble.'

'Isn't Felix a Womble?'

'Felix is a *rabbit*.'

'No, the name: Orinoco . . . Felix . . .'

'No. Will you come inside?' I do not feel that I should leave her here. Not like this.

'Everyone has a favourite Womble,' she muses. 'Deep down.'

'Not me.' I reach for her, squeeze her arm, shake her: 'Now, are you coming?'

'In a minute,' she says, and lies back down on the grass. 'You go. Go and snog Adam Rawlings.' She adds, 'If that's the best that you can do,' and a smirk floats up from the words. But then, 'Listen, Niquie: you're wrong about Adam.'

I shiver, but warmly. 'I can't help myself.'

'No,' she says, serenely, 'I mean, you're wrong about Gilly. About him and her. Believe me. You'll have no trouble. You haven't seen the way that he looks at you. But I have. And, believe me, he wants to have your babies.'

I laugh down at her. 'You're very, very drunk.'

'Yes, perhaps,' she yawns. 'But it's true about the babies.'

A man is walking along the pavement on the other side of the road. An old man, in his fifties or sixties. Small under the streetlamps. A wash of thin hair on his bright, bony head. Brown suit. What is striking about him is the flowers: he is carrying a thin bunch of flowers

47

in a tall cone of paper. He seems too old for flowers. Or for *these* flowers, carried so carefully. He is holding them slightly from him as if he is already offering them: I can see that this bunch is for giving, not for his own vase. Nor is this a formality, a token, not such a simple, homely bunch. No, these flowers are for giving carefully, with love. I want to follow him, to know where he is going, to see her.

'Off you go,' Ornella interrupts my thoughts from a long way below me. 'Go and ask Adam-darling to dance.'

The Wombles' Song has changed into *Bohemian Rhapsody*, which is no better for dancing. 'We can't dance to this,' I tell her.

She sighs, 'I was speaking euphemistically.'

ORNELLA AND I have come in here for Brown Derbys and Coke. An hour or so ago, we were here for chips and tea. I ordered my tea with a slice of lemon, which came curled stiff in my saucer like a dead goldfish. On the wall there is a picture of a Brown Derby. The base of the Brown Derby, the solid foundation, is a doughnut, although I might not have known from the photo, without the help of the menu. The doughnut is yellow, and smooth. Sitting on this base is a tapering twist of white ice-cream. Chopped nuts and chocolate sauce spill over the top and down the sides. The picture has always been here and I have always been curious; but whenever I come in here with Mum and Juliet, Mum says, *No, because there are two of you, and when there are two of you, you can't have everything that you want*. But there are two of us now – Ornella and me – and we seem to be succeeding.

Tapping the menu on the tabletop, Ornella looks across at me and wonders, 'What type of cheese do you think they use in the cheeseburger?'

'Cheese is cheese, surely.'

The tall, thin, shiny menu taps harder; and Ornella pipes, '*You are* irritable.'

'I'm *tired*,' I tell her. 'Thirsty. Hungry.' Deliciously so. Beneath the table I lift my hot feet from their shoes and lower them onto the cold floor tiles.

She says, 'Brown Derby to the rescue.'

We both check the waitress. She is spinning from table to table in the steamy distance, budding white plates.

Ornella to the rescue, too, because I could not have ordered a Brown Derby unless she had offered to pay my bus fare home.

It was Ornella's idea to come shopping. When she rang to ask me, I said no, because Dad had come home from Saudi this morning.

There was a pause before she squeaked, 'Well, have you seen him?'

'Well, yes . . .' Briefly, before he went upstairs to sleep.

'Well?' she concluded.

And, yes, what? I felt that I should stay home, but what would I do when he was awake again? Before he went to bed, Juliet had been talking enough for both Mum and me, chattering to him about everything from school to Felix. She is too young to write to him; or, to write properly, to write as much as she wants to say. Sitting with her at the table, he listened, nodding and laughing. Mum stood with her back against the kitchen cabinets, her hands behind her back. I had never seen Mum so still, particularly not in the kitchen. Standing beside her, I noticed that I was as tall as her.

Ornella had complained down the phone: 'You can't stay home for the whole day,' and then stressed, 'It's the weekend.' Several times during the conversation she repeated, 'I *must* buy some shoes for school, *please* don't leave me to do it on my own.' But mostly she tempted me: 'We can have a laugh . . . we can do whatever we want to do, all day long . . . the sales are on . . .' In the tiny pauses I heard the silence of the house: much more silence than usual, so that Dad could sleep.

She reassured me, 'You have the evening for your Dad.'

I did not tell her that I had been hoping to see Adam this evening. Instead, I agreed to ask Mum if I could go shopping. I left the receiver on the window sill and went to find her. She was hanging washing onto the line which spans the lean-to. Her mouth, when she turned, was sharp with a peg.

I said, 'Ornella's on the phone, she wants to know if I can go and help her to choose some school shoes.'

Mum slurred, 'What, *today?*'

As if a lot was happening at home.

I said nothing.

'Oh, alright,' she gargled, looking disappointed.

And so here I am. Again. The first time that we came in here, when we had finished choosing the shoes, was for toasted teacakes; then, for lunch, milkshakes; then, for late-lunch, because we were still hungry, the chips; and now, to end the day, the Brown Derbys. Between visits we have survived on Ornella's cough lozenges. On each visit we have had more bags to place beside us on the slippery red benches. Firstly, there were Ornella's shoes. Then, a pair of jeans which she bought because they were in a sale, and a pair of footless tights which I bought from the same shop for the same reason. Next, a long cardigan for Ornella, and for me a thin blue Grandad-shirt, reduced because it was missing a button. Finally, three pairs of earrings which Ornella chose from a revolving rack on a counter in the department store, and the top which she prompted me to buy. Whilst she was examining the earrings, I was looking through the clothes. I was holding up the top when she said, admiringly, approvingly, 'That's very you.'

Was it? I returned the glance. She smiled, briefly. A pair of long diamanté earrings were dull in the palm of her hand. What, exactly, did she mean, *Very me*? I returned to the top, held it higher. It was delicate, thin, trim. I ran my gaze down the tiny buttons of pearl. It was lovely. It was like some of my own favourite clothes, but more so. More expensive, too. But it had caught my eye immediately. It had recognized me, I had recognized it. It was *Very me*. Yet it was not *for* me. It would belong eventually to someone who simply happened to have money. When would the time come for me to buy lovely clothes that were *me* rather than those in sales, and necessities? My gaze dipped to lick the creamy sheen of the cotton. If I wore this cotton I would keep as cool as deep water. I would shine, unmarked. Nothing bad could happen to me if I wore such a shirt.

Suddenly Ornella was beside me. 'Go on,' she urged gently, kindly. There was a bag in her hand: she had bought the earrings. I considered the cost of the shirt. I had been fairly careful lately, so I had savings. Which were partly earnings, from babysitting for several families in our street and feeding Next Door's cat for a fortnight. But there was Adam's birthday present to consider. And before Adam, Mum. On the other hand, because Dad had come home, there was a good chance of more pocket money. I slung the top over my arm and told Ornella, 'I'll see how it looks.'

I saw, and I bought.

Now Ornella is saying, 'So, the old man is home, huh?' She is gazing beyond me, presumably to track the waitress.

'Yes.'

She gives up on the waitress, returns to me, asks, 'Can you hear them doing it?'

'Who?' Doing what?

She laughs, reaches again for the menu to tap the table-top. 'Your *parents.*' *Of course.*

I suspect that I have lost track; or, I hope so. The waitress has arrived, swooping between us with the two steel dishes. In response, Ornella is noisily appreciative, before delving with her teaspoon. She sinks with the first mouthful, groaning long and smooth. Which encourages me to start, to carve exactly the correct proportions of ice-cream, sauce, and nuts from the dish with the cool lip of my spoon. Once the spoonful is inside my mouth, some slips, and some sticks.

'Well?' asks Ornella.

'Fabulous.'

She swipes the spoon from her mouth in another laugh. 'No, your *parents*.'

My mouth is momentarily gummed with warm sauce left by the slippery ice-cream.

'Can you hear them doing it?' she asks pleasantly.

Surely she cannot mean what I think that she means. I resist asking *Doing what?* Instead, I say, 'What do you mean, *Hear them?*'

She waves her spoon to hold my attention whilst she swallows a mouthful. 'Hear them; hear them,' she repeats – insists – pointlessly. Frowning down into her dish, pressing down hard with the edge of her spoon onto the doughnut, she explains, 'In your house. I mean, sometimes *I* hear *my* parents doing it, but ours is quite a big house, as you know, and their bedroom is across the landing from mine, so I only hear if I go to the bathroom, in the night.' She slips a chip of doughnut into her mouth, and bites.

I let my spoon sink into the ice-cream. '*Ornella*.'

She looks up sharply, hugely; her eyes are two blobs of caramel. 'What?'

'Well . . .' My spoon, slipping, is swilling in warm

white fluid which bears no resemblance to ice-cream. A minute ago, it was all ice-cream. '. . . how do you know that it's the sound of them doing it?'

She is firmly into the doughnut now. Between mouthfuls she says dismissively, 'Well, they're not putting their hair into rollers.'

Twisting the spoon, she draws it down, slowly and cleanly, from her mouth. 'So you've never heard them?' she asks, more seriously.

'No I have not,' I protest.

She shrugs. 'At least mine *do* do it. Natasha Driscoll's parents don't.'

'She *told* you?' *She told* YOU?

Ornella laughs, mouth closed, then splurts, 'No.' She leans across the table and snips at my indestructible doughnut with her spoon. 'I *saw*.'

I place my spoon in my saucer.

'Separate beds.' She taps my idle spoon with her own.

'I've had enough,' I tell her, 'for the moment.'

Mouth full, she raises her eyebrows.

I suggest, 'Perhaps they have back problems.'

The eyebrows drop heavily: a frown, of incomprehension.

'Natasha's parents: some people sleep in separate beds because they have problems with their backs.'

The eyebrows leap dismissively.

She taps my spoon again, to remind me; and warns me, 'I'll finish yours, in a minute.'

I lift my spoon and scrape the silvery surface, collecting cold dense chocolate. Do Mum and Dad do it? When he comes home, do they do it more, or less, than other parents? How would it sound? Do I hear them in my sleep, perhaps?

Ornella drops her spoon into her own empty dish and slams back in her seat. 'Twenty more of those, please,' she murmurs to no one in particular. Now she smacks her lips, troubled: 'I'm thirsty.'

Steadily, stealthily, I continue my Hunt The Chocolate, carefully drawing brown routes all over the dish. When I glance up, I find Ornella fidgeting and frowning over her open purse.

'Jesus,' she says thoughtfully.

'What?'

'I thought I had a fiver.'

Ridiculously, I crane towards the tiny purse. 'Have you looked in the section for notes?'

She snaps it shut, clamps her hand around it. 'I spent it on the earrings,' she says conclusively. 'I forgot about the earrings. I've nothing left except two five pence pieces and a dime.'

I lay my saliva-sticky spoon gently in my saucer. 'A *dime?*'

'Forget the dime,' she says briskly. 'A dime is no use to us now.'

'*Ornella* . . .'

'I know, I know.'

'You *said* that you had enough money for all this.' I push my dish away from me; it clangs against hers.

Downcast, she is nodding. 'I did, I did. I did say it, I did have enough money.' She stops nodding, looks across the table to me and shrugs, sharp-shouldered, wide-eyed. 'Before the earrings. It was a genuine mistake, Veronica.'

'I don't care what kind of mistake it was! I only have enough money for one of these . . .'

'I'll wash up my dish,' she says, and grins.

'Be serious!' *For once.* And now, hotly, I remember: 'I'm fifteen pence short. For mine. You were going to lend me the bus fare *and* fifteen pence.'

'I was, I was,' she confirms dolefully.

I take a deep cool breath and glance quickly around us: has anyone heard our predicament? No one is looking. But are they listening?

I hiss across the table, 'What are we going to do?'

She continues in her new subdued tone, 'At least you have your top.'

'Oh, I'll wear that for them, shall I?'

'You could try.'

We are looking at each other across the table, but now there is a spasm in Ornella's level gaze. 'Abi and Bev,' she says to me.

I do not reply, because I do not know she means.

'Over by the phone box,' she says.

I twist towards the window, hearing Ornella snapping behind me from her seat, watching her haul open the door and run to the roadside, waving and calling. On the other side of the road, by a phone box, are Abi and Bev. Bev is leaving Abi, stepping backwards, one hand thrown into the air. They turn away from each other, smiling, continuing to smile. As Bev disappears around the corner, Abi sees Ornella. Her self-smile broadens in greeting, and she hurries towards her. When she has crossed the road and reached her, they walk together towards the door. Coming through the door, Abi is all smiles as usual. All midriff, too: her T-shirt is cropped above the waistband of her jeans to show a lean stripe of her brown stomach. 'Helloooo,' she is cooing to me. 'What are you doing here?' She flicks her long thick blonde plait over her shoulder and slips down to sit beside me. I realize that Ornella has not told her of our predicament.

Trying to keep calm and to seem welcoming, I throw back the question: 'What are *you* doing here?'

'Oh,' she sings, taking the menu card into both hands, 'I came to town this morning with Mikey, and he's a love, but boys aren't made for shopping, are they; so after a while he went home to watch the football, and I rang Bev.' A twitch of a smile: 'Girls have their uses.' She peers short-sightedly at the menu. 'I'm glad you're here, I'm *dying* of thirst.'

I snatch the menu from her. 'Abi, how much money do you have?'

She stares at me. 'Enough for a drink,' she says, defensively.

'It's just that we're in trouble.' I flick my hands into the air, feeling for words. 'Financially. Ornella told me that she had enough to pay and now she tells me that she forgot that she'd spent it on earrings.'

Abi smiles appreciatively across the table at Ornella. 'Ornella! You naughty twinkle.'

'We're about a pound short,' I urge. 'I don't suppose

that you can lend us a pound? Please? Until tomorrow?'

She shakes her head, and the plait slithers on the cotton between her shoulder blades. 'I've nothing but a fifty pence piece.'

I turn wildly, helplessly, to Ornella.

'*But*,' Abi soothes, 'I'll ask Bev.'

I whirl back to her. 'Bev's *gone*.'

She faces me with another affronted but patient stare. 'Bev's *going* to the bus stop. So, I'll *go* after her.'

'But what if *she* has no money?' I whine.

On the other side of the table, Ornella is bleating, 'She will have, she will have.'

Abi says sprightly, 'She has. A couple of quid. I know. I saw.' Her smile comes long and slow. 'So, *wait*.' She unbends from the table, stands very tall above us, taps the tabletop with a handful of long red nails. 'And order me a tea.'

And suddenly she is on other side of the door, and running across the other side of the huge window, the plait hooking and dropping through the air with each step.

'See?' goads Ornella. 'See? Everything was fine in the end.'

THIS IS ORNELLA'S weekly nail-filing session: double English Literature, Thursdays, nine until eleven. Miss

Knickers, our teacher, used to ask her to stop, but Ornella argued that she listens better when she is filing her nails. It is soothing, she says. It keeps her nails tidy, too. Which is handy. I am reading Ornella's magazine, which is hidden inside my folder. Reading magazines is soothing, but does not help me to listen. Soothing is the best that I can hope for in this lesson. I do not like English Literature, have disliked it from the very first lesson, last term, which was on the subject of Oberon and Titania. Apparently they are fairies, married to each other. Apparently the play is a comedy. The sole comic moment for me was immediately before last term's exam when Davey Lake was trying to scan the whole of one of our set texts and asking anxiously as we went into the room, 'What happens after page 209?'

To which Ornella replied sadly, 'Everything, I'm afraid, Davey.'

Ornella glances up from her nails, checks sideways with me. I raise my eyebrows in reply. In exhaustion and helplessness. More specifically, my eyebrows are saying, *This is no good, I'm no good at this.* And, *Surely it's eleven o'clock soon?* I glance around the other desks. In front of me, Davey Lake is tapping his feet urgently; or, no, tapping the whole of himself, faintly nodding in his chair to a private rhythm. Could I guess the music, if I concentrated hard? Across the room, Abi is sitting very still with her eyes closed. Miss Knickers is talking about Jane Austen; or, more specifically, Jane Austen's *Emma*, whom she seems to know very well, of whom she seems very fond. Miss Knickers is young, mid-twenties, and nice to us, nicer than most other teachers. Whenever I despair loudly of English Literature to Ornella, Ornella insists that *The trick is to remember that Miss Knickers isn't cleverer than us, she has simply read more books.* Sometimes she adds disparagingly, *Books about fairies.*

Miss Knickers is explaining cheerfully, 'When Jane Austen tells us that he goes to London for a haircut, she is telling us that he's a dandy.'

Ornella says, 'He's a junkie.'

I turn to her. Everyone turns to her. Which she does not see because she is bowed over her hands. The emery board is see-sawing relentlessly on one of her nails. It occurs to me that she may not realize that she has spoken aloud.

'Ornella,' I whisper.

But Miss Knickers is saying eagerly, 'I'm not quite with you, Ornella.'

Ornella looks up, surprised, filing blindly. 'It's obvious,' she says.

Miss Knickers smiles even more eagerly.

Ornella says dismissively, 'No one would go to London for a haircut.'

Across the room, Abi argues, '*I* would.'

Ornella swivels in her chair, frowns towards Abi. '*You* don't *have* haircuts.'

Abi rushes her hand down her plait and seizes the tuft at the end. 'I have trims,' she answers, indignantly. 'And if I *did* have haircuts, I'd go into London.'

'*Would* you?' I ask her. Ornella and I have our hair cut by Bev's older sister in Bev's mum's kitchen.

Miss Knickers says, 'Girls . . .'

'Miss Nichols, where do you have your hair cut?' Ornella asks earnestly.

I know the answer: in *Hats Off*: I know, because I saw her go in there. I tap my copy of the book. 'But *he's* a man, and a *man* wouldn't go to London for a haircut.'

Davey twists around in his chair to remind me, 'He's a *dandy*,' and laughs.

Miss Knickers looks down on him, anxiously, and starts, 'D . . .'

'He's going to London to replenish his supply,' Ornella calls triumphantly. There are murmurs of agreement, and Miss Knickers sweeps her anxious gaze around the classroom.

'No,' I insist. 'He's a *man*, he's going to London for an affair.'

Davey is still laughing, hanging over the back of his chair, and he sends me a wink. 'He's a *dandy*.'

Ornella shrieks, '*No one* would fancy *him*.'

Miss Knickers returns to her, uttering nervously, 'Don't you think so?'

I tap my book again, with relish. 'Emma does.'

Ornella turns to me, her eyes huge and glowing around their dark yolks: 'Emma is drugged out of her mind.'

Miss Knickers sighs disappointedly: 'Ornella.'

The gaze swims from me to her. 'She *is*. She's as *high*

as a *kite*. There's nothing normal about Emma. And her friend Harriet is *utterly spacey*. And her father lolls around all day . . .' She shrugs. 'This book is *riddled* with drugs.'

'Oh, Ornella.'

Ornella announces defensively to all of us, 'It was in their cough mixture.'

Reluctantly Miss Knickers confirms, 'That's true. In general, I mean. About cough mixture.'

Davey flicks through his copy of the book. 'Where? Perhaps I haven't read that bit yet.'

From the back of the class, someone yells, 'Page fifteen.' This is followed by a deep rumble of laughter.

Miss Knickers announces firmly to the class, 'There's no cough mixture in this book.'

Ornella says quietly, 'My dad told me.' And she recommences filing, thoughtfully.

Her dad is a doctor.

Miss Knickers is turning the pages of her own copy, sweeping each page from the others on a moist fingertip. She is frowning into the spinning pages, as if she is searching for something. But what? What will help her, now? But now the bell rings, rattles, clangs, in the corridor on the other side of the door. Our room responds immediately with the noisy grunts of chairs discarded across the tiles. In the same instance Miss Knickers shivers to attention, snaps shut her book, opens her mouth to say something, probably about homework. But I am borne breathless through the newly-opened door, and let loose in the dim Dettol-stinking corridor.

DAVEY, ORNELLA AND I are enjoying the very end of a long hot lunchtime, the last few moments before the start of the afternoon. Perhaps an extra few moments, because we are at the bottom of the field, beyond the sound of the bell. All we can do is watch for the slow sun-stiff movements of those nearer to the buildings. We will be the tail-end twitch of the ripple; we will be last to return to classes. I am teaching Davey to play Cat's Cradle, with laces from my plimsolls. He asked me to teach him. Ornella is lying on her back on the grass, smoking a cigarette. In front of us, there is a large informal game of football, the goal posts made from jumpers. Through my own low hum of concentration I hear the anguished gasps of the players, and the ball flapping around their feet. In the corner of my eye I see the scoop of each kick. I am trying to move Davey's fingers inside the long loop of black string. Baffled, he is groaning, 'Oh my God.'

And I am encouraging, 'Nearly, nearly.'

But I am slightly anxious because I have half a foot of toenails which are so far unpainted. The tiny pink glass bottle is propped beside me in a tuft of grass, the cap slack, the scent sticky in the surrounding air. I relinquish Davey. He groans again, but this time in relief. 'Glad to see you're in touch with the child inside, Vonny,' he says dryly.

'Unlike you, huh?' I do not tell him that I learnt Cat's Cradle from my little sister.

'Unlike me,' he confirms cheerfully.

'I must finish these nails.'

But before I can, he lifts the bottle from the grass, and lifts the lid, the brush, from the bottle. He strokes the thick glass rim with the tiny drenched wing. The rim wells with pink paint which oozes back into the bottle. 'Let me try,' he challenges.

It is easier to submit than to object. But I watch his aim very carefully.

Ornella says, 'I wish someone would paint my toenails for me.'

He replies from low over the first of the nails. 'You're wearing shoes.'

She says nothing. She brings the cigarette briefly to her lips, kisses the filter, breathes hazily into the sky. She is watching the game of football: I can see the reflections of the players moving on the tarnished buttons of her eyes.

Mildly, Davey asks, 'Have you heard of Lights, Prunella? Why settle for slight degeneracy, when you can go all the way? You collect all your fag-ends in a tea-pot, brew them overnight in some water, and drink the result in the morning.'

I try not to shudder; he is holding me hostage with a dripping pink pipette.

'It's called Lights,' he continues, 'because if you drink the brew, that's what you see.' He pauses, returns

64

Ornella's gaze, and smiles. 'You don't believe me, do you.'

She corrects, 'I'm thinking about whether to believe you.'

He shrugs; I cringe, curl my toes.

Ornella wonders, 'Do you think that a boy would ever say no?' She has returned, with a faint twist of her head, to the football game. Her hair is screwed into the ruffled grass. We have all had our hair cut short recently. All except Abi, whose hair seems even longer because she has begun to wear it loose.

'To what?' I ask.

She replies irritably: 'You know.' Discounting me, she asks, 'Davey?'

He pauses, surprised, thinking. 'Depends,' he decides.

She stiffens with impatience and irritation. 'On what?'

'Well *I* don't know. *Depends*.'

'Why?' I ask her. 'Who do you have your eye on?'

By now, we are all watching the footballers.

She muses, 'I'm trying to decide. Who d'you reckon?'

In a far corner of the makeshift pitch a knot of players pulls tight. Ornella is saying, 'You're thinking about Martin Brown, aren't you.'

I turn sharply to find that she is not watching them, but watching me. I snap a defensive, 'No,' which is a lie.

She tinkles with delight. 'Yes you are!' And now she objects cheerfully, 'He's a *snob*, Niquie, a cold-hearted snob.'

'He's *not* a *snob*.' As usual, Ornella understands nothing.

'See?' she crows, increasingly delighted. 'Look how you leap to his defence.'

'He's my *friend*,' I explain.

'He doesn't care about anyone but himself,' she laughs.

Davey reminds me, 'Stay still.'

I freeze. And mutter, 'At least he's different.' Different from the boys whom she likes; different from boys like her brother Guido.

Ornella protests, 'What good is *different* if he's *horrible*?'

I manage, 'Well, that's your opinion.'

'Too right,' she laughs.

I return to Davey, to his bowed amber head. I watch the faint hiccup of his forelock which accompanies each meticulous staccato brushstroke. Suddenly conscious of being watched, he glances up: two nickel coins, flipped. His face is expressionless, striving to read mine. Hurriedly he reassures me, 'Nearly done.'

I smile in reply, and turn my attention to the field. And to my ex, Adam, who is running ferociously into his fellow footballers. Following him with my eyes, I feel the kink in my heart. The kink holds disappointment, dammed and sour. I used to think that Adam was wonderful, but he is ridiculous. I thought that he was full of passion, but he burns with self-importance.

'Not Adam, then?' Ornella has finished the cigarette. Her hands are latched behind her head, she is staring at me, her eyes tensed against sunrays.

'You *know* Not Adam.'

'What do you reckon about James Hendry?'

A simultaneous shriek from Davey and me: 'Oh *no*.'

Ornella is indignant. She is struggling to a sitting position. 'Why not?'

'But *why*?'

Dazed, she rubs her hands through her hair. 'He's nice,' she replies to me. But the tone was unsteady, unsure, shunting this statement towards a question.

Davey says gently, 'He's nothing special, Prune.'

I echo, stress, 'He's nothing.'

She flares, 'He has nice eyes.'

This is untrue. 'He has *normal* eyes.'

'Nice when he smiles.'

'Ornella, *everyone* has nice eyes when they smile.'

She frowns ferociously, and says confusedly, 'Well, he's no exception.'

'You can say that again.'

Very deliberately, she takes a breath to do so.

'No, *don't*. Once is enough.'

Instead, she yanks a daisy from the ground and splits the stem with her thumbnail. The sap is whiter than the nail. She sucks the thumb momentarily.

I remind her, 'He has just started going out with Sarah Dunlop.'

She rolls the stem between index finger and thumb, so that the flower wobbles. 'I know.'

Davey taps my hand with the newly-fastened bottle, and I admire my toenails, and turn them towards Ornella so that she can do the same. She takes the bottle from me.

I start to protest, 'There's no time . . .'

'One little fingernail,' she bargains. 'Just to see if I like the colour.'

She shifts on the grass, collecting one ankle and then the other so that she is sitting cross-legged. Her skirt is taut between her wide high knees. She bends avidly over this green tarpaulin, bottle in hand.

I ask her, 'So you're thinking of propositioning James Hendry?'

She pauses, brush aloft; a brush so tiny and lush that perhaps it is made from eyelashes. She glances, glazed, into my face. 'It's just a thought,' she decides. Crooking a pink-tipped, candied little finger, she turns towards the footballers. 'I wonder what he'd say,' she muses, her eyelids straining against the sun, her tabby pupils stealthy, 'if I went to him and simply said . . .'

At this point, the most interesting point, she stops, shrugs inconclusively.

I want to know exactly what she would say.

But she concludes, 'I'd do anything if I wanted someone badly enough.'

I protest, 'You would not.' But perhaps I am thinking of myself: *I* would not. Or perhaps I am thinking of James Hendry: not for James Hendry.

She mutters, 'I *would*.'

Faintly exasperated, my attention drifts loose. I scan the buildings in the distance. The stones of the older buildings simmer in the sunshine: dry uneven stones, yellow with traces of pink, the colour of rhubarb-and-custard. Presumably the new buildings were impressive on the drawing board: sheer glowing surfaces. Cheap, too. But now, whatever the weather, they are damp, dark. I see Mr Norfolk, coming onto the field from the buildings. He is beckoning with one whole arm, beckoning to the whole of the field. As if he is on traffic duty. Presumably he is on Lunchtime Duty, and the bell has rung. I detect little response to this beckoning, and now he starts to walk into groups of people, reaching out or bending to touch heads, imploring.

'Now there's a lovely man,' I announce.

Ornella twists sharply. 'Norfy!' she squeals appreciatively.

'No,' gasps Davey, this time alone in his scepticism.

'He's so nice,' I enthuse in reply.

'He's so sweet,' Ornella emphasizes.

'And he *does* have nice eyes.'

'*And* a nice body.'

Davey leans forward to suggest timidly, 'Isn't he rather *stolid*?'

'Nooo,' we deride in unison, although I suspect that Ornella is as unsure as me that stolid is the same as solid.

Davey defers to us, shrugging good-naturedly.

Ornella checks with me, 'Is he married?'

'Girlfriend.' And I lean forward to confide, 'Bev's mum told me that his girlfriend is on children's telly, and then said that she didn't know the details. How can she *not know* the *details*?'

Ornella says, 'He'd be good with children.'

'Yes, he would.'

Davey pleads, 'Shut up, you two.'

Ornella's attention is snagged, and tightens around him: 'What attracts you to a woman?'

For a moment he is sleepwalk-woken. A hot dry frond of hair flutters over his eyes.

Ornella prompts, 'Davey?'

He mutters, 'I'm thinking.'

Ornella is incredulous: 'I don't have to *think* about boys, I *know*.'

Davey and I exchange glances, Oh-you-do-sur-prise-me.

I twist up onto my knees. 'We should start to make a move.' My lower legs are burnt with an impression of grass. With my shiny pink toes I scoop my sandals onto my feet.

Behind me, below me, Ornella pipes, 'What about your Adam?'

'What about him?' Across the pitch, he has turned towards the school buildings, his jumper slung over one shoulder, his head slung low, his feet kicking through the short grass. 'And he's *not my* Adam.'

Rising, she is unsteadied by her laugh. 'You're jealous. I thought so.'

'I am *not jealous*.'

'See?' Still laughing, she totters in front of me on her stiff legs like a foal.

'Ornella,' I stress, slapping my grassy skirt, 'you can do whatever you like with Adam Rawlings; I'm simply warning you, you won't like him, he's not very nice.'

'*You've* changed your mind,' she whoops.

'Ten out of ten,' I say wearily.

She folds inwards, frowning down and tidying her own skirt.

'Anyway,' I challenge, 'two minutes ago it was James Hendry.'

She does not look up from her skirt. 'It's no one in particular. I was *simply saying*.'

But why? Why say Adam, in particular? 'And why is Adam so eligible, all of a sudden?'

One hand ploughs her hot brown hair from forehead to crown. 'Why is he so *bad*, all of a sudden?'

'It's *not* all of a sudden, which you *know*.' And *I* know that she is trying to annoy me, but I cannot stay calm.

Davey is light-footed between us. 'Oh no, women arguing!' He bounces away on the grass, laughing, leaving us, telling us, 'I have to fetch a book from Donaldson.' Then calling, 'Save your energy for Lenin, he needs defending from Bailey.'

Lenin, Miss Bailey: Twentieth Century History, our next lesson.

He yells, 'Discuss the role of the proletariat.'

Ornella throws both hands through her grassy hair and mutters irritably, 'Fuck the proletariat.'

I turn on her, 'I *am* the proletariat, so fuck *you*,' before hurriedly calling to Davey, 'We're not arguing; Ornella is trying to wind me up.' This is an important distinction.

'I'm not trying to wind you up. I *asked* you if you were jealous and you *said no* and *now* you're *complaining*.'

I watch the regular white flash of her ankle socks through the grass: the whites of her feet. 'I don't care

71

about *Adam*,' I wail. 'I *care* that you're trying to *upset* me.'

Echoing my tone, she protests, 'I'm *not* trying to *upset* you.'

So she does not know what she is doing. I slide a glance over the rough tufty grass, over the patchy rust of dandelions, to Ornella's dense, clenched, downturned face. I know, everyone knows, that there is no one here at school who knows Ornella better than I do. Yet often I feel that I hardly know her at all; sometimes I feel that everyone else, from their distance, knows more. And there is a possibility that they know something in particular. 'Perhaps it *is* true, what they say about you and your brother.'

Predictably, she looks at me.

Predictably, but terrifyingly. Her eyes glint, and my stomach turns. There is no way out of this. For me.

She asks mildly, but carefully, 'What do they say?'

And I realize that I have not thought about the words, that I have no words ready. I try to remember the words that I heard. But I cannot even remember when I heard, or from whom. It is simply something that everyone knows. Or thinks that they know. Pathetically, I pause, hoping that she knows, too: *Oh, THAT* . . . Hoping that she will come to my rescue. Denial or confirmation, for a moment I do not care.

But she says nothing. Nor do her eyes.

Words and phrases prickle in my mind. Eventually I manage, 'They say that you know each other better than you're supposed to.' Immediately, I feel better: this is what people say, and she should know. And I should be the one to tell her.

She says, 'And how well am I "supposed" to know my brother?' The same cool tone, the same steady gaze. Which knocks me off balance. Surely everyone knows how well they are supposed to know their own brother? Or how well they are *not* supposed to know their own brother. I mutter, 'You know what I mean.'

'Well, obviously not,' she emphasizes, patronizingly.

I look into her sun-speckled eyes. 'Ornella, you *do*.'

'Where's their evidence?'

Which is not exactly what I was expecting. 'Ornella,' I urge, 'this isn't a court of law; I'm telling you what people *say*.'

She looks away, looks up, luxuriating in the sky. 'I don't care what they say.'

No denial.

We continue walking together, scuffing clover. The buildings are looming. Suddenly she says, 'Now you tell me something.' As if there has been a bargain struck between us and this is the second half; as if there is something to which she can hold me.

'What?'

She lights up my face with her dark eyes, and asks, 'Do I love my brother?' She asks in such a way that the only possible answer is yes.

'Yes, you do,' I allow.

She turns back to the sky. 'Well, then,' she breathes, satisfied.

73

Her turned away, up-turned face provokes me. 'Well-then-what?' I demand, 'Well-then it's alright for you and your brother to practise on each other?' *Practise* takes me by surprise: not a bad choice, though; there are worse words.

Ornella whips around, somehow further away from me but leaning heavily into this new space between us. 'Surely it's better than practising on someone I don't know and don't like.'

Was this a reference to Adam, to Adam and me?

She has clamped herself back behind folded arms. 'And when you can say why it's wrong,' she threatens, 'then I'll be happy to hear.'

I watch the grass fizzing around our fast-moving feet. There was – is? – an understanding between us: to tell. She knows, she *simply knows*, that she is supposed to tell me. I cannot believe that she did not tell me. 'What if you have a baby?' I accuse. Not a baby, of course: a not-baby, because brothers and sisters cannot have babies, not real-live babies. Not normal babies.

She twists again towards me, sharply, stiffly around her folded arms. 'God!' she hoots down her little nose, 'You think we do *that*?'

Flustered, I complain, 'How do I know what you do if you don't tell me?' *So, tell me.*

Marching onward, she mutters, 'Don't be a pervert.'

'I don't believe that you just said that.'

'You're quick enough to believe whatever anyone else says.' But before I can reply, deny, she halts to announce, 'We haven't done *that*. Okay? We're not going to do

that. It's not as bad as *that*. In fact . . .' she shrugs, lightly
'. . . it's nothing.' She resumes walking.

So I follow.

We have to be quiet, now, because we are close behind
a group of younger girls who are dawdling, trailing their
cardigans and blazers. They are wearing their hair up,
displaying variations on the same theme, experiments: a
ponytail, high or low or even sideways, or bunches, a
plait or two, and held in bands, combs, ribbons. Their
faces are heavy blooms of hot blood, despite their cool
green summer dresses. The dresses have buttons like peppermint creams. We leave the grass, the girls, and follow
a paved path towards one of the new buildings. The
windows, big squares of blackened silver, are tilted open
into the warm afternoon air. This jagged seam leaks
swimming pool noises, a mosaic of shouts bouncing on
cold hard surfaces. Ahead of us, in the row of windows,
peeking from beneath one of the shiny black blinkers, is
Cathy Sykes, her arms folded on the thin steel sill, her
chin lowered onto one bony wrist. Her eyes track our
approach, and we smile in passing. When we have
passed, Ornella sings, 'Howww much is that dogg-ie in
the win-dow?'

I turn on her, scalding: 'Ornella!'

Our slow steps do not falter. But she has stopped singing. She reflects my wide-eyed stare, but rinsed of my
fury. 'What? I was *singing*.'

'You *know* what. Cathy is a *friend* of mine.'

She startles me with a derisive laugh. 'No she's not.'

And this stings: the contradiction; worse, the dismissal

of my choice of friend. Who is Ornella, to decide for me?

'Nor are any of them, they're nothing to you,' she continues, daringly confident. As if confidence will turn this lie into the truth.

She has gone too far, tried to take me too far from my world. And she has failed, because I am held back by my heart which turns hot and heavy with loyalty: *Love me, love my friends* and *If they go, I go.*

Sensing this, she corrects, quickly, 'Cathy's not a friend *of mine.*'

'*Fine.* But she *is* a friend of *mine.*'

Now she does the worse that she can do: she Makes A Face, *OH-I'M-SORRY,* her eyebrows flicked stiff to the top of her brow and the corners of her mouth wrenched downwards.

'And *you* have to walk into that classroom now and spend the afternoon with her.' I cannot resist arguing, 'Anyway, she *is* a friend of yours.' Because since when has Ornella disliked Cathy?

Ornella whirls ahead of me, in front of me, to plead, 'She *isn't.* Not *really.* Not a *real* friend. None of them are my *real* friends. None of them *care* about me. And I don't care about any of *them.*' By now, her tone has become calm. 'Not *really* care.'

Care? A strange requirement of friends, or of a friend like Cathy Sykes. An unusual requirement. I shrug: Life's-like-that, School's-like-that.

'But *you* do,' she says. '*You* care about me.' She turns and falls into step with me. 'You understand me.' This is somewhere between musing and confiding.

Should I deny it? I do not understand her, I suspect that I have simply developed a feel for her: I think that I know what she is likely to do or say, but not why.

She continues, 'You're not like the rest of them.'

The words slot satisfyingly home, I know that I am not like the rest of them. But, then, who is Ornella to tell me who I am and am not?

'I *trust* you,' she says. 'I don't trust *them*.'

I feel that I should say, 'You're rather harsh on them.'

She pauses on the path. '*They're* harsh,' she is furious, 'On *everyone*.' And suddenly calm: 'But you're different.'

I blow this away in a mixture of a laugh and a sigh. 'No, I'm not. Not really.'

She concedes, corrects, 'Okay, you make a difference. To me.'

Such big words from someone so small. No: small words, but a big sentiment. No one has ever spoken to me like this. She turns to me, and her eyes are the colour of bruises in ripe fruit. 'I don't need them,' she says. 'I don't need a lot of friends. What I need is someone who I really like, really know, can really trust. That's all, that's enough.' Turning away, she adds, 'And I know what you think of Guido, but he loves me and he'll always be there for me.'

We have reached the doors to the building, I reach for the doors. But she stops, and stops me by placing her hand on my outstretched arm. 'Look,' she confides, explains, 'I didn't tell you about Guido because, at the time, I was scared.'

I drop my arm. 'Of me?'

'No,' she admonishes softly, before explaining, 'I was scared that I was pregnant.'

'Pregnant?'

Warningly, she twists my gaze with her own to the open windows: *Keep your voice down.*

'*Pregnant?*'

She looks blankly, perhaps faintly defensively, into my eyes. 'Yes, you know, *pregnant*. I was six weeks late.'

'But you said that you didn't do *that*.'

'Not *that*,' she disparages, impatiently.

Not *that*? Then *what*? 'So there's some other way to get pregnant?'

She breathes hotly, crossly, 'Well I don't know, I was six weeks late so I was scared that it could happen anyway, some other way, after a bit of messing around, because why else was I six weeks late?'

Now I am curious, on several counts. 'Why *were* you six weeks late?'

She shrugs her eyebrows. 'I don't know.'

'Worry, probably,' I say, not very kindly.

She blurts another whispery explanation, 'I was worried that it might have been on his fingers.'

A moment passes before I understand. I decide not to comment.

'Do you think that's possible?' she urges anxiously.

'I don't know.' I try to think back to Biology. 'I don't think so.'

'Well, anyway,' she says pointlessly.

There is something that I must check: 'So you stopped

all this because you were scared that you'd get pregnant?'
Solely because?

'Yes,' she says indignantly.

I switch my eyes skyward and reach for the door.

'Haven't you ever been curious?' she demands. 'Don't you want to know what it's like?'

I check, 'Did Guido make you do any of this?'

She snaps, 'No,' folds her arms. 'And, anyway, stop trying to make me feel bad.' She leans on the door, stands between me and the door. '*And, anyway*, stop trying to change the subject: aren't you curious?'

I back away, and shrug.

But she has seen through me. 'You're *not* curious,' she relishes her own surprise, 'You *know*.'

'Ornella . . .' I warn; and this time I am the one who glances to the open windows.

'Does it hurt?' she squeals, delighted.

'No,' I reply quickly, and reach past her for the door, tap the handle with my fingernails.

Excitedly, she elaborates, 'I mean, the first time.'

'I was talking about the first time.'

She lingers in front of the door, eyes wide. 'Not at all?'

'For one moment. As soon as you notice, the pain's over.'

'Honestly?' Even wider, and freeze-frame.

'Honestly.'

'Why didn't you tell me?'

'I don't know.' I *do* know: she would have been thrilled, she would have asked me questions. And I

79

was not thrilled, I did not want to think about it.

'Adam Rawlings,' she breathes, following with a low whistle of surprise. She checks: 'Were you in love with him?'

'No.' Which she knows. And she knows that it would have been alright if I was in love with him. I had a weakness for Adam Rawlings. I do not like weaknesses, not in myself; I love them in others, I am tender about them in others, but not in myself.

She asks, 'How many times?'

Briefly I consider refusing to answer, perhaps even lying. But instead I tell her the truth, 'Once.' And I stop myself adding *By mistake*. Because there was no mistake. There was the feeling of a mistake – the haste, the doubt, and the desire afterwards to forget – but there was no mistake.

Slightly more serious, much more curious, she asks, 'Why only once?'

'Once was enough,' I suppose. 'Like you, I suppose, I was curious.' But now I ask *her* a question: 'You were six weeks late, and you never said. What did you do, for those six weeks?' *If you were not saying, then what were you doing? For six long weeks?*

She says, 'I thought a lot, I thought about a lot of things.'

The door booms between us and Davey springs from the dim corridor. 'There you are,' he proclaims excitedly. 'She's been in there for five minutes now.' *She* is Miss Bailey, *There* is the classroom. 'I said that I'd fetch the overhead projector from the store cupboard, so that I could come and find you.' He pauses for a breath, in our silence, before asking, 'What's up?'

'Nothing,' I tell him. 'And you're right, we're very late. Thanks, Davey.' I shift, stepping around Davey, orientating Ornella towards the door.

But she resists, wriggles, by stepping back, out, down into the sunshine. 'I'm not going,' she says cheerfully, to both of us.

'Why not?'

'I'm off, this afternoon. Mum wrote a note. I'm due home. Aunty Bernie's funeral.' Her eyes have evaporated in the sunshine, only cracks remain, radiating: two tiny sundials.

'Now?'

'No, not *now*. Four o'clock.'

'Aunty Bernie?' I have never heard of any Aunty Bernie, from anyone, and certainly not from Ornella. And *funeral*?

'Bern*ice*,' she explains.

'But you never *said*.' About the funeral. About the death.

'Well, it's *Great* Aunty Bernie.'

Davey says jauntily, 'A distant relative, now even more distant.'

Ornella laughs briefly, softly. 'Well, yes.'

Stepping backwards, she tells us, 'I'm off, I'm late.'

Wait a minute: 'Will you be back tomorrow?'

Her face narrows. 'Well, of course.' And now she spins away across the grass with waves and smiles, her molten oval crown tipping and swirling.

'Waltzing with sunbeams,' Davey murmurs indulgently.

I tell him, 'I'm not going in there on my own to Miss Bailey, I'll come with you, I'll say that I've been to Sister.'

He shrugs: *Whatever you say . . .*

We begin to retrace the steps that Ornella and I took a few minutes ago along the path, alongside the building, classroom by classroom, teacher's voice by teacher's voice, from Mr Devonshire's bored whine on the subject of standard deviations to Mrs Paley's booming negotiations with the back row of Remedial.

Davey asks conversationally, 'So, what was all that?'

'All what?'

'All, you and Ornella looking furtive in the doorway.'

'Oh, *that.*' I shrug. 'Nothing.' To increase credibility, I add a knowing but weary, 'Boys.' Which, of course, is true.

'Oh, *boys.*'

Glancing sideways, I see one of his faint dimples, a star in the crescent of his smile. I return the smile, but warn him, 'Serious talk about boys.' Gazing into the blue sky, at the long ribbons of faint cloud like X-rays of spines, I realize that this is an opportunity for me to have a serious talk with Davey about boys. Talk is stronger than questions. If I ask questions, he might feel obliged to try denials. So I must let him know that I know. But *do* I know? *How?*

Without thinking further, I say very gently, 'You don't like girls, do you.'

His face is washed with shock. 'Vonny,' he breathes, horrified, pained, 'I love girls.'

True. Looking into his face, my heart reaches for him. Calmly, I explain, 'That's not what I mean.' Or, I fail to explain.

But he understands. 'Oh.' He contemplates the swing of his shoes. 'You mean, I *do* like *boys*,' he says eventually. After a moment he peeps sideways. An incisor holds blood in one half of his lower lip. 'How did you know?'

'I just knew.' Which implies that I have known for a long time. In fact, I think that I was certain for the first time this afternoon, on the field. And I do not remember how, why.

He puffs a humourless laugh. 'That's what friends are for, I suppose.' His gaze is narrow and distant, somewhere on the school field.

I am afraid that he is angry with me. Which, perhaps, I should have anticipated. I follow his gaze, over our lime green field, and further, into the boundary of trees, into the leaves which toss their silvery undersides into the sunshine. 'When did *you* know?' I ask helpfully, interestedly.

'When didn't I know,' he echoes quickly, bitterly, without returning to me.

Lightly, I enquire, 'Does it worry you?'

Which I regret, immediately, because he turns on me, his hard glance a slap in my face: 'Of course it worries me.'

'Why?'

He does not look away again over the field. But nor

does he make an effort to meet me. 'Well, you tell me,' he challenges, apparently to the shrubs lining our route. 'You're the one who brought it up.' And now he mimics me, mocks: 'Does-it-worry-you?'

'Well?' I say meaninglessly, flustered.

He turns to focus on me and says very clearly, 'The whole of the world is made for boy-meets-girl.' As slow and careful as a threat.

And as simplistic. And it is my world to which he refers, the world of which I am a part. So I hurry to defend myself: 'That's not true.'

'It *is* true,' he says. 'So, come and talk to me again when you've bothered to have a think about it.'

Why so many arguments today? Is it the heat? Together we step from the path into the courtyard and pass the centrepiece, the fibreglass sculpture made and donated by an ex-pupil, presumably as an act of revenge. Clouds pearl the windows of the buildings around us. Suddenly he slaps both his hands over his face, into his hair, and moans contritely, 'This is pointless.' Momentarily held high and turned between his fingers, his hair is the colour of dead fern.

Tentatively, I complain, 'I was trying to be nice.'

'Yes, and I wasn't,' he admits readily.

'And I wasn't asking about the world,' I persist. 'I was asking about *you*.'

'Yes,' he agrees: no shift in tone.

I am trying to sense if I can trust him again.

'Yes, I do worry,' he answers, gladly, 'I do worry about what will happen to me.'

84

'Don't we all.' Glimpsing his prickle-eyed surprise, I clarify, 'Don't-we-all wonder what will happen to ourselves?'

After a pause, I dare to ask him, 'Is there anyone?'

His eyebrows twist down hard in his effort to follow.

Coolly, I explain, 'You know, *anyone*.' Anyone whom he fancies. This is a question which I would ask of any other friend, so why not of Davey?

'What's the point?' His tone echoes mine, perhaps even lighter, determinedly lighter. Brave. Nonchalant. Except that there is a world of difference between brave and nonchalant.

'Davey,' I complain irritably. Because we all take risks all the time. Or, one risk, *the* risk: the risk of rejection. I will not allow him to belittle the risks taken by the rest of us. I challenge, 'Anyway, you never know.'

He laughs fondly. 'Oh but I do.'

I shrug: *If you won't help yourself* . . .

He cajoles, 'Come on, Vonny. I've said I'm sorry.'

'Actually,' I pick him up on this, 'you haven't. You haven't actually *said*.' It is only now, in my relief, that I realize how scared I have been throughout this conversation. And, yes, *him*: he must have been afraid. Much more so. But surely I was right to raise the subject? Surely it would have been scarier unspoken?

'Well, I am,' he says. 'Sorry. Very. Vonny.'

But I do not dwell on this. 'Who else knows?'

He blanks, surprised. 'No one else. Or not that I'm aware.'

I remind him, warningly, 'You weren't aware that *I* knew.'

He dismisses this with a wrinkle of his nose.

'You knew that I knew?'

'You know me very well, and you're not stupid.'

So, he knew that I *would* know; sometime, if not now.

He asks airily, 'Does Nella know?'

'I don't know.' Who knows, with Ornella? Momentarily I delve for memories, clues. 'I don't think so.' She would have said.

'Are you going to tell her?' An arc of hair is dabbing regularly from his forehead towards the tip of his nose: an upside-down unicorn horn, infused with gold.

'No, of course not.'

His grey gaze trawls mine.

And suddenly I understand. 'Not unless you *want* me to tell her.'

He turns away, says thoughtfully, 'Perhaps I do.' More jauntily, he finishes, 'I think I'll leave that to you. If you don't mind.'

We pass from the courtyard into the narrow corridor at the quiet end of the Admin Block. My eyes are slow to react to the sudden lack of sunlight. The quietness is noisy: I can hear the hiss of a re-filling cistern, the cough of the caretaker; the ceiling honks with the movements of chairs on the floor above. I cannot stop the feeling that I should – what? – explain Ornella? To reassure Davey? Unsurely, I start, 'She's not as . . .' And I stop. Because Davey is fizzling through the darkness, *Beam-me-up*, and I see that he is watching me very closely. And

I think that I see a smirk. Swallowing my qualms, I press on, try again: 'She's quite . . .' But my tone is horrifying me: it is so apologetic, defensive.

Suddenly, he laughs. And, softer, kind but emphatic, he reminds me, 'I know.'

Thankfully, I drop the subject. And settle into his pace, the long, slow steps, the squash of his soles onto the lino. But questions begin turning inside me. And there is so little time for them, for their answers. Soon our time will belong to Miss Bailey, notorious counter-revolutionary.

Hurriedly, I start, 'You know what you said? That there's no one . . . ?'

He turns his head, confirming, listening: *Go on.*

But I have nothing in particular to say. I am merely troubled. 'Well, there must *be* people . . .' People who . . .

'Around here?' he checks.

I nod.

'No.' He is definite. 'Not many of the boys around here are averse to fun and games in the showers but there's no one to make an honest man of me.'

'Are you serious?' I dare for more confidences, one on top of another.

'Well, no one as far as I know. And I think I'd know.'

I dismiss this with an impatient wave. 'About the *showers*.'

'Oh.' He laughs at me. 'But don't worry your pretty little head about it, eh? Boys will be boys.'

I still do not know if he is serious, so I hurry with a cheerful confidence of my own: 'Girls aren't like that at all.'

'Like what?'

And, yes, like what? 'In the showers,' I manage eventually.

'Oh,' he says, both knowing and nonplussed. 'Well, no, they're not boys, are they.'

'No.' We are getting nowhere. There is something else, something more, which is troubling me. Timidly, I suggest, 'Will girls *do*?' Or, why will girls *not* do?

He laughs, but this laugh is no longer and no livelier than a cough. 'I'm not sure that it's like that.'

How is it, then? I think of the boys for whom I felt nothing and yet had managed to kiss, at parties and discos, for one reason or another, boredom or practice or lack of energy to escape. I think of how I closed my eyes; which is not so very difficult to do. So how, for Davey, is it different? Why cannot Davey close his eyes and make do with girls?

He is saying breezily, 'I *would* like to get married, though, one day.'

'Why?'

His hands stuck down into his pockets, he shrugs untidily, bonily, boyishly. 'Makes life easier.'

Is he joking? I hold his quicksilver eyes in my own. 'For whom?'

His eyes stay level with mine. 'Okay,' he reasons quietly, intimately, 'I'd like a family.'

We are approaching the office from where we will fetch the key to the store cupboard. As always, the door is shut and pinned with a printed notice, *Knock and WAIT*. Davey drops an arm around my shoulders, both

88

heavy and light, and nuzzles my head with his own: 'Marry me,' he laughs.

I can smell his smell, it is the smell of boys: a soft salting of skin and cotton with fresh clean sweat. I tell him, 'It's a leap year.'

I can hear his smile. 'So?'

'So *I* have to ask *you*.'

'You don't *have to* ask me.' He returns his hands to his pockets. 'No strings,' he announces, promises. 'You can do whatever you like, I'll turn a blind eye.'

'*You'll* turn a blind eye?' My words are scratchy with sarcasm. 'How very considerate of you.'

Whoozily pleased with himself, he shrugs expansively, almost stretches.

'Sorry, Davey,' I tell him. 'But I'm going to marry . . .' But who am I going to marry? In a sense, I have always known him, I feel that he has always been with me, born with me, my destiny. But he is a hunch; I have never had to worry with words. In words, who or what is he? Someone interesting, but dependable. With money, of course. And a couple of years older, for good measure. I do not care about tall or dark. But I joke, 'Someone with eyes the colour of a Morning Glory.'

'Morning Glory?'

'It's a flower.'

'A *flower*?' He is sceptical. 'What colour? Mrs Lake will know, of course.' His mum, to whom he likes to refer as Mrs Lake, is a keen gardener.

'An amazing blue,' I tell him, not explaining about the change in shade throughout the day, or that each flower lasts for only one day. On holiday in Majorca, two years ago, my first and only time abroad, the blue flowers covered the whole wall opposite the apartment: a colour so intense that it was hard to believe that it was natural. The best that I can manage is, 'Like something dyed.'

'Something *died*?'

I laugh, '*Dyed*. Artificial. An unreal blue.'

He laughs, too, and says lightly, 'Listen, if we marry, we can have Ornella as our bridesmaid.'

'God, no,' I insist, as the door opens.

EVERYTHING BEGAN TO go wrong for Ornella with Martin Brown. Not that anyone would have known, in the beginning. Because in the beginning, everything seemed to have begun to go right. Contrary to everyone's expectations, it seemed that Martin was right for her, and she was right for him. I remember Ornella's peculiar mood in the first few days of Martin. She was so very quiet. Not secretive, perhaps, but stunned. She told me nothing, and I felt that she did not want me to ask questions. Questions would have been counterproductive, would have shut her up. So, instead, I watched, very carefully. And I saw that every breaktime she went to walk on the field with him. They walked a long slow ellipse. They were walking nowhere in particular, and in cold autumn weather: they were Serious. Their heads were bowed by the weight of their confidences: they were Talking. And I realized that there were secrets again. From me. This time I realized that I would have to be patient if I wanted to know. Martin was buoyant, unusually outgoing and optimistic. For him, everything had fallen into place. Ornella was still feeling her way. But I could see that she was falling in love. I could see that this was the first time. Love shows on girls in a way that it can never do on boys.

I have a memory of them together on the floor in her front room, one Saturday afternoon shortly before Christmas. He is sitting cross-legged, opposite me, and she is lying on her back with her head in his lap. His hands rest on her stomach; no, sometimes they rest but sometimes they rub, and whenever they rub, she ripples like a puppy to follow them. Occasionally he bends to kiss her. And then she cranes upwards, all her concentration in her lips, the rest of her body suddenly and strangely slack. I am sitting opposite them, trying to persuade them to come to a Russian film. Beside me, James is reading the newspaper, moaning quietly in horror: sport, or current affairs? I do not know, I cannot keep asking him, *What*? So I am resigned to not knowing, but this moaning is unnerving.

Ornella is crooning upwards, 'You're such a snob, Brown.'

He laughs down into her face, 'Have you ever *been* into a McDonald's?'

Ornella has said that if we go to a McDonald's

afterwards, she will come to the film. I know that she is not serious, that she is not intending to come to the film. I tell Martin, 'No, she hasn't.'

Her hair swishes on him as she turns on me. She laughs, outraged: 'How do you know?'

I do not bother to answer. I need to know if anyone is coming to the film. I do not care if they do or do not come but they must make up their minds. Because I am meeting Davey at the station in half an hour.

I tell Martin, 'It's the one that had the review in last week's *Time Out*.'

He says, 'I know,' and smiles sadly, to imply that he will not come if she will not come.

She asks James, 'Are you going?'

Without looking up from his paper, he replies, 'Friend's birthday, down the Rugby Club.' Now he glances sideways at me: 'If you and Davey fancy a drink when you get back, we'll be at Dimbo's house.'

I nod, but only in politeness because I cannot imagine that we will want to wander the streets searching for Dimbo's house, nor stand for a couple of hours in the middle of the night in Dimbo's kitchen. Whoever Dimbo is.

Suddenly Ornella yawns, 'If my Marty's a *snob*, you should hear what Veroniquie used to say about *you*, James.'

I slide a smile to James, murmur through melodramatically gritted teeth, 'Isn't she cute?'

He closes and folds the huge paper with ease, and says cheerfully to her, 'I doubt if you can worry me.'

She purrs, 'Oh, I'm not trying to worry *you*,' before smirking at me.

But I respond in kind. 'Miscalculation, Ornella. Because there are no secrets between James and me.' Which she knows. And, anyway, we all know what I used to think of James, or what I thought that I thought. Including James, now. But a few months ago, Ornella had told him, untruthfully, *Veronica fancies you, and she's too scared to say*. Why did she do this? Who knows? Luckily, I was oblivious. We were at Samantha Gregg's party, and, luckily, I was drunk when he made his move. To me, drunk, lying on a pile of dirty laundry in the utility room at Samantha Gregg's party, it-seemed-like-a-good-idea-at-the-time. But, then, anything would have seemed-like-a-good-idea-at-the-time. The difference is that it has seemed-like-a-good-idea ever since. He was so nice to me, so careful with me, he made me laugh and I do not often laugh when I am drunk, I have never been so cheerful whilst throwing up.

Now Ornella has returned to the subject of the trip to the film, and is whining, 'But it's so cosy in here.'

This is true. We have been in here for hours, on this thick carpet, warmed by the gold velvet glow of the floor-length curtains which have wiped away the dark winter window. And because there are so many rooms in this house we have not been disturbed by her parents. Or not often. Her dad appeared in the open doorway when Ornella returned with a tray of tea, and called after her, flamboyantly foreign, 'What is the capital of Yugoslavia?' Ornella replied with a equally flamboyant,

'Ummm.' And he exclaimed, 'The money that I'm paying for your education!' To which she replied, 'Dad, you're *not* paying for my education.' Turning away, laughing, he said, 'And thank God.' In my home there is one living room. There was a dining area which was separated from the living room by a sliding door of crinkly glass, but, on one of his trips home, Dad took the doors away and made an arch. In my home there is nowhere for me to go with my friends. Even if Mum is in the kitchen, my sister Juliet is always in front of the telly.

Ornella yawns and stretches all over Martin. 'I want to lie flat and have things brought to me.'

I know that she is not coming with us to the film but I shrug playfully and suggest, 'We could try to arrange that for you, in the cinema.'

Satisfied, she issues a new challenge: 'But I'd still have to travel there.'

'Wait,' I mutter, 'I'll find a sedan chair.'

She says flatly, 'My mum threw mine out.'

'Mothers! You do your best, and look how they repay you . . .'

She announces, 'I'm not going to move an inch this evening, I think I'll watch *Upstairs Downstairs*,' before a flicker of doubt, a glance upwards into Martin's face. 'You don't mind, do you? You don't mind *Upstairs Downstairs*?'

He laughs. 'Would I mind?'

I rib him, '*Upstairs Downstairs*, very Chekhovian.'

'Miss Georginski,' Ornella says sleepily.

From the back page of his newspaper, James says, 'Miss Georgia.'

We all turn to look at him, but he is busy reading.

Martin says excitedly, 'And Rose is short for Rosa. Luxemburg.'

I laugh, but realize that this will mean nothing to Ornella, who does not do History.

Delighted, Martin continues: '*Mrs Bridges, where's the vanguard? Look in the scullery, Rosa.*'

I correct, 'Mrs *Brezhnev*.'

James slaps down the paper, turns appreciatively to me, 'There *is* a resemblance!'

But Ornella interrupts, 'Why Russian? Why go to a *Russian* film?'

The line of her firmly folded arms mirrors the line of her mouth. Which Martin, above, fails to see. He says jauntily, 'Ornella's Russian isn't up to much.'

She replies immediately, but unintelligibly.

'*What*?'

She smirks, smug, 'I *said*, But my Italian is pretty good.'

In Italian, presumably.

Astonished, I am watching her to see if she will do this again, say something else, anything else. And I protest, 'You've always told me you couldn't speak Italian.'

She sinks into a frown, a tangle of incomprehension and irritability. 'Well, I can speak *some*.' And suddenly she raises her voice to announce, to deride, 'I mean, are you Russian?' Returning us to her point, Why-go-to-a-Russian-film?

I counter, 'Are you American? You're happy to go to American films.'

She says evenly, 'I reckon that *Snow White* was much more difficult to make than a lot of sequences of raindrops splashing into puddles. And I'm more American than Russian.'

'Who said anything about *Snow White*? And which raindrops?'

Her eyes slide away from me, a display of boredom. 'You know what I mean.'

Yes and no. Yes, I know to expect this from her now, although *Snow White* is a new angle. But no, I do not know what these exchanges, these difficulties, mean for us. I do not know if they are serious. We have been having them since she decided to do Sciences in the Sixth Form. Or, more accurately, since she *told me* that she had decided to do Sciences, because, according to Ornella, the decision had been made years ago. When she told me, and I had managed to establish that she was not joking, I had wanted to know why. Because, yes, she had done Maths-Physics-Chemistry for O level: but everyone took Maths, one of the three Rs; and Physics did not feel like a science; and Chemistry did not count, because lots of people took Chemistry O level, for no particular reason that I could discover, because it was simply one of those O levels which was taken by lots of people. But *A level*?

She replied cheerfully, 'Because I'm going to do Medicine.'

'*Medicine*?'

'Yes, you know, Medicine,' and she began to mimic a

mask-muffled surgeon: 'Scalpel . . . Swab . . .'

Incredulous, I wailed, 'You can't be a doctor.'

Her eyes twitched narrow. 'Why not?'

Because doctors are – what? – sensible? Sensitive, even, in a sense? Grown-up, certainly. Utterly unlike Ornella. 'Because you're squeamish,' I lied, desperately.

She shivered with irritation. 'That was *once*, and the rat was *pregnant*; you must admit that it was *extra* gruesome.'

It was in a big jar full of musty yellow fluid on the top shelf of the Biology lab, its unborn babies strung on a long line from its abdomen; the whole display as random and fixed as a stellar formation.

'And, anyway, my patients will be alive. Hopefully. Mostly. And, anyway, I don't want to be a surgeon.'

'That's not what you said.'

She challenged, 'When?'

'You said, *Scalpel*.'

Very seriously, she informed me, 'I was joking.'

I said, 'But you'll have to do Science A levels.'

Flatly, she confirmed, 'As I was saying.'

But what had happened to the old Ornella, the Scienceless Ornella who had sat next to me through years of English and History? 'You never *said* that you were going to do Medicine.'

A spark of irritation, 'What else did you think that I was going to do?'

'Is Guido going to do Medicine?' Guido is doing Sciences, but I had assumed that this was because he was a boy. Boys seem to sprout Science A levels.

'Yes,' she replied. 'If he gets the grades.' The *if* was quick, she did not dwell on the *if*.

Will *she* get-the-grades?

She began to explain patiently, 'It's what we do, in our family.'

I looked for the honeycomb cores of her eyes. '*You* don't have to. You don't *have* to.'

'I *want* to.' Decidedly, she told me, 'I think I'll make a good doctor. Better than Dr Drake, anyway.'

Dr Drake, our local doctor, who tells everyone, *If people learned to blow their noses properly, then we'd have half as much illness in this country.*

'And, anyway,' she continued happily, 'why are you moaning? I bet you come to me when I'm qualified.'

Would I? I blinked, tried to turn her into a doctor, tried to conjure that particular woman-doctors' smile onto her face, a precise smile, crisp. 'I'm not moaning . . .'

'And if you carry on like this,' she relished, 'I won't fit your coil for you.'

'*Ornella*,' I complained, half-horrified, half-heartedly, half-smiling.

But she completed the smile for me: 'I'll tell you to go away and blow your nose.'

'*Then-we'd-have-half-as-many-babies-in-this-country*.' But seriously, 'You love English and History and everything.' And I loved having her with me in English-and-History, asking questions, taking on the whole world: *Why didn't they . . . ? Don't you think they'd . . . ?* Had her enthusiasm been a lie?

She allowed, 'It was nice while it lasted.'

Meaning, *It's over, no discussion.*

But it was not quite over because she returned, with sudden passion: 'What would I *do* with English and History? They're not going to get me a job, are they?'

'*Job*,' I echoed, derisively.

'Well, what are you going to do? For a job.'

'Wait. Until after university.'

Infuriatingly calmly, she stressed, 'Well, I can't wait. Not if I want to do Medicine. I have to decide now. I *have* decided.'

As a last attempt, I insisted, 'But you're so good at the Arts.'

Her eyes were spun smooth in her smile. 'Anyone who has a big mouth can be good at the Arts. And I have a big mouth.' And she widened her smile to ridiculous proportions.

It was not until much later that it occurred to me that, being useless with Sciences, I could never have chosen to do them, that I was the one without a choice.

If Ornella had never become a scientist, would Russian films have been a problem between us?

Now she is saying, 'Don't go. Stay and laze around here.'

Why? Why say this? If she wants to stay home, then fine; but why require me to stay too? Me, as well as Martin. All of us around her, sedan-style. 'What about Davey?' Not a question, but a complaint, a reminder: she is not the centre of our world.

'Go and fetch him, bring him back here.'

No. Rising stiffly, I tell her, warn her, 'I'll have one last cup of tea before I go.'

She rolls her eyes, mutters, 'Big of you,' but immediately unfolds herself from Martin's lap to follow me. At the door, she turns, checks with the boys, in a mock-American drawl, 'Do you-all want tea?'

They mumble their No-thanks. And as the door closes behind us, I hear Martin remarking to James, genuinely puzzled, 'Don't women drink a lot.'

Ornella smiles, says to me, 'Our bodies are made of much more water than men's bodies.'

Our bodies, women's bodies. We float together down the hallway: corporeal mermaids, afloat on our bodies of water.

In the kitchen, she says, 'More fat, too.'

I tut.

'It's true,' she pipes cheerfully, flicking the switch on the kettle.

'True is all very well . . .' I catch my reflection in the glass door of the oven, and turn from side to side for a critical examination.

Emerging from a cupboard with a tin, Ornella says, 'You've *no* problems.'

I dismiss this with an irritable shake of my head, and highlight the fat of my hips and stomach with my hands.

She says, 'It's there for a purpose.'

'Oh yes?' It-had-better-be-good.

'Babies.'

Not good enough. Shrugging off my reflection, I seek solace, 'What else is there to eat?'

She lifts the tin from the table, the lid from the tin. 'These.'

Shortbread. And it is *proper* shortbread, flaky and fat-yellow; not dense, dry and vaguely grey, like the biscuits in our tin at home.

Ornella says, 'But we can have them with cream cheese.'

I look up from the gleaming medallions. 'Cream cheese?'

'*And* strawberry jam,' but there is a dash of doubt in her words. She spins, flings open a cupboard door, scans the shelves, concedes, 'Well, not strawberry jam, because there's none left, thanks to my hog of a brother, who has taken to having strawberry jam on his toast in the mornings.' This last observation lurched under the weight of disgust: *Jam . . . toast . . . mornings.*

I tell her, 'The biscuits will do fine.'

But she has gone into another cupboard, from where she is asking brightly, 'What about Golden Syrup?'

'What *about* Golden Syrup?' When can I have a biscuit?

She turns, the Golden Syrup tin held in both hands. 'Golden Syrup with cream cheese, it's wonderful,' she says appreciatively. And she begins to muse, 'One, sticky; and the other, so smooth . . .'

'Yes, yes,' *I believe you, but just give me a biscuit.*

But she dumps the ingredients on the table and twists around, pushes herself upwards on her hands so that she is sitting on the tabletop. I am left to make the tea. I rinse our two favourite mugs.

Behind me, Ornella says, 'We need to find Davey a girlfriend.'

My stomach prickles with bloodless chill. Which is, presumably, similar to how Mum must have felt when Juliet, five years old, came home from school and said, 'Miranda Dooley's mummy and daddy have had a big fight because the new baby was made by Miranda's uncle Eric and not by her daddy but how can a man make a baby because babies come from mummies, don't they?' I have been delaying the inevitable, and the time has come. It must have been worse for Mum because she knew that I was a thrilled eavesdropper in the next room. Here, now, there is no one but Ornella and me. And the kettle, which is boiling, so that the switch clicks ferociously. I attend gratefully to this interruption, fill the two mugs. The newly-shallow water in the kettle shrivels noisily on the element. And then I surprise myself by saying simply, 'Leave him be.'

Ornella replies mildly, 'I worry about him.'

I fish two teabags from the jar and jiggle them in our mugs of water. I do not know what else to do.

'I mean, he mooches around, going to Russian films,' Ornella continues vaguely.

'German.'

Distracted, she checks, 'What?'

'German. German films. Not Russian. Never Russian, until now.' I turn towards her in the wake of the two teabags which are beading the floor below with amber.

She has been alerted. She is watching me, warily. 'Whatever,' she says carefully. 'Foreign.'

'And, anyway, so what?' I back down, 'So what if he's going to German films?' I stamp on the foot pedal, scoring noisily. At home there is no foot pedal, and the bin lid swings instead to Mum's complaint, *How many times do I have to tell you . . . ?* Although she never tells me, merely points to the lid, the dried brown trickles in the pattern, non-pattern, of bark.

'So he's *unhappy*.' And now Ornella tackles me, 'I'm not worried about the *films . . .*'

'You don't *know* that he's unhappy.'

'I *do* know.' Suddenly a smirk sidles across her face. 'I *know things*. I even knew that you fancied James before you knew.'

I swipe a carton of milk from the fridge: door, milk, door; sigh, snatch, gulp. 'You *didn't* know; you were trying to cause trouble. I *didn't* fancy James.'

Ornella reels, delighted. 'Oh, I see. So, what is it that you do together of-an-evening? Discuss the GLC?'

Throwing a dash of milk into each mug, I complain, 'What is this with the GLC? You're always on about the GLC.' James and the GLC.

She laughs. '*James* is always on about the GLC, it's *James* who is always on about the GLC.'

I turn back, carton aloft, dripping pearls, to counter knowingly, 'Not with me. Not of-an-evening.'

Suddenly Ornella's mother is in the doorway, waiting wordlessly but emphatically: arms folded, pressed; lips pared and hard; eyes, on Ornella, blinkless, peeled. Waiting, but for what? Ornella slips sulkily from the tabletop. And this seems to have been what her mother has been waiting for, because now she smiles, says shinily, 'Hello Veronica.'

'Hello-Mrs-Marini.' I busy myself, slotting the milk back into the fridge. When I look up, she is gone, she is nothing but a shiver of silk blouse in the dark hallway. Ornella pauses before replying with a soft kick to the kitchen door. The door brushes its frame, threatens to bounce back, but settles. Ornella says in a new sharp tone, 'Perhaps you're right, perhaps you don't fancy James, because why are you so concerned to keep Davey without a girlfriend?'

Where do I start? Slowly, wearily, I manage to complain, '*Ornella* . . .'

But she flares, 'Meanwhile, he's mincing around all the arty cinemas in London . . .'

I turn my back on her.

'What?' And now, 'Veronica?' softer, inside a deep curl of curiosity. A reminder, *Veronica*: friends do not have secrets, not from each other.

I take a deep breath, turn back, hand her the mug of tea, and tell her, 'Davey's gay.'

Together we slide through the next moment, in which nothing happens.

Now, uncharacteristically patiently, she wants to know, 'Who says?'

This is easy: '*He* says.'

'To who?'

'Me.'

'When?'

'Sometime in the summer.' I flinch: she will know,

now, that I have been delaying telling her since the summer.

She says thoughtfully, or perhaps thinks aloud, 'He never told *me*.'

'I *asked* him,' I explain. But I admit, 'He said that I could tell you.'

Her attention bounces back to me, loaded with indignation. 'And you *didn't*?'

'Well,' I bluster, 'I would have done, eventually.' And more despairingly, 'What was I supposed to do? Announce it?'

She is not listening to me. 'You've known since the summer and you *didn't tell me*.' She tilts her head to one side, a small smile running smoothly into the slope like the contents of a spirit level. 'Is there anyone?'

'No.' Correction: 'I don't think so.'

A milky swirl of wide eye around her pupils. 'You *didn't ask him*?'

'I *did* ask him, but not *recently*.' I am flustered by this question-and-answer session. 'The answer, when I asked him, was no.'

'*Has there ever been anyone?*' Her face has risen perky from her mug.

If I admit that I do not know, that I did not ask, I will be in even more trouble with her. So I do not answer. And she hurries, conspires, 'We must find him someone. I think we need to keep an eye on Dreamboat Davey. I think we should keep him in the family. So what do you reckon about Guido?'

I manage an amused, '*Your-brother-Guido?*'

'Yes,' delighted, guileless.

'Is that feasible?'

Snatching the still-life of mug and biscuit tin from the table, twitching the door with a taper of toes, she moves into the hallway and sings back to me, 'Oh, don't worry about Guido, he needs broadening.'

I can do nothing but follow. To keep down the volume of her voice. My longer legs concertina the distance between us; I reach her in a step or two. 'But they don't have much in common, do they?'

'Opposites Attract,' she laughs.

One morning, Martin was missing. He should have been in English, with me, with everyone else. When I noticed, I whispered to Davey, 'Where's Martin?'

'Yes,' Mr Donaldson echoed immediately, loudly, 'Where *is* Martin?' Mr Donaldson was trying to explain to us how and why 'The Miller's Tale' was hilarious. His task had been complicated by Abi's explanation of how and why it was exactly the same as a sketch in the previous year's Sixth Form show which our headmaster had termed *juvenile in the extreme* and banned. Thankful for the distraction, Mr Donaldson said, 'No, really, where is he?'

None of us replied. None of us knew.

None of us knew that Ornella was also missing. She should have been in Science, one of her Sciences, in one of the labs in the Science Block. Protected by her white coat and goggles, by washing her hands and tying back her hair. Science is surprisingly dangerous for something which is natural.

When I went into the Common Room for the mid-morning break, I saw Ornella slotting her heavy sciencey folders – full of graph paper, conversion charts – into her locker. She muttered, 'Can I talk to you for a moment?' Which seemed ridiculous: *could* she talk to me? for a *moment*? Without a word, I followed her from the Common Room into the playground. She sat down on a bench. I sat beside her. We faced a playgroundful of children. They were chaotic but graceful, as paradoxically purposeful as gulls on geysers of air. It was impossible to know, from the sidelines, who was playing and who was fighting.

Ornella said, 'It's Martin.'

I was going to say, *Yes, where is he?*

But she said, 'He says he's had enough.'

'Of what?'

'Of me, stupid.' The *stupid* was not unkind. It was nothing. Her eyes were fixed on the whole playground, unfocused.

I knew, from those eyes, that this was not a joke. But if not a joke, then what? 'What do you mean?'

'*I mean,* he's just told me that he has had enough.' And then she added, softly but pointedly, '*Of me.*'

Obviously there had been a misunderstanding. Which would be easy to solve, to resolve. But my heart was cowering. Nothing of Ornella was moving but her eyes, which were washing reflections of the playing and fighting around on their wide open surfaces.

'He told you this just now?'

She answered, sort-of: 'We were around by the pavilion for an hour or so.'

'*Since when* has he had enough?' My question flapped with incredulity and indignation.

Which she took personally. 'Well *I* don't know *since when*.' And suddenly she had moved, once: dipping, or ducking, but hands up, palms up.

And I put my hand, briefly, on her shoulder, which was odd, because I did not wish to still her. And she flinched, which was also odd.

I started again, differently, badly: 'What did you say to him?' *To make him say this to you.*

She informed me, flatly: 'I believe I said *Hello Twinkletoes, I didn't see you this morning*; and he said, *Can I have a word?*'

A *word?* The bastard. And then a sick-flicker in my stomach: because would he, could he really have said this? Surely not, surely he would not have done this, begun the end with *Can-I-have-a-word?* Not my Martin, my friend Martin, made of words: I knew him, knew his words, knew his ways. If he had said this, then I did not know him. But, then, how else is it done? How else do you begin to tell the end to someone? If not with a word.

I changed direction: 'Did he say why?'

She surprised me by replying, 'Of course he said why.' And then she recited, into the playground, '*It isn't right, It doesn't feel right, It's going nowhere, It hasn't been going anywhere for a while*.' She turned to me. 'That sort of thing.'

A momentary breeze had blown a strand of her hair across one cheek, where it had become stuck. One sticky salty cheek. I reached up, loosened, let it fall. I realized that her story was increasingly unpromising. My frightened heart was back by now, plodding. *It isn't right, it's going nowhere.* But it had *never* been going anywhere. They had *never* been suited. And it had never mattered. Because he was in love with her. So why did it matter now? Had he fallen out of love with her? If so, how serious was this, how permanent? Had he merely missed his footing, or was he on a very different track?

Trying to sound confident, I told her, 'It'll be nothing, it'll pass.'

'No it won't.'

Ornella, *defeated*? I looked down at her hands which were motionless in her lap, held by a slack lacing of fingers but split open, showing soft pink flesh, palms. The two thumbs and index fingers were splayed: blunt-sharp ends, loose ends, of tight, clipped stitches. She twisted towards me, in fly-swatting irritation, to check, 'You didn't know anything? He didn't say anything to you?'

'No!'

'No,' she agreed. '*Of course* he didn't.'

True: I, too, sensed the depth of his silence, the careful covering up of fear. What was *I* going to say to *him*, when I saw him? If we did not mention Ornella, then we would be carrying on as if nothing had happened. Which I could not do.

More hopefully, she said, 'Perhaps he has said something to James.'

'No. James would have told me.'

She pushed me with her frown.

'No, really. James is pathetic at secrets.'

She gave up, her focus flipping away from me. Brightly, too brightly, stingingly, she concluded, 'He was very nice about it.'

Martin was very nice about everything. I knew that if I went to talk to him about her, then he would be very nice. Which was why there would be no point. Suddenly Ornella stood, and clasped her upper arms: protective wrapping, ready for the journey back into the world. 'I have Physics next.'

A few minutes later, walking to History with Davey, I was holding the news gingerly, reluctantly, inside myself. It was fluttering in my chest and throat, fizzy but heavy. From time to time I glanced longingly at him; longing to tell him but wondering how to start. Recently his hair had been cut very short, and now I noticed that this showed where the sun had not been reaching him. A short cut should have rejuvenated him but his white borders of scalp and the remaining hair were dry, dusty. And there was a strange shine around each eye which had nothing to do with light. A moon around each eye. Moonshadow. Suddenly concerned, I asked, 'Davey, are you tired?'

He turned to me, alarmed. 'Yes,' he replied indignantly.

Which made me laugh.

'Aren't you?' he continued. 'You should be. You're-only-young-once.'

Still laughing, I asked him, 'Why? What have you been doing?'

'Thinking,' he mused grandly. Then he added, 'And watching a lot of football; did you see last night's match?'

I did not know if he was serious. Warmed, emboldened, I started, 'Listen, I have to tell you something.'

He was alerted by my tone.

So I had to rush to keep ahead of his guesses. 'It's Ornella. Well, no, it's Martin. He's told Ornella that it's over.'

'Are you serious?'

'Yes.'

But he was already correcting, 'I mean, is *he* serious?'

I shrugged: both *How do I know?* and *Seems so.* Also, *Afraid so.*

'*Why?*' More than a question: a protest.

Another shrug from me. Much more than an illustration of my cluelessness: an expression, too, of helplessness. Or perhaps more than that. Anger.

'*When?*' Another almost identical wail of anguish.

'Just now.' More specifically, 'When we were in English.' When Martin was not in English.

'She's just told you?'

I nodded.

'What did he say?'

Looking up unblinkingly into the sky, I began to recite, '*It's-not-working, It-hasn't-been-working-for-a-while . . .*' I could not remember the exact words.

'That's what he said?'

111

Anxious, doubtful, I snapped, 'Well, that's what she said that he said. Or something like that.' Why was Davey questioning me like this? Why *me*? Why not go and question Ornella or Martin?

Luckily he did not take offence. 'What do you think? Do you think there's more to this?'

'I don't know.' And I really *did not know*, I knew *nothing*: I had never felt so unknowing; my world, which lately and until twenty minutes before had been perfectly predictable, now seemed unknowable.

'How is Ornella taking this?'

'Surprisingly well,' I replied unthinkingly. But as soon as this was said, as we were crossing the threshold into History, I realized that my answer should have been *Quietly*, which is not the same as *Well*. Especially not in her case.

When Ornella joined us for lunch, she looked openly and blankly into Davey's face, searching his eyes for knowledge of her predicament and in turn hiding nothing from him. His response was split-beat, like a heartbeat but slower: he raised his eyebrows, pulling wide his eyes, then wrinkled his nose, hard. Which told her that he knew, was shocked, horrified. Which, apparently, was enough because she rolled her eyes in weary but grateful acknowledgement before emphatically changing the subject to the lunchtime menu ('Not that travesty of ravioli again.'). After lunch, Davey left the canteen for the library, with an overdue book. Ornella and I were waiting listlessly for the bell, for the afternoon to start. Our gazes trailed passers-by and we swopped comments across our table: their haircuts, nail colours, safe topics, no love-lives.

Then she said, wheedled, 'Veroniquie.' Signalling a coming confidence.

I obeyed, dropped the passers-by, fixed on her small face. 'Yes?'

She said simply, decidedly, determinedly, 'I have to get him back.'

When I saw Martin, I was on my way to the first class of the afternoon. I turned a corner and there was Martin, in a crowd, walking ahead of me into the classroom. On the back of his shirt were a few sprigs of sticky buds. I joined the door-bound crowd and instinctively peeled off the sprigs. At my touch he turned, luminuous with surprise, to face me and my sparse sticky bouquet. Without having to think about what to say, I asked, 'Are you alright?' Light, yet meaningful.

He replied, 'Uh-huh,' equally light but with an undertone of knowingness. We walked together, with everyone, into the classroom, and no more was said.

I did not see Martin for a few days after I took the buds from his back. Or only from a distance, across classrooms, across the Common Room. Which was not unusual. But I was more aware than usual of that distance between us. Ornella said nothing more to me on the subject of the crisis. She was doing all her talking to Martin. Sometimes I saw them together: two dark dabs on the hedgerow horizon beyond the football pitch; or nearer, in the cloakroom, two rippling raincoats among the deflated ones which hung in dry bunches from the peg-studded wall. I would see Ornella wiping her eyes with the small-fingered tip of a swift hand. I did not see the tears, of course, from my distance. I saw no tears at all from Ornella in those first few days.

I was sure that she was talking to him in the evenings, too, on the phone, because usually when I dialled her number, the line was engaged. I called, every evening, all evening, but whenever I did reach her, she said nothing much. Which was not why I had wanted to call. I wanted to let her know that I was there; and I needed to know that she was okay. Eventually, I was left with nothing to say but, *See you tomorrow.*

At school, she was not withdrawn, if withdrawn means blank. On the contrary, she was careful to smile. These smiles were small, but cleared of sadness; they were brief, bright. Her eyes were everywhere, on everyone, polite. It was me who felt bad. I was lonely without her. I did not want to ask questions, but sometimes I had to ask, *How are you?* Not a question for friends, for everyday friends, every-minute friends. Always her reply was always a considered, cautious, given-the-circumstances *I'm alright.* But I could see that she was far from alright. And whenever I asked, more directly, *Are you alright?* her answer was a simple untrue, *Yes.*

Once, in those first few days, I managed to ask her, 'Have you spoken to Martin?'

She was beside me, busy, loading textbooks into her locker; she was small-person busy: concentrated, compact, abrupt. She looked up at me. Although our lockers were side by side, mine was higher, because I was taller; I was taller than most of the girls in the Sixth Form, so I had had to have a higher locker. Her textbook, suspended in mid-air and momentarily poorly supported, began to sag, the thin pages flopping, flowing. I saw skeletal equations slipping past on those silky pages. Elements, velocities, the components of science. Her scientist's gaze was fearless, optimistic. She asked, 'Have you?'

I shook my head, No.

She said, 'Yes, I've spoken to him.' Then, confidently, diagnostically, 'He needs time, that's all.'

A statement of faith.

She slammed the locker door. Which was exactly how to close one of those lockers: with a slam, because they failed to close with anything less. Everyone knew that the slams which closed those lockers were not slams. Nevertheless, Ornella slammed. She knew it, I knew it. We both knew that the slam said, *Subject closed*.

When she decided to talk to me about Martin, a few days later, she started by announcing, 'So long as there's no one else, he'll come back.'

We were walking to the school gates, on our way home. I had been telling her about Abi's night out with Dominique, who had rarely been seen by any of us since leaving school almost a year before to train as a PA. As far as I was concerned, I had not finished the tale. So, I was thrown by the interruption.

'What do you mean?'

Without lifting her gaze from the bus stop, she replied, 'Martin isn't capable of being on his own. Not for long.' Her eyes drifted to mine. 'So, if he finds no one else, he'll come back to me.'

'Nella,' I murmured, pained, before urging, very gently, 'Is that good enough?'

I watched her misery float to the surface and disperse the hard fear and determination on her face. And she almost smiled. 'Do you hear me complaining?'

I was washed with the chilling realization that I loved Ornella, that I was one of several people who loved Ornella very much, who wanted nothing more than for her pain to stop, but that we did not matter, because no one and nothing mattered now to Ornella but Martin. *Martin*, who did not care.

She asked me over to her house for the evening: the first time that she had wanted to see me since Martin had had-his-word. 'I could use some company,' she added in a soft but very mock-American accent, and slid me a quick self-depreciative smile which slipped beneath my heart. But I was unprepared for the dreadfulness of the evening. I spent the first hour or so half-sitting-half-lying on her bed, then one-quarter-sitting and three-quarters-lying for a while before struggling up, sitting straight, trying to leave. Trying to stem the flow of her words. Refusing to sink back beneath the weight of those words. Not that they were heavy words: they were anything but heavy, they were startlingly insubstantial. But there were so many of them. And the tone, too: the sound of them was suffocating, they were slick, oozing affection. *He's such a baby – but aren't they all babies, really? – and he has to flex his little muscles, has to have his freedom. His Freedom. So, fine, let him have his Freedom. Of course he's afraid of commitment, they're all afraid of Commitment – and do I want commitment? can you imagine? can you imagine anything more ridiculous than ME wanting COMMITMENT? But of course he has forgotten loneliness. They all forget loneliness. They all come back. And don't we have to be patient?* Certainly *I* was patient. I spent the evening listening to this long spell for Martin's return, and I do not believe in spells.

I could do nothing to help her. I was hoping that she would return to a peace of her own accord, that her fears would settle, sink, sleep again. As she talked, I watched her flinching from these invisible internal fears, Ghost Train tickles. The best that I could do was to ease her around the obvious dangers, limit the damage. So I followed, murmuring unceasingly and always in agreement, *Oh yes* and *No of course not* and *I see what you mean.* And in this sense, I stayed close to her.

At school the next morning she was unrested, tired but tense; her face was the colour and texture, the too-hard white, of a knuckle on a clenched fist. The words were stopped up, she went to and from her classes barely saying anything. At lunchtime, though, she turned on one of the dinner ladies. She went to the serving hatch to complain about the custard on her Bakewell tart:

deliberately obstreperous, because school custard was never anything but cool and lumpy, and she never took more than a touch on each spoonful of pudding, she always left the bulk in the bottom of the bowl; custard was nothing to her, she could take or leave it. Until now. By going to complain she was picking a fight, picking a scab, scratching an itch: the serving hatch provided someone on whom she could vent her fury. Which she did, spectacularly.

Across the room, we watched helplessly from our table. Davey's head was low in the corner of my eye, and held hard, his palms pressed to his temples. I could hear him muttering wretchedly, tolling, 'Oh dear, oh dear,' a running commentary. Opposite me, Abi was chewing the index finger of one hand and tapping the other soundlessly on the tabletop, urging the scene onwards to a speedy end. I knew that the three of us sensed that this fight with the dinner lady was the start of something, the start of a different phase. For some reason, no reason, I looked away from the scene to ask Abi, 'Why is Martin doing this? Why now, why like this?' I was surprised that my tone chimed with the argument on the other side of the room, that I sounded so angry.

'Search me,' Abi replied, widening her eyes for the purpose.

I snapped, 'Has Martin said anything to you?'

Her eyes glittered as they rolled. 'Martin,' she repeated disparagingly.

I was not sure that I knew what she meant, but then my attention was torn by the rising voice of the dinner lady, her repeated refrain: 'It's not my fault, don't blame me.'

Ornella returned rather regally to the table with a new bowl, a fresh piece of Bakewell, dry. She seemed satisfied. No one spoke. She sat and started on the Bakewell. There was a scallop of hair behind one ear: the off-balance, lop-sided, jaunty head, along with her suddenly hearty appetite, implied a lighter mood, a gain in confidence. When the spoon rose, however, I could see that her hand was shaking. After a few mouthfuls, she paused to look up into my face. The fluorescent lights clashed with the dark hot cores of her eyes. Waving her spoon towards the kitchen, she reported mischievously, 'In the war, they were grateful for whatever they were given.'

The afternoon passed peacefully but when she rang me in the evening she was crying hard. I had come to the phone from *Aire and Angels*: for English, we had had to chose a Donne poem for Comprehension. I was regretting my choice but by now I was in too deep, it was too late to change my mind. Comprehension of *Aire and Angels*? A contradiction in terms. I was lamplight lazy and woozy from the many seconds which my clock had been trickling for so long into the silence of my bedroom. Ornella's broken words were swilling in the receiver. Momentarily, *Aire and Angels* was preferable; even *Aire and Angels*. Furthermore, I had been smoking when she called, to aid concentration – leaning from my window, holding the burning star into the black sky, intending to throw the stub eventually into the garden next door – and now Mum was lingering around me, suspicious, presumably on the scent. So I was trying to breathe softly, sparsely. Ornella did not ask me to go to her, but I knew that this was what she wanted. 'I'll pop over for an hour,' I said, trying to sound casual for Mum because it was late. 'Give me fifteen minutes,' I said, thinking through the bus timetable. And hoping that one of her parents would give me a lift back home.

I replaced the receiver and went upstairs to my room without saying a word to Mum. Why should I? She had been standing close enough to me to hear everything. But upstairs, checking my purse, I realized that I did not have enough bus fare. So I went onto the landing and called sheepishly over the banisters, 'Mum? Can I borrow some bus fare? To go over to Ornella's?' Mum came to the living room doorway. Juliet came and stood behind her, startlingly infantile in flannelette pyjamas and fluffy slippers. She had had her bedtime bath and her sleek silver head shone. I looked down onto her clean wet parting. Mum did not mention the late hour. Instead, she asked with kind concern, 'Have you done that homework?' She had sensed the tension through the floorboards, if not the smoke. 'Yes,' I lied.

When I arrived, Ornella took time to settle. I followed her into the kitchen where, despite my protests, she made elaborate coffee with hot milk and additional cream. She looped the cream into the cups over the smooth hump of an upturned spoon. Then this fat silky white ribbon curled and sank beneath her finishing touch, cinnamon and brown sugar. She fired the cinnamon from its container with several slaps of the heel of her palm but shook the sugar very carefully from a teaspoon. Momentarily, her shaking was held into those few focused shakes. A precise dosage of shakes, an illusion of control. We took the cups to her room, where she showed me a new jumper. Holding it to herself, framing her reflection in the full-length mirror, she fussed, 'I'm *just not sure*. There's *something...*' *Something wrong*. From the bed, I puzzled politely with her; frowned dutifully across the room at the back-to-front, flat and silvery Ornella. On the dressing table, the warmth coiled free from her cup. Eventually she threw the jumper onto the wicker laundry basket and sat down opposite me, on the dressing table stool, to urge, 'You have to talk to him for me.' There was no trace of tears in her eyes but her voice was rusty.

'But what would I say?' My reluctance was amplified into despair by tiredness.

Her voice, her clear eyes, remained level. 'I don't care what *you* say, I care what *he* says.' And she explained, 'I want to know what he says.'

So now, at last, I could ask: 'Well, what has he been saying to you?'

But she deflated and folded away from me. 'Nothing.' Her head dropped onto one hand and she began to cry. '*Nothing*. He says *nothing* to me.'

The sobs rained down as hailstones. Flustered, I began to protest, to cajole, '*Ornella*, he *must* have been saying *something*.' I should have simply leaned across to comfort her.

'No,' she bubbled. 'Nothing, nothing, he won't talk to me.'

'At all?'

She lifted her head to tell me, 'It's getting that way.' Which told me everything: she had been pushing him and now he was hardening from tolerance to resistance. What had I been thinking? That Martin would ease up, come round, give up, laugh it off? Thanks to Ornella's strenuous efforts, he was discovering the depth of his resistance. Her eyes were huge with fear, watchful. Such a shiny, wide open, wounded gaze: a sitting target. I sensed her queasy anticipation of the dire consequences of her behaviour towards Martin. If only because she could not fail to know. Because everyone knows what happens when you push someone. Nothing happens. Nothing good. Nothing which is not bad. Yet I sensed, too, her justification, her compulsion: *what else could she do?* She could not do nothing.

I looked away and tried to visualize Martin, I wanted to pick over him for clues. But he would not come to me without Ornella: in my mind's eye, he was talking to her, or simply looking, smiling, lit by his affection for her; very bright, but merely a reflection of her. When I gave up, a shard of him lodged and drilled underneath the lowered lid of my mind's eye, cutting an image, a composite image, Martin as he had been during the past week: alone, spectacularly alone in the middle of a crowd, cut loose, turning in on himself and squeezing shut his dry eyes. I saw now that they were painfully dry. Sleepy sleepless eyes. He was touching his forehead with his fingertips, I saw them flex with each press. He was pressing on a specific point, but the point became a time-lapse graze and I saw that this was a random search for relief.

Ornella was quizzing me about whether Martin had talked to anyone else: James, Davey, Abi, anyone? Then she began speculating on the contents of these unlikely – impossible? – conversations. I was sure that her teeth were chattering. She faltered and fell back to her original plea: *He'll talk to you, He'll listen to you.* Inside my eyes were those fingertips of his, those nails, each one a stripe of blood pressed below a stripe of bloodless nailbed. Under pressure. I told Ornella, 'I don't think he'll talk to anyone for a while, I think he needs to be left in peace.'

'*Peace?*' she shrieked angrily: a shorter, more effective way of asking, *Whose side are you on?*

An effective way, too, of drawing my attention to my simmering headache. 'Ornella, *please.*' The resulting, resentful silence was no more comfortable for me, so I tried a hopeful, friendly, 'Shall we talk about this in the morning?'

Ornella began to nod, but the nods fell into sobs.

I sighed, 'Oh, *Nella* . . .' Which was an attempt to soothe her and to exhale the stinging disappointment which her tears caused in me. Doomed, on both accounts, to failure.

She wailed, 'Look what's happening to me! I'm turning into an awful friend. You come around here and I carry on like this.' Her lower lip was swollen with emotion, a huge hot red teardrop. A crease ran down her forehead, a dagger between her eyes. She was straining to hold back more tears. But physically she was very composed. In her lap, her palms were pressed together beneath a crest of folded fingers. The fingers fluttered spasmodically, beating their own rhythm, an unrhythmic rhythm. Fingers, palms, the four chambers of a small lumpy heart, squeezing hard.

I smiled, 'But you made me this wonderful cup of coffee.'

She sniffed an appreciative laugh through her tears.

I said, 'I'll *try* to talk to Martin.' I said this because I wanted to give her something, anything. Perhaps it should have been a hand on her shoulder, or a shoulder to cry on, but this no-promises promise achieved spectacular results.

'You will?' she trilled.

'I'll *try*.' Why was there greater beneficence in this mean qualification than in a simple yes?

I refused to wait for Ornella to search for a parent, to arrange a lift home for me. I did not want to go home. I was tired, but I did not want the silence of a sleeping house, the sinister hush of switched-off household appliances. I did not want to face those few lights which Mum would have left on for me to guide me on my route through the house, from kitchen to bathroom to bed. I did not want to have to think about those lights left on so carefully for me, to have to remember to switch them off, to unpick the stitches and let the house fall into darkness. I craved the bubbling of other people's words around me, the dilution of Ornella's. *Our local* was not, in fact, local for me. It was several miles from my home, so I did not often go, but James was always there. James was always drunk there. Davey often came in time for last orders. If I hurried, I could catch him.

Ornella let me go, waving diligently after me from the doorstep. I walked quickly in the freezing air, breathing faintly, flinching, puffing in protest. There had been rain, earlier, and I did not know if there was likely to be more because the clouds, the clues, were covered with darkness. Head down, I hurried through rainslicks. Entering the pub, I felt conspicuous, with so much sparkling night air running off me, and out of me. As I shut the door behind me, I saw James. He was leaning heavily on the bar, talking to one of his drinking friends whose name I did not remember (Pokey? Pogo?). The friend saw me. His alcohol-burnt face crackled with a smile and he nudged James. James responded, but raggedly, swivelling unsteadily from the bar. Between the bar and me, his expression had stiffened: an attempt to ready himself for whatever he would find, but very ineffectual. So, when he saw me, I was laughing at him. Which tickled an identical, but magnified, response in him. I flared with the usual affection and exasperation. Coming through the crowds, I wished that I had been with him for the evening, I wanted to be thoroughly caked with his thick drunken laughter.

Delighted, he called theatrically to me, 'My darling, my sweet, my honeysuckle-rose, what are you doing here?' He was smoking. He was not supposed to be smoking; he was supposed to be *not* smoking, to be giving up, or to have given up, for the sake of his sport.

Reaching him, indicating the cigarette, I asked, 'What's *this*?'

He grinned, with considerable satisfaction. 'A vice.' He licked the tip of my nose.

'*James*.' How did he find the time to become so drunk? Did he never have essays to write? 'Don't you economists ever do any work?'

Amused, he said, 'Economists *talk about* work. *Other people's* work.'

I glanced around the room. 'Is Davey here?'

'Don't you want *me*?'

Exchanging a smirk with the friend, I said, 'You're joking, surely.'

Enormously pleased with himself, James began to insist, 'But I love you. I love you. I *love* you.'

I had stepped back into someone; I muttered an apology over my shoulder; then, patiently, 'Yes, James, I know.'

'I was just saying to Porky, here . . .' his gaze went giddily in search of the friend. 'I was just saying, wasn't I, my old mate . . .'

Suppressing a laugh, the friend shook his head for me, No.

'*James*. Is Davey here?'

'Davey,' he echoed meaninglessly. Then earnestly, 'Davey: fine man, fine man.'

'Yes.' I took and held his gaze very firmly in mine. 'But have you seen him?'

I had to wait for a lungful of smoke to go down into

him and return. Smoke leaked from his nose and mouth. Finally he managed, 'No sign.'

I tipped onto my toes to kiss him, once, diligently, dryly, before I stepped away. 'Okay, I'll see you tomorrow.'

He lurched in alarm, flailing the cigarette. 'You're not going? Already?'

I knew that he did not know why I was there, where I had been. He was beyond reasoning. I was simply *there*.

He was shouting happily after me, 'Stay with me.'

I turned, laughed, 'Lovely idea, James, but not very practical.'

'Fuck *practical*,' he returned flamboyantly.

'See you tomorrow.'

'Marry me.'

Around us, quite a few people had begun to laugh.

'Tomorrow.'

When I checked back from the door, he seemed to have forgotten that I had been there, he was laughing with a small group of friends. I was reaching again for the door when I saw Martin. He was sitting alone; apparently only recently or temporarily left alone because the tabletop was uneven with glasses and the ashtray petalled with shrunken, dusty cigarette ends. He was low on the bench, half-slipped beneath the table, his head dropped to one side and his arms asleep on his chest. But his eyes were hard, focused hard on mine. I saw that he knew exactly where I had been. And he knew that I knew that he knew. Why did he mind? I knew that he was drunk, and very differently to James. James had been burning, but Martin was sunk. The coldness of his eyes slashed into my breath. Dropping my hand from the door, I could manage nothing but a breathless, pointless, unavoidably abrupt, 'Did you do your Donne?'

He replied with a flat, heavy complaint, '*God.*'

I did not know if this was yes or no.

Suddenly there was more, but slurred, a slurry of words which I failed to catch. Instinctively I went after them, bent down, one hand rising to hold my hair from my eyes. His fingers snapped shut around this flying wrist. I could not see his eyes, because of my fallen hair. I said, 'Let me go.' Pathetic, despite the tough tone.

He threatened, 'Have a drink with me.'

Archly, I reminded him, 'We've had last orders.'

And he let me go. I saw blood springing back immediately beneath his nails, and with a slight delay into his fingerprints on my wrist. I stood, stunned. He seemed reluctant to look at me. So I waited, and when finally his frightened eyes had staggered upwards to mine, I thrust them away with a sharp turn of my head, I slammed away through the door into the street.

I ran across the street to a phone box, thinking nothing but *phone box*. Not thinking, but breathing hard, the sharp air scooping bitter little clouds from my lungs and tearing on the dry seams of my eyes. When I was safely inside the blood red Tardis, I blinked myself back to normal and dropped some of my return bus fare into the slot, condemning myself to a walk home.

Confident that Davey would walk with me. But when the line cracked open, I was hooked by a woman's *Hello?* Mrs Lake. Suddenly Davey seemed very far away, spirited away somewhere behind her; impossibly far away; nowhere. I began to clock up heartbeats. I knew that I should apologize to her for the late hour, but I was desperate to summon Davey. So I slipped a razor of urgency beneath my question, 'Is Davey there, please?'

She said simply, happily, 'I'm afraid not.'

Afraid not? Meaning what? Where was he?

'He's out.'

'*Where?*' Too late, I winced myself into silence.

But she took no offence, replied very helpfully, 'He's with his friend Veronica.'

All the breathing and beating in my body simply stopped. For a moment I made no trace in, on, the cold black air.

Cheerfully, gamely, she said, 'Usually he's back by midnight; if he's back by midnight, do you want him to call you?'

My stomach had begun to settle, but now it failed to stop, it continued to fall, to sink. I sighed, 'No.' Then I caught myself, became belatedly polite, hurried with a breathless explanation: 'Too late.' And hoped that she would hear the slant of my sorry smile in those words, my unspoken apology: the best that I could do, in the circumstances.

And, yes, she did: 'Oh,' she soothed. 'Shall I tell him you called?'

'Yes,' I started automatically. But, *Veronica called*? 'No,' on second thoughts. 'No, it doesn't matter.'

The next morning, I saw the stamp of sleeplessness on Davey's eye sockets. It was nine o'clock and he was sitting opposite me in the Common Room with the mug of coffee which was his small china nosebag. Beside me, Ornella was stirring her coffee with a finger of Kit-Kat. She asked me, lightly, 'Was Martin at the pub last night?'

'Yes.'

She sucked the hot runny chocolate from the wafer, slowly, to steady herself. 'And?'

I looked pointedly at the bald stained wafer. 'Do you have to do that?'

Her loopy expression flattened; her eyes, which had been wide for my reply, narrowed. 'Since you ask,' she said quietly, 'yes.' In the same tone, she continued, 'Did you talk to him?'

'No.'

Instantly, strikingly, her composure was gone and she was insisting, 'But you *promised*.'

I had not promised. But I wanted to explain. I opened my mouth, but already she was flouncing away in disgust.

A beaded curtain of raindrops was swishing on the window. I eased myself forward in my chair, slid towards Davey. 'Where were you last night?' I menaced.

He lowered his mug, surprised. In the steam his face was hazy. *Burning the candle at both ends*: his skin was waxy. 'Nowhere,' he protested weakly.

'Because when I called,' I continued, 'Your mum said you were with me.'

His eyes widened, too big too suddenly. 'You called? She didn't say . . .' And then he stopped. *Veronica called*? After a fortifying sip of coffee he said, 'I went for a walk.' Deadpan, Dare-to-disbelieve-me.

And I dared. 'Until *midnight*?'

'I can't sleep.' Not *Couldn't sleep*, but *Can't sleep*. Can't sleep, *in general. Ever*.

Acidly, I said, 'It's difficult to sleep when you're pacing the streets.'

In retrospect, I realize that I must have been the very last person who he expected to kick him when he was down. And he was down, I could see that he was down. Amazed, he protested, 'What's up with you?' His eyes drifted vaguely after Ornella, unconsciously making the connection.

'Why didn't you *say* that you'd gone for a walk?'

'I don't want to worry Mrs Lake.'

Petulantly, I said, 'She sounded very nice.'

Leaning forward in his chair, he corrected, 'I didn't say that she *wasn't nice*.' Sitting back, he concluded coldly, darkly, 'So, don't take sides.'

My complaint came in a rush: 'And don't *use me*.'

He said defensively, insincerely, 'My mistake, and I'm sorry.' Then he added the sting, 'I needed you to cover for me and I didn't think you'd mind.'

I stood up, spilling my real pain, saying simply, 'I *needed you*.' And then I followed Ornella. No, I did not follow Ornella, I merely moved in the invisible track which she had left across the room, because I was too weary to know what else to do.

Ornella began to follow Martin. She followed him to rugby games on Saturdays, to spectate; to the A level lunchtime play-readings, to listen; to Chess Club after school, where she began to learn to play chess; and to the pub afterwards, after everything, for a drink. She was not stealthy; on the contrary, she was sprightly. It was not her idea that Martin should *not notice* her; it was her idea that he *should notice* her. And how could he fail? She was everywhere. A huge mistake, I could see, because he was beginning to dread her.

I could not keep up with her, but if I lost her, I would look for Martin. Or his friends, because he had begun to ensure that he was rarely alone. He looked for protection in numbers. In the middle of the crowd, I would find Ornella. There was nothing unusual about Ornella in the middle of a crowd. And, to some extent, Martin's friends were her friends, our friends. What was odd was the obviously deliberate nature of her actions. She would set herself down in the middle of Martin's friends. She was, literally, showing herself up.

She was forever smiling. The fewer smiles from us, the more from her. *Making light.* Those smiles of hers were worryingly wide of the mark. Because her situation was serious. Martin never smiled. He seemed to focus inwardly, constantly uncomfortable, as if bothered by a pain. Which, of course, in a way, he was. He was undergoing a real, live haunting. For a few days after our clash in the pub, he did not look into my eyes when we spoke. But, then, we barely spoke. I wondered whether he was looking into anyone else's eyes. So I watched him with James, and with Davey. And I saw that he put his gaze into theirs, but gingerly, on trust. At arms' length. Those eyes were imploring, *Don't ask, just don't ask.* And he limited these exchanges to arrangements, *See you at seven-thirty?* Indisputable, requiring nothing but yes/no answers. Obviously brave, falsely cheery, his eyes had a middle-of-the-night emergency room sheen: in control, but barely. An economical gaze, limited but strong: making clear to all of us that he would see-this-through.

When, finally, he looked into my eyes, we were rattling with the slam of the Common Room door. Ornella had slammed the door, apparently for no reason, although of course the reason was Martin. He was there: for Ornella, this was reason enough. No doubt she felt that the slam spoke volumes but in fact we were merely deafened. When he spoke to me, his voice spoke one message – I forget, perhaps *Can I borrow your Coghill?* – but his eyes contained another. His eyes spoke sadness but I did not know if he was sorry for me or for himself or possibly, more nobly, for everyone, for everything that he had caused to go wrong and for turning our Common Room into a place which was no longer common but noisy, slammy, with fear and loss. This message from his eyes made me want to reach out and hold him. I resisted, of course. I said yes to the Coghill, or whatever it was.

There was something else in the haziness of his eyes. It was the hardness of a resolution: *Despite everything, I would not have done this any differently*. There was more, there was something specifically for me, a little chink, almost a question mark: *You know that, don't you?*

Yes, I knew.

You have to understand.

Yes, I understood. Because who can refuse a silent plea?

I did not see him face-to-face again for some days, and then Ornella said to me, 'It's Martin's birthday on Wednesday.' It was Monday morning and we were waiting together in the Common Room kitchen for the urn to boil the water for our coffee. No one else ever bothered with coffee until mid-morning, so the Monday morning struggle with the cold urn was always ours. I had been struggling, too, with my reflection on the silvery urn, struggling to dampen down some sleep-skewed hair.

'Oh no.' I had forgotten. It did not occur to me, for a moment, to worry about the meaning behind Ornella's words; I was more concerned that I had forgotten. Martin had blinded me to him so successfully that I had forgotten his birthday; he had held me so absolutely from him, I had lost track of him. Then came the heavy hum of dread. Because I realized that his birthday would provide justification for Ornella to talk to him, to dote on him. Cards, presents, the scale could be stupendous. Padded cards, soft toys? Ornella was increasingly difficult to predict. Fearfully I asked her, 'What are you going to do?'

'*I'm* not going to do anything,' she replied cheerfully. '*You're* going to go to the pub with him and everyone else.'

'Ornella . . .'

'*Yes*,' she insisted, although I had not said no.

I was instantly and utterly exhausted by the prospect. But how could I possibly feel too tired to do something so far in the future? Two days, two nights: a lot of sleep, in two regular doses. No, I was not tired, I was afraid.

On the Wednesday, I slipped Martin's card into his locker: a simple action, ordinarily simple, but, in these circumstances, stinking of subterfuge. Inside the card I had written *Martin, Happy 18th, Love, Veronica*: so unusually reticent that it was the equivalent of *No Message*. When he found it, two lessons later, and read it, he turned to me, smiling, and said over several heads, 'Thanks.'

So I said, 'Happy Birthday.' Which seemed the wrong way around. Then, suddenly, he disappeared behind a thick dense web of fingers which came down over my eyes from behind. '*James*,' I decided, accused. Not because I recognized his fingers but because who else would do this?

'*Aha*,' sang James, evidently pleased with himself, although I do not know why, because he had not caught me out.

A little later, Ornella arrived in the Common Room and checked with me, 'Are you going to the pub tonight?'

She had been in Biology; she was tidying her dissection kit, shuffling sharp implements into slots in the wallet which was unrolled across her knees. The soft khaki wallet, lined with scalpels, reminded me of *M.A.S.H.*

'I don't know,' I whined.

She smiled down on the blades, said, 'Oh, go on. What else is there to do?'

Silently, I ran through my homework itinerary. 'I could do the Treaty of Versailles.'

She folded the clanking khaki and tied the two loose laces, lifejacket-mode: cross-in-front-and-behind-and-knot-securely. Although she was busy flipping and tying, she sent me a scornful glance.

So I asked what I had been wanting to ask, but had not dared; what I did and did not want to ask: 'Are *you* going?'

She stood, sighing, and crossed to the lockers; she deposited the dissection kit and turned back to me, leaned back on the lockers and folded her arms. Her lips opened soundlessly and her eyes slid sideways and downwards, nowhere. She was considering. Or making a show of considering. I suspected that she had had a plan for weeks. 'No, I think I'll stay home.' A foolproof plan to snag Martin's attention: sooner or later during the evening, he would notice her absence.

I said, 'Oh, *do* come.' It was a genuine plea, rather than an attempt to foil the plan. I was tingling with missing her. Like the tingling of a lost limb, a feeling with nowhere to go. Lately she had been everywhere but nowhere. We had had no fun together. We were together but we had no fun. She was on the phone to me every evening but she talked but about nothing but Martin.

Now she shook her head, replied knowingly, 'I have to get to grips with photosynthesis.' Words to sound good in place of the stubborn truth, *I'll stay home*.

There was something else which I wanted to ask. 'Have you bought him a present?'

Her eyes widened, took the strain, pushed darkness and confusion to their corners and beyond. The reply came uncomplicated, light and easy: 'Of course.'

My itch of curiosity began to burn; strong enough, now, to kill a cat. 'Have you *given* him his present?'

'Later,' she said, definitely, declining to specify.

So, 'What have you bought him?'

She warmed to this question, leaving the lockers and returning to me. 'A record . . .'

'*Which* record?' Because, famously, Ornella understood nothing of Martin's mania for music, and cared even less. She complained – *had* complained – about the time that he spent in the evenings listening to John Peel. I joked, 'Not another copy of Athletico Spizz's *Where's Captain Kirk?*' To replace the copy that the boys had ruined by over-use on the Common Room record player.

'Patsy Cline,' she said.

'*Patsy Cline?*'

'She's –'

'– I *know* who she *is*. Was.'

Ornella was expressionless, so I prompted, 'Why? Why Patsy Cline for Martin?'

'Oh,' she seemed surprised by the question, 'He *loves*

her.' Now *my* lack of expression made her laugh. '*Seriously.*' She laughed louder, but said more quietly, 'I suspect there's a lot that you don't know about Martin.'

At the end of the day, hurrying from the cloakroom, Davey grabbed my arm. 'You coming tonight?'

Startled, swamped by my raincoat which had cascaded onto me from its peg, I muttered grudgingly in reply.

Suddenly he seemed struck by a thought: dropping my arm, he both straightened and softened to enquire, 'Is Ornella coming?' His eyes were stark with embarrassment.

I dug deep into one of the arms of my raincoat. 'No.'

He hovered in the edge of my field of vision. 'Right,' he said, faintly. 'See you, nine-ish, then.'

I was there by nine. All of us except Ornella were there, but we were diffuse in the noise and smoke. James was drinking with Martin and others. The regular roars from their table – some in triumph, others in derision – implied a drunken contest of some kind. Davey had decided to be one of the boys for the evening: I watched him, mid-conversation, throwing palm-loads of peanuts into his mouth. Bev had come over to sit beside me. She shifted through strange angles in the chair.

Unfortunately she wanted to talk about Ornella. Unfurling from her chair, she confided, 'She seems so *abnormally normal* at the moment.'

I knew what she meant: quite quiet, and oh-so-sociable. 'Yes,' I agreed. Ornella was growing a hard bright surface, and I could no longer locate the centre of her. I had to look from the corner of my eye whilst she was unaware of me, perhaps when she was loading her locker, delving into darkness, her eyes and the corners of her mouth dropped low. Or when she ran her hands through her hair, ran the hair back from her face, her hands momentarily in front of her eyes so that she was hidden but free. She slotted herself back into the world with a purposeful blink: When-I-open-my-eyes-please-let-everything-be-different. Her disappointment, when her eyes opened, was painful. For me, as well as for her: disappointment flares around a wound, and burns onlookers. I made a snap decision to talk to Bev about Ornella, but when I leaned towards her, she turned away, distracted. I traced her gaze across the room to Davey; and to Abi, who was edging carefully towards him through a narrow gap between bench and table. I nudged Bev with a sharp, 'What?' Her eyes flicked back to mine, and she told me, amused, 'Abi is after Davey.'

'No,' I derided. I watched Abi sit down next to Davey.

'Oh yes,' Bev breathed, wonderous, in my ear. 'She told me.'

'Oh no.' I insisted, 'No, Bev.'

She nodded slowly and surely.

'But that's ridiculous,' I protested. 'Davey isn't Abi's type.'

Dutifully, Bev informed me, 'She thinks he's cute.'

'Cute?' I squeaked. 'Well,' I hurried. 'He *is* cute . . .'

'She thinks he's a challenge,' Bev reported soberly.

Yes, but she cannot know how much of a challenge. I

said confidently, 'Davey's not interested in Abi.'

'Oh no?' With an amused twitch of her head, Bev tipped my gaze back across the room. Davey and Abi were laughing hard into each other's faces. His hand lay heavily on her forearm. He was interested. But only up to a point. *His* point, a point chosen by him. Then he would stop. No explanation for Abi, or perhaps an untrue explanation. And unconvincing.

Bev took the opportunity to move on to a related topic: 'Can I ask,' she piped, hopeful, 'How long did you and James wait before you went to bed together?'

Reluctantly, briefly, my eyes left Davey and Abi. Bev's eyes were waiting for me, warm with a mixture of fear and trust. She was serious. I did not want to tell her about my first time with James. I could answer the question about *bed*, our first time *in bed*; but I did not want to mention the utility room. Not even Ornella knew. James and I had tidied the incident into a private joke: a giggle teased from me by his occasional whisper of, *Fabric conditioner*. Davey and Abi had become a bold flicker on the edge of my field of vision, a snag in the corner of my eye. So I asked Bev, 'Why?' I knew why.

She told me why: 'I'm not sure if I want to go to bed with Darren.' She swopped the cigarette from one hand to the other, apparently without consequence: ambidextrous. Then she prompted, 'Vonny?'

I blinked away Davey-and-Abi, bit hard into my lip to sharpen my thoughts. But, shamefully, I was not thinking of Bev; I was thinking *How do I go over there and stop Davey from doing what he's doing?* But why did I want to stop him? I simply knew that I had to stop him. Perhaps I was worrying not for Abi but for Davey. In one sense, yes, Davey knew what he was doing, he was adept even, his laughter gliding low around Abi; but in another sense, no, because what is the expression, *Playing into her hands?* In her lowered gaze, her hands were moving restlessly, pointlessly, glittering over the table-top, around the glasses, her purse, a pen, a few beer mats. She talked to him without once raising her eyes: an assumption of intimacy. A picture of intimacy. *Wrapping him around her little finger*. In the meantime, Bev's question remained. I looked across our table into her eyes, but blankly, and said hurriedly, 'Tell him that you have your period.'

'*Veronica*,' she protested. Then she explained sweetly, 'I didn't mean *tonight*, I meant *in general*.'

I had known exactly what she meant. As she was speaking, I had stood up, suddenly, and she had been reduced to whining upwards. Her words tugged on me; the flare of her upturned eyes burned too bright, wavered; her downturned mouth, denied the conversation, shrank. Poor, sweet, trusting Bev: I was failing her. Miserably. I was failing everyone. I promised, 'Use an excuse tonight, and I'll talk to you properly tomorrow.' As I turned away, I heard her say, 'He isn't even *here* tonight.' This was whispery with wonder, a mere exclamation to herself, because she had given up on me.

On my way to Davey, I was interrupted by Martin. 'Happy birthday!' he shouted to me, a sloshy echo of the words which he had been hearing all day, all evening.

His grin was huge, genial, hazy, a slow-setting sun. His hair was fluffy. I faltered; I did not think, I went to him on instinct. I leaned over his table, laid my hands on his head to hold us both steady, and lowered a kiss onto his hot crown. 'Happy birthday,' I repeated.

'Ahhhhh,' James bleated appreciatively, from somewhere behind the cigarette which was stuck between his lips.

I straightened and Martin's eyes came up after me, opened up to me, clear and bottomless; I stepped back, felt his hand running softly through mine, sliding the length of my palm and slipping from the tips of my fingers.

I turned away, tried to concentrate on my mission, tried to think about what I should say to Davey, decided not to think too hard: I would rely upon inspiration, improvisation. So I stopped in front of his table, fixed on him, and the words which came were, 'Davey, can I talk to you for a moment?' *Pathetic*. And he knew it. His expression hardened with irritation and he asked pointedly, 'About what?' I flinched, flicked my eyes over Abi: was she cross, too, with me? There was no clue in her stilled gaze, but I felt not: she was too sure of herself to be so easily unsettled. I returned to Davey, replied, lied, 'About Ornella.' It worked: I might have spoken the name of a dead person, for the spectacular result which I achieved. Abi's silky hands contracted, withdrew from the table, folded demurely in her lap. She lowered her head, a sign to Davey that he was excused. He was already standing.

He followed me towards the door; the sounds of

people shifting once more, this time for him, followed me to the door: a regular, reassuring split-second delay. Outside, I sat down on the top step, to anchor us. He shuffled in front of me, on the steps below me, blinking away the darkness.

I came to the point: 'Don't mess with Abi.'

He stopped, very still. But the change in the tone of his voice was less dramatic: 'I'll "mess" with whomever I like,' he informed me; but carefully, painfully pleasant. Then he came up the steps, and circled me.

I stood and turned around after him.

He raised one hand, to halt me, to stop my words. 'I won't "mess" with anyone,' he insisted. Lowering the hand, tentatively, he winced. As if I was burning in the darkness and he feared for his eyes.

I wailed, 'You're behaving like an idiot, this evening.' Like a *boy*. 'What's wrong with you?'

He admitted sadly, 'Six pints, is what's wrong with me.'

I tutted extravagantly and stomped up the steps. I did not know what else to say.

Behind me, he gloated over-loudly, 'So you *didn't* want to talk to me about Ornella.'

Ornella? My hand weakened on the doorknob. I had forgotten Ornella. I had used her as my excuse, then forgotten her.

I did not forget her when I left the pub. She was expecting me to phone her as soon as I came home. She wanted news of Martin. All day she had been asking me, reminding me to make the call. At first I had tried to explain that I would have nothing to tell, and to insist that I could not disturb her household so late. 'No problem,' she said firmly, 'I'll be by the phone, waiting.'

I wanted to ask, *What do you expect to hear from me, about Martin? What do you want so badly to hear?* But I said, or probably whined, 'Can't it wait until the morning?'

Was this thoughtless of me? A loud twang of indignation came from Ornella: 'And what do I do in the meantime? Sit up, twiddling my thumbs, for twelve hours?'

But what could she hear from me that would put her to sleep? I tried again, gently: 'There'll be nothing to tell you.'

'Maybe, but I need to be sure.'

Then I decided simply to refuse. 'I'll tell you everything in the morning.' Laying down the law, laying down some boundaries, sensible and sure. Expecting her to surrender, thankful for the relief. But her expression hazed into panic. So I came quickly to the rescue: 'Okay,' I relented, 'I'll ring.'

I rang, wriggling from my coat in the hallway. Four rings, and then Ornella's dad challenged, 'Hello?'

I spluttered, 'Is Ornella there?' before adding a hurried, 'It's Veronica, hello.' My coat, half-mast, held me by my elbows. In a half-nelson.

Ornella's dad picked up the tail end of my utterance: 'Hello, Veronica.' Empty of enthusiasm. Barely tolerant.

A warning. 'No,' he continued carefully, too patiently, 'She's in bed.'

'Right,' I said, thinking about this, around this, trying to see what I should do, what I could say.

'Okay?' Smooth with fake charm. *Can-I-go-now?*

'Okay,' I repeated mindlessly.

He sang a weary, pointed, 'Bye-bye, Veronica.'

'Yes, bye.' No opportunity for me to leave a message, to leave her a rebuke: *Tell her I called*.

The next day, she told me, 'I was *so tired*,' piping a sense of wonder over a bass note of self-pity. No apology. Soon afterwards, she began ringing me with spectacular disregard for routine. The calls came when I was in the middle of eating or when I was in the bathroom, when I was watching television or after I had gone to bed. Why suddenly so wrong? Previously, she had never called during my favourite programmes because they were her favourites too. Now she had stopped watching television in the evenings. Had she stopped doing everything else? Meals, baths, homework, sleep? Also, she was ringing more often, three or four times each evening, so that, inevitably, some of her calls came at the wrong time.

They came as my Welsh rarebit began to blister beneath the grill, to offer up juicy scalding bubbles of cheese. Or they came as I began to blow-dry my hair, or to brush my teeth. The phone would scream briefly in the hallway, before Mum's announcement: *Ornella!* In the beginning Mum had shouted for me, *Veronica*, and

I had responded with a hopeful, *Who-is-it?* Eventually this exchange became unnecessary. *Ornella* stood for *Ornella again*, said *Come here and deal with this*. My hair wet and wayward or my mouth foaming chalk, I would pause and try to hoist my heart into place.

Her calls did not stop coming if I was not there to answer them. I would come home to the evidence, Mum's handwriting on the message pad: *Ornella, Ornella, Ornella*. Once, only once, Mum asked me nervously, 'Is Ornella alright?' A polite, less intrusive, version of the real question: *Why is she not alright? What's wrong?* I smiled ruefully, knowingly, and replied, 'Boyfriend trouble.' Even Juliet seemed knowing and superior, stepping so very carefully and silently around me when I was on the phone.

Often Mum was my excuse; perhaps she overheard, sometimes, and was surprised by my uncharacteristic eagerness to comply with her wishes, that *I'd like to call Aunty Sheila sometime this evening*, or that *I'd appreciate if you could keep the line free this evening because I think your dad may try to ring*. But these excuses to Ornella were useless because the postponed calls piled up in my head, just as the missed calls piled up on the message pad: *Ornella, Ornella, Ornella*. Sooner or later I had to return those calls. Then her voice rattled thin on the line, lacking breath. Her words tap-tapped from the receiver, trying to draw from me whatever she wanted to hear. *You'd think, wouldn't you* . . . Often I tried to oblige, and lied in my aim to lessen her misery. But she was unpredictable. Often there were small silences and

I did not know if these silences stood for tears.

Weekends were different, they broke this new routine and offered respite, returned us to our old ways. There was no school, no Martin, just the two of us in Ornella's room. With her hands pinned to the pillow by her head, she was suspended between restfulness and restlessness. Her only movement was an occasional flex of her toes. Her only problem was the phone: whenever it rang, she would tense, tighten, rising slightly, unconsciously, from her bed; and when she was not called, her recline was slow, fractionally slower than normal. Sitting by her window, I enjoyed a view which was different from the view from my own bedroom window, yet familiar: the intricate garden, haunted in a far corner by the ruins of a swing; and beyond the boundary hedge, the field of sheep. Beside each sheep was a small lamb, like a handbag. My fingers would idle through the tapes which lined the windowsill, teasing out the old favourites which I did not dare to keep in my own collection: soft rock, over-produced. Or I would take the magazine from the top of the pile on her dressing table and search for the Problem Page, the solar plexus of any magazine; scanning for the tell-tale bands of dark and light type, Question and Answer.

There were no problems in Ornella's magazines to match those which were available to us, free, from the men who rang the late-night phone-in on our favourite radio station. In the magazines there was no mention of sex with dogs. The problems in the magazines were emotional, and predictable: jealousy, mainly. For me, the physical problems held the surprises: people who wet themselves, or had hair growing in strange places. I was happy to read aloud the emotional problems, whenever Ornella issued a request from her prone position; but I shied away from the physical problems, and not simply because I did not want to create a freak show. It seemed easy for us to pass judgement on the emotional problems – *How ridiculous! That's pathetic! She should . . .* – but there was nothing to say about the physical problems, they existed, they stayed in the air between us.

Our weekend conversations were normal. Except, perhaps, for Ornella's new enthusiasm for analysing other people's relationships, for being in favour of every, any, relationship. The moral was that these people were sticking together, were working things out between them: they loved-each-other-really, they really-loved-each-other. Usually they were Ornella's parents, with their cross-cultural complications; often they were Guido and his new girlfriend from medical school; sometimes they were people on the telly, no one in particular, or not even real. Whenever she stopped these lectures, our chatter would drift backwards and forwards into our pasts and our futures. And she was happy whenever she was talking about her childhood and her plans for the future, which, miraculously, Martin did not seem to have touched.

Weekdays, though, were different. The row with the dinner lady had indeed been the start of a new phase: Ornella had begun to vent her anger on people who had no involvement in her troubles. Bystanders. She was a terrorist, eager to sabotage the very notion of innocence. *If you're not for, then you're against.* None of the bystanders were *for*, they were happy to allow the world to roll onwards. So she decided to take action, to stop them in their tracks. The bigger the target, the better. The worse. Because she went for teachers. Each successful shot was signalled by, *Ornella Marini, WHAT did you say?* And then, usually, she exercised her right to silence, or sort-of, by replying with a very sulky, 'Nothing.' But there was no right to silence in our school. On the contrary, the rule was *You will speak when you are spoken to*. And, of course, *Speak* stood for *Speak nicely*. Inevitably the initial exchange and Ornella's subsequent refusal to play by the rules brought about the fight that she had wanted. She was in a lot of trouble. And she was failing, refusing, to produce homework. This was mentioned to me in passing, in her absence, by one of the boys with whom she shared a bench in Chemistry and Physics. Her excuse, he told me, admiringly, was simply, *I'm SORRY, but I was TIRED*. No excuse at all. A fanfare of aggression and accusation.

One evening, a fortnight or so after Martin's birthday, she called me specifically to ask me to go over to her house. Her voice was wobbly with panic. When I arrived, she was in her room, crying messily, noisily. As soon as the door clicked into place behind me, her words started to spill over the sobs. She was crying, 'I'll kill him, I'll kill him, I'll fucking kill him.' Her words, her sobs, shook me; I went to her, held on to her. She smelled of her mother's perfume. I was saying, 'Nella, Nella, Nella.' A remonstration? A plea? I did not know, I did not care, I simply wanted her to stop, I would have said or done anything to stop her terrifying noise.

Which, in a sense, was her line, or began to be her line, over the next few weeks: she decided that if he had no strong reason for wanting to be free from her then he should continue their relationship simply to stop her pain. I could hardly bear to hear this, I had never come across anyone who was prepared to settle for so little. And who was so certain to lose. Because pain is soothed only by happiness. And happiness was too simple, by then, for Ornella and Martin: too much had happened. There could be no going back.

Suddenly she stopped slamming doors and causing trouble for teachers. Or more than stopped: she started to float through the days with the high-seriousness of a nun. But after school, and in front of me, came the outbursts, and they were variations on a single theme: *Martin had ruined her life*. I tried to remind her that there had been life before Martin, to tell her that there could be life after him. But she did not believe me.

And what about everyone else? Where were they? They were around, they were there, I knew that they were there: presences, like the people in my dreams; close, very familiar, but not quite visible. I did not talk much about Ornella to James; so he remained a source of light-hearted relief for me. Questions came occasionally from Davey – he checked with me, checked on me – but gener-

ally he seemed preoccupied. I could see that he was working hard: he was rarely without a book from one of our
supplementary reading lists, or that had been vaguely
mentioned in class, or that everyone knew but no one
ever read, like *Das Kapital*. I suspected that he was playing hard, too. His eyes were spectacularly sunken. One
day, his ear was pierced; then pierced again, a few weeks
later, for a second sleeper. This was too much for the
school authorities: he was told to remove the sleepers
or cover them with a plaster. He chose the plaster. He
approached Mr Donaldson, our English teacher, about
putting on a school play, which, with Mr Donaldson's
help, he became responsible for producing and directing.
He chose *The Crucible*. I declined to become involved,
claimed that I was too busy. I was drained. Abi took the
part of her namesake, the main accuser, the ringleader
of the girls. She went to Mr Daly, Head of History, to
ask if she could take fourth term Oxbridge exams. So,
she, too, was preoccupied. Only Bev was watchful over
us, her little face tense but wide open: an ever-present,
luminous question mark.

Ornella began to go to bed early. Earlier and earlier.
Until, soon, she was in bed whenever I rang in the
evening. *Headache*, her mum would whisper down the
line to me, or *Flu*. Non-specific, all-purpose ailments. I
was left with the sense of Ornella, beyond my reach,
turning and turning in her bed. One day, to explain to
me how weary she had become, she said, 'I'm so tired of

everything; sometimes I think that if I have to file another nail, I'll die.'

I tried to make her smile, by telling her, 'They'd still grow.'

She was distracted. 'What?'

'Even if you died, they'd still grow.' I smiled. 'You should know that: you're a scientist.'

She merely rolled her eyes.

One evening, an hour or so after her mum had told me that she was in bed (with *Ladies' problems*), she rang me. 'I'm frightened,' she said immediately. Her voice was feeble. Whatever else was frightening her, I could hear that she was also frightened of me. Of telling me.

I asked, 'What have you done?'

'I don't know.'

But I knew; I knew, somehow, as soon as I heard that reply, wobbly with misery. Calmly, I asked, 'What have you taken?'

She had taken some tablets, a handful, snatched from the bathroom cabinet. Her mum's tablets: she could not, or would not, specify beyond, 'For her head.'

I told her, 'I'll come over.'

'No,' she said, faintly but definitely, 'I'll come to you.'

Carefully, I checked, 'Why? Are your parents there?'

'Out,' she said.

'Ornella,' I was suddenly very angry with her, 'How are you going to get over here?'

'I'll walk.' She sounded tired. 'I want to walk.'

Further protests from me failed to deflect her. She told me that she was fine, that this was nothing serious, but she did not want to be alone, nor to stay home. I left the phone and went into the living room to tell James, who was visiting, that she was coming over. He said, 'I'll fetch her.' On his new motorbike, which was outside on the driveway.

I shook my head, 'She's not feeling well.'

He said, 'I'll be careful.'

So I rang her back and told her the plan. And ten minutes later, with a triumphant roar from the engine, she was delivered, stiff with carefulness and slapped silly by the rush of air, from the soft shiny black wasp-waist of the bike.

When we were alone, when James had reversed and gone from the driveway, she said to me, in explanation, 'I was so depressed.'

Was?

When we were indoors, I tried to find out more about the pills. She said that they were small and green, and that she had taken about ten of them. 'I'm sure that they're nothing serious,' she told me, 'I only took them because I wanted to be out of it for a while.'

Why did I not try to take her to hospital? Perhaps I did not want to give her up. Perhaps I wanted to do this by myself. After all, she had come to me. This was between the two of us. I was easy on her, asked no questions. Simply kept her with me and watched her cold face and bullet-hole eyes. I was waiting for signs. I did not know any signs; but I was sure that I would know, if and when I saw. In the meantime I fed her. Toast, then beans on toast. Then Weetabix: one, then two more with a thick stir of honey. If in doubt, *feed*. I told her to ring her mum, to arrange to stay with me. Her mum agreed: presumably she was delighted that life seemed to be returning so suddenly to normal, that we were back to sleep-overs on put-me-ups. So, I kept Ornella with me through the night, I checked on her through the night. I checked that she was alive, and asleep, and that I could wake her. I woke her every hour. I decided that if she was the same in the morning, then she would survive. In hindsight, my strategy would have been disastrous if she had taken paracetamol, slow poison. In the morning she had nothing worse than a headache, and I decided that the danger had passed.

But, in another sense, the danger had not passed. Because, six days later, she did it again. More so. And this time she did not come to me. She went to no one; her mother found her, sitting on the bathroom floor, very sick and drowsy. When she had taken her to hospital, she came to tell me. She was stunningly polite, on the doorstep: 'Veronica –' a too bright smile '– can I talk to you for a moment?' I obliged, led her into the living room, my heart thumping loopy question marks. She crossed to the sofa and sat, barely, her knees firmly together, her hands together on knees. Mum had slipped respectfully back into the kitchen as soon as she had heard those first few words from the doorstep; but her absence, so diligent, so thorough, was huge in the room.

I was as uneasy as Mrs Marini. I followed her, and when I had sat down, she recited the facts over her own soft murmurs that everything was alright, okay, fine. And this telling was so quick that I could do nothing, I asked no questions, I thought of no questions, I did not think at all; nor did I react. And then suddenly it was over, the telling was over. Her white hand hopped like a bird across her face, along her hairline, and then away through her hair to the back of her head. Politely, interestedly, she added, 'It's Martin, isn't it.'

I said nothing. I may have nodded.

She stood, to conclude, reluctantly, 'Well, you know ...'

I did not know.

Simultaneously she smiled, squeezed together her hands, and her eyes shone with a red glaze. '... keep an eye on her.'

Ornella's version, a few days later, was different. Her eyes were the too-clear eyes of the convert. 'They were so good to me, in there,' she gushed, 'I don't know how they do it, I wouldn't do it, I wouldn't want to be bothered with someone like me. Not when there are so many people, in there, who are really ill.' Borrowed words. Her own account of her experience was short on details: jovially, she mentioned the sore throat which had resulted from the wash-out, 'It kills your throat, I warn you.' As if she was an early initiate, and someday I would follow. Then she told me, 'I have to start seeing someone, there, once a week, from next week.' She concluded with a rueful shake of her head and a declaration: 'I felt *so stupid.*' I presumed that she meant that she would never try again, but, in retrospect, she meant that next time she would be more determined.

A week later, Martin came up to me when I was alone for a moment in the Common Room. Without looking at me, he began to speak quietly and quickly. As if he was pretending that he was not talking to me, or not talking at all. 'I've had a letter,' he said. 'From Ornella.'

I had taken my cue from him, I was frowning down onto my shoes. But with the mention of Ornella, my gaze went to the busy door. She was due to return from Chemistry. I began to watch for her.

'She implies that she's going to do it again.'

Do it. I did not know that he knew. *How* did he know? I was watching the door, dabbing it with glances. Each sweep was bringing one more member of the Chemistry class.

'And that, this time, she'll do it properly.'

I flinched, and my eyes ended up in his.

'And she said not to tell anyone.'

My heart was trying to escape.

He shrugged hugely, helplessly, hopelessly, which was a perfect sketch of how I was feeling. But I had to ask him, 'What are we going to do?'

His reply was jumbled, running scared. 'Nothing. What can we do? She won't do anything. She'll be alright.'

Suddenly disgusted with him, I hissed, 'All you want is for your life to return to normal.'

'Don't you?' he urged.

Yes, yes, yes, more than anything. 'It doesn't matter what I *want*,' I flared, 'We have to *do* something.'

In the corner of my eye, one more Chemist came carefree through the door.

'Talk to her,' I pleaded.

He reeled, incredulous: 'Have you *tried*, lately?' Then he muttered, 'Maybe I don't want to do anything, maybe I'm so sick of her that I don't care.'

I did not know whether to believe him; I made a snap decision to take these words as a silly, sulky bid for attention. For which this was most definitely the wrong time. 'Don't give me that crap,' I threatened. 'What are we going to do?'

We decided that someone should tell Ornella's mother, and that this someone should be me. I rang her from the phone box by the school gates. I could barely stand, I was so weak with fear. I was afraid that, somehow, I was too late. Because where was Ornella? She had not come back into the Common Room from Chemistry. Or perhaps I was too soon: my call would provoke her. But much stronger was my fear of Ornella's fury and the possible loss of our friendship. I was turning her in, turning her away, turning her over. I cried throughout my short conversation with Mrs Marini. If she noticed, she did not say. For which I was grateful. Her voice was weary but warm: 'Thank you very much, Veronica.' No discussion. *Your comments have been noted.* When I left the phone box, I went, late, to English. Lowering myself into the sole vacant chair, lacking the energy to apologize to Mr Donaldson, I nodded at Martin: *It has been done, it has been dealt with*.

I do not know what happened, but several days later Ornella announced to me that she would be going to the hospital three times each week. 'Contacts,' she said, self-importantly, implying that her father was the reason. Then she confided, 'I saw him yesterday.' She was referring to the doctor, or therapist. My whole brain was singing with relief: someone else was going to save her life, someone who knew how.

Very cheerfully, she said, 'Early thirties, I reckon. Very cute.' Just as cheerfully, she added, 'Wedding ring, though.'

I managed to laugh, 'You're incorrigible.'

I never knew if she knew that I had turned her in, that I had let go of her. If she did know, then surely whatever her initial reaction, she would have realized almost immediately that I had to do what I did. And in time she must have been thankful. But *almost immediately*: it was this split-second, untraceable, unknowable, that worried me.

For a while, everything improved drastically with the arrival of Dr Sinclair in Ornella's life, but unfortunately there was some damage which had already been done. Which I discovered on a Saturday morning when I called for her on my way to the shops in town. Her mum opened the front door, phone in hand, and mouthed happily to me, indicated, 'Upstairs.'

Smiling my thanks, I started for the staircase. I was halfway up when I saw. Ornella was coming through the bathroom doorway onto the landing. I saw her bloodless lips and the wet film in her eyes. She had been sick. The remaining stairs seemed to last forever. When, finally, I reached her, I managed to whisper, 'How far gone?' I did not, do not, know how I knew. I simply knew.

She said, sadly, 'Eight weeks.'

Neither of us spoke for a moment, and then I said, 'I don't believe this.'

Quietly, she said, '*You* don't believe it?'

We went together, slowly, along the landing and into her bedroom. Below, downstairs, somewhere, her father was singing, bellowing, *New York, New York*. She closed the door very softly and crossed the room behind me to sit on the far end of the bed. I had the pillows. I took one, hugged it, asked her, 'What happened?'

'A slip-up,' she replied.

'How?' My voice sounded distant, even to me. There was no reproach in my question. I did not know why I was asking for the details. What was done, was done.

She breathed deeply, once, regretfully, thoughtfully. I knew that she was sifting unspoken words. Eventually she went half-heartedly for, 'I didn't want the moment to . . .' The silence rustled with her shrug.

'. . . go,' I finished for her.

She nodded. Then she added, 'I really thought that he was coming back to me.'

This sank heavily into the silence between us.

'It's my fault,' she said, more to herself than to me.

'No,' I said, 'It's not. Not this.'

She said briskly, 'Well, anyway, I'm the one with the problem.'

I asked, 'Are you going to tell him?'

Her eyelids lifted a little in surprise; the tone of her voice, too: 'Oh, he knows.'

He knows? I was awed by the enormity of what I did not know about Ornella and Martin, about what went on between them.

'He doesn't *want* to know,' she added, wry. 'It's one more problem, for him. First, me; now, this.' When she said *this*, her eyes went nowhere, her hands rose but went nowhere. As if *this* was an abstraction. I froze, barely breathing. Realizing that it was not an abstraction, it was something, it was somewhere, somewhere very close. I concentrated on keeping my eyes on her face. I asked, 'What are you going to do?'

'I don't know.' The words were flat beneath her misery.

But we both knew *what* she was going to do; we did not know *how*.

I checked, 'Does anyone else know about this?'

'No.'

'Dr Sinclair?'

'No. Not yet.'

Not even Dr Sinclair. Or did he? He was a psychotherapist: could he detect, spectacularly without a stethoscope, the presence of something else, something very real, beneath her surface?

'But you told Martin.' I was thinking aloud.

'Yes.'

'But not me.'

'No.' She tried, 'I didn't . . .' her concentration flickered, faltered, '. . . have the words.'

She was frowning, trying to squeeze an explanation.

I stopped pressing her, shrugged to release her.

'You don't think I *should*, do you?' she checked with me. Her eyes and mouth, her whole face was wide open to receive my answer.

'Should what?'

No movement in her face. 'Have it.' *Have the baby.*

'No.' I heard the pause before my reply, but in fact I gave the question no thought at all. What I wanted was for our lives to return to normal.

Later that day, when I had gone, she told her mother. So that her mother would tell her father. The abortion followed very shortly: contacts again? I told no one. When she did not turn up for school, I remarked that she had a cold. As I spoke, I looked at Martin, who looked away. But I kept looking, I did not want the moment to go. When I rang her in the evening, she said simply that she was fine and that her parents had arranged for her to stay with relatives in Italy for the summer.

'Lovely,' I tried to enthuse.

'Next week,' she said.

I did not see her before she left. Her parents kept her busy, taking her shopping and to hospital out-patient appointments. And when she was not busy, she was in bed, exhausted. I spoke to her on the phone a few times.

She left without returning to school, missing the last four weeks of term.

At the end of the last day of term, the last day of the school year, Martin followed me into the cloakroom. I reached hurriedly for my raincoat. His voice came from the warm green shadows behind me: 'With Ornella, I made a mistake, and I knew that I was making a mistake. I was stupid, and I'm sorry.'

I did not mean to look at him, I meant not to look, but I could not help myself. His eyes seemed bare, somehow. His hair had been stirred by his restless hands.

He appealed, 'How much longer do we have to go on like this?'

I knew, then, that *mistake* did not mean *mistake in leaving her,* but *mistake in becoming involved with her.* And that *sorry* did not mean *sorry for her.* I knew that he had meant what he said, on the day of her letter, about not caring whether she lived or died.

I tried to walk past him, but he took my arm. Which I wrenched back, with exaggerated force, hurting myself more than him. 'Forever,' I said. And true to my word, although there were times when I came close, I never spoke to him again.

In Ornella's letters from Italy, there were no mentions of Martin or anything that had happened. Instead, she told me what she had been doing, which was nothing much, and included funny stories about her loathed cousin Lucia. At home, I was working hard, and splitting up with James. Ornella did not return until a few days before the start of the Upper Sixth. She was briskly cheerful, glittery not only with a suntan but with smiles, with the gloss of a grown-up. But the bones of her face had risen, hardened, in her skin. And she was taller. Not tall, but not so small any more. She smoked differently, too. Hungrily. At first, I was careful with her, with this new, determinedly clean-slate Ornella. But soon I found that everything was the same, except for the new unspoken rule: no mention of Martin. This was fairly easy because of my split from James. Martin and James kept themselves to themselves, hunched around the Common Room record player, over Martin's Elvis Costello records.

I did not want James but nor did I want anyone else. I wanted to be left alone. Ornella became involved with Matt Chalmers for a term or so: I liked him, had always liked him, he was a nice boy who smoked too much dope and was a rival for the record player with his Stones and Ry Cooder albums. But we did not often mention him, either. Although sometimes I gave her the option, asking, 'How's it going?' She would reply with the quiet whine which means *So-so*, finishing with a wrinkle of her nose, a dwarfed flourish of disappointment. And then, suddenly, she told him that it was over. Which was what she told me: 'I've told him that it's over.' Because, she said, 'I was fed up with it.' With what? I did not ask. She did not say.

'Oh, well,' I said, 'I suppose he was never the love

163

of your life.' Said stupidly: I had intended this to be a comfort.

It was, of course, a reminder. She hitched her eyebrows and looked away.

At the end of the year, she did not do quite well enough in her exams to go on to medical school. Her parents decided to send her to a crammer in London. So, when I went away to university, she stayed home with Abi, who had failed her Oxbridge entrance exam in the previous year and was going to try again. Bev went to London to train as a physiotherapist. James and Martin went to do Law, but in different places, different ends of the country. Davey left the country to travel for a year.

In my first year away, Ornella and I wrote to each other fairly regularly. We both wrote diligently to Davey: we sent letters throughout Europe, later to Israel and eventually to India. I skimmed his replies, the wonderful tales of his travels, verbal picture-postcards, scanning for *him*, for the familar bass note of his voice, his laugh: *Oh, you'd love Greek breakfasts . . . Help, I'm sorry, I left your Plath on a train . . . Send me a cup of PG, Veronichar, poste restante Alexandria.*

At the end of my first term, I had not worried about returning from my new life to Ornella. She had a new life of her own, at the crammer, which was just as exciting as mine because it was in London. As soon as I was back, my time away seemed like nothing but an interlude. A rather fantastical interlude, like a holiday. Not that we did not talk to each other about our new lives. But sitting on Ornella's bedroom floor, hearing about her crammer friends, I felt that I was being told stories: true stories, but stories nonetheless, irrelevant and fun.

But having stayed home, Ornella had some stories of people we both knew. She told me that Abi had a new boyfriend.

'From the library,' she told me, then stopped, laughed, 'Filed under *what?*'

I remembered that Abi had had a summer job at the library. According to Ornella, romance had blossomed – 'Beneath the Issue Desk?' – before the boy had returned to university.

I wondered, 'Do you think it's against the rules?'

She frowned. 'What do you mean?'

'Well, I don't know, but it might interfere-with-your-duties, or something. I mean, would you *fine* your lover?'

Ornella considered, 'She could fine him if *she's* over-due.' Then she confided, 'Actually, from what she told me, in their case, she needed a fine for *early* return. Premature return.'

'*Nella*,' I laughed.

'What she needed was compulsory renewal.'

'*Ornella*!'

Her eyes widened ridiculously. 'I'm only telling you what she told me.'

I choked on my coffee. 'I bet Abi didn't *say that*.'

'Well, okay,' she relented. 'Not those exact words.'

She seemed to have seen a lot of Abi. They had been

left alone together: Abi waiting for the boyfriend; Ornella simply waiting, waiting for everything, exams, results, a life away from home.

Later during the Christmas holiday, Abi arranged to see me, with Bev: Abi and Bev, just like old times. Having left school, we had no home ground. So we sat in my living room, which felt odd. Which felt *small*. Bev's hair was shorter, even shorter; it had crossed an unquantifiable line from shorter to short, had crept up so that suddenly Bev was someone with short hair. Abi's hair was shorter, but only by a couple of inches, too little to invite comment. To me, this cut seemed odd: why cut such long hair *to her shoulders?* More decisive than a mere trim, but not a bob or new style: it had been docked. But then, sitting opposite her in my living room, I began to notice how it moved. How *much* it moved. I began to see how this new length was perfect for movement. Previously it had been too long, hooked deep over her shoulders, down her back. But now she had had her hair cut free. And she had a new mannerism, too, an accessory to match: a toss of her head, to ripple the hair.

But nothing else had changed: Bev did the smiling and Abi did the talking. *'Til the cows come home*: Abi's constant chatter was comforting, involving, enveloping. I remember feeling warm, safe, sitting opposite her; feeling at home. I remember thinking, *With Abi, I know where I am*. She talked about the new boyfriend but did not tell me everything: when I spoke to Ornella, the next day, I complained, 'She didn't mention the "premature return".' Ornella laughed, scornfully. 'She's not going to admit to you that she has picked a sexual illiterate.'

PRESUMABLY WE SAW each other at Easter, but my next clear memory of Ornella is when we met up again for the summer. I had been away for longer, but now suddenly I was home for longer; she was now well on her way to leaving home, yet still a quarter of a year away. In my memory, she is sitting on the blanket box in her bedroom. I am sitting opposite, on her bed. Behind her, the window is open to an early-summer sky which is too hot and too late in the day to be blue but has the colour, or colourlessness, of a newly-picked stem, fresh and tough. The colour seems to have fallen from the sky into Ornella: her face is a sunset; the skin on her cheekbones is high pink cloud. Slumped among the cushions on the box beneath the window, she is silty with so much colour: tan, streaks of sunburn, and freckles. Presumably she has been lying in the sun because lately she has had so little to do: a few odd jobs since receiving her results, but, as far as I know, nothing for a while now; a situation which is not helped by her father's rule, *No bar work*. Across the room from me, she is utterly relaxed, slack: unseen for so long, perhaps, that she has forgotten that she can be seen, that I can see her. She seems permanently on the verge of pulling herself together with a stretch, but so far she has not stirred.

She has been fretting, pressing me to promise that I will visit her at medical school. And I have promised although I know that when she is there she will not need me. (And did she visit *me*, in *my* first year, when she had nothing else to do?) Now her long sigh burns the silky air and she says, 'Two months to go. I can't wait.'

I hum in accord. Although I am still unsure how I feel about my long holiday back here. Both too long *and* too short. I am so pleased to be back here with her, but I am missing my university friends and Mark.

'I've been seeing Abi,' she says.

'How is she?' I have heard nothing from Abi since Christmas, although Ornella keeps me informed, told me that she had finished with the student. I should call her.

'No,' she says. 'That's not what I mean.' Her gaze locks so firmly into mine that I almost hear a click. 'You know what I mean,' she says so coaxingly that her words slip down into me to strike home. So that there is nowhere else for me to go but along with them.

But *do* I know? I hold my suspicion like a held breath, utterly untouched. I cannot go on; I am waiting for a clue.

It is Ornella who blurs this stilled world, chucking a hand through her hair, ruffling her new-found composure with another sigh. This is a sigh of nonchalance, meticulously done. I realize that she is not going to say more, not until I have responded.

But I do not know what to *think*, let alone what to

say. Seeing Abi? As in *Seeing Someone?* Seeing *Abi?* Trusting to luck, I move my lips, put-my-lips-together-and-blow, but manage only, 'Wh . . .'

The start of a question, although I do not have a particular question in mind. I leave her to decide which question.

Very definitely, she replies, 'Here.' Which refers to this room because this is where her eyes go: around the room, mapping a memory, moment, or series of moments sewn onto door, carpet, clock, bed. This specificity confirms for me: incident, or incidents. This is not some tale of shifts and trends in their relationship. No. Something definite has happened.

She says, 'Here, a few times in the afternoons.'

Surprising graphic: I stall my flinch.

But too late, because she has seen. 'Oh for God's sake,' she scowls, but insufficiently to hide her panic. My flinch – my sole, small, stalled flinch – was not what she wanted. Was what she dreaded. What she expected. What she looked for. 'What *is* so *dreadful*,' she shrieks, 'about being in bed with Abi?'

I will not have her take my one stopped moment of squeamishness and turn it into my comment. 'Ornella . . .' I protest: *I didn't say anything; did I say anything?*

She relinquishes, partly; humps her arms into a huffy fold and looks elsewhere. Which is difficult because she cannot see the window; it is me or the walls. Scanning the wall behind me, she complains, 'Oh, but you didn't *have to* say anything.'

Reminiscent of those rows which were happening more frequently between Mum and me before I left for university, the repetition of a few words to skirt around other unspoken words: *Don't give me that look. WHAT look? THAT look.* **WHAT** look? **THAT** look.

But what do I say to Ornella? For once, there are no words in my mind, but pictures, *one* picture, *Abi*. Abi, with whom Ornella has been to bed. In my mind's eye, though, she is fully dressed. Or, as fully dressed as ever, which is not particularly full: bare shoulders and midriffs, and ankles peeking from her pedal-pushers. And the Lady Godiva hair, but cut, no longer quite long enough. I cannot think beyond the question: *What did they do?* But do I want to know? How did *they know* what to do? But, then, if there is a word for Abi, it is *confident*: this is Abi's word, the word which she wears, an invisible version of a name-on-a-necklace, strung hard and bright over the hollow in the base of her throat. There is no word for Ornella. She simply *is*; she is a *phenomenom*. Is there any experience from which she will turn? The word which comes to mind, now, which comes close, surprising me, is *careless*.

She is complaining, 'You're so *straight*.'

I know, we both know – because we have so often had this row, this row of hers – that this *straight* of hers means boring. It has nothing to do with sex. I thought that this complaint had stopped when I went away, when she began to tease me with comments about *wacky-arty-students*. But how can I have been so stupid? Because, left behind, she needs this *You're-so-straight* more than ever, now. This is the backlash.

Wearily, I tell her, 'Look, Ornella, I don't care what you do.'

I see a spasm of surprise in her eyes, or worse than surprise, harder than surprise, the slam of shock. Which has a knock-on effect on me, shocks me, too: because what did I say? That I did not *care*? But she has filled her stark stare with a smile, she fills the air between us with conciliatory babble: 'You should try it sometime,' she says, dares, tightrope-confident. 'Life's short. You should try everything.' A momentary deepening of the smile, a dig, an aside, a personal touch: 'Not with me, though, because I have a golden rule: Never sleep with a friend.'

Blindly I reach for one of her pillows, lay it in my lap, rest my hands on it. I am stunned that she thought – no – that she *said* this. To *me*. Even if only to dismiss it. Is she completely lacking in self-consciousness? I stare down onto my hands to hold them still.

And now something else strikes me: if she never-sleeps-with-a-friend, then Abi is not her friend. I remember the word that she chose to tell me what she has been doing with Abi: *seeing*. A deliberately low-key word, not because she is coy – because she is never coy – but because she was making clear her opinion of Abi. She was telling me that Abi changes nothing between us. And I replied that I did not care. Which was not even true. Now I realize that Ornella has never really even liked Abi. And *do I*, really? Is it not simply that Abi is the sort of person that everyone is supposed to like? She behaves as if everyone likes her, so they do. A confidence trick. She dazzles, her confidence dazzles. Around her, it is impossible to hear yourself think: she sees to that. Her best friend is Bev, but Bev likes her because Bev likes everyone; because *Bev* is nice.

Not long after James and I had split up, there was a brief rumour that Abi had become my replacement; and I remember, now, Bev's cheerful, unbidden comment to me, 'It's nothing, don't worry.' Did I worry? Only for James. Because I did not know if it was nothing to him. Understandably, he did not talk much to me any more, not about anything which mattered to him. And, anyway, he had always been defensive about feelings other than love. He was happy only with declarations. Not with feelings more ambiguous than love, like jealousy and rejection. He never talked to me about Abi, or, as far as I know, to anyone else. Certainly it *became* nothing: never more public than a rumour.

What if there is more to this, for Ornella, than she can admit? She *is vulnerable*, I have seen how vulnerable: suddenly I ache to think, to remember, how vulnerable; and to think how often I am going to be reminded. Tentatively, hugging the pillow, I ask, 'So, what happens now?'

'Oh, *now* everything's different,' she announces, and for the first time this afternoon she smiles properly, a big banana-split of a smile, sunny, ripe.

How, exactly, is everything different? All this new information from her, and I feel that I know less now than ever: I have lost sight of the summer ahead of us, of us and our summer. '*Is* it?'

'Oh *yes*,' she enthuses. And now, finally, from the

smile she swells into her long-awaited stretch, lifts into full flight, every muscle straining towards her splayed fingertips. The slow, grand descent of her arms takes in everything: me, this room, and the summer in the window. 'Because you're back,' she says. She stands, abruptly, energized. 'Let's start,' she says, 'by going downstairs and painting-the-kitchen-red.'

In her second term at medical school, Ornella moved from Halls into a house with her boyfriend Billy. I had not yet met him; she had told me that he was a friend of her brother. One of the other housemates was Leah, who seemed to be Ornella's closest friend at medical school, her equivalent of my own Caitlin. I was halfway through my second year and, when not in Simon's horrid house, I was still in Halls. I started househunting with friends. A few weeks later, when we had found somewhere, I went to stay with Ornella.

Ornella came to fetch me from the station. When we reached the house, only one of her housemates was home: Kendall. Ornella introduced me as, 'My best friend, Veronique.'

Kendall had been reading a book and drinking coffee. She smiled, said, 'Hi, Veronique,' revealing that she was American although I should have guessed from the name and the glasses which were large, sincere. She was old, probably twenty-three or twenty-four.

I smiled apologetically and said, 'It's Veronica, actually.'

The smile was magnified in the glasses. 'Do your friends call you Ronnie?'

'No.' Again, I smiled apologetically. 'Do your friends call you Kenny?'

'Well, no,' she said, apparently genuinely puzzled; then, 'I guess they call me Kendie.'

Suddenly Ornella laughed, 'Oh Kendie-Kendall, if only you knew what *I* call you,' and skipped off into the hallway and up the stairs.

Kendall's glazed face turned after her.

I wondered whether to say something. Whether to apologize on Ornella's behalf. I lowered my bag, which was heavy.

Kendall laid her book beside her on the sofa. 'You want some coffee, Veronica? I made some.'

'No thanks, I've just had some, on the train.'

She laughed, picking up the book again. 'The stuff you get on the train they call coffee, right?'

'Right,' I replied, and hurried towards the stairs.

Ornella was in a bedroom – hers, judging from the familiar contents – clearing books and papers from the desk. 'She's American,' she remarked as I came through the door.

I flopped down onto the bed with my bag. 'You *don't say*.'

'Post-grad.'

'Aren't they all. What's she doing?'

'English.'

'Well, B minus for the oral, I'm afraid.'

Hugging the books and papers, Ornella sat down next

to me on the bed and slipped me a smile. 'You're funny, Veronique,' she said so lightly that I did not know, did not care, if she was serious. Then she nudged me with her armful, said, 'I'm glad you're here,' and this was said seriously.

So I replied in playful sub-Americanese, 'And, boy, am I glad to see you.'

Then I asked her, 'Where's the skeleton?'

'What skeleton?'

'There was a skeleton in *Rising Damp*. Hanging up in the corner of the room.'

She laughed, lowered her head over the bulk of books. 'Well,' she said when she looked up, 'We do have the rising damp.'

'Ha ha.'

She stood up. 'Let me dump this lot in Billy's room and then we can put a sheet on your bed.'

I tweaked the duvet: beneath, bare mattress. Ornella did not sleep in this bed.

'Leave your stuff here,' I told her. 'It's fine.'

'No,' she said, 'I want you to have your own room here.'

Later during my stay, I realized that I could have had Leah's room. Because Leah was only ever briefly home, in the mornings. She spent the nights with her boyfriend: lots of different boyfriends, over the years. For some reason, she referred to them by occupation: *The Dentist, The Translator,* and *Taxi Driver*. Perhaps this was because the occupations were so different from each other that, in spite of the large number of lovers, there was little danger of confusion: occupation seemed to be the lowest common denominator. Apparently there had been two television researchers but they were known by their products, *Crackerjack* and *That's Life*. Leah came home every morning for clean clothes and breakfast: for *our* breakfast; *she* came into the kitchen for nothing but coffee, cigarettes and chat. She claimed to smoke to keep down her weight – 'I *have to* . . .' – although this did not seem to me to have been successful. But what did I know? Because perhaps this *was success*. Damage limitation. Her hair was dyed blonde: nicely but definitely dyed. Once she told me, 'Thank God I'm not a natural blonde, because where's the fun in that?'

The other housemate was Ian, and his hair was dyed, too. Or bleached. Or half-bleached, because half-way through the process from dark to fair, he had stopped. This had not been his initial intention, but then, apparently, he had decided that he liked the half-way colour: It was *different*, he said. And it was *very* different: different both from dark and from fair, different from any colour related to hair or any other phenomena in the natural world. Closest in colour to the yolk of a Cadbury's Creme Egg. Over the few years that I knew him, he treated me genially as an adjunct to Ornella: to him, we were, *You-two-girls*.

How are you-two-girls today? Or, *Do you-two-girls want to come along tonight?*

'We're a single entity,' Ornella laughed to me. 'A two-headed beast.'

So we perfected our favourite duet for him, our

Joanne-and-Susanne routine: *I was working as a waitress in a cocktail bar/ That much is true/ But even then I knew I'd find a much better place/ Either with or without you* . . .

Which, he said, was easier on the ear than Ornella's favourite solo, *I'm in the phone booth/ It's the one across the hall/ And if you don't answer/ I'll just ring it off the wall* . . .

He and I decided that a more appropriate theme tune for her was, *Another Girl, Another Planet.*

But on that first evening of my first visit to her house neither Leah nor Ian were home. I did, however, meet Billy. He arrived whilst Ornella and I were struggling with the sheet for my bed. Below us, the front door boomed in its frame. 'Billy,' Ornella announced.

Digging the sheet into the gap between mattress and springs, I muttered, 'Is it?'

'Didn't you hear?' She was subjecting one of her corners of the sheet to a complicated procedure which, she had claimed, her grandmother had taught her. Yes, I had heard the door, but how did she *know* that it was *Billy*? Did he shut the door distinctively? Or was this a process of elimination (Leah and Ian rarely came in, Kendall rarely went out)?

When we had finished the bed, we went downstairs and he was standing in the kitchen, looking through the window into the garden. Or I presumed that he was looking, because he was not doing anything else. Turning to the sound of us, he seemed startled: I saw that he had been preoccupied, and I saw the preoccupations drop away. I soon learned that this expression was characteristic of Billy, not simply because his eyes were wide and held high on his cheekbones but because the startle in them was genuine. He was always preoccupied, and brought down, back, with every movement or word from other people. His replies, his reactions, were fractionally too slow; they missed, skipped, the beat. There was a syncopated rhythm to him. He spoke only when spoken to, not because he was polite but because his attention was elsewhere. Not that he was *im*polite: when spoken to, he spoke, he did his stint. 'Yes, hello,' he said, when Ornella introduced me.

She went to him, stood next to him, and began to talk to us both about arrangements for the evening. 'I'd like to cook,' she mused. 'But unfortunately I don't have a lot of what you'd call food.'

I was unable to resist: 'What *would* we call it?'

She turned to open a cupboard. 'You'd call it a bottle of brandy,' she said, peering inside, 'And a tin of Whiskas.'

'But you don't have a cat.'

'Rabbit flavour,' she said, still in the cupboard. Then, shutting the door, she added, 'It's for emergencies.' But before I could enquire further she had turned back to Billy, telling him, 'I was hoping that Hayley would come over, and then I could ask her to pick up some shopping on the way, but she rang to say that she had to swop shifts.'

I knew from Ornella's letters that Hayley, a nurse, was *Guido's Latest*. Although Ornella had not used the term. She had used the term for every previous *Guido's Latest*.

From her letters, I knew that she was very friendly with Hayley. Or *matey*: it was a squash-playing, activities-based friendship.

'Is your brother coming?' I asked, carefully cheerful to conceal my disappointment.

'Oh God no,' she said. 'No, it's you, me, and Billy-baby. But what are we going to have?'

Billy murmured, 'I'll get pizzas.'

'*Yes*,' whooped Ornella. 'Quattro Stagioni. Tre.' She whirled to fish a banknote from a cup on the windowsill behind her. 'Take this.'

Which he did.

'And the car,' she said as he turned away.

He turned back.

'*Yes*,' she insisted.

'No . . .'

'*Billy*,' she threw up her hands, to her head; her hair flared through her fingers, 'I *hate* cold pizza.'

'There's *nowhere* to *park*,' he retaliated.

'*Don't* park.'

'I can't leave the car in the middle of the road.' Quieter, he said, 'If I'm going on my own, I'll be quicker if I walk.'

But by now she was flapping him away, 'Okay, okay,' and returning to the cupboard for the brandy.

'Put the oven on, then:' his answer to her earlier complaint about cold pizza.

She continued flapping – with the hand which was not lifting the brandy bottle from the shelf – but she had stopped replying.

As he passed through the doorway, I tried a quick, conspiratorial smile on him. He squashed the banknote into his pocket, and then responded with a hitch of his eyebrows. A flutter of exasperation. Over the years, however hard I tried with him, I never saw more than this. He only ever responded to the moment. For him, there was no trace of one moment in the next. And he would never speculate.

When he had gone, she smiled and said, 'Billy's pretty, isn't he.' I did not know what to say, because this was so obviously true. So, what did she want from me? Why did she need a yes? I never asked her if she was in love with him. She seemed to be in love with him, I had no reason to think otherwise. At the time I was in love, and when I am in love I cannot imagine otherwise, not for me nor for anyone else. It is only when I am no longer in love that I start to wonder.

After the pizzas, we drank the brandy. The next day, I woke mid-morning, not knowing that she had gone to lectures. I knew when I saw the note which had been slipped beneath my door, simply three scrawled twinkles, shorthand for kisses, for *Thinking of you today*, for *Be here when I come home*.

FOR ME, THE big surprise of Ornella's new life was that she had a car. That her father had *given her* a car. 'But

180

what use is a car?' she despaired to me. 'What I need is a washing machine.'

This was true. I had seen the piles of clothes that she dropped on Billy's bedroom floor, elephantine droppings of clothes. But her father had given her a car because, she explained to me, he did not like to think of her travelling by tube. (Why not? For the same reason that the rest of us had lost enthusiasm for travelling by tube? Had he seen *An American Werewolf in London*?) I teased her, 'And he *does* like to think of Guido travelling by tube?' Because he had not bought a car for Guido.

She shrugged. 'Maybe it's that I'm a girl.'

'Most definitely you're a girl,' I said. 'But *I'm* a girl, and no one has bought *me* a car.'

It was not, however, a car for a girl, not cheap, small, square, slow. And it was new. But her father could not buy her a licence. So she decided that Guido could have use of the car in return for lessons. And for half of the money given by her father for lessons. Under Guido's guidance, she passed her test within a few months.

I have a clear memory of my first trip in the car with her. It is a Sunday, and we have had a lunch finishing with chocolate bars melted and poured over ice cream. When she had melted the chocolate, Ornella had to chip the block of ice-cream from the glacier which had formed in the freezer compartment of her fridge. She was certain that the ice-cream was vanilla, but when it was excavated, we saw that it was Double Chocolate Chip. So it was a particularly heavy lunch. Now we are in the garden, sitting on kitchen chairs. Ornella leans – wobbles

– from her chair to tell me, 'When I grow up, I'm going to buy a lounger.'

'When I grow up, I'm going to *be* a lounger.'

'Which neatly sums up the difference between us,' she laughs.

I return to the newspapers, one of which I have bought, the others which I would never buy but have found around the house. Some of which I have already read through to The Week Ahead On Radio, others in which I have not yet even turned to the celebrity profile. Sunlight is uneven in the garden, splashed over one side of a bush, stencilled onto the wall of the house. It is sometime between one and five in the afternoon: I have no notion of the time, except that there is plenty but will have to be plenty more before I can face food again.

Ornella complains, 'I'm bored.'

'Why don't you go and do some revision?'

Turning to me, she replies, 'It's Sunday,' and then turns away again: answer enough.

But my question was genuine: I have no exams in my second year, but everyone else is busy with them. Billy is in the library and Leah has tried to revise in the garden but was distracted by the sunshine. No, she was *intoxicated* by the sunshine: flushed and unsteady, she rose from her chair after a while and returned, mumbling irritably, to the house. She had not been home for long; she had arrived even later than usual, for lunch rather than breakfast. She had announced her arrival by looking in on us in the kitchen and saying, 'I couldn't delay any longer.'

'Revision?' Ornella had called after her.

'The morning-after pill,' she had called back, from the foot of the stairs. 'Let me go and take one and then I'll come down for some coffee.'

I had quizzed Ornella, 'She *has* them, she has *more than one?*'

Spooning honey into her coffee, she had confirmed, 'She has them, she has more than one.'

Her own supply? In her bedroom?

Licking the spoon, Ornella had added, 'A legacy from Family Planning.'

The clinic, or one of Leah's boyfriends?

Now Ornella says, 'Let's go for a drive.'

I turn from Quotes Of The Week to look at her. She seems to have spoken to the sun.

'A Sunday drive? What are you, my grandmother?'

'Not Southend,' she says to the sun. 'Camden, or somewhere.'

'Why?' I slap shut my newspaper.

'Because I'm bored.'

I throw the paper down and bend, groaning, for a magazine.

'You're interested in Elton John's latest transplant?' She has spoken without moving her head, barely moving her lips.

I let the picture of Elton John slip from my fingers, reach hurriedly for another section of the paper. 'I have to read the reviews.'

'Oh, read them to me.'

I know that below this request lurks an iceberg of sarcasm.

'Okay,' I drop the Books section, 'I'll go and hunt for my shoes.'

'Leave them. You don't need shoes: wheels, not heels.'

So I tip-toe to the car, tip-bare-toed behind her, around the house to the car, my soles prickly with abandon.

In the car, she takes my sunglasses from my eyes.

I flinch from the swipe of sunlight. 'Ornella!'

She replies, 'I couldn't find mine.'

Speechless, I tut savagely.

And she wails, 'I can't drive in this sunshine without sunglasses.'

And I can't sit here. So I turn away from the glare. Turn inwards. To find that that I feel sick. That my innards have been hijacked by chocolate.

Several streets later, and she has said nothing more. Is she coping with the driving? I look sideways through the haze of my nausea, see nothing but my sunglasses. I need to see her eyes to know her mood. Mood rings, mood stones, they were a craze when I was a child: the colour of the stone on my finger swilling between brown, green and blue to paint a picture of my mood. A murky picture, though: what was a brown mood? And, in any case, why did I need to be shown my own mood?

I shut my eyes.

Eventually she says, 'Look at these houses,' and her words, after the silence, are surprisingly tuneful.

So I brave the glare, and look around. White houses. Familiar London-white-houses. But not totally white. Nor, on closer inspection, even mostly so. The borders of the windows and doors are white, but the walls are bare brick. The dense brickwork is worn slightly unevenly to give a grain to each wall. Yet it is the white which is striking: wood and plaster vulnerable to chipping and rot but so obviously unchipped and unrotted, so *very white*. And the windows: these are houses of windows. Houses of servants, too, originally, I suppose, to keep the windows clean. The windows are huge silvery leaves, to drink sunlight from doubtful English skies.

'This is the kind of house that I want,' Ornella says.

'Rather different from the house that you *do* have.' I like her house, her little rented house, but sometimes, looking from the end of the street or the garden, I feel depressed. Perhaps because it is an old house, has held so many lives. No, because it is no older than these houses. It is *obviously* old. In poor condition. A terraced house, for poor people. So many short lives of long moments. I turn away from this thought, switch on the radio.

If I can't have you, I don't want nobody, baby . . .

This is familiar: I close my eyes and concentrate. And after a moment, I remember: *Yvonne Elliman*. Not that this means much, not that this was ever much more than a collection of sounds at the end of the record: *EevnEllimnon Cabiddle Radio*. But now I remember: this record belongs to a summer, nineteen-seventy-something. I am certain that it was summer because I remember heat and darkness, which means summer nights. And *big*: this is what comes to mind; but even though I try hard, squeeze shut my eyes, squeeze out the world, squeeze into my memory, I cannot go beyond this simple sense of *big*. Excitement? Nights out? If so, I am remembering a world that I never knew, because there was nothing *big* about my world in nineteen-seventy-something. Suddenly I have a suspicion that I am remembering *Saturday Night Fever:* was this on the soundtrack? Yes. I went to see *Saturday Night Fever* with Abi. It was X-rated, so we had to pretend to be four years older than we were. We relied on our platform shoes.

I open my eyes, ask Ornella, 'Have you seen Abi recently?' Because Abi is a student in London, too.

'Not for a couple of months.'

We have slowed alongside a shop displaying uniforms. I suppose that uniforms have to come from somewhere. Wipe-down overalls, in pastels, for domestics, auxiliaries, caterers. Pinched by those belts which are never worn except by women in uniform: the thick band of elastic with a butterfly of buckle, no loose ends, no sharp edges. No give, either: no good for pregnancy, or water retention.

'How was she?'

'Fine.' But she shrugs to retract this ringing *Fine*, back-tracks to, 'Well, same as ever.'

Same as ever? 'But was her ankle still sprained?'

'Oh,' a short note of surprise, of apology, she had forgotten. 'Yes: same as ever except for the ankle.'

I saw Abi three or four months ago. *What* I saw of her when she stepped into the doorway of the pub was her hair, her *lack of* hair: it had been cut short, she had been shorn. Her ears were exposed. Tipped into the light. Tipped *with* light. And then she looked around the room for me and I saw her eyes, suddenly so big in a head of short hair. There was no smile, merely something to pass for a smile, a spasm of recognition. Then she stepped from the doorway and I saw the limp. Odd for someone who is usually so symmetrical. She came very slowly and unevenly towards me. I did not know which to mention first, the haircut or the injury. Both so drastic, so physical. Even though I knew better, I could not help but feel that the two were connected, that her hair had been cut because of her injury: lack of hair, lack of health; operations, and infestations. When she reached me, she lowered herself carefully into a chair and sent me a little smile across the table. No, not a smile, but something to share, something which I was supposed to understand. Something like an appeal, an admission of failure, a wince of exasperation.

I puzzled, 'Your leg . . . ?'

She corrected, 'Ankle,' explained, 'A sprain.'

'How?'

'Dancing.'

Dancing? I would have loved to know more but it was clear that this was all that she wanted to say. No doubt she had had this conversation many times, and perhaps never at her own instigation.

'You should go to Bev,' I finished quickly, flip: Bev, trainee physio.

A sulky roll of her eyes, 'Bev, God, yes,' *I'd forgotten Bev.* She busied herself with a packet of cigarettes from her pocket.

As far as I knew, she was a non-smoker. I raised my eyebrows, nodded towards her busy hands.

'Well, what else is there to do?' Staccato bitterness, and a nod towards the ankle. Then she cocked the lid of the packet: *Want one?*

'No thanks,' I said, 'I've given up, I'll breathe yours.'

Which she could have taken in any of a number of ways, but which she did not take at all. Instead, she took a cigarette from the packet, and began to complain about the weather.

Now I say darkly to Ornella, 'Abi was *not happy* with that sprain.'

She turns, briefly: a flick of her hard mouth in my direction. 'Strange, because I'd love to sprain mine.'

But her sarcasm has skidded over the point: I had never seen anyone so – what? – so *thrown*? Abi was so *thrown* by her injury. She had been failing to cope with being less than perfect.

But suddenly Ornella is asking, 'Did you see her boyfriend?' the question running with intrigue.

'No, because I saw her when I was home.' And everyone knows that Abi's boyfriends do not come home. I make sure that my boyfriends do not come home with me simply because Mum and Dad expect them to sleep on the settee. Abi's boyfriends do not go with her because they belong to universities, to cities, to other countries, to anywhere but our home town.

'Well, *I* have,' she boasts.

'And?'

'Good-looking, but he makes me uneasy.'

Interested, I turn sharply to her.

For a moment she cannot turn her attention from the

road, but responds with a wrinkle of her nose, a shrug of my sunglasses. 'I don't know why.'

I tease her, 'Perhaps *you* make *him* uneasy.' As soon as this is out, I realize that it could refer to her past illicit liaison with Abi. *Which We Have Forgotten*. But I see that she has not realized, and wonder how I can snatch it back unnoticed.

But she whoops happy sarcasm, 'Oh, *yes*, because I'm *terrifying*.'

And my blood stops because I hear that she believes this. And she is so wrong. Hard little Ornella: I have seen how people's words slide off her; how she knocks their efforts back to them. I know their complaints by heart: *Can't-get-through-to-her*, *Don't-know-how-to-take-her*. Her lack of self-knowledge frightens me, I am frightened *for her*. No, for me, too. But why? Why should the opinions of other people matter to me? Because whatever she feels, I feel, too? But she feels nothing, she remains blissfully unaware. Perhaps, then, because I feel *for her*. I feel for them, too, for missing out on her.

There is an impatient click of her tongue, the belated click of a thought into place: 'No, it's not true,' she revises, 'that Abi was the same as ever.'

I turn again, an eye-hook of attention.

'Because she had a tattoo.'

A tattoo? L-O-V-E, H-A-T-E? *Abi* had a *tattoo*?

She is yawning.

I wait.

Her mouth closes on the yawn, but she continues to savour it.

'Ornella?' Strange to try to hold a conversation with the side of her face.

A sleep-sticky, 'Or so she told me.'

I realize, 'You *didn't see it?*'

The corners of her mouth turn down, flicking up an expression of weariness. 'She said that it was on her shoulder,' she stops, adds, '*blade*, shoulder-*blade*,' before continuing, 'and she was wearing lots of clothes.'

'Unusually.'

Ornella laughs.

'What is the tattoo?'

Her eyebrows contract. 'What do you mean, *what is it?* It's real, if that's what you mean. Real blood and guts. Not a sticker or transfer or something.'

'No, *what's the picture?*'

'Oh.' After a moment, she decides, 'Do you know, I don't know. I think I forgot to ask. I think I was more interested in how it was done.'

'How *was* it done?'

'I don't know,' she replies, happily, stomping on the pedals. 'It was so horrible that I stopped listening after a moment or two so that I wouldn't faint.'

I squeal, 'But you're a *medic.*'

A twitch in the corner of her mouth, the momentary holding down, holding in, of the tickle which turns into her smile. 'Which means that I don't like mutilation. And that I *do* know how to stop myself fainting.'

Suddenly I remember, rush, 'I don't think I told you that I saw Davey.'

'Oh, he never comes to see *me*:' pitched between a sigh and a whine.

'He didn't come to see *me*, *I* went to see *him*.' He is too busy to come away. Too busy, even, to come home for the holidays. His joint course, History and Politics, involves nearly twice as much work as a normal degree. And he directs plays. This term, Brecht. In fact, *last* term, Brecht. 'You have a car, now,' I add, accusingly. 'By car, he's an hour or so away.'

'But he's so busy,' she continues, implores, her head on one side, 'he'd have no time for his old schoolfriend . . .'

I know what she wants me to say: 'That's *not true*.'

'How *was* he?' The wheedling is over; she is perky. 'How *was* the darling boy?'

'Fine.'

In fact, he had a heavy cold, a temporary blight. The lining of his face was scarlet: his nostrils and the rims of his eyes. His pallor could never hide a cold. He blooms a cold. But his indisposition gave him a cheerful air: he should have been in bed; by being up and out all day, he was daring. He survived the day with the help of the appropriate props: in the street, a big scarf wound around his neck, mouth, ears; and then, in the café, he had lozenges, opaque amber pebbles which he popped from a taut skin of clinical silver foil. At all times in the café he held one of these precious gems in his mouth, its presence betrayed by an occasional clink when his tongue turned it against his teeth. We spent the afternoon over a series of teapots, bathing our faces in their rust-smelling steam. Tales of his travels seeped into our conversation:

strange that they came so naturally and so vividly, these tales of the equator, as rain slid down the windows.

I tell Ornella, 'I wish he'd write something about his travels.'

'Noooo,' she derides, 'Davey's not a writer. He's a chat show host, that's what he is.'

I laugh, 'He talks too much to be a chat show host.' And this reminds me, 'I'm worried, because he was talking about giving up, dropping out,' I will not say his words, which were *Getting on with it*, 'Trying for drama school instead.'

'So?' A flash of the sunglasses in my direction. 'What's wrong with that?'

Inside me, a hiss of impatience, infuriation. Because lately she has been playing devil's advocate too often. 'Well, why give up anything? If he stays, he can drama himself silly and still have a degree.'

'But he's not going to *use* the degree.' Said cheerfully. A few words thrown off. Neither here nor there, to her.

'You never know,' I counter.

Her gaze leaves the road to turn to me. 'Davey? A civil servant? A teacher?' Just as suddenly, she drops me and picks up the road where she left off. 'Be realistic, Veronica.'

Me? But this is no devil's advocacy: she means what she said. But why will Davey never be a civil servant or a teacher? His choice, or the choice of others? Where is she, in this? With him, or against? Championing him, or writing him off?

She is saying from the corner of her mouth, 'Did I tell

you that I'm on course to fail anatomy?'

I am surprised. 'Are you?'

No reply. Merely a twist of her mouth, empty of words, sour.

'What will happen?' *To you.*

'I'll be okay,' she says to the windscreen.

Meaning what? That she will pass? Or that if she fails, it does not matter? I realize how little I know about medics, their courses, their exams.

She turns to me with a smile, 'Don't worry,' turns back the smile, to herself, 'I'll have my big house, eventually; I won't be put off by a bit of anatomy.'

The house, these houses, I had forgotten the houses. Momentarily we have lost them because we are beneath the arch of a bridge. Similar brickwork, though: dense and dark. How do square bricks build a curve? As it arcs over us, I think I can see how the bridge is built, how it stands up, I think I can see how the bricks hold together. Their tiny straight edges and sharp angles are swept up into the huge curve. Hard-and-fast. Wedged so close that there is nowhere to move. Bricked up.

In the open air again, I wonder aloud, 'Where are we?' I look to Ornella, but her face is as blank and tough as the windscreen. 'Do you know where we are?' Merely conversational.

She says, 'London.'

Ha ha. 'Are you lost?'

Her lips move: 'I can't be lost unless I'm aiming for somewhere.'

Quite an impressive reply, putting me in my place. Or

not quite. Because I begin to feel uneasy. Hoodwinked. On her blacked-out eyes, one more terrace of houses turns into a train. 'Okay, then: you're not lost, but do you know where we are?'

The lips open a while before the words: 'Trust me.'

Implying that she is doing something untrustworthy. I insist, 'And we *are* going somewhere, we're going *back*. So, do you know the way back?'

The car in front of us slows and stops but Ornella is late and heavy on the brake. Her mouth slacks into a smile as she turns to taunt, 'Do *you* want to drive?'

She knows the answer. And, 'I didn't even want to come for a drive.'

In front of the car in front of us, people are crossing the road. The usual uneven pace on the black and white lines. First, a jogger, a young woman jogger: gone-in-a-flash, or a series of flashes of blonde ponytail and white trainers, ping-pong bounces of ponytail and trainers. Next, a group of laughing people turned inwards around a joke, carrying an invisible joke between them; and a straggler, a small child on the end of an extended arm, resisting, further extending the arm. And, finally, a very old woman, or at least a very crooked woman, the shape of a question mark, moving very slowly: I imagine the driver in front, self-conscious, pretending not to notice how slowly.

I complain to Ornella, 'I could have been reading the papers and listening to the radio in the garden.'

'No,' she says: a change of tone, a drop, as she hitches the car into gear. 'No radio in the garden. Because our neighbour complains. Hates us. Thinks all students are drug addicts.' We move forward, gather speed, the engine takes a deep breath which Ornella relieves by slotting into second gear. 'Or something.' She switches into third. 'Communists.' She shrugs. 'Paedophiles.'

By now I am won over; I am smirking. 'Don't exaggerate.'

She shrugs again. 'Gay vicars.'

'Your neighbour does *not* think that all students are gay vicars.'

The twitch of a curbed smile. 'Well, no,' she says, 'but you know what I mean.'

'And, yes,' she adds, 'I *do* know my way home.'

At last, the reply that I wanted.

'You know,' her pitch rises, to change the subject, 'even when I'm working abroad, I want to have a house here in London, I want to keep a home here.' We turn another corner. She is so purposeful but automatic with the indicators that they could be knitting needles.

I have often heard this *Working Abroad* from her, it is her theme tune. Today, I have time to question her. 'Do you *really* want to work abroad?'

'Well,' her tone floats, even-keel, 'I'm privileged: it would be nice to give something to the Third World.'

Privileged and *Nice* and *Third World*: an odd mix of words. A suspect mix of words: which of them, if any, are her own? Much more importantly, is the sentiment her own? Typical of her, too, driving her brand new car and contemplating a future in Camden, to see her privilege simply in global terms: it would never occur to her that she is privileged in *this* country.

'Anyway,' she adds, briskly, 'I don't want to become a consultant when I'm thirty-five and then fossilize in some London hospital for the next three decades.'

Fair enough. 'Does Billy want to work abroad?'

We have stopped; we are at a crossroads and she has indicated to turn onto the main road. We wait. I follow the regular clinks of the indicator: they seem to fall short, to fall heavy for sounds so light; for sounds potentially so tinkly they finish hard, dull, robbed of any ring. Ornella is leaning forward, flattening herself onto the steering wheel. She is aiming to turn right, to take us across one stream of traffic and into another. 'I don't know what Billy wants to do,' she says to the on-coming traffic.

Fair enough again, I suppose.

Suddenly we have sprung into the main road and hooked onto the line of passing cars. My heart settles slowly, warily. Grudgingly.

Ornella says, 'I think I'd rent it out.'

'What?'

'The house, my house. When I'm away, abroad.' She stretches back into her seat, to muse, holding the steering wheel at arms' length. 'I could rent out the basement. Or, I suppose, I could keep the basement and rent out the house. Or you could be my permanent house-sitter.'

I tell her, 'Never live in a basement, Nella: I have a rule, *Never a basement*. They're unsafe.' My only rule for houses, which I made when I read of the rapist who broke into basements. *So many* basements. So many

196

women alone in basements in London. In a nice area of London, where garden flats do have gardens. An *unprepared* area. *He* was prepared, though. He tracked his women, learned about their lives, planned his attacks. And then he came up and over, through the lax top flaps of the windows. From gardens. From the fresh air. From thin air. To women who were sleeping, turned away from the world.

Ornella protests, 'But we have the Thames barrier, now.'

Floods?

'We do, don't we?' she turns to check with me; her confidence slipped, opening a question.

'I wasn't thinking of floods,' I admit.

'No?'

'I was thinking of –'

'Oh, *intruders*,' she says, happily, hitting on the word. Crossword-happy.

'Yes.' Not quite. Not a word that I would use. A parents' word, a word from the newspapers. 'I hadn't thought of floods,' I admit.

'No, you're right.' Conviction sets her face. Because, for her, this is a matter of fact: the danger of basements is *a thing,* one or the other, intruders or floods. 'I don't know why we need a flood barrier,' she continues. The mouth softens and spins a smile: 'We could do what Londoners have always done to escape from danger, we could go down into the tube stations.'

'Ornella,' I protest, but quietly, so as not to give her the satisfaction. 'That's horrible.'

'It is,' she agrees, reasonably. 'I am.' But she continues: 'It's probably quicker to float along the Northern line than to wait for a train.'

We drift onto the end of a stationary queue. The red traffic light, usually so fierce, so forbidding, is barely visible in the strong sunlight.

Ornella says, 'Okay, I won't live in the basement. Happy now?'

'Very.'

'*Someone else* can live in the basement.'

I wince, chastened.

But she is already laughing, 'The brats can live in the basement with the nanny.' Suddenly she slides her hands together to the top of the steering wheel and lowers her forehead onto her knuckles. 'I can't drive,' she mumbles from the small space between her mouth and hands.

Curious, I follow her, bend forward in my seat: but no improvement in my view, no clues. 'You're doing fine,' I try.

She snaps back in her seat, a whiplash of exasperation. 'Yes, well,' she sighs into the open sunroof, 'I'm going to stop.'

Here? Now? Quickly, I check the lights: still red. 'Why? What's wrong?'

Although we are stationary, she does not turn to look at me when she says, 'Too much wine at lunchtime.'

Wine? I have been trying to catch her eye but now I give up and wail, '*Lunchtime* was before you drove all this way. You mean you've driven all this time when you're *pissed*?'

'I didn't realize,' she moans.

'*Didn't realize?*' is all that I can manage: pathetic, but *loud*.

'Don't, Niquie,' she pleads.

Which implies that I am the unreasonable one.

She hurries, 'I don't know what I'm doing.'

The cars in the queue in front of us begin to pull away, not simultaneously but one by one, a collapsing house of cards. Slow motion. We have time on our side.

'Pull over, then,' I demand, in an effort to grab control of the situation.

'I *am* pulling over:' this comes from a barely opened mouth. Tight with shame, or with concentration, or nausea?

Pulling over requires a few sudden spine-swirling turns in her seat and some scrabbling at the steering wheel. And now we stop in a bus lane: far from ideal.

'But you *said* you were *fine*,' I cannot stop this: I am exasperated with her, and my exasperation will not stop.

'Well, I'm *not*.' Her voice is soft but her face is hard, held towards the road, held away from me.

'I *asked* you –'

'You asked me before we left, and I said I was fine?' She hooks her hands over the top of the wheel, flattens her forearms onto it: a half-slump; a threatened slump.

'Yes:' piqued that somehow I am suddenly on the wrong end of the questioning.

'Well, I *thought* I was *fine* but I'm *not*.' Now *she* is indignant. 'It's hot; and I forgot the glass that I had *before* lunch.'

My complaint whirls onward: 'Why did you have to drink so much in the middle of the day? *I* didn't.'

'I *know*.' Beneath the glasses, the slow curl of a smile, a child's drawing of a smile. 'So, *you* can drive.'

She *is* drunk. 'No *way*.'

Suddenly the sunglasses slot upwards into her hair, and the real Ornella reappears. Startlingly real: the sunshine makes morning stars of her dark eyes. 'You want me to drive?'

'Ornella,' I remind her, resist her, 'I *can't drive*.'

'You *have* driven,' she says, knowingly.

'*Once*.'

'Good,' she turns her attention down to the pedals, 'So when I say *Gear –* '

Stop this. 'I *know* about gears, I *have driven*.'

'Good.'

'*Once*. I am not going to drive *now*. And in case you've forgotten –' more blame '– I have no shoes.'

She lifts her eyebrows to muse, 'As far as I know, there's no law about shoes.'

'I don't care about any *law*. I *can't* drive, and I can't drive *without shoes*.'

'In fact, I think you'll find it easier –'

'*Forget the shoes*.'

'That's right, forget the shoes.'

I ignore her. '*And* I'm not insured.' And why did I not say this initially? What is she doing to my brain?

She takes this up into a shrug: one of those generous, unflappable shrugs. 'If something happens, we'll say that I was driving.'

'Oh, so when they come to cut us out of the wreckage, we tell them that we were thrown into each other's seat by the impact?'

She looks away, slides away on a smile. 'Don't be so melodramatic, Veronique.'

But I pursue her, I want to know, 'Did you do this on purpose? Did you?'

Surprise hitches her gaze back to me. 'You think I *want* to have you drive me through the streets of London?'

Doubly insulted, I huff, frown, fold my arms. No, there was no purposefulness to this. On the contrary, there was thoughtlessness.

She follows my frown with one of her own, and leans over, into no-man's-land, to whisper, 'Do you have any cigarettes?'

'*No*.' She *knows* not. Or does she? Does she know anything, at the moment? I watch her gaze paddling around the windows of the car, hoping to spy a shop where she can buy cigarettes.

'I need a cigarette,' she tells herself, tells the windows.

'A cigarette is not what you need.'

She turns her coppery eyes to me, unguarded.

And this is what I want to say: 'Why do you always do this to me?' *Leave me high and dry, put me on the spot, leave me to pick up the pieces.*

'Why do I always do *what*?' A piping note of panic. She has thrown herself on my mercy so that I can say no more. Not if I do not want to let her down. To upset her. Distress her. And myself, too. What is the point of going on and upsetting us both? But this is a revelation to me: I did not know until now that we are so precarious. We carry on as if there is nothing which is unmentionable between us, but now I know otherwise: we cannot mention how she treats me. Because what does it say of her that she treats her best friend thoughtlessly, carelessly? And what does it say of me, the best friend, who puts up with this? We are in this together.

Quickly, I turn my attention to the car, turn the car into a practical problem. 'Let's leave the car here, or near here, and then come and collect it later.'

'But where's the nearest tube?'

This is the least of our problems. 'We'll find one, we'll walk until we find one; you have legs, don't you?'

The start of a smile. 'Yes, I have legs, but you have no shoes.'

Of course. My toes curl.

She eases the sunglasses from her head and hands them to me: *Booby prize.* 'Come on, you can do it,' she laughs, urges. 'You need someone to push you. With me, you can do it.'

When Ornella began work as a doctor, she would often ring me from the hospital. I did not ring her – I left her to ring me because I thought that she would know when she had the time to talk. But, then, whenever she called, she was bleeped. 'Ignore it,' she would tell me, but we became skilled at short conversations. Sometimes the interruptions did not come via the bleep but in person, another voice joined her own, but thinner, higher, an interference on the line. I could hear a few of the words through Ornella's hand, which cupped the mouthpiece: *He says . . . and I've told him*; or, *Can you come and have a look?* or, *His wife is here now.*

Her reply, leaking louder into the mouthpiece, was almost always cheerful and almost always the same: 'I'll come along in a minute.'

To me, on the other end of the line, day after day, her every next minute seemed forever to have been taken; to have been marked for a reply to a question or a solution to a problem. From what I heard, these questions tended to concern beds and relatives: problems for which she could not have been prepared by years of anatomy and physiology, by the textbooks that I had seen around her room, the pages of fine figures flayed, skeletons bandaged in shiny purple muscle.

She seemed to like to ring me in the middle of the day and then again at the very end. If she was staying at work for the night, on call, she wanted to hear news of the outside world, *What-are-you-going-to-do-tonight?* If she was due to leave work, she wanted to arrange to meet, *Are-you-doing-anything-tonight?* If we could not meet, she simply wanted to speak, *What-have-you-done-today-and-what-are-you-going-to-do-tomorrow?* During all these calls I heard the ward around her, voices raised, information pitched from nurse to nurse, from ward clerk to nurse. I always needed to know if I should brace myself for interruptions: 'What are you doing?'

Always, her sigh came hard and sharp from the

everywhere-and-nowhere rain of noise. 'Sitting in the office, waiting for some test results.' It was her job to know the patients inside-out, from X-rays down to blood composition. 'Writing out some forms for more tests. Six of them, in fact, for Mr Lyndon.'

Often I knew these patients, on *Male Medical*, knew their names, felt that I knew them.

She would continue: '*And* I'm *dreaming*...' a thoughtful pause, 'of...' more pause, more musing, then, 'of *dreaming*, I suppose.'

'Not much sleep, then, last night?'

'Not bad.' Said lightly: a brave attempt to be fair? or a genuine weighing-up and a settling for very little? 'Three and a half hours.'

My heart would swell for her.

'Would have been better *un*interrupted, of course, but I was rung at two o'clock, when I'd been asleep for half an hour: they wanted to know if Mr Richards could have a sleeping tablet.'

'You're kidding.'

'I wish.'

'Can't they decide for themselves?' The nurses, those voices behind her, so efficient, and so many of them. A whole world of them, on the end of the line, and one small Ornella.

A yawn. 'Some will, some won't.' Another yawn. 'Sorry, I started work with a new admission at five o'clock this morning.'

What *was* five o'clock in the morning? *Was* it *morning*? Was it light? Were there cars on the roads? In my mind's eye I saw paper rolling from printing presses, and trains running from tunnels against a backdrop of dawn, and I realized that I had only ever seen five-o'clock-in-the-morning in documentaries, those old documentaries on newspaper production and milk trains, of machines and their workers pulling together to make the world go around. 'Did he *need* to come in at five?' Why not six? Six is different. Six is morning. Just. If-you-must.

But, 'Oh yes,' she would say, cheerfully. 'He was very poorly.'

She had begun to favour this word, *poorly*. For her, a surprisingly gentle, mumsy word. With connotations of *the vapours*. A careful, inoffensive word, for patients and visitors. But I learned that she meant something very different. Whenever she said *poorly*, she meant that life-lines were wavering or fractured. Often she followed with more specific talk of crackling lungs, of hearts which had flown their rhythm. The mechanics of which I did not understand, but I got-the-picture. I never knew what to say about her five o'clock admissions. I knew what I felt: I felt angry for her, that she had had to do it, that there was no one else to do it. 'Could you go back to bed afterwards?'

She laughed, sort of: 'No, it took me a long time to sort him out. When I'd finished, it was time to do the bloods.'

Her first task of the day was to go from bed to bed to collect blood. This was how they started the day, in hospital; the equivalent of checking the weather, picking up the milk from the doorstep, sorting the post.

Once I said, 'You must hate your patients.' So that she could say no and feel good.

'I want them to *die*,' she said, cheerfully.

I did not know if she was serious.

'Not when they're here,' she said. 'But before. I hope they die before they reach me so that I don't have to leave my lovely warm bed.'

She *was* serious.

'You can make the most dreadful wishes in the middle of the night, when you're exhausted.'

And suddenly I did not doubt this.

Usually she would ask me, 'What are *you* doing?'

Not doing. For whom did I feel most sorry? Her, with too much to do, or me, with too little? 'Well, I'm *not* going to the library.'

'No?'

I would lie, 'Too late, by the time I'd arrive.' *Too late to do all that I need to do . . .* Which, in fact, was never very much. I was doing some freelance journalism, which occasionally required research. But more often involved hustling for work, by phone, which I hated.

ONE DAY, AS usual, she asked me, 'Are you coming over for the evening?' And as usual, she sounded enthusiastic.

What else would I do? I was not going to see Pete, I had seen too much of him in the months when I had been trying to leave him. When I had been trying to find somewhere else to go. Trying to save enough money so that I could move away. I had seen several months too much of him. I would need time before I could see him as a friend. And my other friends? My friends from university had jobs which left them too tired to socialize, or had required them to move away. Or had made them so much money that we had less in common. Caitlin had a job in Birmingham. Of my old schoolfriends, Davey did not have a proper job but was working in a restaurant in the evenings, and Abi was busy with an M.Phil. Most of my friends from university lived in the flat, with Pete. The flat which had been mine, too, until a month ago. The flat which I wanted to avoid, for a while. I could not meet them very often in town because I had no money. And they could not come to my box-room, nor to the living room which was full of my two strange flatmates and their six or seven friends, rock-climbers temporarily home from the rocks. Rock-climbers without rocks to climb, and without homes, who stayed over in our living room, bored and doped. The rock-climbers and their three groupies. One of the climbers and one of the groupies had fallen in love in our living room. I had observed the developing relationship during my trips to the kettle, until I bought a kettle for my own room. Now the groupie was pregnant and vomiting for hours in our bathroom.

But I could go to see Ornella, and we could stay in, do nothing, a *nice* nothing: she was too tired after work to leave her room, in which she had a television, magazines, and chocolates. There was a word of my mother's which was perfect for Ornella: *homebody*. And I was at home with her. I reached for my purse, checked that I had enough money for the fare.

She was saying, 'I'll be finished with this lot in half an hour; say, seven o'clock.'

Seven was too soon: 'I have to do some shopping before I come over.' I could not delay the shopping until the arrival of my next dole cheque, as I had hoped. So I would have to write a cheque. Which meant that I could not go to the market in Berwick Street. I would have to go to a supermarket. Which meant spending much more money. The only useful product of my student days had been a bank account which the manager was accustomed to finding empty or overdrawn. I had had some savings, birthday money in a building society, which I had spent on a typewriter: my sole investment in my career.

'Don't bother before you come over here,' she said, 'Because I can drive us to the supermarket and we can do a huge shop.'

I could not afford a huge shop. And how would I carry the shopping home, the next day? But did I care? I was persuaded: anything for a change. Even a trip in a car to a supermarket was a luxury.

Once upon a time, London had been a luxury. An adventure. What had taken its place? Nothing. Nowhere. Whenever Ornella and I had come into London from home, we had begun by heading for a snack bar in Brewers Street, for lunch: our favourite place because of the succulent toasted sandwiches. Was it still there? By now, we rarely went anywhere in London because we had our own places. But *what* did we have? She had a room in a Nurses' Home, I had a room in a horrid flat. When we had lived at home and come into London for the day, we had wanted to wander: Charing Cross Road, Covent Garden, Chinatown, Carnaby Street; shops; the Photographers' Gallery (and sometimes I had even made her go to the ICA); and, in summer, St James' Park. Now we did not tend to go into town, and we never wandered, because we had things to do. Things that we had to do.

I arrive in the corridor and see that her door is open. So she has gone to, or has just returned from, the bathroom or the kitchen: there is nowhere else to go. When I reach her doorway, I see that she is in her room. She has been in the bath, she is wearing her towelling robe; her bare shins, calves, are hot pink and shiny smooth. Turning, smiling, saying, 'Hi,' she pulls a clip from her hair. The damp ends drop in clumps to her shoulders. I know that she has had no time, for months, to go to a hairdresser. She is tired: beneath her eyes, there are gentian shadows. I know that there will be no trip to the supermarket.

'Hi,' I sit down on her bed. 'Is Billy around?' Not that Billy makes a difference. Whenever he is here with us for the evening, he lies on her bed and watches the telly, peers over our heads to the portable television which is on her bookshelf. Or he brings a book to read, sits bent over it, tapping the spine, glancing up, startled, whenever a response is required from him. If he is here when I arrive, he glances up from the book or around from the telly and says, 'Oh, hi.' I realize, now, that he rarely smiles, he looks happy but rarely smiles. Towards the end of the evening, he likes to leave us, to go to the Mess for a drink. Reaching to switch off the telly, or closing the book, he offers his judgement into the room, *Brilliant* or *Crap*, bizarrely definite for someone usually so diffident. We laugh at him when he has gone, when he is down the corridor, on the other side of the double doors.

'No,' Ornella says, in a tussle with her hair and a comb. 'He's on call.'

Once, I said to her, 'But you never see him,' and she countered, 'What would we talk about if we saw each other every day in here? *Did-you-see-the-sarcoma-on-Ward-Seven?*'

She has turned to the mirror above the sink. With her comb she is driving the water from her hair into dark spots on the carpet around her bare feet.

I ask her, 'Have you eaten?'

'Baked potato, from the canteen.' But suddenly, 'Oh shit,' she twists, whirls water over me, 'the *supermarket*.' Her eyes fix on me, wide, her trepidation held for me to see.

'It's okay.' I lie back on the bed because I know that it is impossible to be angry, or at least to look angry, when reclining on pillows.

She steps towards me. 'Oh, Veronique,' she wails, over me, 'I'm *sorry*.' And shrugs, *But*: the shrug is big, to show her state of undress.

'It's *okay*.' Impossible, too, somehow, not to forgive someone who is so wet. 'Just stop *splattering* me.'

She steps back, returns to the mirror above the sink. 'Do you want something to eat?' she calls, conciliatorily, over a damp shoulder.

I lean over and pick up a *Good Housekeeping* from the floor. 'I'll go to the canteen.' Behind my GH, I suppress a shudder: *canteen* is not a word to inspire optimism. But I will practise some survivalist techniques: there will be a bread roll somewhere in the canteen, supposedly to go with soup; and I will plead for the piece of fruit which I suspect is concealed in every canteen for people with diabetes.

In the corner of my eye, in the mirror, she moves. I glance up but now she is in the centre of the frame, face-on. I can see that she has thought better of turning to face me. 'The canteen closed at half past seven.'

I turn over the page, the full-page photograph of strawberry shortcake, and come across conservatories. 'Well, I'll go to the paper-shop on the corner and buy a roll or something.' I turn from the conservatories to consumer rights, *Can you get your money back?*

Her comb clatters on enamel. 'You'll be lucky to find an *Evening Standard* in there,' she admits, turning her attention to the kettle. 'Well, *this* evening's *Standard*; you'll find yesterday's, no problem.'

There is despair in the pit of my stomach. I lower the magazine and sigh, 'The Night Of The Long Hunger Pangs?'

'No,' she replies, juggling two tea-bags, 'Because I have some cheese.'

I am surprised, because Ornella rarely keeps food

which is not a craze. The most recent craze was for Strawberry Mivvies, which she bought in handfuls from the paperless paper-shop and stuffed into the freezer compartment of the communal fridge. There was no problem with theft: hummus, yoghurt, milk and juice went from the fridge but no one ever stole a Strawberry Mivvy. Biting into the red ice, Ornella would announce *Vitamin* C, and I never knew if she was serious. When we were younger, my mother would smile over our snacks and say to us, *You girls should look after yourselves*. Advice which we ignored, because what was there to look after? Advice which Ornella continues to ignore. But for me, now, somehow, there *is* something to look after. Somehow, suddenly, I feel that there is a body to consider: unfortunately, it is not that I am more vulnerable, but more substantial.

My surprise wisens into suspicion: 'How old is this cheese?' *This* cheese: sceptical, dismissive.

She stops, replies defensively, 'Two days. And I haven't opened it. And it's not processed or anything, it's Stilton.'

Too good to be true. 'And it's not one of those tiny wrapped pieces which they sell in canteens to go with crackers?'

'No,' she protests. 'It's big: four ounces or a pound or something,' shrugs. '*Big*.'

So far so good. 'Do you have some bread?'

'Bread,' she says. 'No.'

'Crackers, then?'

A frown. 'Nnnno.' As if she had to think, hard.

'Anything?' But I know that there is nothing. Despair

buzzes through my thoughts. 'Anything that I can put the cheese *on*? Anything that I can *grill* the cheese on?' Because grilled cheese is a hot meal.

The frown flips over into a grin. She throws a tea-bag high and watches this dappled feather fall into the palm of her open hand before she replies, 'A grill pan?' But suddenly, 'Guess what happened to me today?'

Another attempt to distract me. 'What?' I am reluctant but compelled.

She springs back to sit on her desktop, links her ankles and leans forward: storytelling position. 'We were trying to resuscitate a woman on Ward Three,' she confides, 'but the priest was there,' she speeds up, 'giving her the last rites, chucking his water,' she demonstrates, mimes, seems to be scattering birdseed. 'So there we were, rushing around the bed, side-stepping this priest, vying with him for a place at the bedside, and I was *soaked*.'

Over time, I have become immune to her talk of death, resuscitation, *resus, crash*, of *arrests* and *shocks*, and I thrill to this: the stiff black figure dispensing his holy water, conducting his ritual from the foot of the bed in the flurry of white coats intent upon their own frenetic ritual and then their desperate improvisation. 'Really?' I murmur, appreciatively.

Answered by one of her wide, splayed shrugs. 'Look at me.' *In my bathrobe.*

Which brings me back with a bump: the story is untrue; a good story, but untrue. I tut, disappointed, disapproving.

Suddenly alert to this, she strives to reassure me, 'No,

it's *true*, I *have* been in the bath, yes, but it *is* true, it's *still* true, about the priest and the water.'

I perk up, hopeful, better disposed to her. 'Is it?'

She concedes, 'Okay, I wasn't *soaked*, I was *sprinkled*.'

I start to laugh, 'A sprinkle will do.' But I cannot laugh, I need to know, 'Did the woman die?'

She smiles, shakes her head: *no*.

Now I can laugh. 'And now that you've had your sprinkle, will you go to Heaven?'

Her turn to laugh: 'Despite whatever I do from now on? You mean, have I had my last rites?' She laughs again, but this time downwards, an echo. 'Not quite so simple.' But the laugh bubbles in her eyes. 'Not quite so *convenient*.'

I confide, 'I don't think I've ever seen a priest, except on telly.'

She says, 'That summer in Italy, my great-aunt died and the priest was there with his water.'

That summer in Italy. A brief mention of *that summer*. A rare mention. I stiffen, but do not know what to antici-pate. I force a conversational, 'Oh, really?'

She jumps down from the desk but turns to the kettle, to turn it off, feeling over the steam for the switch on the wall. 'Tea?' she shouts to the wall, into the steam.

'Yes, please,' my voice, too, is slightly louder than usual.

If she hardly ever mentions the summer when she was sent to Italy, then she never, ever mentions the reason. But, of course, there has been no need, because I know the reason. There is no need for us to mention so many things, precisely because there are too many to mention, there is so much between us. Often she need only mention something once, and I lock it into my heart. But she told me nothing about a death during her summer in Italy. I had thought of her summer in Italy as a lost summer but now I see that it was lost solely *to me*. I did not know that her great-aunt had died, I knew nothing of any great-aunt, any death. Now I see that anything could have happened to Ornella, during that summer, and I would not know. She only ever mentions the housekeeping tips which she picked up, and then, of course, only semi-seriously: *Call-that-a-pizza?* I have always imagined a summer empty except for sunshine and women's voices.

Her hand shakes as she hauls the heavy, spitting kettle to the two cups. Tipping the spout over the rim of one of the cups, she says, 'I'm going home this weekend.' She has finished her mention of Italy. Now there is an edge of excitement in her words, a purr of longing. She often visits home. Because home, for her, is good food, clean baths, clean bedlinen, soft carpet. A large television. She lowers the kettle, looks up. 'Do you want a lift?' *Home*.

And, yes, me too, I crave the little touches: in my bedroom, when I wake, my thin frayed curtains fuzzy with sunlight; in the bathroom, the soap which smells of nothing but soap; in the living room window, a vase of dried honesty, silverdust on the sill.

'Here,' she hands me a cup of tea.

'Oh, thanks.' And, 'No, thanks,' I mean, 'I don't want to go home this weekend.' Although I do. I do want to wake to those curtains, I do want to wash my hands with that soap, I do want to wonder why the honesty is still there. But Ornella will return home to mothering, or, perhaps, fathering; to living like a princess, simultaneously indulged and left to herself. And if I go home, I will see Mum; and if I see Mum, I will have to arrange to see Dad. Unlike Ornella, I cannot slip home, slip into the hot clean bath, into my old clean bed: I cannot simply slip home. Everything has changed and there is no going back.

Now that Dad has left, even though he was rarely home, the house seems empty. I spend my trips home trying to account for the emptiness, to find what it is that is missing. But when he left, he took very little, or nothing. Some saucepans, I think. A pillow: there is only one pillow on Mum's bed. Why take so little? There is only the two of them, Mum and Juliet, an odd version of Darby and Joan: so why do they need chairs and sheets and cups for four? He has hardly anything in his flat, he seems not to need much, but who knows what he needs? Not me: lately I have been realizing how little I know of him. I am supposed to know why he left, though. He left because Mum asked him to leave. So he says. So Mum says, too, but in a slightly different tone. I have not been told why, apart from Mum's explanation that, *It's over.*

Is this an explanation? I could not help but think, *Well of course it's over, now that you've kicked him out.*

But Mum seemed to have outgrown him. She has her own job, in our old school. Support Worker for Special Needs. Trumped-up toilet duty, but she seems to enjoy it. I see less of her, now, when I go home. Both less and more of her: she is less often home, but when she is, she seems bigger, with her talk of work and friends. *Her* work and friends: she rarely asks about mine. Am I supposed to offer information? She seems shy of me. Juliet is not shy of me, I doubt that she is shy of anyone. Her bedroom has become the centre of the house, the room from which all the noise comes – music and telephone conversations – and then sometimes silence, a firm silence rather than the quietness of child's play. The swollen silence of secrecy. Each time that I see her, she is darker. (Why do blondes darken, but not brunettes?) Her eyes are darker, too: a scowl of eyeshadow has replaced her clear Pears-baby smile.

Juliet has moods, now. There is so much more to her, now, so many sides to her, that when I go home, I never know who I will find. Often she seems more like Mum than me: a small version of Mum, with school, friends, the house. Sometimes there is Juliet the little girl: her teddy bear on the settee, and her rabbit in the garden. Then there is the schoolgirl, conscientious in sky-blue blouse; but sometimes another schoolgirl, the alternative version with the sky-blue detention slip, *For talking*, which she seems never to do with me any more. After school, there is the Juliet of the violin practice, the squeaky, wobbly scales upstairs in her bedroom. But later there is her record player, and a sharp turn of the volume dial. Finally, there is the Daddy's girl; still, but only just. He has a photo of her in his flat, but it is from a year ago, when she was twelve and quite different.

It was strange to visit Dad's flat. His flat, where he *lives*: his flat not simply in name, which is all that our house ever was. Because until then, what I had known of him was his absence and his visits. All or nothing. No little touches. What he had in his own flat, what I noticed when I walked through the door, was a line of empty, clean milk bottles on the kitchen windowsill. Washed, so that he could put them back out onto the doorstep for the milkman. But he had not put them on the doorstep and there were lots of them, seven or eight. Too many: *If-one-clean-bottle-should-accidentally-fall*. This cleaning of bottles for our milkman was something which Juliet and I were brought up to do by Dad, because *Would you like to have to pick up scummy bottles?* Somehow we were brought up to do this by Dad despite his absence: Dad's habit, not Mum's, but his wishes were followed even though he was rarely home. Perhaps *because* he was rarely home. I wonder if Mum still washes her empty milk bottles. I suppose so, because she would have to make a conscious effort to break the habit, the habit which was Dad's but which became her own habit of a lifetime. So that, in a sense, she, too, has been brought up to do it.

The washing of the bottles was one of the few habits of his that I knew, but I did not *know* that I knew until I saw the long line of them on his windowsill. Bottled, concentrated sunshine. Trapped in the squat neck of the bottle on the end of the line was a bubble: made from rich, thin material, almost invisible and almost emerald. I saw that Dad's wash was far more thorough than what

I could remember of Mum's cursory rinse. But, then, unlike Dad, she was a practised housekeeper, she knew what needed to be done and what would do. I do not wash my bottles, I have no deliveries. It is Dad, not Mum, who frets about my home life, my lack of home life. He says that he wants grandchildren, tries to remind me to have children. Whenever I deride Ornella with, *You sound like my mother*, I should say, *You sound like my father*.

Resting against her desk, Ornella is hunched over the cup which she is holding in both hands, in cupped hands, taking tiny sips, wincey sips, wary. Steam coils around the damp strands of hair which have flopped in front of her face.

I cannot stop myself saying, I have to say, 'Why don't you find a flat with me?' A home, my own, our own. It feels odd to have lived with Caitlin and then Jenny-and-Rory-and-Sarah but never with Ornella.

She looks over the rim of her cup, her dark unblinking eyes burning through the faint wet haze; and she replies, without lifting her lips far off the rim, 'You know why not.' She continues her usual reply, in a whine: 'This costs me nothing.' And above the rim, her gaze slides around the room, makes me follow: *this room costs me nothing, and look at it, it's not bad*.

'I know, I know,' I wave away my question, her answer, her eyes. What I could have said was, *I want you to find a flat with me*. I should have said, *Forget bills, forget finances, there are more important things in life*. Then her reply would have been different, if only in tone. She would have been required to take account of me.

I am going to go further: 'And you'll live here for the rest of your life, will you?' Said with a smile, sanitized with a smile; but if I dared to stop smiling, I would say, *Everything costs money, That's life, A life costs money.*

Her wide eyes contract inside a frown. 'You *know* that I'm not going to stay here for the rest of my life.' She puts down her cup, not quite a slam. 'I should be so lucky,' she protests. 'Because, for a start, my job changes every six months, I'll never know where I'm going to be in six months' time.'

She is right, I *do* know. And I know that I am in the wrong, that I should not have raised the issue. I wish that I had said nothing, because I do not want an argument.

'And what could I afford, if I left here now?' She hurries to answer for me: 'Something horrid.'

As I should know.

'So what's the point?'

The point is to live with me. But, 'Yes, yes,' *I'm sorry.*

'Okay,' she allows, having a different conversation, perhaps a conversation with herself, perhaps a re-run of one of ours, 'It's not wonderful, here, but it's warm.'

True: if nothing else, it is warm, very warm, it is hospital hot. So, perhaps she will feel differently in the summer.

She returns to her cup. 'Let me save up,' is as far as she will go.

All this talk of money is a way to say that her world does not revolve around me. I want to tell her that I do not want her world to revolve around me. I want to say, *I am not asking for the world.*

Silence has settled around us. After a moment, I brush at it with, *It's just that*, 'I'd love to share a flat with you.'

Her face opens up into a smile. 'Oh, Niquie, that's very sweet of you.' She has forgiven me, she is delighted with this opportunity to forgive me. She lowers her voice, more intimate, insistent: 'You know that you can come here whenever you want.'

Yes, I know; because she is forever telling me. Yet somehow it is not quite what I want to hear. She is very hospitable, for which I am very grateful, but I suspect that she would never put herself out for me. I laugh it off, 'I'm here all the time.'

'*Stay* here more.'

Nice thought, but not the answer. Not my home.

'You know that I can always go to Billy's room, if I want. Two rooms between the three of us, that's not bad.'

The three of us: me, her, and Billy.

I do not tell her that I am sick of living in rooms, on corridors, off hallways. That I fear that I will spend my life in rooms on corridors, off hallways.

I decide to change the subject. And I do have something to tell her: 'I saw Abi last week.' When did Ornella last see or speak to Abi? I have no idea. Probably she has not seen her since she saw her with me, several months ago, for a quick coffee in the Royal Festival Hall before Abi and I went next door to see a film. But I am always suspicious. Suspicious? No, wrong word; too strong: I am ready for surprises, where Ornella and Abi are concerned. Unsurprisingly. So, my opening line was news but also a test, a toe-in-the-water: I am fishing for a reply, *Yes, she told me*, or *Oh I saw her on Thursday*, or *Haven't seen her for ages*.

But all she says is, 'Abi-synnia.' A nickname from school, which I had forgotten. I remember, now, that *Abi-synnia* came from O level History: a treaty or the Balkans or something. But suddenly she says, 'Wait, I have to go to the loo.'

So I have to wait, and I think about Abi. Unusually, when I had last seen her she had asked me to come to her flat. She let me in, took me into her room, then crossed ahead of me to perch lengthways on her windowsill, her long legs stiff and angular in drainpipe jeans but her feet soft in black plimsolls. She said, 'I'm having my heart broken, Veronica.' So, she wanted to speak to *Veronica* the grown-up, not to *Vonny* from her schooldays. She was setting the tone. She was taking me into her confidence.

Her story came in sharp, shiny little pieces. Picked up, randomly, and dropped. So different from her usual fine-spun narratives. And she did not smile. Usually, her smile comes in reflex to every statement. But this time, she smoked. After every statement, she closed her lips around the tip of her cigarette, and closed her eyes. And what did I manage to pick up? What can I pass on? She started with, 'He's my supervisor, and, yes, I know it's a cliché, we're both well aware that it's a cliché.'

I said nothing, hummed some sympathy. My response,

kept to myself, was a cliché, too, I suppose: *Is this a habit of his? is this a perk of the job?*

'He lives with a woman.'

Oh. Oh dear.

'Has lived with her for five years; has a kid, who's three.'

Grow up, Abi. Steer clear.

'But they haven't had much to do with each other since Pascal was a baby. But they've stayed together for his sake.'

Another cliché?

'She's a high-flier publisher or something, and he's always working, so they see very little of each other.'

Or so he says. So when *do* they see each other? When is this *very little*? At the end of every day, in bed? On holiday? Very little, perhaps, but very important.

'He loves me but he can't leave her because of the kid.' Or words to that effect; I do not remember Abi's exact words. I wondered when he spent time with this beloved child. Between supervisions with Abi?

'He thinks the world of Pascal.'

And I could hear that she was so proud of him; so proud of so much selfless love.

But suddenly, hugging her knees, squeezing, so that her plimsolled feet lifted momentarily from the sill, she said, 'The problem is that I'm so in love with him that I don't know where to *put myself*.' Letting go, she dropped her head back to take a deep breath not of smoke but of fresh air from the open top of the window. And I looked away. Too graphic. *Passion.* Graphic passion, on the dark silver window. Despite her posing, Abi is capable of this, of these flashes: despite herself, on occasions, rare occasions, she has shown me, *this is how it is, this is how life really is*.

Who else have I seen lately, who else can I discuss with Ornella when she returns? *Davey*, my thoughts turn to Davey: I wish that I could live with him, I wish that he would live with me rather than with Chris; or *Freddie Mercury*, as Ornella calls him but not to his face. Not to Chris's face nor Davey's face. Whenever she calls him Freddie Mercury, to me, I feel obliged to counter, *Oh, he's alright*. And then she says, *I know he's alright, did I say that he wasn't alright?*

But, *well, yes*, because there is something about calling someone by another name. About refusing to use a person's name. About *calling names*, perhaps, whatever the name. It is not that we dislike Freddie, but that we are wary. Shocked, even. Because we never expected Davey to be the first of us to settle down. And now, suddenly, he has been spirited away from us: *Dead-and-married*, to use Ornella's expression. She likes to say that they live with *two-point-five cats* but, in fact, there are two cats, Fellini and Dali. The *point five* is a budgie called Karen.

Not that Davey is not careful to spend time with me, in that manner in which married people are careful. He plans, weeks in advance, for me to go to dinner with him, with him and Chris. And he *spends time* on me: a whole evening given over to me; a whole evening, allowed for. He balances two worlds, and makes a show of it. I could drop by, any time, in the daytime, but usually I am deflected by the prior existence of some plan of his for me (*Next Saturday?*). And, anyway, whenever I do drop by, Chris is there. And even when we are away from Chris, Davey's conversation tends to orbit him. They both work evenings, in the same restaurant. Chris introduced him to the restaurant, found him the job. To tide him over while he aims for film school. He did *need* a job. He did need a *home*, he did need a *lover*. I suppose that the only problem, as far as Ornella and I are concerned, is that everything is provided by the one person.

Sometimes Ornella shrieks in horror, *Our Davey, a waiter!*

And I have to remind her: it is his *day job*, his evening job. And once I ventured, 'It's not *so* dreadful: it's better than being a *miner*.'

She puzzled, 'Why? Who's a miner?'

Missing the point, so that I could say nothing but, 'Well, *miners* are.'

She is still not back. Looking down into my cup, I start to think about the flat where I live. No, not to *think*: the flat creeps up on me, the thought of the flat, the thought of going back. A living room full of people who never sleep but are never awake: like an airport lounge, and complete with the sealed-in cigarette smoke of an airport lounge. But without the departures. And my room, my tiny room, the big typewriter in my room. Now, beyond my cup, Ornella appears. I am reached by a ripple of the warmth that is still coming from her, from her bath. The scent of bath oil or lotion melted onto, into, her warm skin. Brand new skin, raised by a loofah, sealed with a fresh sweat from the hot bathwater, cleaner than bathwater. There is something else which comes to me, an idea; I think no further, look up and say to her, 'I have an idea.'

She says, 'My period has started.'

'Oh,' I check, 'Are you alright?'

Sitting down on the bed, she frowns. 'I have had them before, you know.'

'No, I mean, do you have any *sanitary requisites*?' The term that we have relished ever since school, since a typewritten notice appeared in the girls' changing room: *Sanitary requisites available from Miss Stringer.*

She frowns harder. 'Yes, but anyway, this is a *hospital*, *full* of sanitary requisites.' She picks up the newspaper, probably in pursuit of the telly page. 'So, what's your idea? E=Mc2?'

'That was yesterday's idea.'

She looks up, her eyes flash a laugh.

I tell her my idea: 'I could shadow you.'

'What?'

'Shadow you for a day.' A day? Only half the story. 'A day and night. Or whatever. A day and a night and a day, a whole shift. I could write an article about what you do here.'

Slowly, her hand rises from the paper and rakes back her damp hair. 'Surely it's already been done.'

I shrug happily. 'It-ain't-what-you-do . . .'

She starts to smile.

'It hasn't been done *by me*. It hasn't been done *about you*.'

She turns the smile down to the paper. 'You don't need to shadow me,' she murmurs. 'You *know* what I do.'

Perhaps I have gone too far, have pushed her. 'You don't want me to shadow you.'

'Oh, no,' her face flicks up, eyes wide, mouth drawn small, 'I'd love you to come around with me.'

'But you think it would be awkward to have me with you?'

Her expression sinks into a smirk. 'Oh God no, this is a *hospital*, *full* of people coming and going. I'll say that you're a student or something.' As her attention drops back down to the paper, she says, 'I think it's a brilliant idea, we can spend the whole day together, we can have a laugh.' And as she tracks the telly programmes down the page, her voice comes lower still: 'You haven't told me about Abi-cadabra.'

'Oh,' No, 'Well . . .' and I settle down, to start the story.

I REMEMBER THE hospital rooms in which Ornella lived: a new room with each new job, every six months, but so similar, with bed, desk, sink, metal wastepaper bin. I remember pushing my way very carefully into one of them, so as not to hit her head. She is there, lying on her back on the floor, star-shaped, because she cut short her run, turned around behind me to run back to her room. *Turncoat.* Nothing moves but her lungs, which are convulsed. As I step over her, she moans, 'I need a cigarette.'

'Believe me,' I pant, 'the last thing that you need is a cigarette.'

Her eyes closed, and eyelids creasing with passion, she shrieks to the ceiling, 'But it's my last request.'

I laugh, which is painful. 'By the look of you, it's too late for a last request.' In a way, she looks healthier than ever, because she is so pink. Now she opens her eyes, up into mine, and I see the brightness of them, the oxygen in them, the green rust in the brown irises. I nudge her bare leg with my foot, my trainer. 'Get up. Don't make an exhibition of yourself.'

'There's only you here,' she pouts.

I bend down to tackle one of my laces. 'And all the people who are on the other side of the door listening to the heavy breathing and shrieks of torture.'

She rolls over and crawls to the door in a loose tangle of clothing. 'Not like *that*, darling,' she shouts. 'Like *this*.'

Smiling down onto my trainer, I tell her, 'You are *so childish*.'

She rolls onto her side to reply, 'And *you* are so *middle class*.'

Which surprises me because this has not been a favoured insult since we were young, since our Davey-days, and even then it was never favoured by Ornella. Too close to home, for her. Incredulous, I throw back,

'You're the most middle class person I know.'

She rolls over onto her back and links her hands behind her head. 'Even now that you hob-nob with the stars?'

She rarely mentions my work, and I do not know how to take this. I kick my foot free of the trainer, tell her, 'I saw Leo Sayer in the street last week, if that's what you mean.' I know that it was not what she meant.

She crosses her ankles, her trainers. 'Did you?'

'No.'

'Oh.'

I tut. '*Of course* I did. Why would I make up a story about having seen Leo Sayer in the street? I'd say George Michael or someone, wouldn't I. Boy George or someone.'

She asks, 'Who are you interviewing, this week? Anyone interesting?'

I glance up from my second lace to see if this is sarcasm. But her expression is so different from usual, her face so pink and puffy, her eyes so shiny, that it is unreadable.

So, all I say is, 'No.'

She snaps upwards, hugs her knees, changes the subject: 'You *enjoyed* that run,' she mumbles, accusingly, onto her knees.

I counter, 'It was *your* idea.' She had said, *Let's go for a jog before I try to do some revision.*

She straightens. 'Yes, but not because I *enjoy* running. I do it to keep fit.'

Releasing my foot, rubbing my sore arch, I frown ferociously at her. 'What makes you think that I'm such a pervert that I enjoy running?'

Phlegm ricochets inside her chest and she flops back onto the floor. 'Call it intuition,' she rasps.

'No, I won't.' I lever myself off the bed and hobble to the kettle. 'And look at you –' Which I do, derisively, in passing ' – there are easier ways for you to get fit. Quit-the-cigs, for a start.' On the tray, with the kettle, is a small white lump, too round and smooth to be a sugar lump. I pick it up, sniff it, confirm my suspicion: peppermint. 'Nella, you have some *food* here.'

'What is it?' A note of curiosity, behind me, but no movement.

'A mint imperial.'

'Bagsie,' she calls, feebly.

'Bagsie, bollocks,' I reply, lifting the lid from the kettle, checking the water. 'Finders, keepers.' She will know that I am teasing her. For good measure, I add, '*And* I'm your *guest*.'

'But,' she responds by raising her voice, 'you've already denied me my post-coital cigarette. I want the mint.'

I step towards her, stand over her, hold the mint over her. 'Shout all you want,' I whisper down to her, rolling the mint between the tips of my forefinger and thumb, 'Shock the whole corridor. Blackmail won't work on me.'

Below me, she laughs, more convulsions, and wraps her arms over her stomach, presumably to hold the pain of a stitch. 'I've a horrid taste in my mouth,' she laughs, wails, 'I'm dying. Give me the fucking mint.'

I raise the mint a little higher. 'You have a horrid word in your mouth,' I smile, smarm; 'Nice ladies don't say fuck.'

'I'm not nice, so . . .' her lungs whoop around a huge intake of breath before she screams, 'GIVE ME A POST-COITAL MINT IMPERIAL.'

I step back, chucking the mint into the air and catching it; sit back on the desk, swinging my hot feet, the kettle whispering beside me. 'If this is a post-coital mint,' I lecture, 'then it stands to reason that it should go to whoever most recently had sex.' And I know that I will win this contest because Billy was not here last night: he was working, and he works in another hospital, across town.

From the slumped body comes an arm, raised, stretched, the hand snapping on the trail of the mint. 'Midnight last night,' she warbles, giggles, in desperation.

'Liar.' I lean forward to stress, 'And liars are disqualified.'

The arm flops. 'I did,' she pleads, 'I did.'

'A new position, Ornella? Long distance? Billy was on the other side of town.'

She struggles to roll onto one arm, to fold over, to push herself up into sitting position. Her cheeks are pools of blood beneath her skin, she is woozy on so much blood, and blinky. As soon as she is sitting, she bumps over the carpet to lean back on the bed. 'Not with Billy,' she says, trying to smooth her hair with her hands.

Inside, I drop. Stumble from an unseen kerb. Because suddenly the world is not quite as I had thought. 'And you didn't tell me?'

Fussing with her hair, she narrows her eyes, a show of impatience. 'I *am* telling you.'

'*This* is telling me?'

She pauses, shuts her eyes, more impatience: 'No, this is the weather forecast.'

'You're sleeping with someone who isn't Billy, and *this* is *telling me*?'

She opens her eyes. 'Slept,' she emphasizes. 'Once.'

'Oh.' Now I know something. Now I start to get a feel for this; the story starts to take shape. First question: 'Who?'

She tries a grin, tries, 'That's my secret.'

Not good enough, I will not have this. Irritated, I mutter, 'Oh come on, Ornella,' *You know we don't have secrets from each other*.

She drops the grin, admits, 'One of the other SHOs, you don't know him.'

But there is something that I *do* know, now: a *him*.

'What happens now?' This is a story of what? Of a drunken slip-up? Of two people who, from now on, will pass each other in corridors with their eyes low, colour high? A sorry affair? A resolution, Never-again, Once-is-enough? Of a row, recriminations, with Billy?

She hugs her knees again, peeks over the knees, interested. 'You mean, do I do it again?'

Inside me, a twitch of exasperation. 'No,' I explain, carefully calm, trying to calm the twitch, '*I mean*, do you

232

tell Billy?' But I relent; she has the better of me: '*And, do-you-do-it-again?*'

She slots, settles, her chin into the dip between her knees. 'The answer to the first question is no, of course I don't tell him, do you think I'm stupid?' Rhetorical question: her gaze rests in mine, unflinching. 'The answer to the second question?' For the first time in the conversation, her eyes drift, her attention folds inwards. 'I don't know.'

Suddenly the eyes are back. 'Don't look at me like that!' And squeezed into a frown. 'What is it to you who I sleep with?'

I want to say, What-about-Billy? But why? Why do I care about Billy? It is *Ornella* who is my friend.

'Billy's nothing to you,' she counters, reading me.

'That's *not true*,' I am uncomfortable under this sudden spotlight. 'And, anyway, *what matters* is that he's something *to you*.' Yes, this is it, this feels right, this is what I had wanted to say. And now I see her differently, I see the pieces which do not fit into her fearsome frown: the jutting chin, the slick of tears on her eyes.

She wrenches her gaze from mine. 'Leave me to worry about Billy,' she sulks. And manages to add, 'I know my priorities.'

A shock for me, quick and then slower, a brand and an after-burn. Because does *I-know-my-priorities* mean *I'm-in-love-with-Billy*? No. By no stretch of the imagination. No one can use the word *priorities* to talk of love. It will not fit, priorities will not fit over love. Nowhere near. Priorities are black and white, and love is colour.

For the first time ever, it occurs to me that Ornella is not in love with Billy.

She has twisted up her face to plead, 'Don't take me to task for this, Niquie. It *just happened*.'

I have heard this so often from her, I marvel that she lives in a world where her actions *just happen* to her; that she spins through her world; that, for someone so apparently in control, her core is chaos.

'It *happens*, here, in hospital,' she explains, whines. 'It's the Linen Store Syndrome, it happens in the linen store. We're all too close, here: we work too hard and too close, too late at night.' She shrugs: a narrow, knee-hugging shrug. 'I couldn't help sleeping with him. People *do*, here.'

'People do what, here? Go off into the linen store, or go off with Doctor Whatsisname?'

'Oliver,' she says.

There is a silence in which I do not repeat his name.

And now, 'They go off into the linen store.'

I cannot suppress a flicker of interest. 'Really?'

Answered with a flicker of a smile. 'No, not really. Not literally.' A little more of a smile. 'Well, not often.'

I can swop stories with her: 'I had sex in a laundry room, once.'

Thrilled, she squeals, 'With *who*?'

'James.'

'Oh.' She drops the smile, her eyes. 'James.' And nothing more.

So I babble into the silence, 'Samantha Gregg's party, do you remember Samantha Gregg's party?'

To the floor, she says, 'Feels like a million years ago.'

More silence. In which I start to think: *Oliver*. Grudgingly, I ask, 'So, what's he like?'

'Nice.'

Silly question.

She shrugs again, this time more expansively, unclasping her knees and placing her hands on either side of her on the floor. 'It was something to do,' she says.

I realize that the mint is becoming sticky in my hand; I hold it out to her: 'Here.'

She shakes her head.

'But you were *screaming* for it.'

'I was joking,' she says, but barely, and without a smile.

Something to do? 'But you have *so much* to do,' I insist, sympathize, despair of her. If I had to do what she has to do, I would have no energy, even, for chat up lines.

'Yeah,' she complains, moving slowly onto her feet, 'Like revision.'

I rush to talk some sense into her: 'You can't start revision *now*.' Twenty to nine, and no food yet.

'*After* my shower.' She reaches out and pulls her towel from the towel-rail, but reconsiders, 'After a *cup of tea*,' and tips backwards to sit on the bed with her bundle.

'Don't revise *now*, Ornella.'

My plea makes no impression on her, brings no spark to eyes dipped with eyelid. 'If I don't pass this exam . . .' But suddenly this is enough, and she shudders to life: 'I don't want to become a GP stuck in the Shires or in Tower Hamlets or somewhere.'

General practice dismissed in a single sentence.

In her lap she has fistfuls of towel. 'I *must* pass this exam.'

I feel a pang for her: because did she know this when she chose Medicine? But there is something that I can do for her, I can give her some advice: 'Do your revision in the *mornings*.' *When you're awake, so that it's less slow, less painful.*

'I'm too drugged up.'

'Give up the pills, then.'

Sighing to the bottom of her lungs, she hurls the towel to the end of the bed and lies down to lecture the ceiling: 'My sleep's buggered.' Now she challenges me, '*You* try being woken three times a night, every other night, for a few years, and *then* you can tell me to give up the pills.' She closes her eyes, concludes, 'Sleeping pills are my only vice.'

Another pang, but more fond. 'You drink and smoke.'

'Okay,' she revises. 'They're my only vices: drinking, smoking, and drugs.'

I smile to myself: she is so small for so many vices. Her feet are so far from the end of the bed. '*And* sleeping around.' I am enjoying this.

She cranks herself up onto her elbows to send back, '*You* sleep around.'

Which is hardly a defence. And, anyway, 'I *do not*.'

'You *do*.' Her arms collapse but she continues to speak to me via the ceiling, a satellite: 'Since you met John, you haven't stopped having sex for more than ten minutes.'

I have to laugh. 'But I've been *here* for a couple of *hours*.'

'Okay,' she sends via the ceiling. 'But you haven't stopped *thinking about* sex for more than ten minutes.'

In fact, I have been thinking about food. Thinking about the emptiness of my stomach and the corresponding emptiness of Ornella's section of the fridge. Thinking of John's cooking. Thinking how, unconsciously, he will cook for two. Wondering whether he will eat twice as much, or whether there will be some left for me. And whether I can wait. 'Listen, this isn't the point, that's not sleeping *around*.' Which surely she knows, so why am I bothering? Why do I let her draw me in, wind me up? 'Not if it's *one person*.'

An immediate reply from the far end of the bed: '*Words*.' Less a reply, more a dismissive snort.

I will not let her get away with this: 'It's not *words*, Ornella; it's what it *is*.'

'One person *at the moment*,' she goads, suddenly. I cannot see her face clearly from here, but she folds her arms over her chest: the equivalent of a smug smile, *Get out of that*.

But this is nonsense. 'That's the whole point: one person at a time.'

She sits up, straight up, struck by a thought: 'Have you ever tried two?'

'You *know* I haven't.' But now I have to stop and check, 'Have *you*?'

She flops back down onto the bed. 'What do you think I am? A perv?'

I have had enough of this. I will make her a cup of tea and then tackle her about food; if neccesary, I will go down the road to the late night supermarket to buy fake fresh bread and tubs of dips. But, turning my attention to the kettle, I cannot resist an arch, '*I am monogamous.*'

'Mostly.'

I ignore this.

Which she ignores, continuing, 'Monogamous, polygamous,' sing-song and derisive. And now, more sing-song: 'Istanbul, Constantinople.'

Dabbling two teabags into two cups, I ask her, 'Is that your considered comment on the issue?'

Goaded, but with nowhere left to go, she sings, 'Ra-Ra-Rasputin.'

So that I have to laugh.

And she answers back with her own laugh, '*Oh*, but you *do* love me.'

'*Mostly.*'

She waddles to the end of the bed on her knees for her cup of tea. 'Really?' she chirps, but focused firmly on the cup, concentrating on her balance whilst reaching for my hands, 'There are times when you *don't*?'

I lower the cup into her hands. 'I will *forever* if you come on holiday with me: me and John, you and Billy. Because if there are four of us, we can rent an apartment.' Should I have mentioned Billy, future plans and Billy?

But she seems bored rather than upset, sits back onto her heels and speaks into her cup: 'Can't afford it.'

I knew that she would say this. It is her answer to anything that is asked of her. It makes everything unaskable, unarguable. But not this time, because I am going to argue back. '*Won't* afford it.' Because I have seen her spend as much on clothes. And she pays no rent or bills.

Why do Ornella and I never do what normal friends do? Why do we never have holidays, days out, meals out? But I know why not: because I come to her and we do whatever she decides. And usually we stay home. Which she likes to portray as intimacy. Sisterly. She likes to say that I am the sister she never had. But we are not sisters, I have no claim on her, she could walk away from me tomorrow and I would be nothing to her. There would be nothing or no one to remind her of me. And I know what she will do for a holiday, this year: she will make no decision, no effort, and then, at the last minute, on the spur of the moment, there will be an opportunity to go away with some other people, with Billy's friends, or Guido's friends, Guido's girlfriend's friends, Leah's friends, Leah's boyfriend's friends. People with whom she has no involvement but who will provide a change of scenery for her. She socializes with strangers, but makes no effort with Billy and me. She keeps us home with her, but she will not live with us. She does not often even *feed* us.

She unfolds below her carefully held cup, watchful of the slippery surface of the tea, and sidles to the far end of the bed to rearrange herself on the pillows. I sense that she is not going to answer my charge, *Won't afford it*. And I am too hungry to persist.

'Never mind,' I say, turning wearily to the window, 'I suppose that I'll enjoy the villa in Tuscany that you'll buy when you're older.'

'I *am* older,' she says, behind me.

Outside has become dark since we came in from our run. I am surprised by the moon: a thin, tipped moon; an icicle, but hanging from nothing.

'Venus flaring,' she decides, thoughtfully.

Curious, I turn back to her. 'What?'

One leg is outstretched on the bed, slack, and the other is folded. She is bent over the folded leg, holding the ankle in one hand and rubbing her calf with the other. 'Like varicose veins,' she mutters, but looks up to explain, '*Venous flaring*,' her eyes widened by the upwards angle, and blank for facts: 'like varicose veins.'

Beneath her fingertips, I see a few small, faint, red lines like scratches.

She says, 'It's what happens when you start to grow old, when everything starts to go wrong.'

I HAVE A very specific memory from this time, a pinhole memory: I am with Davey in his garden; we are sitting side by side in Directors' Chairs, our faces turned to the sun. The insides of my eyelids are orangeade, lurid and fizzy but warm, summery. We have been silent for a while, sunworshipping. Now I feel his fingers on my wrist: pulse-poised fingers. Through narrowly opened eyes I watch him lean forward, let him roll my wrist towards him so that he can see the face of my watch. When he has seen, he flops back in his chair, flings back his head: a dramatic gesture of despair. I do not dare to ask, but peek, to see for myself: half past four. At five, he will have to start to get ready for work; have a shower, dress properly.

I am in his garden because the weather is too nice for work. We are cast adrift together from the nine-to-five world. I will work this evening. I will encourage John to go to the pub, and then spend the evening running and re-running a conversation which I have had with some-one, which has already been had but is echoed by my tape recorder. It is my job to go over and over conversations. A strange job. Sometimes difficult, too: some of their words move too quickly, others too quietly, evading the sticky molecules of the tape, sliding over them or bubbling beneath them. But, then, speech is for rustling those tiny bones of the ear, not for taping. I feel furtive, going back to someone's words on my own, taking my time to go over and over them.

Beside me, Davey speaks to the sun: 'How's Prunella-babes?' Catching up before we have to leave each other.

'Fine,' I reply without thinking.

'Haven't seen her for *ages*.' A conversational murmur but mildly scandalized, placing himself centre-stage: *I've been so busy lately*.

So I do my bit, tell him, 'I saw her yesterday.' One of us has seen her: this will suffice.

But, 'She's fine? You're sure?'

I open my eyes and flinch from the sun. 'Yes, why?'

'Nothing.' He tries to shrug off my question: sudden sharp shoulders.

Not nothing: I am mildly stirred. I do not sit back and give up; I turn sideways in my chair.

And so he says, 'She seemed quiet, that's all.'

'When?'

'When I last saw her.'

'Which was when?'

But he has had enough of my questions: he tilts back his head, and his face receives another splash of buttery sunshine. Which throws fuzzy shadows into his smoky eyelashes; shadows made not from darkness but from light, like a spider's web. 'Don't remember.'

'I suppose she *is* quiet,' I muse. 'She's tired. She's fed up. The usual.' My turn to shrug. 'You know Ornella.'

It was around this time that Ornella had begun to fail her exam. She failed four times. Which was, apparently, not too unusual; six attempts were allowed. Her failure was insidious: she was forever receiving results, deciding to re-take, and revising. Billy had failed twice, before diverting from mainstream medicine to a career in opthalmology. Guido had settled on psychiatry. Leah was training to become a GP. So Ornella was alone in her failure. And she did not want to talk to me about it: she would always complain, *It's boring*. Otherwise, she seemed to be working well, finding jobs easily; moving on, every six, twelve, eighteen months, with good references.

I do not remember much else in detail: there seems to be nothing in particular to remember. No, not true, I do have a memory: she is standing in the kind of kitchen which is common to hospital accommodation, fire extinguisher and fire blanket on the wall next to handwritten notices about dirty pans and thefts, and she is cramming a marmalade sandwich into her mouth: bouncy cheeks and slithery throat. Her clothes are smart but rumpled. *Potentially* smart: navy blue and white, collars and lapels. The hand which is holding the sandwich has nail varnish on two fingers, has had nail varnish removed from all but two of the fingers, the last two. I am newly-woken, having stayed for the night. Coming into the doorway, I ask, 'Okay?'

Inexplicably, this alarms her. She yells, 'Mascara, one eye?' through a mouthful of marmalade.

I peer, and reassure her, 'No, you're fine,' *mascara on both eyes*.

'Thank God.' She rushes past me, a waft of deodorant and marmalade. I turn after her with my warning about the two red nails but am too late, and simply watch her disappear down the corridor.

Now another memory comes. She was late from work, I do not remember if we were in her home or mine. Probably hers, because she very rarely came to mine. She had come in and sat down in a chair opposite me, knock-kneed and fidgety in her complicated buttons and tucks and cuffs, her slip-on shoes with shoe-bows. Her hair was pinned up, which she hated, and falling down, which she hated even more. When she swiped the loose strands, I saw that her hands were shaking. She said, 'I was the only doctor on duty in the hospital this afternoon.' At the time, she was working in a smaller hospital: four or five wards, two or three doctors. 'The other one was in Outpatients, so there was only me. And just before I was due to come home, I had a crash call. So I ran to the ward, where Sister was furious: *You're the only doctor.* As if this was my fault. There were ten or more nurses around the bed; I had to send some of them away before I could reach him.

'The man had stopped breathing, his heart had stopped. He was new to the ward, I'd never seen him before.' Her eyes were black stones in clean water. 'He hadn't even been clerked, there was no information on him. He'd been on the ward for ten minutes and then he'd stopped breathing.'

Sitting opposite her, closely following her words, I began to feel that *I* had stopped breathing.

'There was no one to help me intubate him. So I tried to push the tube down his throat, but, you know . . .' her hands thrown, and her eyes. She spoke to the window, 'I'm not an anaesthetist, I'm not trained.' Then the hands returned to her lap, and so did her gaze. 'The nurses didn't know what they were doing and knocked the monitor off the trolley.' She looked up to check that I understood: 'Onto the floor.'

'Oh God,' I sympathized.

'So, no readings.' She bit her lip. 'He died, of course.'

She shrugged, emptily, loosely, 'I mean, perhaps he would have died anyway,' another shrug, protracted, shoulders held high and stiff, 'but.'

'Yes,' I said.

'And when I'd tidied him up a bit, I looked around and saw that the nurses had gone.'

Tidied him up? I flinched, shut my eyes.

'*Of course* the nurses had gone,' she added, heavily. This was the first note of emotion. Anger. 'Never there when there's trouble. So *I* had to go and see his wife.'

'*Wife?*' I opened my eyes.

'Sitting in the corridor,' she explained, 'with no idea. So I told her, and she started to cry.'

And suddenly I saw that Ornella had started to cry. Her tears had happened very quickly, sneaked up on me, nearly slipped by me. They were silent because she was noisy with her story; the sound of the story was the rapid regular rasp of her inward breath between her burning words. The sound of sore, dry lungs. Desperation.

'And she started to say *I'm sorry*.' Ornella leaned forward to emphasize this absurdity, '*I'm sorry*.' Her eyes were still but spilling tears of which she took no notice. 'She said s*orry, but*, they'd been married for nearly fifty years.'

I repeated, '*Fifty years*.' But I could not imagine fifty years. A lifetime, but not mine; twice mine.

'*Fifty years*.' She snapped back in the chair, snapped shut her eyes, rubbed her forehead with one hand, and muttered, 'So I took her to him, to the bed.'

My turn to lean forward. 'On the ward?' *In public?*

She opened her eyes, and began to spell it out for me: 'I walked her past everybody else's bed, to the end of the ward. To the curtain. Where I left her.' The words were so separate that they bumped into each other with sinister little clicks.

No, 'But was there nowhere else?'

She sighed, slowed; the pulse of breaths and words slowed down. 'Chapel of rest, across the car park, behind the dustbins.'

Which left me with nothing more to say. Apart from, 'But then where did she go?' *Afterwards.*

Eyes closed, she replied, 'I don't know. Home, I suppose.'

We were silent for a moment, and then she said in a whirr of panic, 'I don't want to end up there, or anywhere like there; I don't want to end up like him, or her.'

I did not know what I could say; I said, simply, 'You won't.' Which, I saw, failed to touch her. She did not believe me. I should have laid my hand on her arm. To steady her. To show her that she could never *end up there* because she was *here*. With me. I should have held her.

She should have given up on a career in hospital medicine rather than hanging on, hating it, and failing so frequently that *it* began to give up on *her*. She should have known, or should have listened to me. She should have made the decision to give up gracefully and go. But she seemed to have stopped making decisions: the only decision that she made was to marry.

*

And it was at her wedding that I realized that every-thing between us was beginning to change. It had been no surprise to me that she had decided to marry. Or not in one sense: I knew that this was part of a plan which she had for herself, for her life. But I was surprised when she told me. Because marriage had always been for the future, not for *now*. One day she rang me and said, pleasantly, 'Good news, Niquie: I'm getting married.'

Surprised, I said, stupidly, 'To Billy?'

She said, 'That's the *bad* news,' and laughed.

I laughed, too, but continued with questions: 'Since when?'

But she misheard me, thought I had said *When?* 'Twenty-seven weeks on Saturday.'

Twenty-seven weeks: so sudden. And, lately, they had seemed settled. They had been renting a flat together for a few months. I wondered if it was an emergency decision. But somehow it did not *sound* like an emergency. I did not want to ask her if she was pregnant. To bring her down to earth with a bump.

'What do your mum and dad think?' I was trying to enthuse, but also listening carefully.

'Oh, they're thrilled.' But this was faintly dismissive.

I checked, 'Church?' Trying to focus on *wedding*, this was what came to mind: *church*.

'Well, you have to, don't you. Who do you do this kind of thing for, if not for your parents? And they want the whole show, don't they.'

You, your: Well, no, not mine. Mine would feel uneasy as joint hosts of a wedding. And if they felt uneasy, then

247

so would I. Perhaps I would feel uneasy in any case, the centre of attention in a big white dress. Suddenly I was unsure that I would want to make a show of my private life.

Then she said, 'Tell you more when I see you.' And I thought she meant that she would tell me the arrangements: *Please, no, not twenty-seven weeks of arrangements.*

But I was wrong. What she had meant, I discovered when we met the next day, was that she would tell me why she had decided to marry Billy. When we had settled at our table, her first words came in a sigh: 'Oh I don't know.' As if I had asked her a question. We were in a patisserie, not our favourite; our favourite was much smaller, more crowded, around the corner. But for today Ornella had chosen this one, *See you in Valerie's, six-thirty*, and there had been no time, on the phone, to argue. Now she repeated, 'Oh I don't know. Marrying Billy: it feels right, now; I feel that it's time.'

Time? Certainly there had been no one else since Doctor Oliver, or not that I knew. Apart from two one-night-stands with an anaesthetist. If it is possible to have two one-night-stands with the same person. *One-night-stand* had been her term. And then there was a fling with a nurse, a woman; a fling which Ornella had defended, or perhaps dismissed, with her claim that *This is different.* So different that she had gone on holiday with her: four days in France. It happened during the holiday, was confined to the holiday, a holiday romance. Whereas Doctor Oliver had been on and off – *Both on duty and off duty,*

Ornella had joked – for the couple of months of his working holiday – *Hard work* was my joke – before he returned to Australia.

Time to *marry*, or to marry *Billy*?

She put down the menu and said, 'I felt that I had to make a decision.'

Had she always intended to marry Billy? What was the decision, exactly? To marry or not, or merely when? Or to marry or leave him?

She leaned forward to confide, 'I felt that I couldn't just go on . . .' she stopped, sat back, shrugged, '. . . indefinitely.'

But life does go on. Indefinitely. Sort of. Would go on, indefinitely, sort of, after she married him. I slid the menu from beneath her hands, although I did not need it; I had seen the cakes and knew what I wanted.

'And I won't marry anyone else, *now*, will I.'

I looked up from the menu and she laughed at me, so I did not know if she was serious. I checked, 'Does *he* want to marry *you*?' Half-serious.

'Oh, yes,' she said, dismissively.

And I did not know if this was dismissive of my question, *Yes, of course he wants to marry me*. Or dismissive of him, *Yes, if only he knew*.

Then she looked down onto her hands, and muttered, 'Anyway, what else *is* there?'

She meant, *In life. To life.*

Which turned me cold. Why did her decision to marry Billy seem like a giving up, a shutting down, rather than an opening up, a moving on? But this was the only downbeat moment in the conversation. When our cakes arrived, she did not touch hers, not until I prompted her; and then, when she ate, she did so mechanically. Because she was here to talk. About why she was marrying Billy. Her reasons were clear: they had known each other for years, for the whole of their adult lives; they liked each other, were close friends; they enjoyed living with each other; they wanted the same from life and had each other's interests at heart.

Did she think that I would want to find fault with her decision? I had never said a word against Billy. Quite the contrary, she knew that I liked him. (There was nothing to dislike.) And, importantly, he was easy to have around. And I had never said a word against marriage. So why do this? Why take me somewhere and *sit me down* like this? Anyway, I could not have found fault because she left me no time or space to say a word. I was *being told*. Quickly, but softly, *deftly*, so that any comment or question from me into those quick soft words would have jarred or whined.

Twenty minutes of words to tell me over and over again that, *This is how it is going to be from now on.* This was a statement of faith. Sitting opposite me, blindly chopping her pavlova with her tiny fork, telling me what she was going to do with her life, she was somehow both so certain and so tremulous that for me to have contradicted her would have been cruel. Destructive. I was nervous for us both. The underlying theme of her speech seemed to be, *Trust me.* Or perhaps, *I trust you.* Whichever, I knew that somewhere in all those words she was making a case for trust. A sort of, *I trust you to trust my instincts*. But talk of trust makes me nervous. She was telling me over and over again that there was no place for questions. Which, of course, was not our usual manner with each other. But, then, this was supposed to be different. Because we were supposed to be talking about love. I did not need to be told not to ask questions about love. So my suspicions were raised. I realized that she was pleading with me not to ask questions. Several times, she said, very quickly, 'You do see, don't you?' *Please see*.

It was not that she did not mention love. Sometimes she said *I love him*, in the middle of her lists of reasons for marrying him. No, she said *I do love him*: an unspoken qualifier; a response to an unasked question. Whenever she told me that she did love him, I heard the weighing up of evidence behind the words: *On balance*. At the end of her speech she said, 'I'm happy.' And I thought of old films, which always seem to end with someone saying, *Well, if you're happy, then I'm happy for you, darling*. I realized that she was asking for my blessing. I think I said, 'That's good.' She was asking me to let her marry him. Because she knew that she was doing wrong. She was asking me to turn a blind eye. And I did because I was frightened of losing her. I could see that marrying Billy was no answer to her desperation, I could see that she was digging herself deeper, but I said, 'That's good,' and I did nothing to stop her.

During the twenty-seven weeks, she did not tell me much about the wedding. She played down the wedding.

Her comment, whenever I pressed her for information, was that she wanted, 'Nothing *big*, just something *nice*.' And for the twenty-seven weeks, we followed our usual routine: a couple of times each week I went around to her flat or, less often, she came to mine, and we watched soaps then stayed in front of the telly to deride the sit-coms; or we shopped in the supermarket and then ate everything that we had bought or found that somehow there was nothing suitable in our carrier bags so that we had to go for a takeaway. And we read magazines, read aloud the Lonely Hearts and speculated. Our boys did not distract us. Billy was often at work; but if he was home, he was unobtrusive. The flat was Ornella's: every-thing in their flat was hers, even the notepad by the phone. Evidence of Billy was confined to temporary sur-face clutter: a newspaper, a jacket, and perhaps a beer can and empty glass scarred lightly with scum. In my flat, John was often only briefly there: he had friends, sports, he had *energy*; these were the days, the evenings, when we had energy for more than each other. Some-times we all went to a film together. *Salaam Bombay!* Or *Annie Hall* again. At weekends, I saw less of Ornella, because she went home to her parents more often, on Mission Wedding.

So when the invitation arrived on my doormat, it could have dropped down, in, from another world. Which, in a sense, was true: it came from home, with the postmark of home. I had seen Ornella on the previous evening and there had been no mention of invitations. Once, when I had asked who would come to the wedding, she had said, cheerfully, 'That's up to them,' meaning her parents, 'because they're paying.' And another time, she had said, 'Not the Italians.'

I had been disappointed, I had been looking forward to seeing the Italians. 'Really?'

'Well, not many of them,' she had revised. 'It's too far for them to come.'

The stiff envelope was not addressed in Ornella's handwriting but in an adult's squirls. And the inky inscription, too, *Veronica and John*. Below, I was informed in silver that I was *invited to the marriage of Ornella Lucia Marini and William Terence Stone*.

'Terence?' I said aloud to myself in my hallway, then laughed: weddings and middle names.

I pinned the invitation to the cork board in my kitchen, calling to John in the bathroom, to remind him. He shouted back, '*When* is it?' As if he would have difficulty fitting it into a diary full of squash games. I ignored him, stepped back and looked over the invitation. Saw that I was being invited to the marriage of Ornella and Billy, not of Ornella *to* Billy: there was no sense that she was going to be dispatched down the aisle to him. They were equals in this endeavour. And she had a silver surname, too: she had not been stripped of her name, left floating in preparation for the ceremonial handing from father to husband. I remembered that Ornella and I had laughed at our invitations to Bev's wedding: *Mr and Mrs Harold Grace invite you to the marriage of their daughter Beverly Clare to* ... To who? I could not remember his name, could never remember his full name; Michael something, somebody. Whenever I wrote Christmas cards to Bev, I had to look up her new name, his name, in my address book. Under her old name, which had been crossed out, because if she was under her new name, I would never remember, never find her. Ornella and I did not go to her wedding, we were both unable to go: it was during my finals and Ornella's elective in Milan. Turning away from the invitation to Ornella's wedding, I wondered whether she had had to fight over the wording. Had there been a fight, about which I knew nothing? Knowing her parents, I suspected so.

It was odd to see her name in print on my board. As if she was someone else, somehow, someone unknown to me. Somehow there was none of her in the silver print, none of her voice. I began to feel uneasy. I wondered if Davey had been invited; and if so, to how much? To the service and reception, or simply to the reception? I needed to talk to him, to confer. To conspire. So I rang him.

'Hello, Chickadee,' he yawned.

'Have you been invited to Ornella's wedding?' Unfortunately, unintentionally abrupt.

'Er . . .' He sounded disorientated.

I urged, 'Have you picked up your post?' *Pick up your post.*

'No.'

'Well, go and do so.' Friendly but firm.

The receiver clunked onto the tabletop. Then there was silence for a moment, then a squeak and a sigh and the steady creep of a sharp thumbnail beneath the frail part of the luxurious envelope, the fold, the fault line. Then, 'Verrrry posh,' as I fidgeted, waited for him to continue.

He read, scanned, '*Dr and Mrs Marini invite, to Seldon Manor* – where's Seldon? – *to celebrate the marriage of.*'

I had a sudden thought, said, 'Invite who, precisely?'

'What do you mean, *who*?' He was sleepily irritated. 'Invite *me*.'

'*Just* you?'

'Oh,' Suddenly he understood, 'Yes.' And he laughed; or approximated a laugh. 'You thought that *Dr-and-Mrs-Marini* would invite *David-and-Christopher*?'

I did not reply, said simply, 'Shit, I'm going to have to go to the church on my own.' Abi would not be going to the wedding: she was in the Sudan for a year.

'On your own? She hasn't invited John?'

'They *have* invited John. On *our* own, then.' But on *my* own, because what use was John? What did he know of Ornella, of Ornella-and-me?

'Buy yourself a nice hat,' Davey soothed, 'and you'll be well away.' I could hear that he wanted to go back to bed, to sleep. 'The key to weddings is: wear a nice hat, and sit back and enjoy the show.'

But this was exactly what was odd about the prospect of the wedding: a friend is for being with, not for watching. Over the next few weeks, contemplating the wedding, I felt similar to when I had stood back from the board in my kitchen and looked over the silvery invitation: I was a long way away from Ornella; or, she was a long way from me. In Davey's words, *Well away*.

255

Which was accurate in another sense, too, because where *was* Seldon? In-the-middle-of-nowhere. Nowhere near the church, which, in turn, was nowhere near home. Ornella told me that because of the short notice – twenty-seven weeks was short notice, apparently – they had been unable to book any of the nearer churches. So, the wedding was fifteen miles from home, in an area to which none of us had ever been. I bought a map, and John arranged to borrow his mother's car, which we had to collect. We were going to have to travel to his parents by train, the day beforehand, and stay overnight. Davey arranged for us to come to collect him from a nearby mainline station. And afterwards we planned to travel back into London together, as soon as Ornella and Billy had left on their honeymoon.

The day before The Day Before, Ornella rang me to remind me, 'Ring me tomorrow, OK?' An unnecessary reminder. The rest of the conversation concerned her trip to Thailand: the shopping for the trip, and the packing which had not yet been done. And, as ever, she finished by saying, trumpeting, 'Two and a half weeks away from work, *two and a half*.' The following evening, when I rang her at her parents' house, she complained that everyone was infuriating her, and then added, 'No word from Billy The Git.'

'You want a word?' For some reason, no reason, I laughed.

'*I want*,' she insisted, no laugh, 'to know that he hasn't *run off*.'

'*Run off*,' I repeated, disparagingly. 'To *where*?' I had

never seen Billy run anywhere. I had rarely seen him *move*. 'And why can't *you* ring *him*?'

'*Be-cause*,' impatient mock-patience, 'I want to see if he'll ring *me*.'

'*Ornella*,' I began to lecture her: 'You're getting married tomorrow, this is no time for games.'

'But I *always ring him*,' she flared. Over-tired.

So I hurried, 'But isn't it bad luck, anyway? On the eve of the wedding?'

'That's if he *sees* me,' she snapped; but then she checked, 'Isn't it?'

'Well, *I* don't know,' *how do I know, because what do I know about weddings?*

We were silent for a moment.

Then she muttered, 'My *mum*'ll know.'

I said with a smile, '*My* mum'll know,' and then I was struck, 'In fact, *Billy's* mum will know, and perhaps she's told him that it's unlucky, perhaps that's why he hasn't rung you.'

A brief pause, before she allowed, 'Perhaps,' but then decided, 'Perhaps *not*. Because sometimes I think that if I'm not there, in front of him, he never even thinks about me.'

Quickly, I soothed, 'That's because he's a boy; that's what boys do.' *Don't do.*

And I heard her smile: heard the space for the stretch of a smile, heard the differently taken breath, hardly taken. 'I wish I was marrying *you*,' she said, before returning to, 'I think it's the *dress*, actually: I think that it's unlucky for him to see the *dress*.'

257

The dress. I did not see the dress until the day. I had known – she had told me – that Leah was making the dress. What she had not told me was that Leah was making one for herself, too: a bridesmaid dress. I did not know that Leah was going to be a bridesmaid until she walked down the aisle with Ornella. I suppose that I had presumed that there were cousins who would be bridesmaids. Tailor-made bridesmaids: suitably-sized little girls who would kick their fluffy hems down the aisle, excitedly gripping their posies. And, on the day, there were cousins, but only two of them, and they accompanied Leah. As Leah's skirt brushed the end of the pew in which we had slumped after our long, hot, rushed journey, John swivelled to face me and whispered, 'Who's that? Her sister?'

I hissed back, 'She doesn't have a sister.' *Sister*? I had never seen two people who looked less alike: small, dark Ornella, still small and dark despite all the white taffeta; and big Leah, copiously blonde, who, in her peach frills, made me think of the Wife of Bath. Throughout the ceremony, I was rarely able to shift my gaze from Leah. She seemed to be doing everything in slow motion. Even her smiling. One never-ending slippery smile. What I had seen as she had passed the end of our pew was her engagement ring. What I had noticed was their rings, hers and Ornella's: two flashes, in sequence. I knew that these were the reasons why she had chosen Leah: Leah would play the part. I knew that, in her own defence, Ornella would have said to me, *You wouldn't have wanted to be a bridesmaid*. Those were the words which came to me in the hush of the church. There was another word which came to my mind as Ornella stood with her back to me, exchanging rings: *underhand*. A word for the sleight of hand by which I had been turned into just another guest.

Outside the church, between poses for photographs, Leah came over to me, dodging the crowds, wobbling on tufts of grass, hauling her skirt so that the frills of the hem bunched and hovered like the suction pads of an octopus. We whooped greetings, during which I introduced John; then I took her hand and twisted it towards the sun so that the diamond crackled with light. 'Wow, Leah,' I exclaimed, and admitted, 'Ornella told me: you're going to marry someone.'

'The Euro Bond Trader,' she laughed, 'Or something. I lose track, I think it's Euro Bonds.'

I laughed, 'Must be a relief to know that you'll never want for Euro Bonds.'

She was still laughing, but she mused, 'Well, there comes a time when you have to admit that you're committed.'

Which took my breath away. Because what was I, if not committed? Committed with John to a joint mortgage. As well as a heavy loan for the deposit. Unlike Leah, who, I knew from Ornella, was planning to move into Euro Bond Trader's flat in Chelsea. And unlike Ornella, whose wedding present from her parents had been a ten per cent deposit for their new home.

Escaping to the car park with John, to fetch Davey, I relished the hush. The trees were spilling a breeze. As

John unlocked the car, I paused in the lacy shade of the leaves and looked towards the horizon to see the sunshine raining through clouds. Rare rays of sunshine: until then, it had been a cloudy day. Cool, but humid. A day of open doors and windows despite the lack of sun, despite the tang of low cloud. The banks of grass which bordered the car park were pearled with damp, curled daisies. I left the trees and walked across this grass, feeling its tickle in the hollows of my ankles. And suddenly I thought of Abi: Abi, in the Sudan.

I had gone to Abi's going-away party with Davey, I had *taken* Davey. At Abi's request. She had asked for Ornella, too, but Ornella had said that she was on call and claimed to be unable to swop, told me that she would *Catch up with her later*. I do not know if she did. Davey had not seen Abi for a year or two. Walking beside me through the streets, he seemed nervous: quick, flat smiles; and an occasional inward creep of his lower lip, which pressed his dimples into his cheeks. As we turned the corner into Abi's street, we heard, saw, that music was pouring from her open windows into the darkness.

As soon as we stepped through the doorway, I saw Abi's tatoo: she was wearing a sleeveless vest with two huge scallops for armholes, to bare her shoulderblades. Which were somehow both sharp and smooth. True *blades*. She turned from her friends and hurried to bring me into the room; and as she looped her arm around my neck, I imagined the tiny blue butterfly in flight in her skin, over the bone. She kept her arm around me as she introduced me to her friends. She introduced me as if I was her best friend. Eventually, she spared some attention for Davey, 'Daaaavey.' This long soft wail was followed by the click of a kiss which they exchanged without touching, their cheeks turned like shields; and then they stood back from each other and gazed appreciatively into each other's eyes whilst they picked their way together through the obligatory questions and answers.

Later in the evening, she beckoned me over to her. She was sitting for a moment on a chair by the table, pinching crisps one by one from a pile in a bowl. Her legs were crossed: below the broad pale turn-up of her jeans, her dangling foot had an arch as high and stiff as a palate. I went over to her, leaned back on the table, my hand alternating with hers in the bowl. We talked for a while, and her lover was mentioned. Often when I saw her we were in company and could not mention him. I had lost track of him, I did not even know if he still existed. For her. 'I need a break from him,' she told me. 'If he still wants me when I come back, then okay, I'll think about it.'

And I thought, *But you ARE thinking about it.*

Was she thinking of him now, in the Sudan? Would she marry him, if she could? And like this?

When we returned with Davey to the wedding reception, I saw very little of Ornella. Or I saw a lot of her, but mostly from a distance. At one point, she came over to me, moving carefully in her dress across the dance floor, the dancers giving her a wide berth. I heard the creaks of the stiff material as she approached. Her cheeks were full of hot alcohol-rich blood, and her lips hovered

261

apart, around a vacuum: she was quite breathless. She was hot or drunk or both.

I shouted over the music, 'How are you?'

She said, allowed, 'Oh, okay,' and then admitted, 'Drunk. Hot. Tired.'

So I said, 'You're *supposed* to be drunk, hot and tired.'

And she laughed, before she was interrupted by someone who I did not know, had never seen before.

I had not bought Ornella and Billy a present from the wedding list. She had not allowed me to see the list, had not even owned up to a list, until I brought up the subject and pushed her. I promised her that I was simply curious, pretended that I agreed with her when she explained, 'A list is useful for the people who don't know me, have no idea what to buy me.' She had listed what I considered to be luxury items, finishing touches. How did she have such a complete picture of a finished life? And it was her own vision, not her mother's. She told me that she had gone to the store with a bored Billy and strolled through the departments with pen and paper, noting items. Spending other people's money. People who, by her own admission, did not know her. If I had not seen the list, I would not have known that she was hankering after expensive place mats and silver napkin rings.

I began to wonder whether my parents had had many wedding presents. I knew of a few, but because they were remarkable enough to require explanation: a large tray painted with a view of Venice, a lamp made of a globe, and a chrome coffee percolator which had been fetched from the cupboard-under-the-stairs for rare dinner parties. It struck me that, once upon a time, their home must have been up-to-date, but had never been up-dated. There had been no drive for efficiency in my mother's household, she had had very few gadgets. She had been a housewife, she had had all the time in the world for housework.

Having taken on the mortgage, John and I had very little money and any spare tended to be spent on luxuries. Clothes, usually. Glassware never crossed my mind until I saw Ornella's list, and then I began to wonder, to notice glasses in other households and to look in shops. To wonder if I *did* want proper glasses. And I thought that Ornella was right when she claimed that homemaking was, 'A question of priorities;' but that, currently, with little money and little prospect of improvement, my priorities were for non-priorities.

I had decided to buy a garden for Ornella and Billy. Their new home came with a small patch of overgrown land. I did not tell her my plan. I told her that she would have to wait for her present until she came home from Thailand. That it would not keep. And then, while she was away, I went to a Garden Centre, to look. I had never been to a Garden Centre. I was there for an hour and a half and came away in a taxi with a honeysuckle, a rhododendron, and an apple tree. I went back, a few days later, having decided that I could not do without a rosebush, and then I failed to resist the lavender, for which I chose a warm terracotta pot.

I kept the plants in my hallway. And when I was out and about, I looked into gardens, noticed plants. One day, I saw white foxgloves. I had not seen foxgloves for years, and was certain that I had never seen *white* foxgloves, pure white: I longed to slip my fingertips into those flowers, so much more like real gloves than the florid varieties. Sometimes I quizzed Davey, who would complain, 'Mrs Lake's Question Time'; but usually he had the answers, and seemed surprized by how much he knew from her, how much he had remembered. I went back to the Garden Centre and my eye was caught by angelica. To which I added cornflowers and an oriental poppy. I was beginning to find memories that I did not know that I had: *cornflowers, poppies*. In my hallway, the collection grew. John complained: '*Stop* this.' I added a lemon tree, which, I knew, would have to remain an indoor plant.

Whenever I was in the Garden Centre, I was amazed that people were there for so many purposes other than buying plants. Some of them seemed to come for lunch: inside the main greenhouse, there was a small café; white plastic garden furniture sprouting pastel-coloured, tassled parasols. When I was choosing the lemon tree, I had to stand close to the café, trying not to notice the smell of steak and kidney. What I could not help but notice, as I turned away with the tiny tree, were two hands in the lap of a nearby diner: the bones in the hands were curved like stems. Of course I had seen gnarled hands before but they had always been red and this woman's hands were white. Her *nails* were red: polished and very long, expertly shaped, they were probably false. I had never seen rheumatoid hands so cultivated. I wondered whether she came to the Garden Centre, to the greenhouse, for the warmth.

I took Ornella's lemon tree to the till and immediately saw the hands of the boy in the queue in front of me: they were inflexible too, but utterly differently; they could have been made of no bones at all, they were featureless, huge, thick. He was holding a birthday card which he must have chosen from one of the revolving racks. He was holding the card in both hands and frequently looking down onto, over, the illustration. I could see that his tongue was too large for his mouth. His neck was too short: he had to peep over the collar of his anorak. He seemed delighted by his choice, or perhaps the pleasure was anticipation: taking the card home to write his own message, to seal and hand to someone, perhaps someone who was very important to him. The queue was moving, and moving him towards the girl on the till. She was a similar age to him, late teens. But there the similarity ended: in contrast to him, she was made of movement. Her tongue whirled around gum; her hands clattered over the keys of the till, and slammed the cash drawer.

He was shunted to the head of the queue. He began to hand over the card, slowly: the simultaneous polite glance into her face was a feat of co-ordination for him. But suddenly the card was gone, snatched by her and slipped into a paper bag. Suddenly she was waiting for him to hand over the money. Apparently this was much quicker than he had expected: she had not admired the card, as he seemed to have expected her to do; she had

265

not stopped to smile, to encourage him, to congratulate him. His slow movements fractured under pressure, he jerked the purse from his pocket, jerked the zip of the purse. She waited, but pointedly: exaggeratedly motionless, her slight weight transferred to one hip, and her head, too, inclined. She did not smile, did not slip him a smile to help him on his way. I reminded myself that she had a boring job, told myself that this was only a minor thoughtlessness, but nevertheless I had to try hard not to confront her: *Do you know how difficult this is for him? Do you know how important this is, to him?*

Ornella and Billy had begun to move into their new flat a month or so before the wedding. A month of painting and decorating and plumbers, of arranging for the reconnection of the phone, of waiting for furniture and kitchen appliances to be delivered. The flat was the first floor, top floor, of a large Victorian villa in a tree-lined street close to the centre of the town. A market town, thirty miles from London. A town on a main railway line to London. I had been to see it once before they had signed the contract. It had been home to an elderly lady. The walls were the colour and texture of parchment. The rooms smelled of furnishings and upholstery and the many slow days which had settled onto, into, them. On my first visit, checking a window for a lock, I remarked to Ornella, 'I'm glad that it's not ground floor.'

'You *are* a *worrier*,' she complained.

I smiled. 'Worry makes the world go round.'

266

She was examining a floorboard. 'Spin.'

'What?'

She looked up, and now she was smiling. 'I think you'll find that it makes the world *spin*, which is not quite the same.'

After Ornella and Billy took over the flat, the smell was different, sharp, new: a rich brew of sticky paint and varnish, but, beneath, a burning dust from the holes drilled into walls and the sanding of floorboards. On my second visit, the walls were newly iced, magnolia, a temptation to fingertips. Glistening but dry. The floors were the skins of giant conkers. The old carpet had been ripped up and thrown out: the pile lay in the driveway, a slain dragon.

In the town, Ornella and I had found a teashop with wonderful cheesecake. Our other favourite shop was kitchenware, with cascades of chrome appliances from hooks: high above our heads, the colanders swung and shone like planets. But we had not found much else of interest. Except, perhaps, the health food shop which was staffed by women with blue rinses and plastic pinnies but had a window display of dubious dietary supplements next to cardboard cut-outs of bodybuilders. There was a recently-built redbrick shopping arcade with the usual selection of chain stores, and several pubs whose most important function, judging from the declarations on their chalkboards, was to offer Sunday lunches.

Ornella and Billy had not been back long from Thailand when they discovered a much more serious problem: the distance of their new home from London. This was supposed to have been the advantage: Ornella had told me that she wanted to escape from London, and had given all the usual reasons. But they were having to leave by six-thirty in the morning and they were rarely home before eight in the evening. Ornella told me that she was planning to find a job closer to home. But there were so few jobs. Or there were lots of jobs but so few that she would want to do. Billy was not even halfway through his three-year job in Hampstead, a job that he had wanted very much and did not intend to leave.

Ornella's travelling left less time for talking, so we did not speak to each other in the evenings more than a couple of times each week. But we accounted for the silences: she would tell me that I would not hear from her, the next evening, because *There's clinic so I'll be home later than usual* or *I have to do a late night shop* or even simply *I'm going to go to bed very early to catch up on some sleep*; or I would warn her that I was going out and would be gone before she was home. There was still a rhythm to us, if syncopated.

On the phone, she sounded tired. Not a glamorous tired, not overtired. Her expression for her state was, '*Tired* tired.' Essence of tired. Doubly tired. Tiredness compounded. When she spoke, she was quiet and mono-tonal. Her lungs seemed to lack energy, her voice came stale from somewhere smaller. From the air which was left behind after each breath and came scratching over her voice box. She continued to ring briefly every day from work. To ring in, to check in. Simply so that we could hear each other's voice. The contents of the conversations were unimportant: *Doing anything tonight? Did you see Brookside last night, wasn't it ridiculous? Have you seen that article in the paper today, do you want me to keep it for you? Did you buy that skirt, in the end?* The long-distance equivalent of over-the-fence conversations, to keep us in touch throughout the day, throughout the days.

When she called from home, Billy was in the background. I knew this, because I would ask: *Where's Billy?* And she would reply, *Watching football*, or *Upstairs, reading*. Her replies were cheery, but without elaboration. I had no sense of them together, no idea of what they might do together: the shopping? watching telly? Or of how they would talk. Because whenever I was there, she shopped with me, watched telly with me. Talked with me. Billy was almost always there but she span around him. But she found his presence a reassurance, it seemed to me, rather than an annoyance.

Soon there was something that they began to do together: they began to go to Ornella's home, to visit her parents. They had moved nearer to her parents, they were a mere forty minute drive away. They went on Sundays. Sundays, the minutes so slow that they pool to become the whole day: their Sunday lunches lasted all day. Unlike my parents' home, my mum's home, where Juliet was not awake by lunchtime and Mum lounged around with *The Archers* and the newspapers, liberated from Sunday lunch and relishing slapdash sandwiches.

I had an open invitation from Ornella for the weekends. But her Sundays were already spoken for, and

Saturdays were busy days for both of us, taken up by everything that had not been done during the week; shopping and laundry. She had an open invitation from me for the weekdays, but she always wanted to go home. And I did not blame her. She worked so often overnight, and spent so much time travelling, that she was never in her new home for very long. We had plans to meet but they stayed as plans, stuck in the future, moving forward with the future: *We should go to the Cotswolds for a weekend; We should go shopping in London.* Even phone calls became an inconvenience. If I rang her, she was too busy to talk, she had just arrived home and she was cooking a meal or running a bath; but even if she rang me, she was brief because the bath had to be run, or the meal had to be cooked. During each call we promised that we would talk soon, properly. Which we believed. Which, I suppose, we had to believe.

We believed wrong. Over the weeks, the syncopated rhythm became more syncopated, became less of a rhythm. Often I heard nothing from her for three, four, or five days at a time. Nothing except the words on her new answering machine. Words to which I was happy to add my own, every few days: I liked to reply to her mechanical wheeze, to do as I was told and leave a message for her, slipping it onto the thin black tape for her to unwind later into her home. To let her know that I was thinking of her. I had my own machine but she did not usually reciprocate. Usually I came home to a clutter of messages, but none from her. The counter would have clocked up a square number four and I would wait through three messages until Davey spoke, fourth, and I knew. I knew that there was nothing from her. And whilst Davey spoke, and when he finished and the machine began to lay a new trap for tomorrow's voices, I wondered what Ornella was doing. What she was doing instead of ringing me. Was she working late? Was she unwell? Was she with her parents, perhaps, for a day or two?

I kept whole conversations on the tip of my tongue, for her; I put whole evenings on hold for her unmade calls. I began to realize how unsettled I am by anything which is unmade. An unmade bed. Unmade promises. An unmade call would distract me the next day like an unfinished dream.

She took a job in a Casualty department, which she regarded as a step backwards, or several steps backwards, an emergency measure, drastic and temporary. She hated the work. In one of her rare calls, she complained, 'Suicide attempts, endless suicide attempts.'

I was taken aback.

'Always the same people,' she was whining, 'and no one knows what to do with them.' Then she laughed, momentarily, humourlessly, a mere exclamation: 'Or *I* know what we should do with them, but I have to remember my Hypocritical oath.'

I replied with a sniff of laughter, but only because I did not know what to say. My real response was a mix, a mess, a deep unease. Because, for a moment, I did not know her, she did not know herself.

As weeks passed into months, I wondered why Ornella

would not simply ring more often to leave messages: why not call quickly sometimes to say that she could not call later? This was all that I needed. A passing touch, tape to tape. Even before our answering machines, our calls had rarely been more than this. So why, suddenly, so much silence? Why the cold shoulder? But whenever we did speak, there was no answer to my question. She would not hear the question, built tentatively of hints, *Haven't-heard-from-you-for-days*. She blasted these hints with fierce sighs. And she gave the same answer to my one question that I did dare to ask, *So-what-have-you-been-up-to?*

'Nothing.' And suddenly it had become not defensive, but accusatory.

But then she called me one morning, said, 'Hi, it's me,' in a voice rusty with tears.

The world slowed and my heart quickened. 'What's happened?' I asked.

'I should never have married Billy,' she said.

All of a sudden? All of a sudden, she had decided that she should not have married Billy? Had he done something? I realized that she had whispered, but I could hear no other sound so I was fairly sure that she was not calling from the hospital. Was she calling from home? Was he there? I checked: 'Is he there?' *With you.*

'No,' she said, surprised, loud. 'He's gone to work.'

'Are you home?'

'I've taken the day off,' she admitted, sniffed. 'Told them I have flu.' The implication was, *Told them a lie.*

This was an inconvenient time for me to have a proper

272

conversation, because I had a friend with me. Hearing the snap of my bathroom door, I shifted to allow Fleur to pass me on her way back down the hallway. She had arrived a few minutes earlier to leave her baby, Poppy, with me while she went to the dole office to sign on: a regular arrangement of ours. As soon as she had arrived, she had gone to the bathroom with Poppy and a big bag of toiletries. Since the baby had been born, I had not seen Fleur free from this blue vinyl bag. Inside the bag nestled a colony of disposable nappies, shiny thin white shells full of soft folds and puckers. As she passed me on her way back from the bathroom, I smelled the toiletries, milky and sweet. I re-focused my attention onto the phone. I did not know what Ornella was trying to tell me: was she going to tell me of rows, sinister secrets, affairs? Gently, I asked her, 'What do you mean, you should never have married him?'

'I *mean*,' she emphasized, but her voice wobbled, 'it's *all wrong*.'

'Since when?'

'Does it matter *when*?' Anger steamed in her sigh. 'What is this, a fucking *interview*? I'm trying to tell you a *fact*: my marriage is a *mistake*.' Then she relented, perhaps by way of an apology, and replied, 'Since the day we came back from Thailand.' Then she revised, 'No, it's *always* been wrong, I should *never* have married him. There's only one person I've ever loved.'

Framed in the open doorway, Fleur was lowering Poppy onto the living room floor, settling her down. Carefully, I reminded Ornella, 'You told me that you

273

loved Billy.' And I had tried to believe her. To trust her.

'I *had to* say that I loved him,' she whined, 'Because I was going to marry him.'

Oh come on, 'You could have *told me*.' I saw that Fleur had stepped away from Poppy, turned away and dipped down into the big bag. Poppy looked up and around the room, her head turning rather too much. Rather too much for a human, more like an owl. Her mouth was a bobble, full of surprise, to match her eyes.

Years before, when I had told Ornella that I was going to leave Pete, she had said *Nothing's perfect,* implying that I was unreasonable. She had said, *As long as you know what you're doing,* to imply the contrary. But beneath those smooth words I had heard the vibration of fear. She had been afraid of change. And I had been infuriated with her. Was I behaving in the same manner, now, to her?

She said, 'I couldn't tell you because I didn't know. I was telling *myself* that I was in love with him.'

'Because you wanted to marry him.' This was about marriage. Not about love. Why had she not been honest and told me simply that she wanted to marry him? Then I could have reasoned with her. But she had cited love, which is indisputable; love is not a decision.

'Yes,' she said, sniffed. 'I did. I did want to marry him.'

I watched Fleur fold her arms and turn aimless in the space between the bag and the baby. She had ten minutes before she was due to leave. I waved, flagged down her attention, then mimed drinking and pointed to the kitchen: *Make yourself some coffee.* She smiled her thanks.

Ornella said, 'And now I don't want to be married to him.'

'Why not?' I had switched to a coaxing tone.

'I can't explain, *but*,' she sighed, *but I'll try*, 'I feel as if my life has come to an end, that there's nothing more to happen, that nothing will ever change.'

I could not stop myself from protesting, 'That's ridiculous.'

But she continued, wearily, 'I go to work, and then I come home, and then I go to work again.'

I flashed with anger for her: *But you knew this, surely you should have known this, should have anticipated this, should have taken better care of yourself.* But inside this infuriation, a hard pip of fear. Because of course I understood.

She tried to explain, 'Billy is part of this going-to-work and coming-home-again.' And before I could speak, she finished, 'What else *is* there?'

Don't ask me: not me, who works for myself; not me, who is unmarried. Not me, who took care to avoid a normal career and home life. How could she have failed to come up with whatever people find to keep themselves alive in normal lives, and yet gone ahead regardless? Did she expect me, now, to find the answer for her?

But then she explained: 'I thought everything would be okay; I thought it would just happen; that, in the end, I'd just find that I was happy.'

Blind faith, which never fails to dazzle me. Momentarily inspired, I told her, 'Well, perhaps you *will* be happy, in the end.'

'No,' she said, very definitely. Then her voice frayed as she complained, 'Although everyone else seems to manage.'

My heart leapt for her. 'Oh, *Nella*.'

'I married for security.'

'I know.' But why did she feel that she needed security? She had *had* security, had *always* had security.

'Security's not quite the right word,' she fretted.

'I know.' *I know what it was, I know why you married.*

She admitted, 'Yes, I knew you knew.'

And I was left with nothing to say. The silence said, boomed, *I told you so.* Which was untrue. I had *not* told her. I had said nothing. I had watched my words, and in doing so I had failed her.

Her splintery voice came again, 'This is driving me mad because I *do* love him, in a way; and every moment that I stay with him, I'm hurting him.' And then she pleaded, 'I *don't* want to hurt him, Niquie.'

Loves him, loves him not. 'Is that what he says? That you're hurting him?'

Her words came softer, 'Oh, he says nothing, he knows nothing.'

Was this true? I felt for him, poor Billy. Poor, shadowy, faraway Billy. At this moment, Fleur stepped into the kitchen doorway, holding aloft a jug of fresh coffee, and raised her eyebrows into question marks, *You want some?*

Distracted, I replied aloud, involuntarily, 'No thanks.'

Ornella asked, 'Who's there?'

Ridiculously, I felt caught out, tripped up. 'Just my friend Fleur. And her baby.'

'Oh.' She blew her nose, and I realized that this was a decisive end to her tears. 'I'll speak to you later.'

I hurried, 'No, honestly, it's fine to talk now. Fleur's fine.'

Turning away, Fleur tipped a thumb in confirmation.

Intrigue bubbled through Ornella's sniffles: 'Did she ever go back to the father of that baby?'

'No,' I replied, watchful of the vacant doorway. I tried to explain, 'He wasn't.'

'Wasn't what?' Ornella piped, infuriatingly.

'What you said.' *The father of the baby.*

She caught on, but doubtfully: 'The father of the baby wasn't the father of the baby?'

Watching for shadows around the doorway, I confirmed, 'You're right.'

And then she understood. 'Oh, I *see*, someone *else* was the father of the baby,' and wanted to know, 'was he the one who came to your flat, once, when I was there?'

'No, that was . . .' *the other one, but this is impossible so,* '. . . shall I ring you back in half an hour, when I've settled Poppy?'

'No,' she said, her tone flat again, 'because I've decided to go shopping for the day. I'll call you tonight.'

'No you won't,' I had to remind her. 'Because I'm off to France this afternoon.' Three days in Paris and then a week in the South West.

And she remembered with a nasal yelp from inside her tissue: 'Oh, God, yes, *France*. You *do* have a life, don't you.'

In the end, I insisted upon giving her the telephone number of my hotel in Paris. And I made her promise: 'Will you ring, if you're in a state? *Will* you?'

'*Oh* yes,' she said, sniffing a laugh, implying that I would have no rest from her.

But I did not hear from her. Whenever I approached my hotel, I wondered if there was a message waiting for me. Walking into the lobby, to the reception desk to fetch the key to our room, my hands sticky from pastries, I smiled into the eyes of whoever was on duty, hoping to jog his or her memory: *the phone message*. But in response their eyes narrowed with suspicion. Upstairs, in our room, in the late afternoons and early evenings, as I lay on the bed listening to John in the shower, I was conscious of the deep sleep of the phone by my head; and when we swopped and I went into the shower, I listened for the bleating ring through the clatter of the water and the murmur of the television. On the occasions when we were in the shower together, I had to listen harder.

When we left our room to return to the streets, I carried the silence with me and turned it over and over in my mind: was Ornella feeling better, or merely not feeling worse?

On the first evening I had told John over the table, 'Ornella rang me this morning and she was in a bad way, saying that she should never have married Billy.' And he had replied through a mouthful of bread, 'Oh God.' Nothing else. *Oh God* and a frown down onto the menu; *Oh God* and, 'Do we need a mixed salad with this?' So I learned to keep my wonderings to myself. On the fourth day, we took the TGV to the South.

For the next week, we stayed in a converted barn in the grounds of a farm. The landscape, an alluvial plain, was densely cultivated, with fields the colour of sand which, in the distance, seemed to have been neatly raked by fingers. The only extravagance was the irrigation, silvery arcs of water stroked by a regular pulse. Arcing over their own individual rainbows. Whenever I closed my eyes, I lost track and could not tell if I was listening to the pulse of the water in the air above the fields or the tapping of the farmer's dog's paws on the hot flagstones of the yard. Nothing much moved in the landscape except the water. And the bees, dropping into flowers to baste themselves in nectar. John and I did very little; rarely spoke, even, but lay side-by-side in the sunshine, reading books. There was one day of drizzle, but still John and I did not speak much: we continued with our books, indoors, looking up sometimes to watch the weather system drain away into the horizon. For a week, I gave up my own life to live the lives that ran through my books; my books took me over, lived life for me, let me rest and recover. Like tiny life-support systems.

All the evenings were spectacular, the horizon filling with colour, the colour of the juice of blood oranges. We ate in the yard, distracted by the distant flashes of a white horse's tail catching the low sun. When darkness came, the sky was dusty with stars and smeared with the Milky Way. Unbleached by the burn of a city. I marvelled that the stars were so uniform in size. I wondered how people had ever known that they were so far away and not simply just out of reach. Tidying away our supper, I would hear the whines of occasional trucks on the main road down by the river. Then, slipping into bed, I would glance up into the small, deep window at the huge spider in its dense web – a strange, spiny fruit wrapped in muslin – and relish the relief that we were safely on the other side of the glass. I had not seen a spider so huge since those which had loomed from ceilings when I was a child, when Dad had rarely been there to save us and Mum had had to call the neighbours.

When I came home, I was full of a warm feeling: the certainty that Ornella and I had begun to talk again, that *she* had begun to talk again. This was similar to the tipsy bathtime warmth that I knew from childhood on the rare occasions when I had told Mum a worry and she had shown me that the dark, dense world into which I had sunk was nothing but a trick of the light. Which was odd because it was Ornella who had come to me. I had gone to no one with my problem. I had no problem. It was Ornella who had the problem.

I had been back home for a few hours when I rang her. John had said, 'I must have a pint of bitter,' and gone to the pub. I spent an hour or so on my own recovering from travel sickness. Then I sat on the floor in the hallway with the phone, and dialled Ornella's number. It was Sunday evening and in the kitchen the washing machine was grumbling over my delayed Saturday wash. 'Nella,' I called over the noise, when she answered.

'Oh, hiya,' she said.

'How are you?' I crooned, full of enthusiasm. The washing machine began its spin cycle, whinnying.

'Oh, okay. How are you? Did you have a nice time?'

'Yes, very, thanks.'

'Good. Can I call you later? We haven't eaten, yet.'

'Yes, fine. But,' I checked, 'you're okay?'

'Oh yes,' she confirmed, wearily, 'I'm okay.'

She did not return my call for five days. And then, when she did call, she gave no explanation or apology for the delay. I waited for one, my heart thumped a slow drum roll, but eventually rolled over, gave up, settled down. I listened to her tale of a row which she had had with one of the Sisters on one of the Geriatric wards. She was calling from work, so she could not speak to me for long. When she had finished her story, she asked, 'How was France?'

'Oh, fine.'

This seemed to suffice, because she switched to the topic of Guido's forthcoming holiday in Antigua.

Of everything that she did to me over the following year, this phone call seemed the worst because it was the first sign of her neglect and I was so unprepared. She had not chosen me to be her bridesmaid, but I had been able to explain away her decision. And, anyway, bridesmaidery was not important to me. But I could not explain why she did not want to talk to me. Talk was all that we had ever done. It struck me that whenever I came home from a holiday, I went to her. Until I had talked to her, I was never properly home. She was my source of farewells and homecomings; she was home, to me.

During those days of silence from her, those five cold days, I had begun to lose heart. To realize that we did not seem to feel the same about each other. I had been thinking of her, while I was in France, but she had not been thinking of me. When I returned, her failure to call me broke an unspoken rule. No, not a rule, we had never had rules. We had never needed rules. But she broke *something*. Faith, I suppose.

Over the following weeks, she made no effort to repair this. Whenever I rang her, she would say, 'Look, can I call you tomorrow?'

I could not say no. Not if I wanted to talk to her. I began to dread and loathe this line of hers: the *Look* meaning *Listen*, so very abrupt; and the *tomorrow*, which was a lie. She put me in my place. Which was usually the middle of the following week. Perhaps if she had not called back, I could have given up on her, but the calls came. Often oddly timed, often early in the morning. And occasionally oddly pitched: 'Hi,' she would whisper, suspiciously dolorous. So that I could ask, 'What's up?' To which she gave one of two responses: *Nothing*, or *I'm fucking fed up*, the first to shut me out, the second to shut me up. But I would struggle on: 'Fed up with what?'

'Life.'

Occasionally, I dared to ask how she was feeling about

Billy. And she would say, 'The same.' And then, usually, 'Look, can I call you tomorrow?' I began to suggest that we meet, but she said, 'Look, not next week, maybe the week after next, ask me again next week.' Sometimes I had a simple story to tell her or a small favour to ask, which was delayed by days and days, and when I did manage to tell her or ask her, she would want to know, *Why didn't you say?* Which left me speechless. Did she really not see what had happened to us, what was happening to us? Sometimes I tried to tell her, but her response was always the same: to slot me down into the rest of her resented life by snapping that she was tired and had no time for anything any more. *Anything* included me, presumably. But finally, suddenly, on one occasion she stopped snapping back and said mildly, 'Okay, I'll tell you what: why don't we leave our calls until the weekends?' At last I had had a response. And suddenly we had a rule: weekends.

Then John noticed. Or mentioned that he had noticed. We were in the living room, one evening: he was in the armchair and I was sitting on the floor in front of him. He was finishing a yoghurt: over my head, his teaspoon was clocking the slippery walls of the empty carton. He was watching *The News*. Or perhaps, like me, he was looking above and beyond the telly and through the window into the evening sky. A sediment of deep pink, then a thin layer of green, then the blue. A dark blue, minutes away from blackness. The colours were so strong that they seemed both natural and false, like chemicals in a test tube. I had never seen such a sky in this country, this country of moderation-in-all-things including skies, especially skies.

Of course John and I had remarked upon it; but then it had been said, and there had been nothing more to say. So I did not know if he was watching with me. In a few minutes, this sky would be over; quick, like a chemical reaction. I knew that this change was happening, and rapidly, but I could not see how. I was trying hard, perhaps too hard, holding the whole sky in my eyes. Somewhere beyond me, I could hear *The News*, some verbal strutting on the satellite link: *If you look at the figures, I think you'll find ... Yes, but would you not agree ...*

John said, 'What's up with Ornella?'

Involuntarily, I stiffened. His hand came gently onto the top of my head and I thought, *Don't touch me*. No, nothing so conscious as a thought: it was my body, not my mind, that came out with, *Don't touch me*. Because I had been thinking of Ornella. Unconsciously. Thoughts of her had been ticking away, behind, beneath, inside my other thoughts. All around my sky. Had John read my mind? I did not want him to read my mind. There had been a time when I would have loved him to, but not now. Looking down onto the newspaper which was spread across the floor around me, I said, 'What do you mean?'

His hand twitched: a half-hearted, half-handed ruffle of my hair. 'Well,' he ventured, sounding nervous, 'she hasn't been ringing.'

I half-wanted to talk to him. Half of me pulled hard

on my silence. But I knew why I wanted to talk: I wanted reassurances. And I doubted that there were any to be had. And if I talked, he would listen, he would respond, he might complain about her, and I could not risk this, I did not want him to voice my thoughts, I did not want to have to hear them.

I had assumed that he would not notice Ornella's absence, but I had been stupid. Of course he would have noticed: no messages from her on the answerphone; no coming across her when he picked up the ringing phone. Until now, I did not know that I had been trying to hide. Or *what* I had been trying to hide. And now I knew that what I had been trying to hide was humiliation.

I said, 'She's preoccupied, at the moment.' And added, sharply, 'I *told* you.' Meaning, *In Paris*. Meaning, *I told you everything in Paris*. Which was untrue but I knew that he would not remember. I turned a page of the newspaper, to show him that I was not intending to speculate, that I was intending to read. But I was unlucky enough to land on Home News. I busied myself trying to find an article to read. Water quality. Domestic violence.

I was wondering whether he really liked her. Perhaps he did not quite *like* her, but was drawn to her. Whenever he had picked up the phone to her, he had remained bent around her voice until I had come into the hallway and taken the receiver from him. And if ever I asked him, later, what she had been saying to him, he would seem puzzled and say *Nothing*. But whenever I found him speaking to her, he shone; and I was fleetingly jealous, although I was never sure of whom. Sometimes he had complained to me about her, but affectionately: he said that he did not know *how to take her*. And I had been puzzled: because what was there to take? She had been second nature to me. But now I was beginning to think that he had had a point. He said nothing more, but stayed sitting behind me, above me, watching *The News* over my head, and suddenly I despised him for this. I looked up from the newspaper and saw that the sky was dark.

It had been Ornella's idea that we should keep our calls for the weekends, but she rarely rang. Perhaps every third weekend. As yet another silent Sunday came to a close, I would wonder if I should call her. Again. I did not want to call her if she did not want me to call her. Or not too often. Something which had been second nature to me had become very conscious, very complicated. Artificial or impossible, even, like a conscious effort to breathe.

Of course I asked questions: *Are you in a mood with me? Have I done something wrong?* Very gently, because I did not want to annoy her. Whenever I asked, she denied that there was a problem. My questions were genuine, not complaints: I wanted an answer, not an argument. I wanted everything to be fine again. But I was becoming afraid of her. Once she wrote to me and I fished her handwritten envelope from the others on the doormat and went into the bathroom with it because I wanted to face it without having to face John. I did not know why I could not face John, I simply knew that I had to get away from him while I read the letter. Inside the envelope was a card of pressed forget-me-nots, in which she had written: *Hello Sweetsie, Dashed up here to Grasmere to spend a weekend with my bro and Hayley before they go off to H. Kong, lucky bastards. Their friends have a cottage here. (Lucky bastards). Good tea shops, bad weather. Thinking of you. Lots of love, Nella. Billy says Hi.* And along the bottom of the card, in different handwriting, was, *Hi V. Love Leah and Hubby!*

I began to feel that John was watching me. I did not mention Ornella to him. Hoping to hide the gaps, I said less, overall, to him. And I wondered about Billy: surely he had noticed? Surely even Billy would have noticed by now that, over the last six months or so, Ornella had slipped from ringing me every evening to ringing me once a month? What did he know, what was his role, where were his sympathies? On the rare occasions when he answered the phone to me, he gave nothing away: *Oh, hi, Veronica, you okay? Good. Yes, fine. Hang on and I'll go and find her for you.*

So, one time, after the obligatory pleasantries, I asked him, 'Is Ornella okay?' Much more than a polite enquiry. Heavily question-marked.

He did not say, *What do you mean?* He said, 'Ye-es,' *on balance.* 'Tired. You know. She's *busy*, Veronica.'

Busy, Veronica: this said it all; this was a ticking off. They were in this together.

It was then that I decided to confront her. I considered writing to her but did not want to wait for a reply, to risk that she would not reply at all. I would have preferred to meet with her, but she continued to be evasive. I knew that I would have to do this by phone. I decided to wait for an occasion when Billy was not home with her, and when I was also alone. And because our conversations were so few and far between, I knew that I would have to wait for a couple weeks.

In the meantime, I spoke about her to Davey. We had arranged to meet in a sandwich bar in Covent Garden, from where he was going to go on to a lunchtime play. In advance, I had declined his offer to accompany him to the play; decided that I should go on to the library to do some work, because I had not been working well. When I arrived at the sandwich bar, he was already there, sitting inside at a small circular marble-topped table, reading *Libération*. He did not see me in the doorway. He looked so grown up: this was exactly what came to my mind, *grown up*. Strong, perhaps. Very different from how I was feeling. As I came through the doorway, I saw a woman on another table look at him, look for slightly too long. I leaned over his table and flicked his newspaper. 'Since when do you speak French?' I demanded, choosing not to apologize for being five minutes late, not to whine about the traffic.

'*Read* French,' he corrected, smiling upwards. 'And I have to start somewhere.'

'With *Libération*? It's full of Parisian slang.' Someone had told me about the Parisian slang. 'Make it easy for yourself, Davey: rediscover Monsieur Lafayette,' our reading scheme in school. Sitting down, I pronounced knowingly, 'Il est ingénieur.'

He laughed, 'And busy working on the Channel

Tunnel, now, no doubt.' Folding away the newspaper, he backtracked to greet me, 'Hello, Chickenfeed.'

'*Chickenfeed*? You're losing your English.'

'Good,' he took one of my hands from the cold table-top, 'I could do with losing a little,' and he turned over my hand so that it was open. Absently, his eyes nowhere in particular, he laid a kiss on my palm.

Which felt more intimate than anyone had been with me for a long time. Gently, I began to slide my hand back to me, but then changed my mind and left it half way across the table between us. I asked him, 'Are you having another coffee?'

'Yes,' he replied, cheerfully, '*and* a doughnut.'

Having fetched coffees and a doughnut, we chatted for a while: gossip and plans; the reviews of the play to which I was not going; even the traffic had a mention, because Davey had the explanation, *Security alert*. All this time, I was waiting for an appropriate moment to mention Ornella. Half of me was waiting, the half of me that was not chatting. The wait was hurting me. I was trying to judge an appropriate moment, but my stomach had turned into an egg-timer, was becoming heavy with the slowness. Eventually, I asked, 'Have you heard any-thing from Ornella?'

He put down his coffee cup and switched his grey eyes onto mine. 'I never hear from Ornella, unless through you,' *which you know very well, so why do you ask*?

'Well, I'm not hearing from her very much, nowadays, all of a sudden.' I exhaled a breath which I did not know I had been holding: *There, said*.

He did not move. 'Why not?'

'She rings me perhaps once a month.'

His eyes widened. 'How long has this been going on?'

'Six months,' said with an upwards inflection: not quite queried, but an estimate.

He blinked his eyes away from me for a second, then demanded, almost wailed, 'Why didn't you say?'

I shrugged; now I was unable to say anything at all. He put a hand over mine. I looked away and saw the woman on the other table, I saw her eyes on us and in them I saw her conclusion: *Love troubles*. I looked away from her, back to him. 'I don't know why I didn't say,' I answered, although I did know, by now I knew most of what there was to know about silence. But I knew, too, now, that I *should have* said. And I burned with this realization, with optimism.

'*Why* isn't she speaking to you?' he urged.

'I don't know.'

He took away his hand, leaned back in his chair, frowned, 'Depressed?' He meant her.

'I don't know.' Then I revised, '*Yes*, but . . .'

'But she'd be more likely to call you,' he confirmed, '*more* often, if she was depressed.'

'Yes. *Unless*.'

He came forward in his chair, checked with me, 'Unless she's *very* depressed?'

I shrugged this off. 'I don't know.'

'So, what do you think?' *Is she very depressed?*

'I don't know.' I poked my teaspoon into the bowlful of sugar. Again and again. Crunch, crunch.

'What does Billy say?'

'Nothing.' I looked up, drawn to his eyes. Our eyes yanked on either end of an invisible thread, a single notion.

'*Billy*,' he voiced our shared despair.

'I know.'

Not much more was said; there was not much more to say. In the end, he came up with nothing better than, 'Give her time.'

Beating the sugar smooth with the back of my spoon, I smiled sourly and assured him, 'I'm giving, I'm giving.'

Later, I went, as planned, to the British Library. But in the lobby of the British Museum, approaching the door to the Reading Room with my pass ready in my hand, I could not face work and veered instead into the Library's exhibition galleries. I had never been into the galleries. I walked into a hall which contained horizontal display cases, their thin frames of dark wood punctured regularly by tiny keyholes. Leaning over the shiny glass and peering down through my own faint reflection, I saw the huge old books. How had the curators chosen where to open these books? Were the closed pages equally elaborate? These books were from the Dark Ages, but they were illuminated in vivid colours. Pigments which, in patches, had burned away the paper. Toxic, too, I knew. Verdigris. Vermillion. I wondered whether the scribes had died from recording their stories.

I went from case to case, and came upon a pale illustration of a man with zodiacal signs around his body, Aries' ram on his head, Leo's lion leaping to his chest, his feet on two fish. Beside the book, a note typed on white card said that this was a medical manuscript from the fifteenth century: the body mirrored the stars, the universe; surgeons would prefer to wait for favourable stars before attempting a particular procedure, *such as bleeding*. I turned away from the case, struck by this notion of bodily excess and therapeutic reduction; the contrast with modern medicine, made of supplements, the channelling of chemicals into the body. I left the gallery, went into the shop, browsed and bought a pamphlet on astrology, before returning to the gallery to read. My booklet began with the construction of the calendar: we cannot use the day as the basic unit of time, not from sunrise to sunrise, because the sun rises at different times throughout the year, nor from midday to midday, because the sun travels through the sky at different speeds throughout the year. I read that the first calendars were lunar, from new moon to new moon, but the moon moves differently from the sun: when England switched from the Julian to the Gregorian calendar in 1752, the error was eleven days, midsummer day fell on 11 June. We had to lose eleven days. But we remain in error by 26 seconds per year. I looked up from the booklet, took a deep, steadying breath: I had had no idea that this was so complicated, I had known nothing of this, had never given the calendar a moment's thought: to me, until now, a day had been a day, and a night, a night.

I watched someone going into the Manuscripts Library, flourishing a special pass. And for a moment, I yearned to have done History. Like John, working in the War Museum? I was shocked to realize that I had not once thought of John whilst I had been in here. But he was Modern History. Twentieth Century. His job was in Exhibitions: collections of objects, and stories told on glossy vinyl boards. No, I wanted to have spent years *in here*, with these manuscripts, I wanted to touch and turn their pages, to study them instead of the real world. No, *this was* the real world. *The Babylonians spent many centuries watching the sky until they were able to make a calendar, to project the movements of the stars*: I looked up from the book, over the room, and realized that these preoccupations – our place, permanence – had existed *for ever*. It was *my* world that was the unreal one, the one that had been made up on the spur of the moment. On my way home, on the bus, I read more of my little book, and learned about astrology. I read that everything had changed when people discovered that the sun did not move around the earth, that the stars did not move in perfect circles around us; that we were not the centre of the universe, our bodies were not tiny replicas of the universe. So, we could learn nothing from the stars, they showed us nothing about ourselves.

I began to learn to live without Ornella. Life continued to happen to me: I had my purse stolen, had to cancel and replace my cards, even my library cards; my favourite tutor from university died and I went to his funeral; John and I decided to move home because I could afford to buy somewhere bigger, and we began to look around. Ornella knew none of this. I told other friends, but they were not her, and I realized how much I missed her. I could not talk to other friends about how much I missed her, because they rarely or barely knew her: only Abi, Bev, and Davey knew her and would know how bad this was for me. Abi was a long way away; I no longer ever saw Bev; and Davey already knew. Occasionally, he would ask, *Any better, with Ornella?* I would wait for him to bring up the subject, I had used up my chance in the sandwich bar: I did not want to mention her again unless there was something new to say. Whenever he asked, I would have to tell him, *The same.*

When I eventually confronted her, I said, 'You never ring me any more; you used to ring me every day and now it's only once a month.' If she had been my lover, I could have asked, *Do you still love me?* But she was not my lover.

She said, 'Look, I don't ring because there's nothing to say. Nothing ever happens to me, I do nothing, I have nothing to say.'

But I have.

And she *did* have something to say, the day she had rung and cried and told me that she should never have married Billy. Plenty to say. And then nothing more. What was happening to her? So I started, 'But you *did* have something to say, the day you told me about Billy –'

'And you've heard it,' she interrupted, 'so what's the point in saying it again? Nothing has changed. I've made my bed and I have to live in it. Okay?' Not a nice *okay*. Not a reassurance, but a threat; not a chuck of a chin, but a twist of an arm, a tweak of an earlobe.

And I wanted to say, *No, it's not okay. Talk to me. I don't care what you do or don't say. Just keep talking to me.*

But I did not. And she did not.

A few days later, she did ring me. It was late at night and I was in bed when I heard her speaking to the answerphone. I could not remember having heard, was not conscious of having heard the ring of the phone. Only her voice, in the hallway, which for a moment I mistook for a dream. I could not hear the words, but I knew her voice. I left my bed, left John asleep and ran towards the hallway to catch her before she had had time to leave her message. But as I ran into the hallway, I realized that she was not leaving a message. She was crying, and calling, 'Niquie ...? Niquie ...? Niquie ...?' My name was followed each time by a deep inward breath rippling with shudders. I swooped on the receiver in the darkness and managed to announce myself, 'Yes.'

And she exhaled hugely with, 'Thank God you're there, thank God you're there.'

'Of course I'm here.' And I urged, 'What *is it*?' I had been swirled by my rush, my heart was bumping around the bones of my chest: naked and cold in the dark hallway, I was all heart.

'I do love you, you know,' she said.

'Are you alone?' I was worried.

Her laugh splashed into her tears, and she said, 'Except for you.'

Still laughing and crying, she said, 'I've been so awful, lately; and I don't know why, I don't know what's been the matter with me.'

I soothed, 'It doesn't matter, it doesn't matter.' There was nothing else that I could have said, but, of course, it did not matter, then, suddenly, in the hallway, in darkness.

I said that I wanted to see her.

And she said, 'Look, not this week, but how about next Tuesday?'

We arranged to meet on her way home from work, in the coffee shop in the station. 'The station?' I complained, feeling cheated.

'Think about it,' she insisted: 'Gives us more time.'

But I decided that this would not do: 'Why? What's the hurry?'

'Oh, nothing, except that I should go along to choir practice later.'

And I was amazed: 'You don't sing.'

She laughed. 'You-don't-*say*. I *do* sing. Nowadays. Sort of. Starting to. You should hear me.'

She was late, slightly. I had had one coffee, and was wondering whether to order another or to wait. For her. I watched the man making the cappuccini. Not Italian, but Spanish: I knew this from his conversations with the various women who appeared behind the counter with brooms and cloths from time to time; women who were Spanish too, probably relatives. I had been buying coffee from him for years on my way through this station. I liked him. Whenever I came to his counter, he seemed to recognize me; but no, this was ridiculous, because I passed through this station no more often than once every few months. And he served hundreds of people every day. He managed to look delighted whenever anyone ordered. There must have been a trick to this. Or perhaps the job was not so bad: but for him to look so pleased, this would have had to occur to him every minute of every day. Impossible, surely? I wanted to interview him.

I listened to some of the words of two women on the table behind me.

'What did you buy?'

'Pillowcases.'

'You're *always* buying pillowcases.'

'I'm *not*. And, *anyway*, what's wrong with *that*?'

I wanted to turn around, to see them, but the space between us was too small, I would loom, too obvious. Not wishing to catch the eye of the coffee man, to have to make my decision about the next coffee, I turned my gaze to the woman at the table in front of me. Middle-aged, she was wearing a single long loop of black beads – small, shiny, square beads – which reminded me of childhood, of Mum's discarded jewellery, of my dressing up. She was alone, and the chair next to her was occupied by several plastic bags. Glossy plastic: department store rather than supermarket. She had been on a day out, a trip to town; a rare trip, perhaps. Her skirt and blouse were not new, yet stiff, seldom worn.

She was nervous about missing her train, she had been checking her watch more often than necessary. I watched her stir a half-teaspoonful of multi-coloured sugar crystals into her coffee and frown down into the cup, perhaps watching for a rainbow to rise in the froth. Hoping. Then she looked at me, so I looked away. I had sensed her watching me earlier. Neither of us had much to look at, nearby, except each other. What did she see, when she looked at me? No beads. No skirt, but jeans. So, I was unlike the workers who were walking purposefully through the station in their suits. No purpose; but no bags, either, so I was not a day-tripper. No children. How old did I look? I was not young, not old. Nor middle-aged. So what was I? I looked out of the coffee shop onto the opposite wall, to the poster, to the model on the poster: was she younger than me? I knew that models were supposed to be younger than me, but she looked so grown up, so much more grown up than I looked.

Was the theory true, that men want girls of seventeen, eighteen, nineteen, twenty? Unfortunate, because girls of seventeen, twenty, tend not to want men, they want boys. Men seem too solid, somehow. I had wanted boys, had gone for hands that were pliable enough to rope to my own with my fingers. I had wanted the veins to be fluid beneath the skin, not knotted. I had wanted, I had had, bodies that were gangly, unpredictable: bodies not yet cut down to size by life.

I had been to the local swimming pool, the day before – my first swim for many years, for something to do –

and become captivated by a boy who was no older than sixteen. He was sitting alone on a bench on the poolside with a towel around his shoulders. He had done too much, his eyes were unfocused and he did not stop shivering. The blood had run so low in his skin that his other colours ran high: the blue sheen of his wet hair, the blurred blue of his eyes. I wondered whether he would notice me. Whether I could market myself as an older woman. No, because I had never been able to market myself, and I was not yet an older woman. It was only now, in the station, that I was struck that I had not wanted *him*, I had wanted *his youth*. I had forgotten – I yearned to know again – how it felt to have a skin which was both so firm and so soft.

And now three teenage girls came to the coffee counter; I could hear that they wanted matches, not coffee. Sixteen or seventeen years old, loopy limbs, their faces unset, they were turned inwards around a serious discussion of a friend's PVC trousers. How many years since I thought about PVC trousers? These days I thought of mortgages. If they turned, now, and saw me, what would they see? But they would *not* see me, they would see no one in particular. How could I have become nothing, no one, without noticing? Was I living in a different world? But which world? There is only one world.

Then I saw Ornella coming across the concourse, through the crowds. Looking like a twelve-year-old. Or perhaps not twelve, but young, youthful: what I saw of her, first, was her wide smile – because she had seen me – and the flopping of her loafers on the tiles as she jogged towards me. Then I noticed the inky linen jacket and shorts: I had never seen this beautiful suit before; but, then, I rarely recognized her clothes, they were so often new. Coming towards me, she was no longer the tight, wire-thin voice that I had learned to dread. Anything but. And watching her, the word that came to my mind was *tomboy*. Which was new: she was not, had never been, boyish; she was all girl. How, why, *all girl?* Because she tended to look into people's faces in that manner which is unique to girls: she looked hard, to find motives. But not now, when she was running.

As she came closer, I saw that she had had her hair cut: almost pudding basin, but shaped around her ears. Closer still, I saw a big pearl bobbing on each earlobe. *Those* pearls? Her mother's pearls, worn years ago when she tried to seduce Guido's French pen-friend? Perhaps, perhaps not: I remembered that her mother's pearls were bigger; but, then, we were smaller in those days, and everything was bigger. These pearls were a cream risen from the colours of her face, lipstick lips and dark eyes; they were globules of a dispersed halo. Reaching me, she laughed, an appreciative laugh, sounding like a response to a joke that I had not made; and her hand came onto my shoulder, partly to return me to my chair, partly to steady us both as she leaned to kiss my cheek. She laughed, 'Good to see you, you old tart,' and I laughed, too, seeing the sudden stiffening of the beaded woman in the corner of my eye.

Immediately, and then for the hour or so that we spent together, the joke was the time that we had spent apart:

silly, needless, inexplicable. There was not much else to say about it, so we did not dwell on it. Ornella did not try to tell me that she had nothing to say. She talked about herself and Billy, about work and home, about everything. I told her about the flat that I was hoping to buy. When we were exhausted by the serious talk, we switched to talk of men, ours and others. After an hour or so, she left, laughing, for choir practice; laughing about the choir, explaining, admitting that by joining the choir she was making an effort to make an effort. She laughed, 'Remember how I would listen to nothing but The Clash?' *After Martin*, because The Clash had been a favourite band of Martin's. 'And now, ten years on, I'm reduced to this.'

As we walked away from the coffee shop, we vowed to keep in more regular contact. And from the ticket barrier, she called, 'I'll call you in the next few days.'

I smiled, shrugged, 'Whenever. Or I'll call you.'

She frowned. 'I'm going home for Mum's birthday, the day after tomorrow. So, the weekend: I'll call you at the weekend.'

I decided to wait to see if she would call, and I waited for twenty-three days. Twenty-three days: I counted, I was reduced to counting. And when she called, after twenty-three days, it was as if we had never had our meeting: she spoke briefly, about nothing.

Over the previous months I had stored news for her, not that this had ever been appreciated: when I had told her that Davey seemed to be splitting up with Chris, she had simply said, 'Thank God for that.' She rarely reciprocated, and tended to forget what she had and had not told me. And contrary to her claims, there was always plenty for her to tell me: weekends away, dinners, shows. I would have to say, 'I didn't know,' and then she would reply, 'Oh, yes,' implying that this was old news, that somehow I *should have* known. Implying, perhaps, that she did not care if I did or did not know. When she rang after the twenty-three days of silence, she mentioned that she was just about to go to Italy.

I had to tell her, 'I didn't know.'

'Oh, yes,' she said.

'For how long?'

I heard her musing, 'Mmm . . .' before deciding, or not quite deciding, 'Three, three and a half weeks?' And explaining, or not quite explaining, 'Between jobs.'

I knew that she was due to finish her job. When we had met in the station, I had asked her but she had had no news of any other work. 'You have a new job?'

'Oh, yes,' she said, 'temporarily. Back here, for a few months.'

Seven weeks passed before I heard her voice again. I moved flats. Our new home was on the top, seventh, floor. I looked over the whole of London, from Crystal Palace to Hampstead Heath. Surprisingly small. My new locality was so quiet that the only sounds reaching me, seven floors up, were those that would have been soaked up anywhere else: car alarms, mostly. All the cars nearby were stationary, there was no traffic. Because there was nowhere to go, this was dockland: this was as far as anyone ever went; residents only ever climbed back into their cars to drive into town, to work. Leaving me behind. From my windows I looked out over this lunar landscape, flat and pale but dappled with peaks: church spires and tower blocks. I could see no movement on the ground except for the occasional metallic strip of train briefly visible between buildings, running from reel to reel. And the piecemeal demolition of waterfront warehouses. From my balcony I could look up and see what was happening above: sometimes there were hot air balloons, liquid-bright beads run off the hills of the North into the sky; and always planes, small silvery fish in an upturned blue basin. Below my balcony was the river, slow barges snagging the silky surface of the water.

And I thought of Ornella. I thought that I was right to expect her to speak to me – her best friend – every week. To expect her to check with me like I checked the sky for weather. I wanted her to think of me every day, I needed her thoughts of me to run through her daily life to keep me alive. But I tried to hide these thoughts; I tried to keep my thinking to darkness. I would wait for John to roll over into sleep. Lying in wait, my breaths were shallow so that I could detect the start of his deep sleep breathing. And then I would allow myself to think. But darkness did not help. Every night, my thoughts buffeted the darkness, and were made real, or more real than they should have been. And when morning came, darkness slipped no further than the half moons which were beginning to haunt my eyes: my misery was pooling, coagulating, beneath my eyes.

I decided that I should spend less time on my own in the flat, in the sky; that I should come down onto the ground every day. But where could I go, locally? There was a swimming pool. So I began to go swimming every day. I began to avoid dry land for my thinking. I did not know that I was thinking; I thought that I was swimming. But I was thinking how losing a friend is worse than losing a lover because everyone expects to lose lovers. Because a lover will leave, eventually, for someone else. But why should a friend stop being a friend? These thoughts went nowhere but back and forwards with me in the pool. Crawling, I watched bubbles returning to the air from my hands in front of me. As if my fingertips could breathe for a moment, before they were too deep. Doing breaststroke, I watched my bare arms push purposefully into nothing: no struggle, no bubbles. Less speed, though. More drag. Over the weeks, I began to crawl much more, improving, impressed by my strength. Vulnerable only for the second when I had to turn my head to the side to breathe. The danger came from children, who would jump into the water in front of me. Disobeying their parents, probably, but beneath the surface I could hear nothing of this, none of their cries and counter-cries, *Don't run* and *Five more minutes*. Suddenly they would appear in front of me, in puffs of bubbles, with surprise slapped onto their faces. Then they would shoot upwards, away, the bubbles becoming Tinkerbell trails. Otherwise, I saw only the limbs and torsos of elderly people, their blubber and blue barnacles of veins, their belief that *This is good for me*.

When I began my daily swimming, I remembered the words of my swimming teacher from twenty years previously: *Fish don't splash*. I had believed her, trusted her, because she possessed the most important secret of all: she could teach me how to stay alive when something was trying to pull me down and close over me. But I had not understood this favourite cry of hers, *Fish don't splash*. Now, as I improved, day by day, I realized what she had meant: I realized that I was not to waste my energy, not to fracture it on the surface of the water, not to send it foaming across the water, but to keep it to myself. Day by day, I was aiming to reduce splash. Developing not only strength, but stealth.

I sent a card to tell Ornella of my change of address. During the seven weeks of silence, I heard nothing from her except a postcard from Pompeii: *Due to an incident, the 08.45 from Pompeii to Rome has been cancelled. Ha ha! Having a nice (fattening) time, but the grannies are dismayed by my lack of bambini. (I suppose than if I become fat enough, I can pretend). Watch EastEnders for me. See you soon.*

After seven weeks, I wanted to know if she was home. According to my calculations, she had been back for weeks. But had she? If I rang her, I would probably have to leave a message on her machine, and unless she returned the call, I would not know. And I did not want to *talk to her*, not if she did not want to talk to me; I simply wanted to *know*. So I decided to ring her at work, where she would have to answer.

I rang her hospital.

'Could you bleep Dr Marini for me, please?'

No word from the operator, no hesitation: I was plugged into thin air, crackly purgatory. This operator was confident that Ornella could be found. But I was used to the initial swagger of switchboards, before the eventual apologies, *I'm sorry, but Dr Marini doesn't seem to be on duty*. Or the surprise answers from other doctors, a sudden *Dr Grant* or *Michael-Walters-here*: crossed wires, although there are no wires. So I did not take the operator at her or his unspoken word. After a minute or so, a woman snapped into the silence, 'Who do you want?'

'Dr Marini.'

And then nothing.

But then, suddenly, she was there, her voice mild and enquiring, 'Ornella Marini speaking?'

I put down the phone.

I hurried away from it, across the room. Shaking, I sat down, but for some time I could not haul my gaze from it. I could sense, on the end of the line, the molten silky bubble of Ornella's life, billowing with work, home, family, friends and acquaintances, but not with me. She was there, but she was not there for me. Then, in the evening, she rang me. She was breezy, her conversation was sparkly with laughs. I wondered if she knew that the disappearing caller had been me. Surely not: how *could* she know? And yet. As I listened to her rattling on, I realized that she *was rattled*. I listened, amazed. I had been so afraid of her, but not now. Moreover, I seemed to have passed it on to her. Suddenly, from nowhere, came, 'We're still best friends; you do know that, don't you?' A quiet confidence, a coax.

My weariness fell into a sigh, 'No.'

'Well,' she slid her promise into my ear, 'we are.'

'No,' I had to stop her, to explain, 'I meant, no, we're not.' Because suddenly I was sure of this.

'What?'

Gently, I told her, 'I've learned to live without you.' I was surprised by the absence of recrimination in my words.

She tried to laugh this off, 'Don't say that.'

But it was true. I survived week by week; and I had a sense, now, of a life without her.

The first time that I had cut her off, had shut away her politely enquiring voice, my slam of the receiver had been little more than a reflex: I had not known what else to do. But as soon as I had done it once, I planned to do it again. And I did so, the next day; and then, in the following few weeks, it became something that I had to do: ring the hospital, ask for her, wait for her to answer, then replace the receiver. Why? At the time, I did not think. I did not want to think. It was enough that it pleased me. And that it was easy. My life had not been pleasant and easy for a while. It was not easy, I knew, for her: the squeal of the bleep in her pocket, the interruption of whatever she was doing, then the hunt and perhaps the queue for a phone. She could not refuse a call.

I did not know if she felt the impact of these silences: perhaps stray bleeps from the switchboard were commonplace. I did not call too often: usually daily, but usually only once. She rang me a few times but did not mention the silent calls; but, then, she did not mention much at all.

In our other calls, our conversations, I tried to persuade her to meet me: *Would you like to come along to . . . ? Do you fancy . . . ? How about . . . ?* She never replied directly, she sighed and muttered irrelevancies, cast a spell so that, within seconds, these requests of mine, these opportunities that I had created so carefully, were turned to nothing. Eventually I decided that I would have to present her with a meeting. I was certain that if she could see me, I would reach her. So I decided to go to the hospital, in time for the end of her day. My intention was for her to come across me, as if by coincidence. Because I knew that she would hate me to come for her.

I was losing my touch, on the ground: whenever I came down the seven floors and tried to cross town, I became disorientated. My journey to the hospital took an hour, and required my *A to Z*. From the tube station, I zigzagged through terrace after terrace of brick bow-fronted houses, occasionally coming across a street of shops: kebab shops, the sweaty brown thigh of meat pirouetting above tendrils of dead cabbage; shops proclaiming *Discount Office Furniture*, filing cabinets dumped on the pavement; travel agents without display windows, purely practical sources of trips to relatives, not holidays. It struck me that a supposedly chance meeting with Ornella, here, was an impossibility: why on earth would I be here? So, a last minute change of plan: if I could not meet her around here, I would have to meet her on her way home. Not in the mainline station: too obvious; she knew that I knew that she would leave the station every evening on one of the three or four trains between six o'clock and seven. We would have to meet en route: I would need to know her route to the station. Examining the tube map on the back of the *A to Z*, I found several possibilities. This was my chance to trace her exact route.

When I reached the hospital, I stayed across the road and walked around a corner from where I could see the main lobby. The hospital was an old building, with *Save Our Hospital* posters tied to the gates. I checked my watch: twenty past four, perhaps too late. Because I knew that, in some hospitals, on quiet days, the doctors leave when the work is done, sometimes by four; but then there are bad days, and clinics which do not finish until seven o'clock or later. This was when I realized that I had forgotten something: sometimes Ornella would not leave at all because she was on call. And even if I had not yet missed her, even if she was due to leave, I did not know if there were other exits from the building. All I could do was hope. After ten minutes, my legs were hot and heavy with pooled blood. But there was nowhere to sit. And I could not pace properly back and forwards, could not risk her leaving the building behind my back. I began to worry, woozily, that I would faint and be taken into the hospital as a casualty. I wished that I had brought a drink with me. I wondered if the people at the nearby bus stop were looking at me.

At ten past five, Ornella left the hospital. I was sure that it was her, but I peered hard to check because I did not know the clothes; ivory jacket, ice-grey skirt, and proper shoes with small heels which, from my distance, I could not hear. When I was doubly sure, I followed. Following her was as difficult as trying to ride a bike slowly. But I had the stealth of a swimmer, I held my breath but not too hard. She went into a newsagent and emerged with sweets which slowed her down, stopped her on several occasions: the careful peeling back of the tube of paper to expose the top sweet; the thumbing of this sweet away from the others. At the tube station, I stayed on the stairs until a train came, when I slipped into the end carriage. And then, when we drew into likely stations, I watched from the window, watched the platform for her. When I saw her, the doors had closed and the train was leaving. Which did not matter: I knew what I needed to know, I knew where I would have to be.

The next day, I stood at the bottom of the main escalator for an hour, but she did not pass me. After an hour, I gave up, I had to give up. I had never done anything so draining: standing, craning, being buffeted, in the mere ghost of air which came with the trains through the tunnels. *Five more minutes:* every five minutes I told myself, *Five more minutes*. When I finally made the decision to leave, I hurried home; home, I lay in the bath for a long time, listening to John's arrival, his attempts at greetings, at conversation, *What have you been doing today?* I tried to drown my replies, lies, in splashes. Then, later, I tried not to hear his complaints: the bangs in the kitchen, bites of empty kitchen cupboards, snap of the gums of the fridge door, and his yells, *God, when did anyone last do any shopping?*

The following day, I rang the hospital, bleeped Ornella, and she answered: so, I knew that she was there; not sick, nor on holiday. I did not know if she was on call, but I took a chance and went to the bottom of the escalator again. After an hour, I gave up, allowed myself to be drawn up the escalator, and then I found a phone. I rang the hospital and was told immediately, 'Dr Marini's off duty now; do you want to speak to someone else?'

'No,' I said, loudly, through the noise of the ticket hall; and only just remembered to shout, 'thanks.'

So, she had had somewhere else to go; or she was varying her route; or, quite simply, I was somehow missing her. I realized that I would have to watch her leave work, and follow her, before bumping into her: I realized that I could take no short cuts. The next day, I rang the switchboard to ask if Dr Marini was due to be on call. The operator answered me with a question, a worried, 'Dr Marini, is she A, B, or C rota?'

I admitted, 'I don't know.'

The operator could manage only, 'Ummm...' a buzz threatening a sting, *If-you-hang-on-I'll-put-you-through* ...

So I interrupted, told her, 'Don't worry, I'll call her

later.' I decided to go to the hospital, but, a few hours later, I had to abandon my plans because of rain. I could not stand for hours in the rain.

It was a Friday, and then the rain ran through the weekend. It was a thorough rain, sliding down the windows all day, then tapping into my dreams. I went outside rarely, reluctantly, hurrying breathless beneath my umbrella. The streets were noisy with the gasps of tyres, with the fuss of rainwater in gutters and drains; but still, somehow, the whole world was hushed, perhaps because the people were blotted out.

I was supposed to see Davey on the Saturday afternoon but he cried off: an old friend was briefly home from the States. Late on Sunday afternoon, my sister rang from Leicester Square. She had been to a spa to celebrate a friend's twenty-first birthday, and now that the party was going on to see a film, she had decided to come over to see me. 'But don't you want to go to the film?'

'Seen it.'

I whirled from the phone in a panic, telling John that I would have to tidy the flat. Meaning that he would have to help me to tidy the flat. During the weekend, mess had accumulated in our rooms, like the rainwater in the street. Our resistance had been lowered by the weather. The living room floor was puddled with newsprint. In the kitchen sink, breakfast crockery was soaking; not only Sunday's, but Saturday's. Looking up briefly from a newspaper article, probably on the subject of the New Man, John complained, 'It's not your Mum who's coming.'

I confirmed, 'No, worse.'

Juliet had not yet seen the flat, she had not come along when Mum came to visit. I had not seen Juliet for a long time. Not even at Christmas because I had gone to John's family, and Mum and Juliet had gone to Spain. Juliet's boyfriend of a few months, her fiancé, Paul, had been due to go with them, but they split up six weeks before the trip.

'The only problem,' Mum had told me, on the phone, 'is that nice set of yellow towels.'

'What nice set of yellow towels?'

'Her engagement present from Aunty Hester.'

I had never thought of engagement presents: people had bought engagement presents for Juliet and Paul?

'She should return them,' Mum continued, 'but I'm afraid we've used them.' Then, suddenly, she said, 'Your sister has finally seen sense over Paul.' Which so surprised me that I failed to ask questions, and then it was too late. I had had no notion that Paul was wrong for Juliet: I had never met him, and Mum had never said anything adverse to me. Later, when I asked Juliet, she seemed to tell me a lot but later I realized that she had told me nothing: *We had drifted apart. We had begun to want different things from life.* As if they had been an old married couple rather than newly-met twenty-year-olds; but, then, perhaps it was better for her to be speaking these doleful clichés about Paul when they were twenty rather than waiting years, wasting years. Since then, I had heard nothing of romance in Juliet's life. And I was fairly sure that there was no one in Mum's life. And that this was how Mum wanted her life. Dad had been taken over by a divorcée called Sheila who cooked him Sunday lunches. This was how Mum referred to Sheila: *the divorcée*, dee-vor-cee, a term that came from my childhood. This was how Mum replied to my questions about her own possible divorce: *Well, I suppose the divorcée will want us to get a move on.*

When John folded away his newspaper, it was to say, 'I'll make a cake.'

Wiping a surface, I shouted, 'I don't believe that you just said that.'

He came across to me and soothed a wayward strand of my hair. 'You don't want a cake?'

'A cake would be lovely but –'

'Good.' He smiled.

And I relented. And as I cleaned, he made a new mess; but a fresh, sweet, old-fashioned mess.

Juliet arrived immaculate despite the rain. In clothes designed for rain. The rain seemed to have run off her and shined her smooth hair. I had not had my hair so long or so simple since I was a schoolgirl. She had never had her hair any differently, or not that I knew or remembered. When she was small, her hair had been the colour of coconut. Had smelled of coconut, too, in the days when I been close enough to know. Not the manufactured smell of coconut shampoo but real coconut, the milk.

During her visit, she sat cross-legged on the sofa and enjoyed several slices of cake. She had turned to the sofa after admiring the view: she rushed away from the streaky french windows, enthusing, 'Oh, I *like this*.' She had never criticized my furnishings, she had merely been selective in her praise. Which must have been taxing for her, at times, because she had never lived in a student flat and so her standards were different from mine. My sister, the legal executive: when she had told me of her plans to become a legal executive, I had tried, I had said, *You could be a lawyer*. And she had replied, *All that work but no pay for years and years, why would I want to do that?* To which I had no answer. Now, between bites of cake, she asked me, 'Interviewed anyone interesting in the last few weeks?'

Gently, I told her, 'No one you'd know.' I explained: 'An actress.'

Licking her fingers, she yelped, 'Try me; who?'

I told her. Her mouth full, she wrinkled her nose to concede defeat: the name meant nothing to her. So then I leapt in with my usual question, 'How's Mum?' Why did I ask? I knew that Juliet could not tell me what I needed to know. She had been eleven when Mum and Dad separated. For her, it was normal for Mum to be on her own. Also, she lived with Mum, so that although in one sense she saw more of her, in another she saw less, was too close to see.

'She's fine,' she hummed, happily.

'And Dad?'

A hand rose to hold the moment as she finished her current mouthful. 'Moaning that I don't save enough money.'

'Yes, but how *is he*?'

She waved the hand, dismissively. 'Doing fine.'

Sometimes when I was questioning her, I would want to know, *And do you think that I abandoned you?* And then I would tell myself that perhaps she had more than I had had: growing up with two parents, two separate parents; Dad taking an interest, framing photos of her. I grew up in the years before the separation, and had only one: Mum.

'Oh, God,' she roared, slapping her forehead, 'I forgot to tell you: *Mum* has *a friend*.'

I sat forward in my chair. 'A *friend* friend?'

She was nodding her head in time to each chew. 'That's what she calls him: *my friend*.' She added, for my information, 'Len.'

I looked across the room for John. I widened my eyes; he raised his eyebrows. Returning swiftly to Juliet, I demanded, 'What's he like?'

'Old.'

'*How* old?'

Still cross-legged, she swooped to lay her empty plate on the floor; a strange movement, a strange position, the dying swan in Swan Lake. 'I don't know,' she puffed. 'Fifty or something.'

I should have known that she would be a poor source of information. I objected, '*Of course* he's fifty-or-something; *Mum's* fifty-or-something.'

She shrugged. 'Listen, *I* wouldn't fancy him.'

Which was even less help.

So I changed tack, asked her, 'Do they . . . ?' Failed to ask.

But, 'No,' she replied, very definitely.

'No?' But was this information reliable?

'Well, whenever he comes round to ours, he leaves by ten; I see him leave, I hear him leave.'

Poor Mum, trying to live her life so closely to Juliet.

I laughed, 'And what about when she goes to his house?'

'She never goes to his house.'

'Why not?'

'He has kids.'

I laughed more: '*Mum* has kids.' And corrected, 'Well, *kid*.'

'I'm a *big* kid,' she informed me. 'They're small, eleven or something. But,' her eyes smiled, 'not small enough not *to know*.'

'But what about when you're not home?'

I heard John despairing, '*Veronica* . . .' *What is this, twenty questions?*

Juliet slumped, melodramatically miserable: 'I'm always home, believe me.'

I persisted, 'Why aren't his kids with their mother?' I did not care that this was a sexist assumption: Juliet would not notice, and I was happy to ignore John's huffs and sighs from the corner of the room; this was easy for him, we were not talking about his mother. And surely not even he could deny the fact that children tend to stay with their mother.

'She's dead.'

'*Dead*?' People – mothers of young children – do not die, nowadays, surely?

'Cancer.'

'When?'

'Years ago. Three or four years ago.'

Juliet was still young enough for *three-or-four-years-ago* to be *years-ago*; still young enough for anyone over forty to seem old enough to die.

Suddenly she enquired, very politely, 'Can I smoke in here?' And hauled her handbag towards her.

'No.'

Her hand returned to her lap.

I added, 'Nor can you shoot up in the bathroom.'

Her face swelled with surprise. 'I don't do drugs.'

I exchanged a smirk with John.

'I *don't*,' she yelped, indignant.

I told her, 'It was a *joke*. To make a *point*.'

She was reluctant to relinquish my gaze; she stayed unsure. Then, looking down onto her hands, she said, 'I saw your friend.'

I wriggled from my chair, intending to fetch her plate, to offer her more cake. 'Which friend?'

'Ornella.'

Her name hit home. I was careful to sound casual: 'Oh yes? When?'

She clicked her tongue, shook her head, became a blur of frustration, *You don't understand*, 'Just now.'

I stopped on the edge of my chair. 'Where?'

'At the tube station.'

'*My* tube station?'

'Two or three down the line.'

'Was she coming here?'

'*How do I know?*'

Which is when I realized that I had been sharp with her. So I tried to soften my approach: smiled quickly and sank back into my chair. 'You didn't speak to her?'

'No.' She was satisfied with my new tone. 'Doesn't she live around here, then?'

'No. Not even in London.'

She frowned over this. 'I don't suppose that she was coming here, because she'd be here by now.' The frown lifted, questioningly: 'Where else could she be going, around here? What else is there around here?'

I ignored this. 'What was she doing?'

She shrugged, 'She was wearing a wonderful mac –'

'Was she with anyone?'

'Yes. A bloke.'

I could hear that John had returned to his newspaper: I heard the turn of pages, the lick of paper on paper.

'What did he look like?'

'Blond.' She shrugged, noncommittal, 'Nice looking, if thirty-year-olds are your scene.'

Which made me smile, briefly. 'Nowadays, they have to be.'

'Billy,' she said, thoughtfully.

'Billy?'

'His name was Billy; that's what she called him.'

I rose again in my chair. 'You were *that close*, and you didn't say anything to her?'

She rose, too, hurling this back to me: 'She wouldn't have known me. And, anyway, what would I have said?'

I wailed, '*Of course* she'd have known you.' *You're my kid sister. She's my best friend.*

Juliet countered, even more loudly, 'She would *not* have known me. And why would I want to talk to one of your old friends?' Then, probably afraid that she had gone too far, she lowered her voice: 'As I said, what would there have been to say?'

A few hours later, she returned to the rain with a chunk of John's cake wrapped in kitchen towel. She had insisted that she did not want to be accompanied around the corner to the tube station, so I waved to her from my balcony. Even from so far away, she looked substantial; even in all those clothes, I could see how her body had become more than the mere bare bones of womanhood.

For hours, I wondered whether Ornella would call from nearby, or call in, but she did not. I felt that the rain would never stop. But the next day came as a shock, flaring like the flesh of a dark, washed peach. So I went to the hospital for four o'clock, with a bottle of mineral water and a book. I was determined to become better at waiting. I had been waiting for an hour and twenty-five minutes when I looked up from my book to see her leave. I realized that, very quickly, I had become better at recognizing her from a distance: it did not matter that I did not know the plain, cool little lemon dress.

I had become skilled at following her, too. I followed her to the tube station, onto a train, then off, and onto another platform. The electronic board told us that the next train was due in three minutes, I had three minutes. I began to wander along the platform. Difficult, because my legs were shaking: the shakes seemed bigger, to me, than the steps that I took. Difficult, too, because there was no reason to move. I worked my way towards her by pretending to scrutinize the map on the wall, to peruse the range of chocolate bars in the dispenser, to look for rats on the track: a pitifully limited number of attractions. My heart was noisy. Eventually I estimated that I was within range. But I could not look, to check. So I waited, blind. *Give her time.* If she did not notice me, I would have to notice her. Then I heard her: 'Niquie?'

I turned, said, 'Oh my God.'

And she laughed. 'I *thought* it was you.' Laughing louder, she kissed my cheek. 'What are *you* doing here?'

'Waiting for a train,' I insisted.

She laughed harder, higher, and I realized how silly this reply had sounded. Silly, to her. To me, suspicious. Hurriedly, I tried to laugh off my mistake, tried another lie: 'I've been to the library.'

Her laughter had burned down into a smile. 'Come and have coffee with me.' She reached for me; patted, squeezed, my upper arm.

'Fine,' I popped a smile, 'where?'

'The station.'

'Station?'

'Yes, you know, the place where there are trains.' A whirl of eyes and eyebrows: '*Sometimes.*' Then she added, 'The Italian man.'

Surprised, I said, 'He's not *Italian. You're* Italian.'

'And there's only one Italian in the world?'

'No,' I explained, 'but he speaks Spanish,' I tried harder, 'and you speak Italian.'

The smile drifted back to me. 'He doesn't speak, he makes coffee; I've never heard him speak.'

Because you never listen. I implored her, 'Not the station.'

The smile flattened. 'I have to go home.'

I salvaged the sprightly tone: 'Why?'

She faltered, then hauled this lost moment into a big shrug. 'Same reason as everyone has to go home, I suppose: I have to cook.'

I tightened my smile. 'Come and eat with me.'

'What about Billy?'

'What *about* Billy? I'm sure he'll manage.'

Flickering self-consciousness, she coughed a laugh, 'I can tell that you've never been married to him.'

I whispered, urged, '*Ornella*,' a reminder, but of what? I did not know what I was saying, but she seemed to understand.

She whispered, but differently, weakly, 'I want to go home.' And clamped shut her eyelids for a second. When they opened, she said, 'Come with me.'

'I can't,' I said, sadly.

She copied my low tone: 'Why not?'

'Too far.'

'Yes,' she admitted.

We both checked the destination board, saw that the train would arrive in one minute.

Then I returned to her. 'Are you okay?'

322

'Yes,' she rolled her eyes, a feeble approximation of a shrug, 'tired.'

I sympathized, 'A lot of on call, in this job?'

'Hardly any, actually.'

'Oh.' I felt cheated.

The prediction on the board had not changed.

I indicated her dress: 'Lovely dress.'

Her face flew into a smile. '*Isn't* it.' She looked down, lovingly, over the dress. 'It's my new favourite.' She told me, 'It's original; 'fifties; my mother's.'

I agreed, 'Very Audrey.'

The smile turned over into a frown. 'My mother isn't *Audrey*.'

'*Hepburn*,' I explained, hissing exasperation.

'Oh,' this smile came slower, snagged by an eye tooth.

Boldly, I said, 'This is such a coincidence, because my sister saw you, yesterday.'

'Juliet?' she piped.

I heard that, for her, the very fact of Juliet was amazing, not that Juliet had seen her: she had forgotten Juliet. She raised her eyebrows but her eyes were unfocused, she was scanning memories of her. The train hummed in the tunnel, blew hot air over us. I pressed on, 'She was on her way to see me.'

The train catapulted from the tunnel. 'Oh, yes?' Ornella was not listening to me; her eyes had begun to scan the carriages for space. We joined the train, and I followed Ornella to some vacant seats. 'But how are you?' she chirped, hopefully, as I sat down beside her.

I wrinkled my nose.

She was continuing, 'Hayley's on and on about your piece in last week's paper, I'm not sure that she has ever seen one before, and suddenly she thinks that you're really famous.'

I flinched, laughed politely, mumbled, 'But I have had a lot of flak for that interview.' *Not that you'd know, not that you know anything about my life.*

'*Why?*' Her question was both hard and soft with dismay; her eyes, too.

I did not want to have to explain, now. 'Some people think I should have been harder on him.'

She tipped her gaze to the row of adverts running above people's heads, and mused, 'That's not your style.' Added, 'Having a row with you is like having a row with a pillow.'

I opened and shut my mouth.

Slowly, she brought her gaze level with mine, and half-smiled. 'Perhaps you should have been the doctor, and I should have been the writer.'

'Truth isn't your strong point.'

She stiffened to counter, 'I'm *famous* for speaking my mind.'

My turn, now, to smile. 'Which isn't quite the same.'

When we had arrived, found a table and settled with our cups of coffee, I asked her, 'When do you have to go?' *How long do I have?*

'I can catch the twenty past.' She dabbed a fingertip onto her tongue, into the crunchy coloured crystals in the sugar bowl, and back onto her tongue. Closed her mouth on this pinker, sweeter tongue. Then her gaze flattened over the concourse, and she sighed, 'I'll be back here in twelve hours' time.'

'Why do we never see each other any more?'

Her eyes did not register the question, absorbed the words, did not move. 'Oh . . .' momentarily she pressed shut her lips, to breathe a sigh so weak that there was no sound, 'You know.'

Quietly, I insisted, 'I *don't* know.'

The eyes snapped towards me. 'It's different, nowadays,' she informed me.

'How?' I whispered.

She folded her arms, lowered them onto the tabletop. 'We're not sixteen any more:' a murmur, but the careful cadence of a threat.

'No,' I despaired, 'we're nearly thirty: but how does this make any difference?'

Her eyes were slow to move, emptying before her gaze fell away. 'I don't know,' she spoke down into her coffee, 'I don't know, I can't explain. But it does.' Irritation drew up her face, then a frown, 'Do you have to start this now? I thought that we could have a nice quarter of an hour.'

Oh, I'm so sorry . . . I held back, down, on this sarcasm, but failed to contain something else: 'I don't *know* you any more.' These words hit me as hard as they hit her.

She had been lifting her cup, but now, suddenly, it was back in the saucer. '*Of course* you do,' she breathed, or tried to breathe. She pleaded, 'I haven't changed; my *life* has changed, *I* haven't changed.'

I said, 'I can't even...' I shut my eyes and the expression that came was, '*see you*, any more'; and I tried to explain, 'Whenever I look for you, in my head, or in my life, I can't see you, I can't find you.'

She leaned onto the table, her looming eyes chipped sparkly by fierce emotion, and urged, 'But I'm still there, Niquie; I still love you.'

'I *want* you to be my *friend*,' I stopped sharp, 'You *were* my friend.'

'I *am* your friend. *You're* my *best* friend.'

'No,' I answered her back, took her firm tone and turned it on her, 'I'm someone whom you ring once a year in the middle of the night, in tears,' *you keep me in the back of your mind, the back of your life, a piece of gaudy jewellery, solely sentimental value.*

She tried to lecture me, 'Okay, so we speak *less often* –'

I shouted, 'We *never* speak.'

Her lips lost shape, fell small; the words were a hiss, 'You're finding a problem where there *is no problem*.' She stood up.

'That's *a fucking lie*.'

A flash of shock from her: under any other circumstances, I would have laughed.

'I've had enough of this,' she informed me, quickly, stiffly, 'I'm very tired.'

I shouted, '*Sit down*.'

She sat down, instantly realized what she had done, and rose again. This time she did not straighten, but leaned low over me to threaten, 'I wish that you could hear yourself.'

I stood suddenly, so that she jerked backwards. She managed, 'I wish you could hear how ridiculous you sound.'

So I hit her.

It was closer to a push than a slap; it came close to her face, but lower, onto her upper arm, catching the swell of her shoulder in the palm of my hand, her bare skin noisy on mine. A breath shot from her, mixed with mine. And from the Spanish man: somehow I knew his gasp, behind the counter, from all the others. And, oddly, it was for him that I felt: he had welcomed me here, always, and this was how I behaved. I had not hit anyone since Juliet, when we were children, when she had been annoying me, taunting me, and the slap had always bounced back, immediately, unwisely because she was so much smaller than me. Ornella did not move. Her eyes burned, dry and solid, and she did not move them away from mine. But then she reached slowly onto the table for her purse, to the back of her chair for her jacket, to the floor for her bag.

I did not watch her walk away, I turned and hurried in the opposite direction. Although I did not know where to go, or what to do. When I reached the doors, I decided that I needed Davey. I was due to see him in a few days' time: he had rung to say that he needed to see me about something, and after some hopeless manoeuvring of diaries – *No, not unless it's before six, No, not unless you can meet me in Camden* – I had realized that I could add a visit onto a previously planned trip to another friend on the same side of town. But now I turned from the doors, went back across the concourse to find a phone, and rang him. 'It's me,' I said, when he answered, 'are you in, now?'

He laughed. 'Seems so.'

'I mean, can I come over?'

'*Of course* you can come over.'

I decided to take a taxi.

Opening his door, he exclaimed, 'How do you manage to keep so cool?' And he swooped with a congratulatory kiss.

He smelled wet and warm, he had had a shower, his hair lay in an odd, damp frown. 'Look at you,' I fussed, fluffing his hair as I stepped through the doorway. Then I admitted, 'I took a taxi.'

'Ah, cheating,' he said, approvingly. 'But, then, you *always* manage to look so cool: what do you do, eat ice cubes for breakfast?' With both hands, he smoothed his hair from forehead to nape: three quick, vigorous strokes.

I followed him into the bedsit, where he had been living since leaving Chris. He reached across his desk into a tiny rubble of single earrings next to a collection of drawing pins.

Distracted, I said, 'I must have *so many* single earrings; I should pass them on to you.'

'Yes,' he said. 'But please, none of your chandeliers.'

'I have to talk to you about something,' I told him, sitting down on his bed.

'Me too.' The earring slotted into place. Then he picked up a bottle of mineral water; raised it, questioningly. 'From the fridge: cold.'

'Mmm.' For a moment, I could think of nothing better. Air shot from the bottle beneath his twisting hand.

'You first,' I suggested. 'What do you want to tell me?'

He poured: translucent globes of liquid rolling over each other down the tall glass. 'I'm going to Prague.'

'Oh yes? When?' I gazed through the window, I liked the view of fire escapes, they reminded me of *West Side Story*.

'About a month, I suppose. I mean, I have the job, but –' having filled the glass, he glanced up and froze. Because he saw that I had misunderstood, but that now I understood. He began to confirm, slowly, awkwardly, 'I'm going to live there. Work there. You know, teach. English.' Then he began to apologize, 'All this is very sudden for me, too . . .'

'Don't,' was all that came from me. My body had become ribbon, fluttery.

Without moving his eyes from mine, he put down the bottle and tried, slowly, 'There's a lot going on in Prague.'

I said, 'Don't leave me.'

He came across the room to me; three barefoot steps. He turned into warmth, an arm across my shoulders, holding me together. 'Heyyy,' he breathed into my hair, 'What's up?'

I said, 'Stay with me.'

His damp hair slid on mine, I heard a smile slide

through his reply, 'It's not a leap year.'

I said nothing, but he drew away from me with my tears on him, a few drops on his free hand, others blotted by the cotton on his shoulder. He drew back further so that he could see my face. 'What *is* it?' he urged, his hold on my shoulder turned into a grip. 'What *is* it?'

So I told him, 'I need you here, you're all that I have.'

He was incredulous: 'You have work, you have a home, you have John . . .'

'I'm leaving John,' I decided.

His eyes became even wider. 'Are you serious?'

I squeezed mine shut. 'It's done, decided.'

His grip lessened: I knew that he was casting around for something to say, for his first question.

So I opened my eyes and said, 'That's not what I want to talk to you about. Not now. What I want to tell you is that I hit Ornella. Just now.'

After a pause, he considered, 'Well, I'm sure that she deserved it.'

'Be serious.'

'I *am*.' But then he checked, 'Did you really?'

I admitted, 'In public.'

'Not too hard,' he said, hopefully.

'Not hard,' I assured him. But, 'That's not the point, is it.'

I gave up, lapsed back into tears. I ached with them, having held on to them for too long, having soured in their salt.

He rocked me, soothed me, 'You *are* low.'

I could have told him about feeling low. I could have

told him about feeling abandoned. But now I did not want to talk. What I wanted to do was cry. Which he seemed to know, because he tipped me over, laid me down, lay with me, held me. I did not realize for a while, not until he stopped, that he had been crying, slightly, silently, too.

And then I realized how bad a friend I had been to him, lately. So we began to talk about Prague. He started by explaining, 'I have to get away,' but did not have to explain further, because of course I knew: his split from Chris, his work, lack of work, the bedsit. London. Britain. We stuck to the subject of Prague, to the future: questions from me and replies from him, muffled because they were spoken into each other's bodies; and, because they came between sniffs, a rickety rhythm. When there was nothing more to say, we were silent. I could not remember ever having been so warm.

We must have dozed, because suddenly I woke. Dusk was pooled around us, around the room. I rose on one elbow, to look down on him. I ran my gaze over and over his closed eyes: bumps, hard with fluid; bony, though boneless; bruisy. I marvelled at the sea-green veins in the thin skin of his eyelids, temples, and the crooks of his arms. The colour of poison. The coldest colour that I could imagine. I wondered if this was the closest that I could come to his heart. Very lightly, I traced the veins along the underside of his arms. When they went deep, they were hazy, ripples in shot silk.

I turned my head to find the window, the sky: a summer sky in the last long minutes before darkness. The sky of an over-long day, spun thin. And yet *so light*: a drenching of fine, white light. So much lighter than the world below, of shadows. For a while, I watched the slow evaporation of the day into the sky. So utterly unlike the darkness of winter, which comes from above, presses down. This summer sky was one huge star. When I turned back to Davey, his eyes were open, his colourless eyes: it was never the colour of them that was striking, but the cut, the simultaneous smoothness and sharpness of them.

I smiled, said, 'You go to Prague, then; I'll wait for you.'

'Wait-for-me?' Now he smiled, too. 'Sounds like something in a book.'

'And what do you have against books?'

I lay back on the bed, on my back, and wondered into the darkness, 'But do you think that we'll *always* be friends?'

'If we try.'

Which meant, *I will try*.

I said, 'I do love you, you know.'

'I love you, too.'

'You're not just saying that?' I turned to him.

He laughed, briefly. 'I'm not just saying that.'

And I noticed, 'You have teeth like an advert.' How had I never noticed? So many years. Such perfect teeth.

He closed his mouth, hard.

So that, suddenly, I was suspicious: 'Are they false?'

'False?' he yelled, indignant.

I tried for the correct terminology: 'Capped, crowned, whatever; I don't know.'

He shook his head. 'Natural,' he said. Surprisingly shy.

When I came home, John did not ask where I had been. But if he had asked, and I had replied that I had spent the evening with Davey, then of course he would have suspected nothing. I came home, I did not leave him; but nor, for the next few days, did I quite stay. I kept out of the flat, away from him; and away from the phone and Ornella's silence. After the sudden warmth of Davey, I was more chilled than ever. So I kept busy. And I tracked down Bev.

Why? I do not know, I did not think: I simply wanted to see her. I needed to see her. In retrospect, perhaps I was seeking a reassurance that nothing had changed. And perhaps I would have gone to Abi, rather than to Bev, if Abi had not been in the Sudan. Perhaps I had wanted to talk about Ornella. Which, in the end, we did not do. Perhaps I had wanted to reminisce, to sink back into our old world, but this was not what happened. None of this matters, because none of this happened. Bev did not seem to require an explanation for my sudden call. On the contrary, she seemed almost to have been waiting for me. Making the arrangement to meet was surprisingly easy, much more so than with other friends. At the time, I assumed that she must have less to do.

We met two days later, in a restaurant which I had

chosen. She had made me choose. I arrived five minutes before her. When she arrived, she came very quickly towards me with a smile too big for her little face. The smile drew me from my chair, I stood up for her. And I wondered: did she look older? Older than what? Older than when I had seen her a few years ago? Older than me? Coming across the room, her small dark eyes were creases. When she reached me, we kissed, which had never been part of our repertoire when we had seen each other almost every day. The kiss was my first inkling that this was going to be different, that this had to be new.

'*Well*,' she sighed through the smile, stepping backwards to remove her coat. The coat, like the smile, was too big for her. And too big for the weather, yet she shivered as it dropped down her back. She hung it over the back of her chair, settling it quickly, thoroughly, but gently, as if it was a child. Her white face fluttered above me like a disc of honesty, brittle but glowing. She slipped down into her chair and a waiter appeared to ask her if she would like to order a drink.

'Oh, yes, mineral water, please,' she ran her long hands down her skirt, but then her gaze glittered on my glass. 'No,' she said, 'wine,' she turned the smile up to him. 'A glass, please. House. Red.'

'Wine,' she exclaimed, appreciatively, to no one in particular. With the palm of one hand she pushed up her hair as if it was stuck with sweat to her forehead. But it was dry, clean, it fell feathery from her fingers. 'You look so *glamorous*,' she enthused, leaning onto the table so that her thin body was slung low between two high, sharp shoulders.

'I *do not*,' I said, truthfully.

'You *do*.' Her gaze skidded past me, hopped from table to table. 'It's so nice to be here,' she whispered. Then she refocused on me, 'And how *are* you?'

'Oh, fine,' *you know*.

She smiled mischievously. 'My mum tells her patients that you're famous.'

I laughed, exclaimed, 'Your mum is lying to her patients.'

So, she laughed, too, and snapped back in her chair, retracting her arms and shoulders. I heard her cross her legs, heard the stubbing of the loose, thrown shoe on the tiled floor beneath our table. 'No,' she said, 'because, remember, my mother knows the truth about everyone.'

By now I was laughing harder, thinking of her mother: *Sister*. I was remembering how, when she was Sister, she had seemed to know everything about everyone in our school. Not that she had an air of secrecy. She was not stifled by these secrets; they buoyed her up, blew her uniform bright and tight.

'Yes,' I said, in wonderment, 'She *did* know *everything*.'

And her mum's secrets were not secret. Or not from everyone. Not forever. She could not keep secrets. Why did people trust a woman who was so obviously open? Only now did I realize that the secrets were not passed to Sister for her to keep. She was immune to secrets. She spent her days very gently curing people of them.

There was so much of Bev's mum in Bev; although, now, sitting opposite Bev, I was struck by the lack of physical similarities. Her mother had been so rounded, with a shine to her ripe tangy rind, a body utterly unlike Bev's bones loosely wrapped in a skin of rice paper. But her mum had been *girlish*. Not that I had known this when I was a girl myself. But now I knew, and I saw that this was the quality that they shared. Even though Bev looked frail, her two front teeth were so often on her lower lip in a twinkle of shy daring. And there was her enthusiasm, however quiet: I had not seen such enthusiasm in anyone for a long time. And I could see that this enthusiasm was for me: opposite me, her warmth burned white.

She was saying, 'And I do keep meaning to read something of yours . . .'

'Oh, Bev, for God's sake, *stop this*.'

She tightened her mouth, which merely sent the smile to her eyes. She placed her hands in the middle of the table, then withdrew them to the rim. There were tiny patches of eczema between her fingers: a red hot sand, impossible to wash away. Her ring, her one ring, was silvery – platinum? – and reminded me of a tag on a homing pigeon. I saw that there were pieces to her life that I could not place.

'My mother reads you, faithfully, and *I* will, I *will*, but lately everything has been so . . .' She threw up her hands, and then suddenly they were on the menu.

I hurried to tell her, 'Don't have the . . .' I had forgotten the name of the dish, but I knew its location on the menu so I leaned to point, '. . . because it's slimy.'

'Slimy . . .' she considered, gravely, following my fingertip.

I backtracked, 'Well, *in my opinion* it's slimy.'

'Nothing else is slimy, in your opinion?'

'No.'

Her smile widened across her downturned face.

'Anyway, how are you?' I asked her.

She lowered the menu, looked up, and blew through rounded lips. And then, politely, she asked, 'You know that Mike has cancer?'

'Mike . . . ?' But I could go no further. *Mike? Her husband?*

She was smiling again: a faded but deeper smile, the stain of a smile. Nothing to do with happiness. Everything to do with kindliness. For me. Carefulness, of me. 'Has cancer,' she repeated, quietly, 'yes. I didn't know if you knew.'

I began to stall, to protest, 'You're kidding.'

'No, unfortunately.' The smile tilted, wry.

'He has cancer?' I checked. But I knew that this was true because she had told me, twice. What I wanted to know was: *Mike, your husband?* I wanted to know about *Mike, the husband*. I had never met him. Had never even thought about him. Not as a real person. *Mike*: I did not yet know him as a normal person, a well person; I needed to know other things about him before I knew that he had cancer, I was not ready for this. I had not come here for this; this was not what was supposed to happen when we met up again after a few youthful years apart. I was frantic for a re-wind button.

But despite my confusion, my brain was pulsing, sending me the essential facts: *Bev, here; her husband; has cancer*.

'Spinal,' she said. 'It's hard to know how to tell people. No, *when* to tell people.'

When. Spinal. Everything was reaching me in the wrong order but I was realizing that I had been asking more when I checked, *He has cancer?* I had not been asking for confirmation, but for information: *What cancer? Since when? Will he die?* And I wanted Ornella. But what could Ornella do? If nothing else, she could tell me the statistics and the science; she could tell me if this would happen to me or John; she could tell me that this would *not* happen to me or John.

Bev smiled: sympathy, for me. 'I'm really sorry that I didn't tell you, but, you know, I couldn't have written it in your Christmas card, could I.'

So I said what she wanted me to say: 'No.' But for a moment I was certain that she could have, should have written it in my Christmas card. Because what was the point, then, of Christmas cards? But I knew that this impatience was for myself: how could I not have known that the husband of one of my oldest friends was dying? Of course she could not have settled down on her sofa with her crisp Christmas cards to write over and over again, *Happy Christmas, Mike has cancer*.

She was saying, 'And we thought that everything would be okay, for a long while we thought that everything would be okay. And if everything had been okay then there would have been no need to say anything to anyone. To the people I don't see so often.'

Which meant me.

'Because what would have been the point in worrying people?' The words stopped suddenly, the eyes dropped fractionally later, and I heard what she could not say, *I was hoping that I would never have to tell people.*

I managed, 'Yes, of course.'

'He's home, now,' she said.

She meant, *Until he dies.*

I worried, 'Is it okay for you to come here?'

'Vonny, it's wonderful for me to come here.'

I tried to return her smile.

She explained, 'Mum is sitting with him.'

I tried and failed to imagine how my mother and I would rally, if ever required to do so. 'But what if . . .' *something happens?*

She reassured me, firmly and kindly, as if I was a patient, 'Nothing will happen while I'm here.' Mysteriously sure of the timing, certain of a rhythm.

Which struck me, oddly, as an echo of the more usual talk of my other friends, their calm talk of the chaos of childbirth, *three centimetres.*

Then she saw the waiter approaching, and returned dutifully to the menu. But she glanced up, fleetingly, to add, 'Not how I'd ever expected to have my heart broken before thirty.'

During the meal, we talked of Mike, of the two years of his illness. And of the future, *her* future. Then we exchanged news of our families and she moved on to ask after Ornella and Davey. I began by telling her of Davey's plans for Prague, and we drifted into a discussion of whether we would want to work abroad for a while. Suddenly I noticed that she was sitting taller, stiffened, poised to pass me some news, her eyes sparky. 'What?' I demanded.

'And *Abi's* having a *baby*.'

'*Abi*?'

She crumpled, in a show of contrition, '*Oh*, you didn't *know*: I was trying not to tell you, I was trying to wait to see if you mentioned . . .' she faded. 'Abi *said* that she was going to tell you.'

But, 'She's in the Sudan.' *Out of contact with you. On the trail of adventure.*

Bev laughed, knowingly. 'Not for much longer. She says that she can't take the risk, says that she's taking no risks.' Leaning towards me, she widened her eyes, emphasized in wonder, '*Abi, no risks.*'

'How do you know this?'

'She told me. In a letter, about three weeks ago. And she said that she'd write to you.'

'I haven't heard from her in . . .' *In the Sudan*: she had never written to me from the Sudan.

Bev mused, 'She has written fairly often to me. It's odd: I hear much more from her now than when she was in London.'

'Absence makes the heart grow fonder,' I quoted, lightly. Gently, because I did not want to imply that Abi had not been fond of her.

After a moment of consideration, she said, 'Makes the heart prioritize, perhaps.'

'Was the baby a mistake?' I asked: her cue for the whole tale.

'She didn't know that she was pregnant, not for a long time, a few months,' she halted, to add thoughtfully, 'you don't have periods when you're abroad, or not properly.'

I tried not to laugh at her.

'No. So,' she continued, oblivious, 'it was a huge shock, but now she's quite excited.'

She had left out a crucial detail: I looked closely at her – her gaze washed into the rising tide in her raised wine glass – and wondered how to ask. Without mentioning love, without mentioning a man.

She lowered the glass, and replied with a smile, 'Someone over there, one of her fellow workers.' A spasm of surprise threw her eyebrows as she added, 'She seems to quite like him.'

I laughed.

Which made her laugh. 'And he's coming back with her,' she finished.

'Trust Abi,' I remarked, cheerfully, 'to be the first of us to have a baby.'

She twinkled into her glass of wine but did not sip; she put it down, to say, 'And trust you to say that.'

'What do you mean?'

She was very amused. 'You two have always been *so competitive*.'

I countered, indignantly, '*She* has always been so competitive.'

Now Bev was interested: 'Why are you like this about her?'

I tried hard; I would like to know: 'I don't know. But I don't trust her an inch.'

She returned to the wine glass, laughing.

I corrected, 'Or decimal equivalent.'

Her lips momentarily closed on wine, she shook her head. 'That's exactly what she used to say about you and Ornella: *They don't give me an inch*.'

'She *did*?' I was baffled; I tried to imagine her saying it, why she might have said it, how she might have said it, but I failed. 'Why? What did she mean?'

'That you shut her out. You and Ornella.'

I laughed this off, '*No one* has *ever* been able to go *anywhere near* Abi,' but allowed, 'Except you,' and knew why: nice, kind Bev.

She shrugged lightly, sweetly. 'She's nervous of people.'

I rolled my eyes in utter derision, but Bev continued, 'I don't think that she cared so much about Ornella. Because, I mean, Ornella is Ornella. But you two, you and Abi, you're *so* alike. Which makes you rivals.'

I yelped, 'We are *not* alike.'

'You even *look* alike.'

'We do *not*.'

'You *do*.'

'We do?' How? Which bits?

'You do.'

'But Abi's so . . .' I had rushed, so that now I had to stop, to think. 'She's so in control of her life,' was the poor best that I could do.

'And she thinks the same of you.'

After a pause, I said, in wonder, 'Tell me that all this isn't true.'

In reply, she laughed, and her fingers flew up and then down, away, through her hair. 'You *know* it's true.'

And she was right, in a sense: I did know; had known, in a way, without knowing.

She was asking, 'How *is* Ornella? You haven't talked about *Ornella*.' Her eyes were glossy with fondness.

I looked into those eyes and could not fail her. 'Fine. Married to Billy. Working. Hard.' I could not talk about Ornella, here, now; I simply could not. So I sidetracked, asked her for news of James and Martin. Her mum was no longer School Sister, but she would know, because she knew everything about everyone. Any news of James or Martin would be my first news in nearly ten years.

'Well,' she said, apparently pleased to be able to oblige, 'Abi's not the first of us to have a baby, because James is married with a kid.'

I tried not to flinch. Not to think of how his child would look. To remember nothing of James. But I did remember that his favourite name had always been Estelle, that he had wanted us to have a daughter called Estelle.

'Called?'

Bev looked up, startled. 'What?'

I tried to sound casual: 'What's the baby called?'

'Oh I don't know what she's called.'

'And Martin?' I hurried onwards, 'News of Martin?'

'Ah, Martin,' she murmured, full of mystery, so

343

that I was ready for anything. 'No news.'

I stopped tapping my teaspoon on my saucer, I did not realize that I had been tapping until I stopped, until the silence. '*No news? Never?*'

'Never.'

I was stunned; her word took away everything but my realization, *He has gone.*

When we left the restaurant, Bev started again: 'It has been *so* nice to see you, it was *so* nice of you to ring me, I'm *so* sorry that I've been so out of contact for so long.'

Wincing inwardly, I grabbed her, squeezed her arm to shut her up.

And my hand stopped her, turned her towards me. Her eyes held mine as she said, 'You'll understand if you don't hear from me, now, for a couple of months?'

She meant, *Until he has died, and then until I can cope.* Understand? I insisted, '*Whenever.*'

We hugged. All I could feel was the coat; but a moment later, when we began to move apart, I felt her leaving me, I felt her bones fold down and away.

'A couple of months,' she reiterated, and the tone of her words was unlike anything I had heard from anyone for a long time: not to put off, but to bring the future firmly into view.

'See how you feel,' I said.

'Oh, I know how I feel,' she said, as she turned away.

Perhaps surprisingly, the time that I spent with Davey and Bev did not make me calmer or kinder. But I was much stronger. And clearer about Ornella. I saw that she did not care, not only about me but about them, her old friends; she did not care about *anyone*. She did not know about Bev's Mike, or Abi's baby; nor did she know how unhappy Davey had been, and that he was going away. She would never know if I did not tell her. From my sudden strength and certainty came fury. I tried to confine this fury to the flat, stayed home for a few days and turned my attention to housework. For one whole afternoon I stripped pleated lampshades of dust, raking each groove with a fingertip wrapped in a damp rag.

And so for a few days I ticked over, bided my time. Avoiding John's eyes, because I was not yet ready to face him. I was too busy thinking. Or so I thought. In fact, I was raging. Because Ornella had been so dishonest with me. She had tried to insist that the distance between us was an inevitable consequence of time. But we had not grown apart: this was not what had happened, I had not been replaced and nor had her old friends. She had always thought that I did not need to bother with other friends and now I saw that she had kept me away from them for all those years, had held me back from them, made me miss out on them. But no longer. Because everything was going to change. The only person I did not need, now, was her.

And yet I had not quite finished with her. I was determined that she would not get away with this, not so easily. Drawing my wrapped fingernail down lampshades, I decided that I was going to get through to her, to make her see what she had done, if this was the last thing that I did. I was going to force her to face the truth. But, first, I would have to catch her. The ideal place was the hospital: I craved the anonymity and neutrality of a hospital, I did not want to have to go to her home, to confront her in her own home, and I did not want Billy there. And if she was in the hospital, on call, she could not leave. So, I decided to catch her when she was on call. I could cope with the interruptions, I could wait; if I had learned nothing else over the past few months, I had learned to wait.

On the fourth day after my lunch with Bev, I phoned the hospital in the evening to ask the switchboard operator if Dr Marini was on call. I was ready to go, if the reply was yes. The reply was no; and was no for the next four evenings. When, finally, I heard, 'Yes,' I managed a mere and falsely cheerful, 'Thanks,' before slamming down the receiver. *She was there.* I had her, now.

When I arrived, I stood for a while in the darkness on the other side of the road from the hospital, and the building seemed different. Comforting. Much less busy, presumably: less of a busy car park; fewer busy porches and doors. And so many lights, softly yellow rather than institutional electric white: every window was glowing. And there was the dial in the clocktower, which I had barely noticed before: it was lit, the colour of the moon. I was very taken with its roundness, which I knew was ridiculous, because of course it was round. Perhaps the old-fashioned roundness of its numerals, then: reminiscent of old signposts, of a quaint notion of the public good; no statements about design, no hidden agenda. I ran my gaze over the rows of golden windows: what was Ornella doing, now, behind them? She was unsuspecting, doing her checks on the wards, whiling away a few late hours so that problems with the patients could occur when she was awake, so that she was less likely, later, to be woken. She was looking over charts, hardly looking and then verifying them with her signature, routinely granting permission. My blood flared: how *could* she have been so careless with me? Everything had so nearly been fine between us. I had asked nothing of her; she had had to do so little to keep our friendship going, and still she had failed me.

I called her, but not from the hospital, not from the reception desk: I called from a phone box, watching the hospital, those windows. The phone box smelled of urine, was scribbled with fossilized claims to fame, *Trix and Jay 8.6.89*. When Ornella answered, I told her, 'It's me, I'm here, I need to talk to you.' Somehow I made this sound as if I did not intend to talk *about her*; my tone was urgent but bright, free from accusation.

'Oh . . .' not much more than half an *Oh*: I could hear that she was genuinely puzzled, properly impressed; and that she was thinking, quickly. 'Okay, I'll come down and give you the key to my room; give me another hour, and I should be finished.'

When she came into reception, she was cheerful, but brief. Her hair was dulled by frequent sweeps of her fingers, and her eyes were luminous in the bruised and slack skin of their sockets. She asked me if I was alright, then gave me the key and directions to her room. One

347

of her nails was newly and spectacularly broken, white forced down into the pink, dried blood peeping from the fracture. Before I went, I nodded towards the nail and said, 'You should do something about that.'

She shrugged, threw the hand: *Later*; or, *Doesn't matter*.

I spent the next hour alone in her room, on her bed, drinking instant coffee and reading two magazines, one of which I had retrieved from the wastepaper bin. When she came in, I was glancing over her horoscope: *Keep a close eye on a close friend*. My own said the equivalent of, *Get a grip*. She fanfared herself with a huge sigh, flopped down onto the chair to kick off her shoes, one and then the other, each one spinning to the floor in a somersault. 'You don't believe in the stars,' she said, peering down the page.

'Sometimes I do.'

She laughed. Properly. As if I had said something funny.

'Coffee?' I checked, slipping the magazine back into the bin.

She shook her head, closed her eyes, murmured longingly, 'Bed.' Then opened her eyes, focused on me, wanted to know, 'But what's up? Are you okay? Why did you need to see me?'

I said, 'It's about us.'

Her eyes closed again. And she complained, 'Oh God.'

But I leaned towards her lid-blinded eyes to urge, 'Why don't you talk to me any more?' This was not a whine: I wanted the answer.

She snapped open her eyes, replying fiercely, 'I *do*.'

But I would not suffer this lie. '*When?*' I challenged.

Her eyes fluttered towards the door, and she muttered, 'Keep your voice down.' Then she replied, loudly, 'I'm talking to you *now*, aren't I?'

'*Ornella*,' I exclaimed, 'I've had to come across London in the middle of the night to your on-call room in order to make you talk to me. When *else* have you talked to me?'

She stiffened in her chair, hardened her mouth, folded her arms. 'The last time that I talked to you,' deceptively smooth, close to cracking, 'you hit me.'

Of course she would have had to mention this sooner or later: my turn, now, to look away, but in exasperation.

She followed my exasperation with her own: 'You're being ridiculous about this.'

As if there was something about which I could have been reasonable. As if something had been put to me and I had refused to meet halfway. But none of this was true: there was no halfway, there had never been any negotiation. I told her, 'You use people.'

Her eyes slid down and away from mine, her lips blurted a sigh before they closed. I saw that her face was mottled with tiredness.

'You use me, you use Billy . . .'

She jerked to attention. 'Oh *don't* bring *Billy* into this,' she said, disgusted.

'You don't bring him into very much at all, do you.'

Outraged, she replied defensively, 'I *married* him.'

'And then wished that you hadn't.'

Now she knew that this was serious. That *I* was serious. That I was not going to forget whatever she wished to be forgotten, to keep the silences that she had dictated and tell the lies that she told. She gathered herself for her reply, leaned hard from her chair towards me so that she was almost doubled up. 'Yes,' she said, slowly, viciously, 'But I *get on* with things. Unlike *you*. I *live* my life.'

But this was my point: 'You *don't* get on with things. This is a *life*?' I disparaged, 'You're not *living*, not really. You're not even *trying*.'

Suddenly she was up from her chair; her back turned on me. '*Right*,' a crisp announcement, 'I'm going to bed.'

But I could not stop. 'What's happened to your *passion*, Nella? You had so much *passion*. That was what *made* you. Was what made you *different*. Made you *you*.'

She whirled around to face me, and her fingers tipped her hair behind her ears in one small, clean, clinical movement; and then she said somehow both quickly and slowly, 'Passion kills people, Veronica.'

'No,' I rushed back, as she turned back. 'No, that's *not* what it does. It keeps you alive. You can't live without it: that's not the answer.'

With her back to me, she repeated, tonelessly, 'I'm going to bed.'

I was lost, she was lost to me, I could only appeal, uselessly, hopelessly, '*Look* at you.'

She was busying herself with bedding, hauling blankets and a pillow from a corner of the room. She said, 'Have these,' dumping them at the foot of her bed.

'Sleep here. You can't leave, now; you can't roam the streets around here at this time of night.'

'Fat lot you care,' I muttered.

'Of course I care,' she replied. Without looking up. Without conviction.

She placed the bleep by her alarm clock, and then threw back her duvet so that I had to move from the end of the bed. She was going to sleep in her clothes, ready for any crash calls. I slid down from her bed onto the pile of blankets.

'You can stay up,' she was saying, over the puffing duvet. 'Makes no difference to me if you keep the lamp on. I'll sleep through anything.' She added, 'Except the bloody bleep,' then her head was down, and she was gone.

I was exhausted, but I knew that I would be unable to sleep. My anger was firing, shaking my limbs and thumping my head. So much louder and faster than the breaths which I could hear from her. She was asleep. She was next to me in a state of complete surrender and still I could not reach her. And if I could not sleep, what else was I going to do, here, in this tiny room which was not mine, which was so far from mine? I began to panic, did not turn off the lamp but pulled the blankets around me in the hope that they would somehow trick my body into rest. And then suddenly I hit on the word for all this, for everything that had happened. Or it hit on me, coming from nowhere but utterly right. The word was *betrayal*: Ornella had *betrayed* me. Which was so melodramatic that I had to stop myself from laughing. But betrayal was exactly what it was; it was what I had been looking for, without realizing; it explained why I was so furious with her. All the others ways that I had been thinking of this – she had let me down, given up on me, dropped me, gone off me, had turned away from me, turned me away, turned cold – were not nearly strong enough. They failed to do her justice. She was supposed to have been my best friend, she *had been* my best friend for most of my life, the whole of my adult life, and then in a matter of months, without a reason, without a word, she was no friend at all. That was betrayal.

I stood up, stood over her. She was lying on her side, turned away from me. I leaned closer, saw that she was frowning hard: her face was aggressive even in sleep, and tightly closed from me. And I saw that nothing was going to change. I would have to go away in the morning and try again to do what I knew that I was unable to do: I would have to carry on with my life without her as if I had never known her. Suddenly I was more tired than I had thought. I sat down on the edge of her bed. She did not stir, there was no shift of the copper shine on her hair, no flicker of her eyelashes. Mascara had drifted from the lashes onto her lower lids and darkened the shadows below them. If she had died, living without her would have been easier. If she had died, I could have kept good memories of her. I could have mourned her. My friends would have talked to me about her, would have let me talk about her, they would have sympathized and helped me through this. For a moment, too tired to think, I heard the noises of the hospital: like the low, irregular noises of sleep, shivers, coughs, turnings and sighings. I was cold, which was odd because I knew that the room was warm. I drew a blanket from the floor and around my shoulders. If she had died, I would have been less alone. And if she had died, she would not have betrayed me. Everything would have been so much easier. I hated her for her coldness.

I felt cold, but I was burning, too. I lifted my pillow from the floor, held it in my lap. It was cool and smelled clean in the way that only clean pillowcases can smell, the very smell of cleanliness. The scent of the moment before sleep, of the promise, the certainty of sleep, of peace. I cooled my hands on the soft, tough cotton, they sank deep into the firm down. *There could be an end to this pain, this could be so very easy.* I settled the pillow over Ornella's head, her face, and gently pressed down. I watched the cotton cover become taut but dimple around my hands. For a moment, there was nothing from her. Then suddenly her head turned very sharply towards me. Or tried to. Her body tried to turn, but locked into the folds of the duvet beneath me. I felt her hands slam up into the duvet for the fight that she could not have. It was an instant, only an instant, over in an instant; because, trying to hold on to her, to squeeze down, I lifted my head and glimpsed my face in the mirror above her sink. Saw my eyes. Next I saw the green veins in the backs of my hands as I took the pillow from her face. I turned and threw the pillow to the floor. The sound of its impact was the punch of air into her hollow lungs, the fizz of oxygen in her blackened blood.

I walked to the door, slipped my feet into my shoes. As I turned to go, her eyes found mine, and they came with me as far as they could through the doorway. But they were washed blank by the shock of surfacing and I do not know if she really saw me, I do not know what she saw.

I walked, my mind on nothing. I must have walked for hours but I do not remember feeling tired. I do not remember feeling anything except perhaps a lightness, oddly similar to an initial fall into love: wakefulness and sleepiness did not come into this; I simply *was*, and so much more than ever. I was a slow-sluicing of adrenaline. I was warm, when the temperature dropped and dropped; I was body-warm, my warm blood hummed in the splintered silence of the streets.

I found my way home. Or home found me. From the street, I saw the lit window: a solitary light, seven floors up; John had forgotten to turn off a lamp in the living room. I went up by the stairs; becoming slower and slower, flight by flight. And when I walked into the flat, I stopped short: John was sitting on the settee. He was wearing his pyjamas, which he only ever wore on Sunday mornings for staying home. Momentarily, I wondered if this *was* a Sunday morning, very early; realized that I had lost track of the days. 'Good God,' I hurried, cheerfully, 'you're up.'

He asked, 'Where have you been?' and miraculously this was utterly free from accusation. An echo of Juliet, when she was small, when I would come home late and she would wake and walk from her bedroom into the hallway and ask me the same question, 'Where have you been?' *With whom, and what did you do? Tell me your tale.* I could see that he was trying, he was trying so hard: his face was held wide open for whatever I could tell him, and wiped of everything except warmth. I could see that he had not been to bed: the skin of his face and the surfaces of his eyes too clear and hard to have been in bed, not sleep-softened or dream-dusty. I sensed that he was not quite sober, perhaps I *smelled* that he was not quite sober: an empty bottle of bourbon shone from the floor. He did not like spirits.

I had no idea what was going to happen. As a delaying tactic, I took off my coat, turned away from him in my dropping coat, turning further to hang it up, and did not return to him when I asked, 'Did you go out, this evening?' When I knew that he had been nowhere except the bottom of a bottle.

'No –'

His reply was cut short by a click from the tape deck, the slam of a tape coming to an end. Having finished its frantic re-wind, the tape bounced back, began to scrape slowly over the head, to crank music into the room. I knew it from the first wobble of sound: Joy Division's *Love Will Tear Us Apart*.

'*Goodness,*' I said, turning, to the room, to the sound; and laughing, thrilled to hear something forgotten but so familiar. And then, to him, 'Where did you find *this*?'

He seemed surprised, too; his own laugh was a sound-sparkle of surprise. 'I've been going through your old tapes, the old compilations, the ones in the boxes that you haven't unpacked. And this one was unlabelled.'

I leaned back, closed my eyes, listened. Knew the words.

When routine bites hard/ And ambitions are low/ And resentment rides high/ But emotions won't grow

I heard him say, 'Veronica . . .'

I opened my eyes, marvelled, 'This is *years* old.'

He paused, briefly, to allow this, laughing once more, but quickly, and downwards. When his eyes came back up to mine, they were still warm. 'From before I knew you.'

'Yes.' Standing there, in front of him, with my back against the wall, I had a sense that I was standing my ground. But over what?

By now there was no expression in or around his eyes, but they were not cold. 'Odd to think that there was a time when I didn't know you.'

'Yes,' because, put like that, 'True: me, you, too.'

Suddenly he stood up but failed to balance. One hand dabbed down onto the settee. As he tried again, straightening more carefully, I turned my fingernails into my palms, held back. I had to let him do this on his own, he would not want me to rush over and tidy him away.

'Where have you been, lately?' he said in a whisper that did not ask for an answer.

But I rushed to reassure him, 'Nowhere.'

His trusting gaze tilted into disbelief.

'No, really: nowhere.'

He edged towards the door, not turning from me but keeping the distance between us. 'Are you coming to bed, now?'

I tried to explain, 'I can't sleep, John . . .'
But in the doorway, he flickered, '*Just* . . .'
Come here. Talk to me. Be with me.
And my heart rose and turned.

I DECIDED to stay with him, to have a baby. The baby took time, but eighteen months later she split from me and flew momentarily in his hands before coming back down to me with her own hands folding from stars to fists and her first breath switching to a cry. Ornella does not know about my baby: she knows nothing about my life, now, and I know nothing about hers. We have not spoken to each other since I walked away from her room; we have had no contact. And apart from the other day, no one has ever mentioned her. I have told no one about what happened. *Of course* I have told no one, because until the other day I did not even think about what I had done, I had turned so thoroughly from what I saw in her mirror. I had never wished anyone dead, before, and I have never done so, since. I have never again been murderous, and I *will* never again be murderous. But the other day, Davey wanted to know if I miss her. That was all: 'Do you miss Ornella?' His question came in the middle of a conversation about other friends. I had to think hard and fast before I could reply, and in the meantime I slipped him a pained smile to indicate that this would be my last word on the subject. And then the truth came to me and I told him: 'I do and I don't.'

Suzannah Dunn

Tenterhooks

'I really love *Tenterhooks* . . . Divinely sarcastic and packed full
of perky observations, it is very hard to resist.'

PHILIP HENSHER, *Mail on Sunday*

In *Slipping the Clutch*, Miranda walks out of Boots one day
into beautiful, beloved, fast-living Uncle Robbie who, years
beforehand, taught her to drive in his Alpha Romeo and then
died in his Lagonda. Well, what's past is past. Or is it?

In *Stood Up and Thinking of England*, Gillian's family are
refugees from the 70s recession, bankrupted in Britain,
surviving in Spain. But then from back home come the King
family, very definitely on holiday. And it is at the local disco
with Tracey King that Gillian catches sight of Pedro . . .

Possibility of Electricity, was the dubious claim made for the
Spanish farmhouse that becomes the Paulin family's holiday
home. Arriving the following summer as company for
Renee's frazzled mother is Auntie Fay. Bond-girl blonde,
injecting insulin, tanning to the hue of a blood-blister, and
telling Irish jokes. Summertime, but the living isn't easy; and,
soon, electricity is the least of their problems.

'Dunn has a sharp eye for the quiet moments of conversation
that contain emotional truths.'

SYLVIA BROWNRIGG, *The Times*

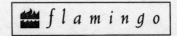

Suzannah Dunn

Quite Contrary

Elizabeth, a young, overworked hospital doctor, gets a phone call from her father late one Friday night telling her that her mother is dangerously ill. Over the weekend that follows, Elizabeth, on duty as ever and confronting the barely controlled chaos of a busy casualty ward, finds moments to reminisce about her childhood, its joys and its miseries. Past and present are interwoven into a series of vivid tableaux, drawing the reader into an intimate understanding of Elizabeth's life as a whole.

'In this vivid picture of "normal" life, Dunn's Elizabeth, the oldest of three sisters, is a witty, down-to-earth female whom you really care for. *Quite Contrary* isn't a weepy slice of bedtime reading, it's a well-observed chapter on growing up – and it proves a touching and remarkably unpredictable read.'   *Time Out*

'The writing is loaded with vibrant, visual images of so strongly evocative, so poetic a quality that they seem about to burst and to yield up a weight of hidden meaning.'
                                                                                                Literary Review

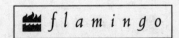 *flamingo*

Suzannah Dunn

Commencing Our Descent

'An enchanting love story of how love happens without itself, a tender reminder that there is nothing more scandalous than an innocent friendship.'
Daily Express

'The heroine of *Commencing Our Descent* is Sadie, comfortably married to amiable, dependable Philip, and with the crippling feeling that life is just not happening. Then she meets Edwin, a reserved, unsmiling historian, and falls painfully in love . . . Dunn powerfully evokes the abyss opening up in the midst of the most mundane and surface-contented surroundings. She is a remarkable writer, a lyricist of ordinary life and ordinary people transfigured by extreme emotions.'
Daily Telegraph

'Suzannah Dunn's writing is as English as treason – a world of twitching net-curtains, furtive sherry and baffled heterosexuality . . . Wonderfully evoking the erotics of 1471 and the terrors of "the caller has withheld their number", Dunn excels at exploring just how thin the line is between innocent conversation and erotic yearning . . . She keeps us in a state of suspended enamouration, constantly hovering between what might be and what never can be. In this sense she reads like an adulterous version of Jane Austen, but without the adultery. Like all innocent liaisons, this one proves to be as dangerous as the rest.'
Daily Express

'The descriptions of marriage and other relationships are as probing and as subtle as anything in Henry James. Dunn's dazzling use of language is a pleasure in itself.'   *The Tablet*

flamingo